THE
LOCKED ROOM

THE
LOCKED ROOM
THE STORY OF A CRIME

Maj Sjöwall and Per Wahlöö

Translated from the Swedish by Paul Britten Austin

VINTAGE BOOKS

A Division of Random House, New York

First Vintage Books Edition, March 1980

Library of Congress Cataloging in Publication Data
Sjöwall, Maj, 1935—
     The locked room.
     Translation of Det slutna rummet.
     Reprint of the 1st American ed., 1973, published by Pantheon
Books, New York.
     I. Wahlöö, Per, 1926-1975, joint author.   II. Title.
[PZ4.S61953Lo 1980]   [PT9876.29.J63]   839.7'3'74
ISBN 0-394-74274-5   79-21993

Manufactured in the United States of America

THE LOCKED ROOM

1

The bells of St. Maria struck two as she came out from the subway station on Wollmar Yxkullsgatan. Before hurrying on toward the Maria Square she halted and lit a cigarette.

The din of the church bells reverberated through the air, reminding her of the dreary Sundays of her childhood. She'd been born and grown up only a few blocks from the Church of St. Maria, where she'd also been christened and confirmed—the latter almost twelve years ago. All she could remember about her confirmation classes was having asked the vicar what Strindberg had meant when he'd written of the "melancholy descant" of the St. Maria bells. But she couldn't recall his answer.

The sun was beating down on her back. After crossing St. Paulsgatan she eased her pace, not wishing to break into a sweat. All of a sudden she realized how nervous she was and regretted not having taken a tranquillizer before leaving home.

Reaching the fountain in the middle of the square, she dipped her handkerchief in the cool water and, walking away, sat down on a bench is the shade of the trees. She took off her glasses and rubbed her face with the wet handkerchief, polished her glasses with the hem of her light-blue shirt, and put them on again. The large lenses reflected the light, concealing the upper half of her face. She took off her wide-brimmed blue denim hat, lifted up her straight blond hair, so long it brushed against her shoulders, and wiped the nape of her neck. Then, putting on her hat, she pulled it down over her brow and sat quite still, her handkerchief crumpled up into a ball between her hands.

After a while she spread the handkerchief out beside her on the bench and wiped the palms of her hands on her jeans. She looked at her watch: half past two. A few minutes to calm down before she had to go.

When the clock struck 2:45 she opened the flap of the dark-green canvas shoulder bag that lay in her lap, picked up her handkerchief, which by now was completely dry, and without folding it slipped it into the bag. Then she got up, slung the leather strap of the bag over her right shoulder, and started walking.

Approaching Hornsgatan she grew less tense; everything, she persuaded herself, would work out fine.

It was Friday, the last day of June, and for many people the summer vacation had just begun. On Hornsgatan, both on the street itself and on the sidewalks, the traffic was lively. Emerging from the square, she turned off to the left and went into the shadow of the houses.

She hoped today had been a wise choice. She'd weighed the pros and cons and realized she might have to put off her project until next week. No harm in that, though she wasn't too keen on exposing herself to such mental stress.

She got there earlier than she'd planned and halted on the shady side of the street, observing the big window opposite her. Its shiny glass reflected the sunshine, and the heavy traffic partially blocked her view. But one thing she noticed. The curtains were drawn.

Pretending to be window shopping, she walked slowly up and down the sidewalk, and although there was a large clock hanging outside a watchmaker's shop nearby she kept looking at her watch. And all the while she kept an eye on the door on the other side of the street.

At 2:55 she walked over to the crosswalk at the intersection. Four minutes later she was standing outside the door of the bank.

Before pushing it open, she lifted the flap of her bag. Walking in, she let her gaze sweep over the office, a branch of one of Sweden's major banks. It was long and narrow; the front wall consisted of the door and the only window. To her right a counter ran all the way from the window to the short wall at the other end, and on her left four desks were fixed to the long wall. Beyond them were a low, round table and two stools upholstered in red-checked material. Furthest away were some stairs, rather steep, disappearing below to what presumably was the bank's safe deposit vault.

Only one customer had come in before her—a man. He was standing at the counter, stuffing banknotes and documents into his briefcase. Behind the counter two female clerks were sitting. Further away a male clerk stood leafing through a card index.

Going up to one of the desks, she fished out a pen from the outer pocket of her bag, meanwhile watching out of the corner of her eye as the customer with the briefcase went out through the street door. Taking a deposit slip out of the holder, she began doodling on it. After a little while she saw the male clerk go over to the door and lock it. Then he bent down and flicked the hook holding open the inner door. As it swung closed with a hissing sound, he resumed his place behind the counter.

She took her handkerchief out of her bag. Holding it in her left hand and the deposit slip in her right, as she approached the counter, she pretended to blow her nose.

Then she stuffed the deposit slip into her bag, brought out an empty nylon shopping bag, and laid it on the counter. Clutching her pistol, she pointed it at the female cashier and, holding her handkerchief in front of her mouth, said: "This is a holdup. The pistol's loaded and if you make any trouble I'll shoot. Put all the money you've got into this bag."

The woman behind the counter stared at her and, slowly taking the nylon bag, laid it down in front of her. The other woman stopped combing her hair. Her hands sank slowly. She opened her mouth as if to say something, but couldn't get a sound out. The man, who was still standing behind his desk, gave a violent start.

3

Instantly she pointed the pistol at him and yelled: "Stay where you are! And put your hands where I can see them."

Impatiently waving the barrel of the pistol at the woman in front of her, who was obviously paralyzed with fright, she went on: "Hurry up with the money! All of it!"

The cashier began stuffing wads of bills into the bag. When she'd finished, she laid it on the counter.

Suddenly the man at the desk said: "You'll never get away with this. The police will——"

"Shut up!" she screamed.

Then she threw her handkerchief into her open bag and grabbed the nylon shopping bag. It felt nice and heavy. Backing slowly toward the door, she pointed the pistol at each of the bank's employees in turn.

All of a sudden someone came running toward her from the stairway at the far end of the room: a tall, blond man in well-pressed pants and a blue blazer with shiny buttons and a big gold emblem stitched to the breast pocket.

A loud bang filled the room and went on thundering between the walls. As her arm jerked upward to the ceiling she saw the man in the blazer being flung backward. His shoes were brand new and white, with thick, grooved, red rubber soles. Only as his head hit the stone floor with a horrible dull thud did she realize she'd shot him.

Dropping the pistol into her bag, she stared wild-eyed at the three horror-stricken people behind the counter. Then she rushed for the door. Fumbling with the lock, she had time to think before emerging into the street: "Calm now, I must walk perfectly calmly." But once out on the sidewalk, she started half-running toward the intersection.

She didn't see the people around her—she was only aware of bumping against several of them and of the pistol shot which went on thundering in her ears.

She rounded the corner and started running, the shopping bag in her hand and the heavy satchel bumping against her hip. Jerking open the door of the building where she'd lived as a child, she took the old familiar way out into the yard, checked herself, and fell to a walk. Passing straight through the porch of a gazebo she came out into another back yard. She descended the steep stairway into a cellar and sat down on the bottom step.

She tried to cram the nylon bag down on top of the automatic in her shoulder bag, but there wasn't enough room. She took off her hat, glasses, and blond wig, and stuffed them all into the shoulder bag. Her own hair was dark and short. She stood up, unbuttoned her shirt, took it off, and put that too into the bag. Under her shirt she was wearing a short-sleeved black cotton sweater. Slinging the shoulder bag over her left shoulder, she picked up the nylon shopping bag and went up the stairs to the yard again. She climbed over a couple of walls before at last finding herself in a street at the far end of the block.

Then she entered a small grocery, bought two liters of milk, put the cartons into a large paper bag, and laid her nylon shopping bag on top of them.

After which she walked down to Slussen and took the subway train home.

2

Gunvald Larsson arrived at the scene of the crime in his own strictly private car. It was a red EMW, which is unusual in Sweden and in many people's eyes far too grand for a detective inspector, especially when he uses it on the job.

This beautiful Friday afternoon he'd just settled down behind the wheel to drive home, when Einar Rönn had come rushing out into the yard of police headquarters and dashed all his plans for a quiet evening at home in Bollmora. Einar Rönn too was a detective inspector in the National Homicide Squad and very likely the only friend Gunvald Larsson had; so when he said he was sorry but Gunvald Larsson would have to sacrifice his free evening, he really meant it.

Rönn drove to Hornsgatan in a police car. When he got there, several cars and some people from the South Precinct were already on the spot, and Gunvald Larsson was already inside the bank.

A little group of people had gathered outside the bank, and as Rönn crossed the sidewalk one of the uniformed patrolmen who stood there glaring at the spectators came up to him and said: "I've a couple of witnesses here who said they heard the shot. What shall I do with them?"

"Hold 'em a moment," Rönn said. "And try to disperse the others."

The patrolman nodded and Rönn went on into the bank.

On the marble floor between the counter and the desks the dead man, his arms flung wide and his left knee bent, lay on his back. One trouser leg had slipped up, baring a chalk-white Orlon sock with a dark blue anchor on it and a deeply sunburned leg covered with gleaming blond hairs. The bullet had hit him right in the face, and blood and brain matter had exuded from the back of his head.

The staff of the bank were sitting together in the far corner of the room, and in front of them Gunvald Larsson half stood, half sat, one thigh across the edge of a desk. He was writing in a notebook while one of the women spoke in a shrill, indignant voice.

Seeing Rönn, Gunvald Larsson held up his right palm at the woman, who immediately broke off in the middle of a sentence. Gunvald Larsson got up, went behind the counter, and, notebook in hand, walked over to Rönn. With a nod at the man on the floor he said:

"He doesn't look too good. If you stay here I can take the witnesses someplace, maybe to the old precinct house on Rosenlundsgatan. Then you can work here undisturbed."

Rönn nodded. "They say it was a girl who did it," he said. "And she got away with the cash. Did anyone see where she went?"

"None of the bank staff anyway," Gunvald Larsson said. "Apparently there was a guy standing outside who saw a car drive off, but he didn't see the number and wasn't too sure of the make, so that's not much to go on. I'll talk with him later."

"And who's this?" asked Rönn with a curt nod at the dead man.

"Some idiot wanting to play the hero. He tried to fling himself at the robber, and then of course, in sheer panic, she fired. He was one of the bank's customers and the staff knew him. He'd been in here going through his safe deposit box and came up the stairway over there, right in the middle of it all." Gunvald Larsson consulted his notebook. "He was director of a gymnastics institute, and his name was Gårdon. With an 'å.' "

"I guess he thought he was Flash Gordon," Rönn said.

Gunvald Larsson threw him a questioning look.

Rönn blushed, and to change the subject said:

7

"Well, I guess there are some photos of her in that thing." He pointed to the camera fixed beneath the ceiling.

"If it's properly focused and also has some film in it," Gunvald Larsson said skeptically. "And if the cashier remembered to press the button."

Nowadays most Swedish banks are equipped with cameras that shoot when the cashier on duty steps on a button on the floor. This was the only thing the staff had to do in the event of a holdup. With armed bank robberies becoming ever more frequent, banks had issued orders to their staffs to hand over any money demanded of them and in general not to do anything to stop robbers or to prevent them getting away that might risk their own lives. This order did not, as one might be led to believe, derive from any humanitarian motives or any consideration for bank personnel. It was the fruit of experience. It is cheaper for banks and insurance companies to allow robbers to get away with their haul than to be obliged to pay out damages and maybe even support the victims' families for the rest of their lives—which can so easily be the case if someone gets injured or killed.

Now the police surgeon arrived, and Rönn went out to his car to fetch the homicide bag. He used old-fashioned methods, not unusually with success. Gunvald Larsson left for the old police station on Rosenlundsgatan, together with the staff of the bank and four other people who had identified themselves as witnesses.

He was lent an interrogation room, where he took off his suede jacket and hung it over the back of a chair before beginning the preliminary examinations. The first three statements given by the bank personnel were as good as identical; the four others diverged widely.

The first of these four witnesses was a forty-two-year-old man who, when the shot had gone off, had been standing in a doorway five yards from the bank. He'd seen a girl in a black hat and sunglasses hurry past, and when, according to his own statement, half a minute later, he'd looked down the street, he'd seen a green passenger car, probably an Opel, rush out

8

from the sidewalk fifteen yards away. The car had disappeared quickly in the direction of Hornsplan, and he thought he'd seen the girl with the hat in the back seat. He hadn't caught the car's registration number but believed it to be an "AB" plate.

The next witness, a woman, was a boutique owner. When she heard a shot she'd been standing in the open door of her shop, wall-to-wall with the bank. First she thought the sound had come from the pantry inside her boutique. Afraid that the gas stove had exploded, she dashed inside. Finding it hadn't, she returned to the door. Looking down the street, she'd seen a big blue car swing out into the traffic—tires squealing. At the same instant a woman had come out of the bank and shouted that someone had been shot. She hadn't seen who had been sitting in the car or what its number was, but she thought it looked more or less like a taxi.

The third witness was a thirty-two-year-old metal worker. His account was more circumstantial. He hadn't heard the shot, or at least hadn't been aware of it. When the girl emerged from the bank he'd been walking along the sidewalk. She was in a hurry, and as she passed had pushed him aside. He hadn't seen her face but guessed her age to be about thirty. She was wearing blue pants, a shirt, and a hat and was carrying a dark bag. He'd seen her go up to an "A"-marked car with two threes in its registration number. The car was a pale beige Renault 16. A thin man, who looked something between twenty and twenty-five, had been sitting at the wheel. He had long, lank, black hair and wore a short-sleeved cotton T-shirt. He was strikingly pale. Another man, who looked a little older, had stood on the sidewalk and opened the back door for the girl. After closing the door behind her, he sat down beside the driver in the front seat. This man was strongly built, about five foot ten, tall, and had ashen hair—fuzzy and very thick. He had a florid complexion and was dressed in black pants with flared legs and a black shirt of some shiny material. The car had made a U-turn and disappeared in the direction of Slussen.

After this evidence Gunvald Larsson felt some-

9

what confused. Before calling in the last witness he carefully read through his notes.

This last witness turned out to be a fifty-year-old watchmaker who'd been sitting in his car right outside the bank, waiting for his wife who was in a shoe store on the other side of the street. He'd had his window open and had heard the shot, but hadn't reacted since there's always so much noise on a busy street like Hornsgatan. It had been five after three when he'd seen the woman come out of the bank. He'd noticed her because she seemed to be in too much of a hurry to apologize for bumping into an elderly lady, and he'd thought it was typical of Stockholmers to be in such a rush and so unfriendly. He himself came from Södertälje. The woman was dressed in long pants, and on her head she'd been wearing something reminiscent of a cowboy hat and had had a black shopping bag in her hand. She'd run to the next intersection and disappeared around the corner. No, she hadn't gotten into any car, nor had she halted on her way, but had gone straight on up to the corner and disappeared.

Gunvald Larsson phoned in the description of the two men in the Renault, got up, gathered his papers, and looked at the clock. Six already.

Presumably he'd done a lot of work in vain. The presence of the various cars had long since been reported by the first patrolmen to arrive on the scene. Besides which none of the witnesses had given a coherent overall picture. Everything had gone to hell, of course. As usual.

For a moment he wondered whether he ought to retain the last witness, but dropped the idea. Everyone appeared eager to get home as quickly as possible. To tell the truth, he was the most eager of all, though probably that was hoping too much. So he let all the witnesses go.

Putting on his jacket, he went back to the bank.

The remains of the courageous gymnastics teacher had been removed, and a young radio patrolman stepped out of his car and informed him politely that Detective Inspector Rönn was waiting for him in his office. Gunvald Larsson sighed and went over to his car.

3

He awoke astonished at being alive. This was nothing new. For exactly the last fifteen months he'd opened his eyes every day with the same confused question: How come I'm alive?

Just before waking he'd had a dream. This too was fifteen months old. Though it shifted constantly, it always followed the same pattern. He was riding. A cold wind tearing at his hair, he was galloping, leaning forward. Then he was running along a railway platform. In front of him he saw a man who'd just raised a pistol. He knew who the man was and what was going to happen. The man was Charles J. Guiteau; the weapon was a marksman's pistol, a Hammerli International.

Just as the man fired he threw himself forward and stopped the bullet with his body. The shot hit him like a hammer, right in the middle of his chest. Obviously he had sacrificed himself; yet at the same moment he realized his action had been in vain. The President was already lying crumpled up on the ground, the shiny top hat had toppled from his head and was rolling around in a semicircle.

As always, he'd woken up just as the bullet hit him. At first everything went black, a wave of scorching heat swept over his brain. Then he opened his eyes.

Martin Beck lay quietly in his bed, looking up at the ceiling. It was light in the room. He thought about his dream. It didn't seem particularly meaningful, at least not in this version. Besides which it was full of absurdities. The weapon for example; it ought to have been a revolver or possibly a derringer; and how could Garfield be lying there, fatally wounded, when it was he himself who demonstrably had stopped the bullet with his chest?

He had no idea what the murderer had looked like in reality. If ever he'd seen a photo of the man, the mental image had been wiped out long ago. Usually Guiteau had blue eyes, a blond moustache, and sleek hair, combed back; but today he'd mostly resembled an actor in some famous role. Immediately he realized which: John Carradine as the gambler in *Stage Coach*. The whole thing was amazingly romantic.

A bullet in your chest, however, can easily lose its poetic qualities. So much he knew from experience. If it perforates the right lung and then lodges near the spine, the effect is intermittently painful and in the long run very tedious.

But there was also much in his dream that agreed with his own reality. The marksman's pistol, for example. It had belonged to a dismissed police patrolman with blue eyes, a blond moustache, and hair combed diagonally back. They'd met on the roof of a house under a cold, dark, spring sky. No words had been exchanged. Only a pistol shot.

That evening he'd woken up in a bed in a room with white walls—more precisely in the thorax clinic of Karolinska Hospital. They'd told him there his life was in no danger. Even so, he'd asked himself how come he was still alive.

Later they'd said the injury no longer constituted a threat to his life, but the bullet wasn't sitting too well. He'd grasped, though not appreciated, the finesse of that little "no longer." The surgeons had examined the X-ray plates for weeks before removing the foreign object from his body. Then they'd said his injury *definitely* no longer constituted any danger to his life. On the contrary, he'd make a complete recovery—providing he took things very easy. But by that stage he'd stopped believing them.

All the same, he had taken things pretty easy. He'd had no choice.

Now they said he'd made a complete recovery. This time too, however, there was an addition: "Physically." Furthermore he shouldn't smoke. His windpipe had never been too good, and a shot through the lung hadn't improved matters. After it had healed, mysterious marks had appeared around the scars.

Martin Beck got up. He went through his living room out into the hallway, and picking up his newspaper, which lay on the doormat, went on into the kitchen, meanwhile running his eyes over the front-page headlines. Beautiful weather, and it would hold, according to the weatherman. Apart from that, everything seemed, as usual, to be taking a turn for the worse. Laying down the newspaper on the kitchen table, he took a yogurt out of the icebox. It tasted as it usually did, not good and not exactly bad, just a trifle musty and artificial. The carton was probably too old. Probably it had already been old when he'd bought it —the days were long gone when a Stockholmer could buy anything fresh without having to make a particular effort or pay an outrageous price. Next stop was the bathroom. After washing and brushing his teeth he returned to the bedroom, made the bed, took off his pajama trousers, and began to dress.

As he did so he looked listlessly around his apartment. It was at the top of a building on Köpmangatan, in the Old City. Most Stockholmers would have called it a dream home. He'd been living here for more than three years, and could still remember how comfortable he'd been, right up to that spring day on that roof.

Nowadays he mostly felt shut in and lonely, even when someone dropped in on him. Presumably this was not the apartment's fault. Often of late he'd caught himself feeling claustrophobic even when he was outdoors.

He felt a vague urge for a cigarette. True, the doctors had told him he must give it up; but he didn't care. A more crucial factor was the State Tobacco Company's discontinuance of his usual brand. Now there were no cardboard filter cigarettes on the market at all. On two or three occasions he'd tried various other kinds, but hadn't been able to accustom himself to them. As he tied his tie he listlessly studied his ship models. There were three of them standing on a shelf over his bed, two completed and the third half-finished. It was more than eight years now since he had started building them, but since that April day last year he hadn't even touched them.

Since then they had gathered a lot of dust. Several times his daughter had offered to do something about this, but he'd asked her to leave them alone.

It was 8:30 A.M., the third of July, 1972, a Monday. A date of especial importance. On this particular day he was going back to work.

He was still a policeman—more exactly, a detective chief inspector, head of the National Homicide Squad.

Martin Beck put on his jacket and stuffed the newspaper in his pocket, intending to read it on the subway—just one little detail of the routine he was about to resume.

Walking along Skeppsbron in the sunlight, he inhaled the polluted air. He felt old and hollow. But none of this could be seen in his appearance. On the contrary, he seemed healthy and vigorous, and his movements were swift and lithe. A tall, suntanned man with a strong jaw and calm, gray-blue eyes under a broad forehead, Martin Beck was forty-nine. Soon he'd be fifty. But most people thought he was younger.

4

The room in the South Police Headquarters on Västberga Avenue testified to the long residence of someone else as acting head of the Homicide Division. Though it was clean and tidy and someone had taken the trouble to place a vase of blue cornflowers and marguerites on his desk, everything vaguely suggested a lack of precision—superficial yet obvious, and in some way snug and homey. Especially in the desk drawer. Clearly, someone had just taken a lot of things out of them; but a good deal was still left. Old taxi receipts and movie tickets for example, broken ballpoint pens and empty candy packets. In several of the pen trays were daisy chains of paper clips, rubber bands, lumps of sugar, and packets of saccharine tablets. Also, two packets of moist towelettes, one pack of Kleenex, three cartridge cases, and a broken Exacta watch. And a large number of slips of paper with scattered notes written in a clear, highly legible hand.

Martin Beck had gone around the station and said hello to people. Most, but by no means all, were old acquaintances. Now he was sitting at his desk, examining the watch, which appeared to be utterly useless. The crystal was misty on the inside, and when he shook it a gloomy, rustling noise came from within the watchcase, as if every one of its screws had come loose.

Lennart Kollberg knocked and entered. "Hello," he said. "Welcome."

"Thanks. Is this your watch?"

"Yes," said Kollberg glumly. "I happened to put it in the washing machine. Forgot to empty my pockets." He looked about him and went on apologetically: "Actually I tried fixing it last Friday, but someone interrupted me. Well, you know how it is. . . ."

15

Martin Beck nodded. Kollberg was the person he'd seen most of during his long convalescence, and there wasn't much new for them to tell one another. "How's the diet coming along?"

"Fine," said Kollberg. "I was down a pound this morning, from two hundred and twenty-nine to two hundred and twenty-eight."

"Then you've only put on twenty since you began?"

"Seventeen," said Kollberg with a look of hurt pride. He shrugged and went on grumblingly: "It's goddam awful. The whole project flies in the face of nature. And Gun just laughs at me. Bodil too, for that matter. How are you, by the way?"

"Fine."

Kollberg frowned but said nothing. Instead he unzipped his briefcase and extracted a light red plastic folder. It seemed to contain a none-too-extensive report. Maybe thirty pages.

"What's that?"

"Let's call it a present."

"Who from?"

"Me, for example. Although it's not, actually. It's from Gunvald Larsson and Rönn. They think it's terribly funny."

Kollberg laid the file on the table. Then he said: "Unfortunately I have to go."

"What for?"

"N.P.B."

Which was the new National Police Board.

"Why?"

"These goddam bank robbers."

"But there's a special squad for them."

"The special squad needs reinforcements. Last Friday some thickheaded goof got himself shot again."

"Yes, I've read about it."

"And so the State Police immediately decide to strengthen the special squad."

"With you?"

"No," said Kollberg. "Actually, I think, with you. But this order came in last Friday, while I was still in charge here. So I made an independent decision."

"Namely?"

"Namely to spare you that lunatic asylum, and move in myself to strengthen the special squad."

"Thanks." Martin Beck really meant what he'd said. To work in a special squad presumably implied a daily confrontation with, for example, the National Police Commissioner, at least two department heads, assorted superintendents, and other bombastic amateurs. Kollberg had voluntarily taken these trials upon himself.

"Well," Kollberg said, "in exchange I got this." He put a thick index finger on the plastic file.

"What's that?"

"A case," said Kollberg. "Really a most interesting case, not like bank holdups and things. The only pity is . . ."

"What?"

"That you don't read detective stories."

"Why?"

"Because if you did you might have appreciated it more. Rönn and Larsson think everyone reads detective stories. Actually it's their case, but just now they're so overloaded with misery that they're inviting applications for their little jobs, from anyone who wants one. It's something to think about. Just sit very still and think."

"Okay, I'll look it over," said Martin Beck dispassionately.

"There's been no word about it in the papers. Aren't you curious?"

"Sure. 'Bye then."

"See you," said Kollberg.

Outside the door he stopped and stood still a few seconds, frowning. Then he shook his head in a troubled way and walked over to the elevator.

5

Martin Beck had said he was curious about the contents of the red file; but this was not really the truth. Actually it was of no interest to him whatever. Why, then, had he chosen to give an evasive and misleading answer to the question? To make Kollberg happy? Hardly. To deceive him? Even more far-fetched. For one thing, there was no reason to do so; and anyway it was impossible. They'd known one another far too well and for too many years. Besides which Kollberg was one of the least gullible men he'd ever met. Maybe to deceive himself? Even this thought was absurd.

Martin Beck went on chewing over this question as he completed his inspection of his office. When he'd finished with the drawers he passed on to the furniture, moved the chairs around, turned the desk to another angle, shoved the filing cabinet a few inches nearer to the door, unscrewed the office lamp and placed it on the right-hand corner of his desk. Obviously his deputy had preferred to have it on the left, or else it had just gotten that way. In little things Kollberg often acted haphazardly. But where important matters were concerned he was a perfectionist. For example, he'd waited till he was forty-two to get married, with the explicit motivation that he wanted a perfect wife. He'd waited for the right one.

Martin Beck, on the other hand, could look back at almost two decades of unsuccessful marriage, to a person who certainly didn't seem to have been the right one. Anyway he was divorced now; he supposed he must have lingered until it was too late.

Sometimes in the last six months he'd caught himself wondering if the divorce, all things considered, hadn't been a mistake. Maybe a nagging, boring wife was at least more exciting than no wife at all?

Well, that was of no consequence. He took the vase of flowers and carried it in to one of the secretaries. This seemed to cheer her. Martin Beck sat down at his desk and looked about him. Order had been restored.

Was it that he wanted to convince himself nothing had changed? A pointless question, and to forget it as soon as possible he pulled the red file towards him. The plastic was transparent, and he saw immediately that it concerned a homicide. That was okay. Homicide was part and parcel of his profession. But where had it happened? Bergsgatan 57. Almost on the very doorstep of the police headquarters.

Usually he would have said it was no concern of his or of his department, but of the Stockholm Criminal Investigation Department. For a second he felt tempted to pick up the phone, call up someone on Kungsholmen, and ask what all this was actually about. Or quite simply to stuff it all into an envelope and return it to its sender. He felt an urge to be rigid and formal —an urge so strong that he had to exert all his strength to suppress it. He looked at the clock in order to distract himself. Lunchtime already. But he wasn't hungry.

Martin Beck got up, went out into the washroom, and drank a mug of lukewarm water.

Coming back he noticed the air in his office was warm and fetid. Yet he did not take off his jacket or even loosen his collar. He sat down, took out the papers, and started to read.

Twenty-eight years as a policeman had taught him a lot of things, among them the art of reading reports and rapidly sifting through repetitions and trivialities— the capacity to discern a pattern, if any existed.

It took him less than an hour to read conscientiously through the document. Most of it was ill-written, some was downright incomprehensible, and some sections were formulated particularly badly. He immediately recognized the author. Einar Rönn, a policeman who, stylistically speaking, seemed to take after that comrade in officialdom who in his celebrated traffic regulations had declared, among much else, that darkness falls when the street lights are lit.

Martin Beck leafed through the papers once again, stopping here and there to check certain details. Then he laid down the report, put his elbows on the desk and his forehead into the palms of his hands. Frowning, he thought through the apparent course of events.

The story fell into two parts. The first part was everyday and repulsive.

Fifteen days ago, viz., on Sunday, June 18, a tenant at Bergsgatan 57 on Kungsholmen had called the police. The conversation had been registered at 2:19 P.M., but not until two hours later had a car with two patrolmen arrived at the place. At most the house on Bergsgatan was no more than nine minutes' walk from the Stockholm Police Headquarters; but the delay was easily explained. The capital was suffering from an atrocious shortage of policemen; besides which it was vacation time, and a Sunday to boot. Moreover, nothing had indicated that the call was particularly urgent. Two patrolmen, Karl Kristiansson and Kenneth Kvastmo, had entered the building and talked to the caller, a woman living two flights up in the part of the house facing the street. She had told them that for several days now she'd been irritated by an unpleasant smell in the staircase and expressed a suspicion that all might not be as it should.

Both patrolmen had instantly noticed the odor. Kvastmo had defined it as arising from putrefaction; according to his own way of putting it, it was strongly reminiscent of the stench of rotten meat. A closer sniff —Kvastmo's again—had led the men to the door of a first-floor apartment. According to available information, it was the door of a one-room apartment, inhabited for some time by a man of about sixty-five, whose name might be Karl Edvin Svärd. The name had been found on a handwritten piece of cardboard under the doorbell. As it might be supposed that the smell arose from the body of a suicide, or of someone who had died from natural causes, or of a dog—still according to Kvastmo—or possibly of some sick or helpless person, they had decided to break in. The bell

20

seemed to be out of order, but no amount of banging on the door had evoked any reaction. All their attempts to contact a janitor or representative of the landlord or anyone else holding master keys had been unsuccessful.

The policemen therefore requested instructions to break into the apartment and received orders to do so. A locksmith had been called, causing yet another half-hour's delay.

On his arrival the locksmith had found that the door was equipped with a jimmy-proof lock and that there was no mail slot. The lock was then drilled out with the aid of a special tool, but even this had not made it possible to open the door.

Kristiansson and Kvastmo, whose time had now been taken up by this case far beyond their normal working hours, asked for new instructions and were ordered to open the door by force. To their question whether someone from the Criminal Investigation Department ought not to attend, they received the laconic answer that no more personnel were available. By now the locksmith, feeling he had done his job, had left.

By 7:00 P.M. Kvastmo and Kristiansson had opened the door by breaking the pins of the hinges on the outside. In spite of this a new difficulty had arisen; for the door was then found to be fitted with two strong metal bolts and also with a so-called fox-lock, a sort of iron beam sunk in the doorposts. After a further hour's work the policemen had been able to make their way into the apartment, where they were met by stifling heat and the overwhelming stench of corpse.

In the room, which faced the street, they found a dead man. The body was lying on its back, about three yards from the window overlooking Bergsgatan, beside a turned-on electric radiator—it was the heat from this, in conjunction with the prevailing heat wave, that had caused the corpse to swell up to at least twice its normal volume. The body was in a state of intense putrefaction, and there was an abundance of worms.

21

The window facing the street was locked from the inside, and the blind had been pulled down. The apartment's other window, in the kitchenette, looked out over the yard. It was stuck fast with window tapes and appeared not to have been opened for a long while. The furniture was sparse and the fittings plain. The apartment was in a bad state of disrepair as regarded the ceiling, floors, walls, wallpaper, and paint. Only a few utensils were to be found in the kitchenette and living room.

An official document they had found suggested that the deceased was the sixty-two-year-old Karl Edvin Svärd, a warehouseman who had been pensioned off before reaching retirement age, some six years back.

After the apartment had been inspected by a detective sergeant called Gustavsson, the body was taken to the State Institute for Forensic Medicine for a routine postmortem.

The case had been preliminarily assessed as suicide; alternatively, death from starvation, illness, or other natural causes was suspected.

Martin Beck groped in his jacket pocket for some nonexistent Florida cigarettes.

Nothing had been mentioned about Svärd in the newspapers. The story was far too banal. Stockholm has one of the highest suicide rates in the world—something everyone carefully avoids talking about or which, when put on the spot, they attempt to conceal by means of variously manipulated and untruthful statistics. The most usual explanation is the simplest: All other countries cheat much more with their statistics. For some years now, however, not even members of the government had dared to say this aloud or in public, perhaps from the feeling that, in spite of everything, people tend to rely more on the evidence of their own eyes than on political explanations. And if, after all, this should turn out not to be so, it only made the matter still more embarrassing. For the fact of the matter is that the so-called Welfare State abounds with sick, poor, and lonely people, living at best on dog food, who are left uncared for until they waste away and die in their rat-hole apartments. No, this was nothing for the public. Hardly even for the police.

But that wasn't all. There was a sequel to the story of this premature pensioner, Karl Edvin Svärd.

6

Martin Beck had been in his profession long enough to know that if something in a report appears incomprehensible it's because in ninety-nine cases out of a hundred someone has been careless, made a mistake, is guilty of a slip of the pen, has overlooked the crux of the matter, or lacked the ability to make himself understood.

The second part of the tale of the man who had died in the house on Bergsgatan seemed shadowy, to say the least. At first, matters had followed their usual course. On Sunday evening the body had been taken away and put in the morgue. The next day the apartment had been disinfected, something that was certainly needed, and Kristiansson and Kvastmo had presented their report on the case.

The autopsy on the corpse had been made on Tuesday, and the responsible police department had received the verdict the following day. Postmortems on old corpses are no fun, least of all when the person in question is known in advance to have taken his own life or died of natural causes. If, furthermore, the person in question enjoyed no very eminent status in society—if for instance he had been a prematurely pensioned warehouseman—then the whole thing loses its last vestiges of any interest whatever.

The postmortem report was signed by a person Martin Beck had never heard of, presumably a temporary. The text was exceedingly scientific and abstruse. This, perhaps, was why the matter had been treated rather drowsily. As far as he could see, the documents had not even reached Einar Rönn at Homicide until a week later. Only there had it aroused the attention to which it was entitled.

Martin Beck pulled the telephone toward him to make his first duty call in a long time. He picked up the receiver, laid his right hand on the dial, and then just went on sitting. He'd forgotten the number of the State Institute for Forensic Medicine and had to look it up.

The autopsist seemed surprised. "Of course," she said. "Of course I remember. That report was sent in two weeks ago."

"I know."

"Is something unclear?"

He thought she sounded slightly hurt.

"Just a few things I don't understand. According to your report, the person in question committed suicide."

"Of course."

"How?"

"Have I really expressed myself so badly?"

"Oh no, not at all."

"What is it you don't understand, then?"

"Quite a bit, to be honest; but that, of course, is due to my own ignorance."

"You mean of terminology?"

"Among other things."

"If one lacks medical knowledge," she said consolingly, "one always has to expect certain difficulties of that type." Her voice was light and clear. On the young side, certainly.

For a while Martin Beck sat silent. At this point he ought to have said: "My dear young lady, this report isn't meant for pathologists but for quite another kind of person. Since it's been requested by the Metropolitan Police it ought to be written in terms that even a police sergeant, for example, could understand." But he didn't. Why?

His thoughts were interrupted by the doctor, who said: "Hallo, are you there?"

"Yes, I'm here."

"Is there something special you want to ask about?"

"Yes. Firstly I'd like to know your grounds for assuming suicide."

When she answered her voice had changed, had

25

acquired an undertone of surprise. "My dear commissioner, we got this corpse from the police. Before carrying out a postmortem I was personally in telephone contact with the police officer I assumed was responsible for the investigation. He said it was a routine job. There was only one question he wanted answered."

"What was that?"

"Whether the person concerned had committed suicide."

Irritated, Martin Beck rubbed his knuckles against his chest. The spot where the bullet had gone through him still hurt at times. He'd been told it was psychosomatic, that it would pass over as soon as his unconscious had relinquished its grip on the past. Just now, it was the present that, in high degree, was irritating him. And that was something in which his unconscious could hardly have any interest.

An elementary mistake had been made. Naturally, the postmortem ought to have been done without any hints from the police. To present the forensic experts with the suspected cause of death constituted little short of breach of duty, especially if, as in this case, the pathologist was young and inexperienced.

"Do you know the officer's name?"

"Detective Sergeant Aldor Gustavsson. I got the impression he was in charge of the case. He seemed to be experienced and to know what he was about."

Martin Beck knew nothing about Detective Sergeant Aldor Gustavsson or his possible qualifications. He said: "So the police gave you certain instructions?"

"One could put it like that, yes! In any case the police made it quite clear that it was a question of suspected suicide."

"I see."

"Suicide means, as you perhaps know, that someone has killed himself."

Beck did not reply to this. Instead he said: "Was the autopsy difficult?"

"Not really. Apart from the extensive organic changes. That always puts a somewhat different complexion on our work."

He wondered how many autopsies she had carried out, but he refrained from comment. "Did it take long?"

"Not at all. Since it was a question of suicide or acute illness I began by opening up the thorax."

"Why?"

"The deceased was an elderly man."

"Why did you assume death to have been sudden?"

"This police officer gave me to understand it was."

"In what way?"

"By going straight to the point, I seem to remember."

"What did he say?"

" 'Either the old boy's taken his own life or else had a heart attack.' Something of that kind."

Another false conclusion crying aloud to heaven! There was nothing to suggest that Svärd, before dying, might not have lain there paralyzed or helpless for several days.

"Well, so you opened his chest."

"Yes, and the question was answered almost immediately. No doubt which alternative was correct."

"Suicide?"

"Of course."

"By?"

"He had shot himself through the heart. The bullet was still lodged in the thorax."

"Had the bullet hit the heart?"

"Come very close, anyway. The main injury was to the aorta." She paused briefly, added a trifle acidly: "Do I express myself comprehensibly?"

"Sure." Martin Beck formulated his next question carefully. "Have you an extensive experience of bullet wounds?"

"Enough, I guess. Anyway this case presents hardly any complications." How many autopsies might she have carried out on victims of bullet wounds in her life? Three? Two? Or maybe only one?

The doctor, intuiting perhaps his unvoiced doubts, explained: "I worked in Jordan during the civil war, two years ago. No shortage of bullet wounds there."

"But presumably not so many suicides."

"No, not quite."

27

"Well, it just so happens," Martin Beck said, "that few suicide cases aim at their hearts. Most shoot themselves through the mouth, some through the temple."

"That may be. But this guy was far from being my first. When I was doing psychology I was taught that suicides—especially the romantics among them—have a deep-rooted instinct to aim at their hearts. Apparently it's a widespread tendency."

"How long do you think Svärd could have survived with this bullet wound?"

"Not long. One minute, maybe two or three. The internal hemorrhage was extensive. At a guess, I'd say a minute. But the margins are still very small. Does it matter?"

"Maybe not. But there's something else that interests me. You took care of the remains on June 20?"

"Yes, that's correct."

"How long do you think the man had been dead by then?"

"Mmm ..."

"On this point your report is vague."

"As a matter of fact it's not easy to say. Maybe a more experienced pathologist than myself could have given you a more exact answer."

"But what do *you* think?"

"At least two months, but ..."

"But?"

"But it depends what things were like at the scene of death. Warmth and damp air make a big difference. It could be less, for example, if the body was exposed to great heat. On the other hand if disintegration was extensive, I mean ..."

"And the actual entrance wound?"

"This business of the disintegration of the tissues makes that a difficult question, too."

"Was the gun fired in contact with the body?"

"Not in my view. But I could be wrong, I must stress that."

"What is your view, then?"

"That he shot himself the other way. After all, there are two classic ways, aren't there?"

"Sure," said Martin Beck. "That's correct."

28

"Either one presses the barrel against one's body and fires, or else one holds one's arm with the pistol or whatever it is stretched right out, with the weapon reversed. In which case I guess one has to pull the trigger with one's thumb."

"Precisely. And so that's what you think happened?"

"Yes. But with every reservation imaginable. It's really very hard to be sure a gun was pressed against a body which had changed so."

"I get you."

"Then it's only me who doesn't understand a thing," the girl said lightly. "Why are you asking all these questions? Is it so important which way he shot himself?"

"Yes, it seems so. Svärd was found dead at home in his apartment, with all the windows and doors closed from inside. He was lying beside an electric radiator."

"That could explain the advanced putrefaction," she said. "In that case a month could be enough."

"Really?"

"Yes. And that could also explain why it's hard to find any powder burns from a point-blank shot."

"I see," said Martin Beck. "Thanks for your help."

"Oh, that's nothing. If there's anything else I can explain, please call back."

"Good-bye." He put down the receiver. She was an old hand at explanations. Soon there'd only be one thing left to explain. But that was still more bewildering. Svärd could not possibly have committed suicide. To shoot yourself without a gun—that's not easy.

And in the Bergsgatan apartment there'd been no weapon.

7

Martin Beck went on with his phoning. He tried to get hold of the original radio patrol that had been summoned to Bergsgatan, but neither of the two patrolmen, it seemed, were on duty. After some calling around it transpired that one was on vacation and the other absent from duty to give evidence in a district court case. Gunvald Larsson was busy with meetings, and Einar Rönn had gone out on a call.

It was a long while before Martin Beck succeeded in contacting the detective sergeant who had finally sent the case on to Homicide. This hadn't happened till Monday the 26th, and Martin Beck found it imperative to ask him a question: "Is it true the autopsy report came in as early as that Wednesday?"

The man's voice wavered noticeably as he answered: "I can't really say for sure. Anyhow I didn't read it personally until that Friday."

Martin Beck said nothing. He waited for some kind of explanation. It came:

"In this precinct we're hardly up to half strength. There wasn't a chance of clearing up any but the most urgent matters. The papers just pile up on us. It's getting worse every day."

"So—no one had looked at the autopsy report before that?"

"Yes, our commissioner here. And on Friday morning he asked me who'd taken care of the gun."

"What gun?"

"The one Svärd had shot himself with. I knew nothing about any gun, but I assumed one of the patrolmen who'd taken the call had found it."

"I have their report in front of me," Martin Beck

said. "If there'd been a firearm in the apartment there should be some mention of it."

"I can't see how this radio patrol could have made any mistake," the man said, at once on the defensive. He was disposed to defend his men, and it wasn't hard to see why. During the past year criticism of the regular police had been growing steadily. Relations with the public were worse than ever before and the burden of work had almost doubled. As a consequence, any number of policemen had simply given up. Unfortunately they were generally the best. In spite of massive unemployment in Sweden it was impossible to get new men, and the recruiting base was getting smaller than ever. Those policemen who stayed felt an even stronger need to stick together.

"Maybe not," Martin Beck said.

"Those guys did exactly what they should have done. After they'd let themselves in and found the dead man, they called in one of their superiors."

"This Gustavsson guy?"

"Exactly. A man from the Criminal Investigation Division. Apart from the actual finding of the corpse it was his business to draw conclusions and report observations. And I assumed they'd shown him the gun and he'd taken care of it."

"And then not even bothered to report it?"

"Such things can happen," the policeman said dryly.

"Well, it appears now there was no weapon inside the room."

"No. But I didn't find that out till Monday, a week ago, when I was speaking to Kristiansson and Kvastmo. Whereupon I immediately sent the documents over to Kungsholmsgatan."

The Kungsholmen police station and the C.I.D. offices lay in the same block. Martin Beck took the liberty of saying: "Well, that wasn't very far, anyway."

"We've made no mistakes," the man said.

"Actually I'm more interested in what happened to Svärd than in who might have made a mistake," Martin Beck said.

"Well, if a mistake's been made, it hasn't been by the Metropolitan Police, anyway."

This retort was insinuating, to say the least. Martin Beck found it best to terminate the conversation. "Thanks for your help," he said. "Good-bye."

The next man on the line was Detective Sergeant Gustavsson, who seemed to be in an incredible rush. "Oh that," he said. "Well, I don't understand it at all. But I assume things like that do happen."

"What things?"

"Inexplicable things, puzzles to which there's quite simply no solution. So one sees at once one might as well give up."

"Be so kind as to come over here," Beck said.

"Now? To Västberga?"

"That's it."

"Unfortunately that's impossible."

"I think not." Martin Beck looked at his watch. "Let's say half past three."

"But it's simply impossible. . . ."

"Half past three," Martin Beck said, and put down the phone. Getting up from his chair he started pacing his room, his hands clasped behind his back.

This opening skirmish said volumes about the trend during the last five years. More and more often one was obliged to initiate an investigation by trying to sort out what the police had been up to. Not infrequently this proved harder than clearing up the actual case.

Aldor Gustavsson made his entrance at 4:05. The name hadn't meant a thing to Martin Beck, but as soon as he saw the man he recognized him. A skinny guy, aged about thirty, dark-haired, with a tough, nonchalant air. Martin Beck recalled having seen him now and then in the orderly room of the Stockholm C.I.D. as well as in other less prominent contexts.

"Please sit down."

Gustavsson sat down in the best chair, crossed his legs, and took out a cigar. He lit it and said: "Crazy story, this, eh? What did you want to know?"

For a while Martin Beck sat quietly, rolling his ball-point pen between his fingers. The he said: "At what time did you get to Bergsgatan?"

"Some time in the evening. About ten."

"What did it look like then?"

"Goddam horrible. Full of big white worms. Smelled to high heaven. One of the patrolmen had thrown up in the lobby."

Where were the policemen?"

"One was on guard outside the door. The other was sitting in the car."

"Had they guarded the door the whole time?"

"Yeah, at least according to their own account."

"And what did you do?"

"I went right in and took a peek. It looked too goddam awful, like I said before. But it could have been something for C.I.D., one never knows."

"But you drew another conclusion?"

"Sure. After all, it was as clear as daylight. The door had been locked from inside in three or four different ways. It had been as much as those guys could do to get it open. And the window was locked and the blind drawn down."

"Was the window still closed?"

"No. Obviously these city police had opened it when they'd come in. Otherwise no one could've stayed in there without a gas mask."

"How long were you there?"

"Not many minutes. Just long enough to establish the fact that it wasn't anything for the C.I.D. It must have been either suicide or natural death, so all the rest was a matter for the city police."

Martin Beck leafed through the report. "There's no list of any objects being taken into custody here," he said.

"Isn't there? Well, I guess somebody ought to have thought about that. On the other hand there was no point in it. The old boy hardly owned a thing. A table, a chair, and a bed, I guess; and then a few bits of junk out in the kitchenette."

"But you looked around?"

"Of course. I inspected everything before I gave them the go-ahead."

"For what?"

"What? How do you mean?"

"Before you gave the go-ahead for what?"

"To take away the remains, of course. The old man had to have a postmortem, didn't he? Even if he was a suicide, he still had to be dissected. It's regulations."

"Can you summarize your observations?"

"Sure. Simple. The body was lying about three yards from the window."

"About?"

"Yeah, the fact was I didn't have a yardstick on me. It looked about two months old; putrid, in other words. In the room were two chairs, a table, and a bed."

"Two chairs?"

"Yeah."

"Just now you said one."

"Oh? Yeah, well it was two anyway, I guess; and then there was a little shelf with some old newspapers and books, and in the kitchenette a couple of saucepans and a coffee pot, and then the usual."

"The usual?"

"Yeah, a can opener, knives and forks, a garbage can, and so forth."

"I see. Was anything lying on the floor?"

"Not a thing, apart from the body, I mean. I asked the patrolmen and they said they hadn't found anything either."

"Was anyone else in the apartment?"

"Nope. I asked the boys, and they said not. No one else went in there, apart from me and these two. Then the guys with the van came and took the body away with them in a plastic bag."

"Since then we have come to know the cause of Svärd's death."

"Sure. Quite so. He shot himself. Incomprehensible, I say. And what did he do with the gun?"

"You've no plausible explanation?"

"None. The whole thing's as idiotic as can be. An insoluble case, like I said. Doesn't happen so often, eh?"

"Did the patrolmen have any opinion?"

"No, all they saw was he was dead and that the place was all shut up. If there'd been a pistol, either they or I'd have found it. Anyway, it could only have been lying on the floor beside that dead old guy."

"Did you find out who the deceased was?"

"Of course. His name was Svärd, wasn't it? It

34

was even written up on the door. You could see at a glance the type of man he'd been."

"What type?"

"Well, a social case. Old drunk, probably. That type often kill themselves; that is, if they don't drink themselves to death or get a heart attack or something."

"You've nothing else of interest to add?"

"No, it's beyond comprehension, like I said. Pure mystery. I guess even you can't fix this one. Anyway there's other things more important."

"Maybe."

"Yes, I guess so. Can I go now?"

"Not quite yet," said Martin Beck.

"I've no more to say," said Aldor Gustavsson, stubbing out his cigar in the ash tray.

Martin Beck got up and walked over to the window, where he stood with his back to his visitor. "I've a few things to say," he said.

"Oh? What?"

"Quite a lot. Among other things the criminologists inspected the place last week. Though almost all traces had been destroyed, one large and two smaller bloodstains were immediately discovered on the carpet. Did you see any patches of blood?"

"No. Not that I looked for any."

"Obviously not. What *did* you look for?"

"Nothing special. The case seemed quite clear."

"If you failed to see those bloodstains, it's conceivable you missed other things."

"Anyway there was no firearm there."

"Did you notice how the dead man was dressed?"

"No, not exactly. After all, he was completely putrid. Some kind of rags, I guess. Besides, I didn't see it made any difference."

"What you did immediately notice was that the deceased had been a poor and lonely person. Not what you would call an eminent member of society."

"Of course. When you've seen as many alcoholics and welfare cases as I have . . ."

"Then?"

"Yes, well, then you know who's who and what's what."

Martin Beck wondered whether Gustavsson did.

35

Aloud he said: "Supposing the deceased had been better adapted socially, perhaps you might have been more conscientious?"

"Yes, in such cases one has to mind one's p's and q's. The fact is, we've one hell of a lot to attend to." He looked around. "Even if you don't realize it here, we're overworked. You can't start playing at Sherlock Holmes every time one comes across a dead bum. Was there anything else?"

"Yes, one thing. I'd like to point out that your handling of this case has been atrocious."

"What?" Gustavsson got up. All of a sudden it seemed to have dawned on him that Martin Beck was in the position to mar his career—perhaps seriously. "Wait a minute," he said. "Just because I didn't see those bloodstains and a gun that wasn't there . . ."

"Sins of omission aren't the worst ones," Martin Beck said. "Even if they, too, are unforgivable. To take an example: you called the police doctor and gave her instructions built on erroneous and preconceived ideas. Further, you fooled the two patrolmen into thinking the case was so simple that you only had to walk into the room and look around for the whole matter to be cleared up. After declaring no criminological investigation was needed, you had the body carried away without even having any photos taken."

"But, my God," Gustavsson said. "The old guy *must* have taken his own life."

Martin Beck turned around and looked at him.

"Are these official criticisms?" said Gustavsson, alarmed.

"Yes, in high degree. Good day."

"Wait a minute. I'll do all I can to help. . . ."

Martin Beck shook his head, and the man left. He seemed worried. But before the door had quite had time to close, Martin Beck heard him utter the words: "Old bastard . . ."

Naturally Aldor Gustavsson ought never to have been a detective sergeant, nor even a policeman of any sort. He was untalented, impudent, conceited, and had a completely wrong approach to his job. The best of the uniformed force had always been recruited into the C.I.D. And probably still were.

36

If men like him had made the grade and become detectives even ten years ago, what were things going to be like in the future?

Martin Beck felt his first working day was at an end. Tomorrow he'd go and have a look at this locked room himself. What was he to do tonight? Eat something, anything, and then sit leafing through books he knew he ought to read. Lie alone in his bed and wait for sleep. Feel shut in.

In his own locked room.

8

Einar Rönn was an outdoor type. He had chosen a career in the police because it kept him on the move and offered lots of opportunities to be outdoors. As the years had passed and one promotion had followed another, his working day had progressively tied him to a sedentary position behind his desk, and his moments in the fresh air, insofar as the Stockholm air can be called fresh, had become steadily rarer. It had become crucial to his existence to be able to spend his vacations in the wild mountain world of Lapland he had come from. Actually he detested Stockholm. Already, at forty-five, he had begun to think about his retirement, when he'd go home to Arjeplog for good.

His annual vacation was approaching, and already he was beginning to be apprehensive. If this bank business, at least, hadn't been cleared up, he might at any moment be asked to sacrifice it.

In order to cooperate actively in bringing the investigation to some sort of conclusion, he had taken it upon himself, this Monday evening, to drive out to Sollentuna and talk to a witness, instead of going home to Vällingby and his wife.

Not only had he volunteered to call on this witness, who could just as easily have been summoned to the C.I.D. in the customary way; he had even showed such enthusiasm for his mission that Gunvald Larsson wondered whether he and Unda had had a quarrel.

"Sure, of course not," Rönn said, with one of his peculiar *non sequiturs*.

The man Rönn was to visit was the thirty-two-year-old metal worker who had already been examined by Gunvald Larsson on what he'd witnessed outside the Hornsgatan bank. His name was Sten Sjögren, and he lived alone in a semidetached house on Sångarvägen. He was in his little garden in front of the house, watering a rose bush, and as Rönn climbed out of his car he put down his watering can and came over to open the gate. Wiping the palms of his hands on the seat of his pants before shaking hands, he went up the steps and held the front door open for Rönn.

The house was small and on the ground floor, apart from the kitchen and foyer, there was only one room. The door to it stood ajar. It was quite empty. The man caught Rönn's look.

"My wife and I have just been divorced," he explained. "She took some of the furniture with her, so perhaps it's not too cozy for the time being. But we can go upstairs instead."

At the top of the stairs there was a rather large room with an open fireplace, in front of which stood a few ill-matched armchairs grouped around a low white table. Rönn sat down, but the man remained standing.

"Can I get you a drink?" he asked. "I can heat up some coffee. But I guess I've some beer in the refrigerator."

"Thanks, I'll take the same as you," Rönn said.

"Then we'll take a beer," said the man. He ran off downstairs and Rönn heard him banging about in the kitchen.

Rönn looked around the room. Not much furniture, a stereo set, quite a few books. In a basket beside the fire lay a bundle of newspapers. *Dagens Nyheter, Vi,* the communist paper *Ny Dag,* and *The Metal Worker.*

Sten Sjögren returned with glasses and two beer cans, which he set down on the white table. He was thin and wiry and had reddish, tousled hair of the length Rönn regarded as normal. His face was spattered with freckles, and he had a pleasant frank smile. After opening the cans and pouring them out he sat down opposite Rönn, raised his glass to him, and drank.

Rönn tasted his beer and said: "I'd like to hear about what you saw on Hornsgatan last Friday. It's best not to give your memory time to fade." That sounded real good, thought Rönn, pleased with himself.

The man nodded and put down his glass. "Yes, if I'd known it was both a holdup and a murder I'd sure have taken a better look both at the chick and at the guy in the car."

"You're the best witness we have so far anyway," Rönn said encouragingly. "So you were walking along Hornsgatan. Which way were you heading?"

"I was coming from Slussen and was heading for Ringvägen. This chick came up from behind and bumped into me quite hard as she ran past."

"Could you describe her?"

"Not too well, I'm afraid. I only really saw her from behind—and for a split second from the side view as she climbed into the car. She was shorter than me, about six inches I guess. I'm five foot ten and a half. The age is a bit hard to specify, but I don't think she was younger than twenty-five and hardly older than thirty-five, about thirty I figure. She was dressed in jeans, ordinary blue, and a light blue blouse or shirt, hanging outside her pants. What she had on her feet I didn't think about, but she was wearing a hat—a denim hat with quite a wide brim. She had fair hair, straight and not quite as long as a lot of chicks wear it these days. Medium length, one could say. Then she had a green shoulder bag, one of those American military bags."

He took out a packet of cigarettes from the breast pocket of his khaki shirt and held them out to Rönn, who shook his head and said: "Did you see if she was carrying anything?"

The man got up, took down a box of matches from the shelf above the open fireplace, and lit a cigarette. "No, I'm not sure of that. But I guess she could have been."

"Her body build? Was she thin, or fat, or . . ."

"Medium, I reckon. In any case neither particularly thin or fat. Normal, one might say."

"Didn't you catch her face at all?"

"I suppose I saw it very fleetingly as she climbed into the car. But for one thing she was wearing that hat, and for another thing she had big sunglasses on."

"Would you recognize her if you saw her again?"

"Not by her face anyway. And probably not if

I saw her in different clothes, in a dress for example."

Rönn sipped his beer thoughtfully. Then he said: "Are you perfectly certain it was a woman?"

The other looked at him in surprise. Then he frowned and said hesitatingly: "Yes, at least I took it for granted it was a chick. But now you mention it I'm not so sure. It was mostly a general impression I got, one usually has a feeling who's a guy and who's a chick, even if nowadays it can be hard to tell 'em apart. I can't actually swear it was a girl. I didn't have time to see what sort of breasts she had."

He fell silent and peered at Rönn through the cigarette smoke. "No, you're right about that," he said slowly. "It didn't have to be a girl; it could very well have been a guy. Moreover, that would be more plausible. You don't often hear of girls who rob banks and shoot people."

"You mean, then, it could just as well have been a man?" Rönn asked.

"Yes, now that you mention it. In fact it must have been a guy."

"Well, but the other two? Can you describe them? And the car?"

Sjögren took a last drag at his cigarette, then threw the butt into the fireplace, where a large number of cigarette ends and dead matches lay already.

"The car was a Renault 16, I know that for sure," he said. "It was light gray or beige, I don't know what the color's called; but it's almost white. I don't remember all the number, but it was an 'A' registration and I've a mental image of two threes in the number. There could have been three, of course, but two at least, and I think they stood one after the other, some place in the middle of the row of figures."

"Are you sure it was 'A'-registered?" Rönn asked. "Not 'AA' or 'AB' for example?"

"No, just 'A.' I remember that clearly. I've a hell of a good visual memory."

"Yes, it's very good," Rönn said. "If all eye-witnesses had one like yours, life would be much simpler."

"Oh yes," said Sjögren, *I Am a Camera.* Have you read it? By Isherwood."

"No," said Rönn. He'd seen the film, though he

didn't say so. He'd seen it because he admired Julie Harris. But he neither knew who Isherwood was nor even that the film was based on a novel.

"But you must have seen the film?" said Sjögren. "That's how it is with all the good books around. People see the film and don't take the trouble to read the book. Now this film was damn good, though it had a stupid title. How about *Wild Nights in Berlin,* eh?"

"Oh," said Rönn, who was sure it was called *I Am a Camera* when he'd seen it. "Yes, it does sound rather stupid."

It was getting dark, and Sten Sjögren got up and lit the floor lamp behind Rönn's armchair. When he sat down again, Rönn said: "Well, suppose we go on. You were going to describe the men in the car."

"Yes, though when I caught sight of them there was only one of them sitting in it."

"Well?"

"The other was standing on the sidewalk, waiting with the rear door ajar. He was a big guy, a good bit taller than me and powerfully built. Not fat, but heavy and powerful looking. He could easily have been my age, roughly between thirty and thirty-five, and had lots of frizzy hair—almost like Harpo Marx, but darker—mouse-colored. He wore black pants, which looked very tight, with those flared leg bottoms, and a shiny black shirt. The shirt was unbuttoned quite far down the chest, and I think he had some sort of silver thing on a chain around his neck. His face was pretty sunburned or, to be more exact, red. When the chick—if it was a chick—came running along, he opened the rear door for her to jump in and then slammed it shut, sat down in front, and the car sped off at a terrific pace."

"In which direction?" Rönn asked.

"It swung right across the street and headed up towards the Maria Square."

"Oh," Rönn said. "I see. And the other man?"

"He was sitting behind the wheel, so I didn't see him too well. But he looked younger, can't have been much over twenty. And he was thin and pale, that much I did see. He was wearing a white T-shirt, and his arms were real scrawny. His hair was black, pretty long, and seemed dirty. Greasy and straggled. He had sunglasses on, yes, and now I remember he had a wide black watch strap on his left wrist."

Sjögren leaned back in his chair, beer glass in hand.

"Well, now I think I've told you all I can recall," he said. "Or do you reckon I've forgotten something?"

"I don't know," Rönn said. "If you should happen to remember anything else, I hope you'll call me. Will you be at home these next few days?"

"Yes, unfortunately," Sjögren said. "In fact I'm on vacation but haven't any dough to travel anywhere with. So I guess I'll just have to hang around here."

Rönn emptied his glass, got up. "Good," he said. "It's very possible we'll be needing your help again a little later on."

Sjögren, too, got up and followed Rönn down the stairs. "You mean I'll have to go through it all again?" he said. "Wouldn't it be best to tape it once and for all?" He opened his front door and Rönn stepped outside.

"What I was thinking was that you might be needed to identify these characters when we catch up with them. It's also possible we may be asking you to come to the C.I.D. to take a look at some pictures." They shook hands, and Rönn went on: "Well, we'll see. We may not have to trouble you further. Thanks for the beer."

"Oh, that was nothing. If I can be of any help, I'd be pleased to oblige."

As Rönn drove off, Sten Sjögren waved amicably from his steps.

9

Police dogs apart, professional sleuths are rarely more than human. Even during the most important and serious investigations they can evince typically human reactions. The tension when some unique and conclusive item of evidence is to be studied, for example, can often become unbearable.

In all this, the special bank robbery squad was no exception. Like their eminent and self-invited guests, they were holding their breath. All eyes in the half-dark room were fixed on the rectangular screen where the bank's film of the Hornsgatan robbery was shortly to be shown. With their own eyes they were not only about to see an armed bank robbery and a murder, but also the person who had committed it and to whom the alert and inventive evening press had already attributed every peculiar trait, dubbing her "the sex-bomb murderer" and "the blond gunwoman in sunglasses"—epithets which only revealed how journalists, lacking any imagination of their own, find inspiration elsewhere. The reality of the case—armed robbery and murder—was too banal for them.

The last sex queen to be caught robbing a bank had been a flat-footed, pimply lady of about forty-five. According to reliable sources, she had weighed 192 pounds and had more double chins that there are pages in a book. But not even the false teeth she lost in front of the court gave the lie, in the press's opinion, to its own lyrical description of her appearance. And a horde of uncritical readers were to remain convinced through all eternity that she was a winsome, starry-eyed creature who should have entered the Miss Universe contest.

Always it had been like this. When women draw

attention to themselves by committing a flagrant crime, the evening papers always make them sound as if they've come straight out of Inger Malmroos's school for models.

The pictures of the robbery had only just become available. This was because the cassette, as usual, had been faulty, and the photo lab had had to take extreme care not to damage the exposed negative. In the end, however, they had managed to pry it loose from the spool and develop it without even fraying its edges. For once the exposure, at least, seemed to have been correct and the results were being predicted as technically perfect.

"What's it to be?" Gunvald Larsson quipped. "A Donald Duck?"

"The Pink Panther's funnier," said Kollberg.

"Some guys, of course," Gunvald Larsson said, "are hoping for the Nazi rallies at Nuremberg."

They were both sitting in the front row and spoke in loud voices, but behind them prevailed only a deep silence. All the potentates present, notably the National Police Commissioner and Superintendent Malm from the National Police Board, held their tongues. Kollberg wondered what they were thinking.

Weighing up their chances, no doubt, of making life hell for refractory subordinates. Perhaps their thoughts were even harking back to the days when there'd really been some order in things, when Heydrich had been elected president of the International Police Association by acclamation. Or perhaps they were thinking how much better the situation had been only a year ago, even, before anyone had dared to doubt the wisdom of once again entrusting all police training to military reactionaries.

The only one who sniggered was Bulldozer Olsson.

Formerly Kollberg and Gunvald Larsson had had very little to do with each other. But in recent years certain common experiences had to some extent changed the situation. Not to the point where they could be called buddies or where the notion of associating outside their work would ever have occurred to them; but ever more frequently they found they were on the same wavelength. And here, in the special squad, they unquestionably had to stick together.

The technical preparations were over. The room was vibrating with suppressed excitement.

"Well, now we'll see," Bulldozer Olsson said enthusiastically. "If the pictures are as good as they say they are, we'll put them on television tonight, and that'll give us the whole gang in a little box."

"Longlegs is passable, too," Gunvald Larsson said.

"Or Swedish Sex," said Kollberg. "Fancy—I've never seen a blue movie. You know, *Louise, Seventeen, Strips,* all that sort of stuff."

"Quiet over there!" snapped the National Police Commissioner.

The film began. The focus was perfect. None of those present had ever seen anything like such excellent results. Usually the thieves only resembled vague blobs or poached eggs; but this time the image was perfect.

The camera had been artfully placed to show the cashier's desk from behind, and thanks to a new type of hypersensitive film they could see with perfect clarity the person standing on the other side of the counter.

At first there was nobody there. But only half a minute later a person had come into the field of vision, then stopped and looked around—first to the right then to the left. Whereafter the person in question stared straight into the lens, as if purposely to give a full-face view.

Even the clothes showed up clearly; a suede jacket and a well-cut shirt with long, soft points to the collar.

The face itself was forceful and grim, the blond hair was combed back, and the fair eyebrows were shaggy. The eyes wore an air of discontent. Then the figure raised a large hairy hand and, extracting a hair from one nostril, scrutinized it at length.

At once they all saw who it was.

Gunvald Larsson.

Then the lights went up.

The special squad sat speechless.

The National Police Commissioner was the first to speak.

"Nothing of this must get out."

Naturally. Nothing was ever allowed to get out.

Superintendent Malm said in a shrill voice: "Absolutely nothing of this must be allowed to come out."

Kollberg let out a guffaw.

"How can this have happened?" Bulldozer Olsson asked. Even he seemed a trifle put out.

"Well," the film expert said, "there could be a technical explanation. The trigger may have gotten jammed and the camera started up a bit later than it should have. These are sensitive gadgets, you know."

"If I see so much as a single word in the press," thundered the National Police Commissioner, "then . . ."

". . . then the Ministry'll have to order another new carpet for someone's office," said Gunvald Larsson. "Maybe there's a kind with a raspberry flavor."

"Fanstastic get-up she was wearing," snorted Kollberg.

The National Police Commissioner dashed for the door. Superintendent Malm wagged out after him.

Kollberg gasped for air.

"What's one to say about this?" said Bulldozer Olsson.

"Though I say so myself," Gunvald Larsson said modestly, "I think that film was real good."

10

Kollberg had collected himself and was looking dubiously at the person who, for the time being, he had to regard as his boss.

Bulldozer Olsson was the special squad's main engine. He was in love with bank robberies, and after the past year's avalanche of such events he'd blossomed out as never before. It was he who had all the energy and ideas. Week after week he could go on working eighteen hours a day, without once complaining, getting depressed, or even becoming noticeably tired. At times his exhausted colleagues wondered whether he wasn't himself managing director of the Swedish Crime Co., that sinister organization which there was so much talk of. To Bulldozer Olsson police work was the most enjoyable and exciting thing imaginable.

This, no doubt, was because he was not a policeman.

He was a district attorney, who was in charge of preliminary investigations into a wholly impenetrable skein of armed bank robberies. One of these was already half-solved, and a few more-or-less guilty persons were being held in custody, and some had even been charged. But now things had got to such a pass that new holdups were occurring several times a week, and everybody realized that many of them were in some way and to some extent connected, though just how nobody could say.

Furthermore, banks were not the only targets. There had been an enormous increase in assaults on private persons. Every hour of the day and night people were being struck down in the city's streets and squares, in their own boutiques, in the subway, or in their homes, indeed, everywhere and anywhere. But the bank robberies were deemed by far the most serious. To violate society's banks was to commit an outrage against its very foundations.

The existing social system was obviously hardly viable and only with the best of will could be described as functioning at all. Even this could not be said of the police. During the last two years Stockholm alone had had to shelve 220,000 criminal investigations; and even of the most serious crimes—only a small fraction of the total—only a quarter were ever cleared up.

This being the state of affairs, there was little that those who bore ultimate responsibility could do except shake their heads and look thoughtful. For a long while everyone had been blaming everyone else; and now there was no longer anyone to blame. The only constructive suggestion put forward recently had been that people should be prevented from drinking beer. Since Sweden is a country where beer consumption is rather low anyway, it can be seen just how unrealistic was the so-called thinking of many representatives of the country's highest authorities.

One thing, however, was plain. The police had largely only themselves to blame. After the 1965 nationalization, the entire force now came under a single hat, and from the outset it had been obvious that this hat was sitting on the wrong head.

For a long time now many analysts and researchers had been asking themselves what the philosophy might be that was guiding activities at National Police Headquarters. A question which, of course, went unanswered. In accordance with his doctrine that nothing must ever be allowed to leak out, the National Police Commissioner, on principle, never gave answers to anything. On the other hand, he was only too fond of speechifying—speeches which, even as samples of sheer rhetoric, were totally uninteresting.

Some years ago someone in the police force had discovered a way of manipulating crime statistics. The methods used, though simple, were not immediately transparent, and without being directly mendacious were nevertheless utterly misleading. It had all started with demands for a more militant and homogeneous police force, for greater technical resources in general, and for more firearms in particular. To get this it had been necessary to exaggerate the hazards that policemen faced. Since verbiage had not proved politically effective enough, recourse had then been made to another method: namely, the manipulation of statistics.

At this juncture the political demonstrations during the second half of the sixties had opened up magnificent possibilities. Demonstrators pleading for peace had been suppressed by violence. Hardly ever armed with anything but their banners and their convictions, they had been met by tear gas, water cannons, and rubber nightsticks. Few were the nonviolent demonstrations that had not ended in tumult and chaos. Those individuals who had tried to defend themselves had been mauled about, arrested, and prosecuted for "assaulting the police" or "resisting arrest." All this information had been fed into the statistics. The method had worked perfectly. Each time a few hundred policemen were sent out to "control" a demonstration, the figures for alleged assaults against the police had rocketed.

The uniformed police had been encouraged, "not to pull their punches," as the expression went, orders with which many a patrolman had been only too delighted, in all possible situations, to comply. Tap a drunk with a nightstick and the chances of his hitting back are always fairly high.

A simple lesson, which anyone could learn.

These tactics had worked. Now the Swedish police were armed to the teeth. All of a sudden, situations that formerly could have been cleared up by a single man equipped with a lead pencil and a pinch of common sense required a busload of patrolmen equipped with automatics and bullet-proof vests.

The long-term result, however, was something no one had quite foreseen. Violence breeds not only antipathy and hatred but also insecurity and fear.

In the end things had come to such a pass that people were going about being scared of each other and Stockholm had become a city containing tens of thousands of terrified individuals. And frightened people are dangerous people.

Many of the six hundred patrolmen who suddenly no longer existed had in fact resigned because they were scared—yes, even though they were armed to the teeth and for the most part just sat locked inside their cars.

Many, of course, had fled from Stockholm for other reasons, either because they'd come to dislike the place in general, or because they were disgusted with the treatment they were now obliged to mete out.

The regime had backfired. As for its deepest motives, they remained shrouded in darkness—a darkness, however, in which some people detected a tint of Nazi brown.

Examples of similar manipulations abounded, and some bore witness to fargone cynicism. A year ago there had been a drive against people passing bad checks. People were overdrawing their accounts, and some money had ended up in the wrong pockets. The figures for unsolved petty fraud were regarded as discreditable, and called for radical measures. The National Police Board objected to checks being accepted as legal tender. Everyone knew what this would mean: people would have to carry a lot of cash with them, and this would give the green light to muggers on the city's streets and squares. Which was precisely what had happened. Fraudulent checks, of course, disappeared, and the police could boast of a questionable success. The fact that numerous citizens were daily being beaten up was of minor importance.

It was all part and parcel of the rising tide of violence, to which the only answer was ever more numerous and still better armed police.

But where were all these policemen to come from?

The official crime figures for the first six months had been a great triumph. They showed a drop of two percent, although as everybody knew there had really been a massive increase. The explanation was simple. Nonexistent policemen cannot expose crimes. And every overdrawn bank account had been counted as a crime in itself.

51

When the political police had been forbidden to bug people's telephones, the theorists of the National Police Board had hastened to their aid. Through scare propaganda and gross exaggeration Parliament had been prevailed on to pass a law permitting phones to be bugged in the struggle against narcotics. Whereupon the anticommunists had calmly continued their eavesdropping, and the narcotics trade had flourished as never before.

No, it was no fun, thought Lennart Kollberg, being a policeman. What could a man do as he witnessed the gradual decay of his own organization? As he heard the rats of fascism pattering about behind the wainscoting? All his adult life he had loyally served this organization.

What to do? Say what you think and get the sack? Unpleasant. There must be some more constructive line of action. And, of course, there were other police officers besides himself who saw things in the same light. But which, and how many?

No such problems afflicted Bulldozer Olsson. Life, to him, was one big jolly game, and most things as clear as crystal. "But there's one thing I don't get," he said.

"Really?" said Gunvald Larsson. "What?"

"What happened to that car? The roadblocks functioned as they ought to, didn't they?"

"So it appears."

"So there should have been men on all the bridges within five minutes."

The South Side of Stockholm is an island, with six points of access. The special squad had long ago devised detailed schemes by which each of the Stockholm downtown districts could quickly be sealed off.

"Sure," said Gunvald Larsson. "I've checked with the Metropolitan Police. For once everything seems to have clicked."

"What kind of a car was it?" Kollberg asked. As yet he hadn't had time to catch up on all the details.

"A Renault 16, light gray or beige, 'A'-registered, and with two threes in its number."

"Naturally they'd given it a false license plate," Gunvald Larsson put in.

"Obviously. But I've yet to hear of someone being able to respray a car between Maria Square and Slussen. And if they switched cars . . ."

"Yes?"

"Then where did the first one get to?"

Bulldozer Olsson paced the room, thumping the palms of his hands against his forehead. He was a man in his forties, chubby, well under average height, with a slightly florid complexion. His movements were as animated as his intellect. Now he was addressing himself: "They park the car in a garage near a subway station or a bus stop, then one of the guys beats it with the dough; the other one gives the car a new license plate. Then he beats it too. On Saturday the car guy comes back and does the respraying. And yesterday morning the car was ready to be driven off. But . . ."

"But what?" asked Kollberg.

"But I had our people check every single Renault leaving the South Side right up to 1 A.M. last night."

"So either it had time to get away, or else it's still here," said Kollberg.

Gunvald Larsson said nothing at all. Instead he scrutinized Bulldozer Olsson's attire and felt an intense antipathy. A crumpled light blue suit, a piggy-pink shirt, and a wide flowery tie. Black socks and pointed brown shoes with stitching—notably unbrushed.

"And what do you mean by the car guy?"

"They never fix the cars themselves. They always hire a special guy, who leaves them in some prearranged spot and gets them afterwards. Often he comes from some completely different town, Malmö or Göteborg, for example. They're always very careful about the getaway cars."

Kollberg, looking even more pensive, said: "They? Who's they?"

"Malmström and Mohrén, of course."

"And who are Malmström and Mohrén?"

Bulldozer Olsson gazed at him, dumbfounded. But then his gaze cleared. "Ah yes, of course. You're new to the squad, aren't you? Malmström and Mohrén are two of our smartest bank robbers. It's four months now since they got out. And this is their fourth job since.

53

They beat it from Kumla Prison at the end of February."

"But Kumla's supposed to be escape-proof," Kollberg said.

"Malmström and Mohrén didn't escape. They just failed to return from weekend parole. As far as we can see, they didn't do any jobs until the end of April —before which they must certainly have gone on vacation to the Canaries or Gambia. Probably a fourteen-day round trip."

"And then?"

"Then they equipped themselves. Weapons and so forth. They usually do that in Spain or Italy."

"But it was a woman who raided that bank last Friday, wasn't it?" Kollberg remarked.

"Disguised," said Bulldozer Olsson didactically. "Disguised in a blond wig and falsies. But I'm dead sure it was Malmström and Mohrén who did it. Who else would have had the nerve, or been smart enough to make such a sudden move? This is a special job, don't you see, hellish intriguing really. Frightfully exciting. Actually it's like . . ."

". . . playing a game of postal chess with a champ," said Gunvald Larsson. "But champ or not, both Malmström and Mohrén are as big as oxes, and that's something you can't talk yourself out of. Each weighs 209 pounds, wears size twelve shoes, and has hands like hams. Mohrén is forty-six inches around the chest—that's five more than Anita Ekberg in her prime. I find it difficult to imagine him fitted out in a dress, wearing falsies."

"Wasn't the woman wearing pants anyway?" asked Kollberg. "And rather on the small side?"

"Naturally they sent in someone else," Bulldozer Olsson said placidly. "One of their usual tricks." Running over to one of the desks he grabbed a slip of paper. "How much dough have they gotten hold of?" he asked himself. "Fifty thousand in Borås, forty in Gubbängen, twenty-six in Märsta, and now ninety. That makes over two hundred thousand! So they'll soon be ready."

"Ready?" Kollberg asked. "Ready for what?"

"Their big haul. Big with a capital 'H.' All these

other jobs are just to get some finance. But any time now it'll be the big bang." Seemingly beside himself with enthusiasm, he practically flew around the room. "But where, gentlemen? Where? Let me see, let me see. We must think. If I were Werner Roos now, what move would I make? How would I attack his king? How would *you* do it? And when?"

"Who the hell's Werner Roos?" Kollberg inquired again.

"He's an airline purser," said Gunvald Larsson.

"First and foremost he's a criminal," Bulldozer Olsson shouted. "In his own way Werner Roos is a genius. He's the one who plots out everything down to the last detail. Without him Malmström and Mohrén would be mere nonentities. It's he who does all the thinking. Without him plenty of others would be out of work. And he's the biggest skunk of the lot! He's a sort of professor of—"

"Don't shout so damn loud," said Gunvald Larsson. "You're not in the district court."

"We'll get him," Bulldozer Olsson said, as if he'd just hit on some genial idea. "We'll grab him now, right away."

"And release him tomorrow," said Gunvald Larsson.

"Never mind. It'll be a surprise. Catch him off his guard."

"You think so? It'll be the fifth time this year."

"No matter," said Bulldozer Olsson, making for the door.

Actually Bulldozer Olsson's first name was Sten. But this was something everyone, except possibly his wife, had long ago forgotten. She, on the other hand, had very likely forgotten what he looked like.

"There seem to be a lot of things I don't understand," Kollberg complained.

"Where Roos is concerned, Bulldozer's probably right," Gunvald Larsson said. "He's a smart devil who's always got an alibi. Fantastic alibis. Whenever anything happens he's always away in Singapore or San Francisco or Tokyo."

"But how does Bulldozer know these Malmström and Mohrén guys are behind this particular job?"

"Some sort of sixth sense, I guess."

Gunvald Larsson shrugged and said: "But where's the sense in it? Here are Malmström and Mohrén, known to be a couple of gangsters, who, though they never confess, have been inside any number of times. And now, when at last they're behind lock and key in Kumla, they're granted weekend parole!"

"Well, we can't really keep people locked up in one room with a TV set for all eternity, can we?"

"No," said Gunvald Larsson. "That's true enough."

For a while they sat silent. Both men were thinking the same thing: how it had cost the state millions to build Kumla Prison and equip it with every conceivable refinement designed to insulate social misfits from society. Foreigners with experience in penal institutions from far and wide had said that Kumla's internment department was probably the most inhuman and personality-deadening in the whole world. Lack of lice in the mattresses or worms in the food is no substitute for human contact.

"As for this murder on Hornsgatan . . ." Kollberg began.

"That wasn't murder. Probably just an accident. She fired by mistake, maybe didn't even realize the gun was loaded."

"Sure it was a girl?"

"Yeah."

"What about all this talk of Malmström and Mohrén, then?"

"Well, it's just possible they sent in a girl. . . ."

"Weren't there any fingerprints? As far as I know, she wasn't even wearing gloves."

"Sure there were fingerprints. On the doorknob. But before we had time to lift them one of the bank people had been there and messed it all up. So we couldn't use them."

"Any ballistic investigation?"

"You bet your life there was. The experts got both the bullet and the cartridge. They say she shot him with a forty-five, presumably a Llama Auto."

"Big gun . . . especially for a girl."

"Yeah. According to Bulldozer that's another bit

of evidence on this Malmström and Mohrén and Roos gang. They always use big, heavy weapons, to cause alarm. But . . ."

"But what?"

"Malmström and Mohrén don't shoot people. At least they've never done so yet. If someone causes trouble they just put a bullet in the ceiling, to restore order."

"Is there any point in holding this Roos guy?"

"Hmm, well I guess Bulldozer's reasoning goes like this: If Roos has one of his usual perfect alibis —for instance, if he was in Yokohama last Friday —then we can be dead sure he planned the job. On the other hand, if he was in Stockholm, then the thing's more doubtful."

"What does Roos say himself? Doesn't he get mad?"

"Never. He says it's true Malmström and Mohrén are old chums of his and he thinks its sad things should have turned out so badly for them in life. Last time he asked if we thought he could help his old chums in some way. Malm happened to be there. He almost had a brain hemorrhage."

"And Olsson?"

"Bulldozer just roared. He loved it."

"What's he waiting for, then?"

"The next move, didn't you hear? He thinks Roos is planning a major job which Malmström and Mohrén are going to carry out. Presumably Malmström and Mohrén want to scrape enough money together to emigrate quietly and live the rest of their lives on the proceeds."

"And it's got to be a bank robbery?"

"Bulldozer thinks everything except banks can go to the devil," said Gunvald Larsson. "It's his orders, so they say."

"What about the witness?"

"Einar's?"

"Yeah."

"He was here this morning, looking at pictures. Didn't recognize anyone."

"But he's sure of the car?"

"Damn right."

Gunvald Larsson sat silent, tugging at his fingers one after the other until the joints cracked. After a long while he said: "There's something about that car that doesn't jell."

11

The day looked like it was going to be a hot one, and Martin Beck took his lightest suit out of the closet. It was pale blue. He'd bought it a month ago and only worn it once. As he pulled on his pants a big, sticky chocolate mark on the right trouser knee reminded him how, on that particular occasion, he'd been chatting with Kollberg's two kids and how they'd indulged in an orgy of lollipops and Mums-Mums chocolate balls.

Martin Beck climbed out of his trousers again, took them into the kitchen, and soaked one corner of a towel in hot water. Then he rubbed the towel against the stain, which immediately spread. Yet he didn't give up. As he gritted his teeth and went on working away at the material he thought to himself it was really only in such situations that he missed Inga—which said a good deal about their former relationship. At least one of the trouser legs was thoroughly soaked, and the stain seemed at least partially to have disappeared. Squeezing his thumb and forefinger along the crease, he hung his pants over a chair in the sunshine which was flooding in through the open window.

It was only eight o'clock, but already he'd been awake for several hours. In spite of everything, he'd fallen asleep early the previous evening, and his sleep had been unusually calm and free of dreams. True, though it had been his first real working day in a long time, it had not been a particularly strenuous one; even so, it had left him exhausted.

Martin Beck opened the refrigerator door, inspected the milk carton, the stick of butter, and a solitary bottle of Ramlösa—reminding himself that on his way home tonight he must make some purchases, beer and yogurt. Or maybe he ought to stop having yogurt in the mornings; it really didn't taste all that good. On the other hand, that would mean he'd have to think up something else for his breakfast. The doctor had said he must put back on every pound he'd lost since he'd come out of the hospital, and preferably a few more.

The telephone in the bedroom rang. Martin Beck closed the refrigerator, and going in, picked up the receiver. It was Sister Birgit at the old people's home.

"Mrs. Beck is worse," she said. "This morning she had a high temperature, well over 101. I thought you'd want to know, Inspector."

"Sure. Of course. Is she awake now?"

"She was, five minutes ago. But she's very tired."

"I'll be over immediately," Martin Beck said.

"We've had to move her into a room where we can have her under better observation," Sister Birgit said. "But come to my office first."

Martin Beck's mother was eighty-two and had spent the last two years in the sick ward of the old people's home. Her illness had been of long duration. Its first signs had been slight attacks of dizziness. As time had gone by, these had become more severe and occurred at closer intervals. In the end she'd become partially paralyzed. All last year she'd only been able to sit up in a wheelchair, and since the end of April hadn't left her bed.

Martin Beck had visited her quite often during his own convalescence, but it pained him to see her slowly wasting away as her age and illness slowly dazed her. The last few times he'd been to see her she'd taken him for her husband. His father had been dead twenty-two years.

To see how lonely she'd become in her sickroom, and how utterly cut off from the outside world too, had pained him. Right up to the time when the spells of dizziness had started she'd gone out, even gone into town, just to visit stores and see people around her, or to call on those few of her friends who were still alive. Often she'd gone out to see Inga and Rolf in Bagarmossen or visited her granddaughter Ingrid, who lived by herself out at Stocksund. Naturally, even before her illness, she'd often been bored and lonely in the old people's home, but as long as she'd been healthy and on her feet she still had an occasional chance to see something besides invalids and old people. She'd still read the papers, watched TV, and listened to the radio—occasionally she had even gone to a concert or the movies. She kept in touch with the world around her and had been able to interest herself in what was going on in it. But once isolation had been forced upon her, there had been rapid mental deterioration.

Martin Beck had watched her becoming slow-witted, ceasing to interest herself in life outside the sickroom walls, until in the end she'd lost all touch with reality and the present. It must be some defense mechanism of her mind, he assumed, which nowadays tied her consciousness to the past: there was nothing heartening about her present reality.

When he had realized how her days passed, even as long as she'd still be able to sit up in a wheelchair, he'd been shocked—even though she had seemed happy to see him and aware of his visits. Every morning she was washed and dressed, put into her wheelchair, and given her breakfast. Then she just sat there all alone in her room. Since her hearing had deteriorated she no longer listened to the radio. Reading had become too strenuous, and her hands had become too weak to hold any needlework. At noon she was given her lunch, and at three the attendants finished their working day by undressing her and putting her back to bed. Later she was given a light evening meal, but she had no appetite and often refused to eat at all. Once she'd told him the attendants were cross with her for not eating. But it didn't matter. At least it had meant someone had come and talked to her.

Martin Beck knew that a lack of staff constituted a difficult problem for the old people's home, not least the shortage of nurses and ward assistants. He also knew that such personnel as did exist were friendly and considerate to the old folk—despite wretchedly low wages and inconveniently long working hours—and that they did their best for them. He'd given a great deal of thought to how he could make existence more tolerable for her, maybe by having her moved to a private nursing home where people would devote more time and attention to her; but he'd quickly come to the conclusion that she could not expect much better care than where she was already. All he could do for her was to visit her as often as possible. During his examination of the possibilities for improving his mother's situation he'd discovered how much worse off an incredible number of other old people were.

To grow old alone and in poverty, unable to look after oneself, meant that after a long and active life one was suddenly stripped of one's dignity and identity —fated to await the end in an institution in the company of other old people, equally outcast and annihilated.

Today they were not even called "institutions," or even "old people's homes." Nowadays they were called "pensioners' homes," or even "pensioners' hotels," to gloss over the fact that in practice most people weren't there voluntarily, but had quite simply been condemned to it by a so-called Welfare State that no longer wished to know about them. It was a cruel sentence, and the crime was being too old. As a worn-out cog in the social machine, one was dumped on the garbage heap.

Martin Beck realized that in spite of everything his mother was better off than most of the other old and sick people. She had saved and stinted and put aside money in order to be secure in her old age and not become a burden to anyone. Although inflation had catastrophically devalued her money, she still received medical care, fairly nutritious food, and, in her large and airy sickroom, which she was spared from sharing with anyone else, she still had her own intimate belongings around her. This much at least she had been able to buy with her savings.

Now his pants had dried slowly in the sunny window and the stain had disappeared almost completely. He dressed and rang for a taxi.

The park around the old people's home was spacious and well kept, with tall, leafy trees and cool, shady paths winding between the arbors, flowerbeds,

62

and terraces. Before his mother had fallen sick she had liked to walk there, leaning on his arm.

Martin Beck went straight to the office; but neither Sister Birgit nor anyone else was there. In the corridor he met a maid carrying a tray with thermos bottles. He asked after Sister Birgit, and the assistant informed him in sing-song Finnish-Swedish that Sister Birgit was occupied at the moment with a patient. He asked her which was Mrs. Beck's room. She nodded toward a door further down the corridor and went off with her tray.

Martin Beck looked in at the door. The room was smaller than the one his mother had had before and looked more like a sickroom. Inside, everything was white except the bouquet of red tulips he'd given her two days ago, which were now standing on a table beside the window. His mother was lying in bed, staring at the ceiling with eyes that seemed to grow larger every time he visited her. Her skinny hands plucked at the bedspread. Standing by the bed, he took her hand, and she moved her eyes slowly up to his face. "Have you come all this way?" she whispered in a scarcely audible voice.

"Don't tire yourself by talking, Mom," Martin Beck said, releasing her hand. He sat looking at the tired face with the wide feverish eyes. "How are you, Mom?" he asked.

She didn't answer immediately—just looked at him and blinked once or twice, as though her eyelids were so heavy it was an effort to lift them. "I'm cold," she said at last.

Martin Beck looked around the room. A blanket lay on a chair at the foot of the bed. He picked it up and spread it over her.

"Thank you, my dear," she whispered.

Again he sat quiet, looking at her. Not knowing what to say, he just held her thin, cold hand in his.

There was a faint rattle in her throat as she breathed. Gradually her breathing became more calm, and she closed her eyes. He went on sitting there, holding her hand. A blackbird sang outside the window. Otherwise all was quiet.

63

When he had sat there, quite still, a long while, he gently let go of her hand and got up. He stroked her cheek. It was hot and dry. Just as he took a step toward the door, still looking down at her face, she opened her eyes and looked at him.

"Put your woollen cap on," she whispered, "it's cold out." And again she closed her eyes.

After a while Martin Beck bent down, kissed her on the forehead, and left.

12

Today Kenneth Kvastmo, one of the two patrol-men who had broken into Svärd's apartment, had to give evidence again in the district court. Martin Beck looked in on him where he sat waiting in a corridor of City Hall and had time to get answers to two of his most important questions before Kvastmo was called into court.

Then Martin Beck left City Hall and walked the two blocks to the house where Svärd had lived. It was a short stretch, but as he walked down it, he passed the two large building sites on either side of the police building. Outside the south wing the new subway line to Järvafältet was being excavated, and further up the hill blasting and drilling operations were going on into the bedrock for the foundation of the new police build-ing, where soon he would have his office. Right now he was grateful that his office was in the South Police Headquarters and not here. The noise of traffic from Södertäljevägen outside his window was no more than a quiet hum compared to this cacophony arising from excavations, pneumatic drills, and trucks.

The front door to the first-floor apartment had been put back and sealed. Martin Beck broke the seal and walked in.

The window over the street was closed, and he perceived a slight but penetrating smell of putrefaction that had bitten its way into the room's walls and sparse furniture.

He went over to the window and examined it. It was an old-fashioned type, opening outwards and fitted with a clasp whose ring-shaped swinging latch hung from a fitting in the window frame and fit over a catch when the window was fastened. There were two latches, but the lower catch was missing. The paint had worn off, and the woodwork of the lower part of the window frame and sill had been damaged. Presumably both rain and wind entered through the crack.

Martin Beck pulled down the blind. Originally dark blue, it was old and faded. He went over to the door and looked into the room. This was how it had looked when the two patrolmen had broken in, at least according to Kvastmo. He went back to the window, gave the cord a slight jerk, and with a tired creak the blind rolled up. Then he opened the window and looked out.

On his right was the noisy building site, and beyond it he could see among other things the windows of the C.I.D. in the Kungsholmsgatan building. To his left Bergsgatan went on a little further, then just above the fire station the street came to an end. A short stretch of street joined Bergsgatan and Hantverkargatan. Martin Beck reflected that that was the way he'd walk after finishing his inspection. He couldn't recall what the street was called or ever having walked along it.

Opposite the window was Kronoberg Park. Like most other Stockholm parks, it was laid out on a natural rise in the ground. In the days when he'd worked at Kristineberg, Martin Beck remembered often taking a short cut across it. It had been his habit to cross the park between the stone steps in the corner by Polhemsgatan and the old Jewish cemetery on the far side. Sometimes he'd stopped to smoke a cigarette on a bench beneath the linden trees at the top of the hill.

Feeling a craving for a cigarette, he felt in his pockets, knowing full well he had none on him. He gave a resigned sigh and reflected that he should start chewing gum or sucking cough drops instead. Or chewing toothpicks, like Månsson down in Malmö.

He went out into the kitchen. Its window was in an even worse state than the one in the room; but here the window cracks had been plugged with strips of tape.

Everything in the apartment seemed worn, not only the paint and wallpaper but also the furniture. Looking around the apartment, Martin Beck felt a dull feeling of infinite sadness. He opened all the drawers and closets. There wasn't much there, only the basic household utensils.

66

Going out into the narrow foyer, he opened the door to the toilet. There was no wash basin or shower. Then he examined the front door and found it was fitted with the various locks mentioned in the report. It seemed probable that they had all been locked when the door had finally been lifted out of the way, or "forced" as it was called in police jargon.

It was all really most perplexing. Door and both windows had been locked. Kvastmo had said there was no weapon to be seen anywhere in the apartment when he and Kristiansson had gone in. Moreover, he had said that the apartment had been under constant guard and that for anyone to have been there and removed anything was out of the question.

Once again Martin Beck stood in the doorway looking into the room. Along the inner wall was a bed, and beside it a shelf. Above the shelf was a lamp with a crinkled yellow cloth shade, a broken green glass ash tray, and a large box of matches. On the shelf lay a pair of much-thumbed magazines and three books. By the right-hand wall stood a chair upholstered in green and white striped material with spots on its seat, and against the far wall were a brown table and a straight wooden chair. On the floor stood an electric heater with a black cord coiling away to a wall socket. The plug had been pulled out. There had been a carpet too, but it had been sent to the lab, where, among innumerable other stains and particles of dirt, they'd found three bloodstains of Svärd's blood type.

A closet adjoined the room. On its floor were a dirty flannel shirt of uncertain color, three dirty socks, and an empty worn brown canvas bag. On a hanger hung a fairly new poplin coat, and on hooks in the wall were a pair of flannel trousers with empty pockets, a knitted green sweater, and a gray vest with full-length sleeves. That was all.

That Svärd could have been shot somewhere else, then come into his apartment, locked and bolted the door behind him, and then lain down to die, was—according to the pathologist—something that could not wholly be ruled out. Martin Beck, admittedly, was only a layman; but he'd had enough experience to see she was right.

But how had it all happened, then? How could Svärd have been shot if no one had been in the apartment and he hadn't done it himself?

When Martin Beck had first discovered how carelessly the whole matter had been handled he'd been convinced that even this mystery could be explained in terms of someone's carelessness; but now he was beginning to feel sure there'd never been a weapon in the room, that Svärd had locked the door behind him, and that consequently his death appeared utterly inexplicable.

Once again Martin Beck went through the apartment with meticulous care; but there was nothing there to explain what had happened. Finally he left, intending to find out whether the other tenants had anything to tell him.

Three-quarters of an hour later, none the wiser, he came out into the street. Obviously the sixty-two-year-old ex-warehouseman, Karl Edvin Svärd, had been a very solitary person. He had lived in the apartment for three months, and only a few of the other tenants had even been aware of his existence. Those who had seen him come and go had never seen him with anyone else. None of them had ever exchanged a word with him. He had never been seen drunk, nor had they heard any disturbing sounds or noises coming from his apartment.

Martin Beck remained standing outside the main entrance. He looked up at the park, which rose up green and leafy, on the other side of the street. He had a mind to go up there and sit a while beneath the linden trees; but then he recalled his decision to examine the little street on the hillside.

"Olof Gjödingsgatan." He read the name on the street sign and recalled that many years ago he had found out that Olof Gjöding had been a teacher in the Kungsholmen School back in the eighteenth century. He wondered whether the school had stood on the same site as the high school down on Hantverkargatan.

On the slope down to Polhemsgatan was a cigar store. He went in and bought a pack of filter cigarettes. On his way to Kungsholmsgatan he lit one and thought it tasted bad. He thought about Karl Edvin Svärd. He felt none too well and rather confused.

13

When the midday flight from Amsterdam landed at Arlanda that Tuesday there were two plainclothes policemen stationed in the arrival lounge to meet the plane's purser. They had orders to behave discreetly and take no unnecessary measures; and when, finally, the purser came walking across the tarmac in the company of a stewardess they decided to bide their time and stand aside.

Werner Roos, however, spotted them at once. Either he recognized them from some earlier occasion, or simply sensed them to be police, instantly comprehending that their presence there had something to do with him. He stopped, said a few words to the stewardess, and then walked into the arrival lounge through the glass doors.

With firm steps Werner Roos went up to the two policemen. Tall, broad-shouldered, suntanned, he was wearing his dark blue uniform. In one hand he held his cap, in the other a black leather bag with broad straps. He had blond hair with long sideburns and a tousled fringe, and his bushy eyebrows frowned threateningly. Thrusting forward his chin he gave them a cold, blue look. "Well, and what kind of reception committee is this?" he asked.

"District Attorney Olsson would like to have a little talk with you, so if you'd be so kind as to accompany us to Kungsholmsgatan . . ." one of the policemen said.

Roos said: "Is he crazy? I was there only two weeks ago, and I've nothing more to add today to what I said then."

"Okay, okay," said the older of the two. "You'll

have to talk to him about that, we're only following instructions."

Roos shrugged his shoulders in annoyance and started walking towards the exit. When they got to the car he said: "And you'll damn well have to drive me home to Märsta first, so I can change my clothes. You know the address." Then he sat down in the back seat with a grim look on his face and his arms crossed over his chest.

The younger policeman, who was driving, protested at being ordered about like a cab driver; but his colleague calmed him down and gave him the Märsta address.

Following Roos up to his apartment, they waited in the foyer while he changed into light gray pants, a turtleneck sweater, and a suede jacket. Then they drove back to Stockholm and the police station on Kungsholmsgatan, where they escorted him to the room in which Bulldozer Olsson was waiting.

As the door opened Bulldozer sprang up from his chair, dismissed the two plainsclothesmen with a wave of his hand, and drew up a chair for Werner Roos. Then, settling down behind the desk, he said cheerfully: "Well, Mr. Roos, and who would have thought we'd meet again so soon!"

"You, I suppose," said Roos. "Really it's not my fault. I'd like to know what reason you may have for arresting me this time."

"Oh, don't let's take it all so solemnly, Mr. Roos. We could say I want a little information from you. At least to start with."

"I also regard it as unnecessary to send out your henchmen to bring me from my place of work. Besides which I might very well at this moment have had a flight, and I've really no desire to lose my job just because it suddenly amuses you to sit there talking nonsense to me."

"Don't take it so hard. I know you're off duty for forty-eight hours, Mr. Roos. Isn't that so? So we've plenty of time, and there's no harm done," Bulldozer said amiably.

"You can't keep me here for more than six hours," said Werner Roos, glancing at his watch.

"Twelve, Mr. Roos. Even longer, if circumstances demand it."

"In that case would you be so kind, Mr. District Attorney, as to tell me what I'm suspected of," Werner Roos said arrogantly.

Bulldozer extended a pack of Prince cigarettes to Roos, who scornfully shook his head and took a pack of Benson & Hedges out of his pocket. He lit his cigarette with a gold-plated Dunhill lighter and waited while Bulldozer Olsson struck a match and lit his own filter cigarette.

"As yet I haven't said I suspect you of anything, Mr. Roos," he said, pushing forward the ash tray. "It was merely my intention we should have a little talk about this job of last Friday."

"Job? What job?" said Werner Roos, pretending to look mystified.

"At that bank on Hornsgatan. A successful job, in so far as ninety thousand is a tidy sum, but less successful at least for the bank customer who unfortunately got shot," said Bulldozer Olsson drily.

Werner Roos stared at him in amazement. Slowly he shook his head. "Now you're really out on a limb," he said. "Last Friday, did you say?"

"Exactly," said Bulldozer. "At which time you, Mr. Roos, were of course on your travels. Flying, I should say. Where were we last Friday, then?" Bulldozer Olsson leaned back in his chair and looked at Werner Roos in amusement.

"Where *you* were last Friday, Mr. Olsson, I do not know. For my part I was in Lisbon. You're welcome to check with the airline. We landed in Lisbon at 14:45 hours, after being delayed ten minutes. At 9:10 on Saturday morning we took off and arrived at Arlanda at 15:30. Last Friday I had dinner and slept at the Hotel Tivoli, another fact you're welcome to check up on." Werner Roos, too, sat back in his chair and looked triumphantly at Bulldozer, who was beaming with delight.

"Pretty!" he said. "A very pretty alibi indeed, Mr. Roos." Leaning forward, he stubbed his cigarette in the ash tray and went on maliciously: "But surely

71

Messrs. Malmström and Mohrén weren't in Lisbon, were they?"

"What the hell should they be in Lisbon for? Anyway, it isn't my business to keep track of what Malmström and Mohrén may be up to."

"Isn't it, Mr. Roos?"

"No, as I've told you many times before. And as far as this job of last Friday is concerned, I haven't even had time to read the Swedish newspapers these last few days, so I know nothing whatever about any bank robbery."

"Then I can inform you, Mr. Roos, that the job was carried out at closing time by someone who, disguised as a woman, first appropriated ninety thousand kronor in cash, then shot down a man who was a client of the bank, and then fled from the scene in a Renault. This shooting business of course places the crime in quite another category, as you, Mr. Roos, will appreciate."

"What I don't understand is how I am supposed to have anything to do with all this," Roos said irritably.

"Mr. Roos, when did you last meet our friends Malmström and Mohrén?" Bulldozer inquired.

"I told you that last time, didn't I? I haven't seen them since."

"And you've no idea of their whereabouts?"

"None. All I know about them is what you've just been telling me. I've not seen them since before they were put away in Kumla."

Bulldozer gave Werner Roos a straight look, then wrote something down on a pad in front of him, closed it, and got up.

"Oh well," he said nonchalantly. "That shouldn't be so hard to find out." He went over to the window and lowered the blinds against the afternoon sun, which had begun to shine into the room.

Werner Roos waited until he had sat down again. Then he said: "This much I can say, anyway. If there was any shooting involved, then Malmström and Mohrén weren't mixed up in it. They're not that stupid."

"It's possible Malmström and Mohrén wouldn't start shooting; but that doesn't rule out their being mixed up in it—like sitting outside in the getaway car, for example. Eh?"

Roos shrugged his shoulders and glared at the floor, his chin buried firmly in the collar of his sweater.

"Moreover, it's not beyond the limits of possibility that they used a companion, a female companion maybe," Bulldozer went on enthusiastically. "It's a possibility we must take into account, yes. Wasn't it Malmström's fiancée who was in on that job they were put away for last time?" He snapped his fingers in the air. "Gunilla Bergström, yes! She got one-and-a-half years, so we know where we have her," he said.

Roos glanced at him without raising his head.

"She hasn't escaped yet," Bulldozer explained parenthetically. "But there are plenty of other girls, and obviously these gentlemen have nothing against female accomplices. Or what do you say, Mr. Roos?"

Again Werner Roos shrugged his shoulders, straightening his back. "Hmm, what should I say?" he said indifferently. "After all, it's no concern of mine."

"No, of course not," said Bulldozer, nodding thoughtfully, his eyes on Roos. Then he leaned forward and laid the palms of his hands before him on the desk top. "So you maintain you haven't met Malmström and Mohrén or even heard from them in the last six months?"

"Yes, I do," said Werner Roos. "As I've said before, I'm not responsible for anything they may be up to. We've known each other since grade school, we never denied that. Since then we've gone around together from time to time, that's something else I've never tried to conceal. But that doesn't mean we bump into each other every quarter of an hour or that they tell me where they're going or what they're up to. I'm the first to be sorry if they've gone off the rails, but as to any criminal activities, I've nothing to do with them. And as I've said before, I'd be glad to help them back onto the straight and narrow path. But anyway, it's a long time since I ran into them."

"You do realize, Mr. Roos, that what you're saying could become extremely incriminating and that you may also find yourself in a highly suspect position if it turns out that you've been in touch with these two?"

73

"I can't see why."

Bulldozer smiled at him amiably. "Oh yes, I'm sure you can!" He banged his palms down on the desk and got up. "Now I've some other matters to see to," he said. "We'll have to interrupt our talk and resume it a little later. If you'll excuse me, Mr. Roos?" Bulldozer walked briskly out of the room, throwing a glance at Werner Roos before closing the door behind him.

Roos had impressed him as being very troubled and disconcerted. Bulldozer rubbed his hands together in delight as he hurried off down the corridor.

After the door had closed behind Bulldozer Olsson, Werner Roos got up, drifted over to the window, and peered out through the venetian blinds, whistling slowly and melodiously to himself. Then he glanced at his Rolex, frowned, quickly went over to Bulldozer's chair, and sat down. Drawing the telephone toward him, he lifted the receiver and dialed a number. While he was waiting he opened the drawers of the desk and looked through them one by one.

Someone answered and Roos said: "Hi kid, it's me. Look, can we meet a little later this evening, instead? I've got to have a talk with a guy, and it may take a couple of hours."

Roos took a pen marked "state property" out of a drawer and picked his other ear with it as he listened. "Sure," he said, "and then we'll go out and eat. I'm hungry as hell." He scrutinized the pen, tossed it back, and shut the drawer. "No, I'm in the bar now. It's a kind of hotel; but the grub's lousy here, so I'll wait and eat when we meet. Seven, okay? Good, then I'll pick you up at seven. So long for now."

Roos put down the receiver, got up, thrust his hands in his trouser pockets, and started to saunter around the room—whistling.

Bulldozer went in to Gunvald Larsson. "I've got Roos here now," he said.

"Well, where was he last Friday, then? Was he in Kuala Lumpur or Singapore?"

"In Lisbon," Bulldozer said delightedly. "He's sure got himself the perfect cover job for a gangster. Who else could come up with such fantastic alibis?"

"What else did he have to say?"

"Nothing. He knows nothing at all. Anyway nothing about the bank robbery, and he hasn't met Malmström and Mohrén for ages. He's slippery as an eel, crafty as a crayfish, and lies as fast as a horse can trot."

"In other words he's a traveling menagerie," said Gunvald Larsson. "Well, what are you going to do with him?"

Bulldozer sat down in the chair in front of Gunvald Larsson. "I intend to let him go," he said. "And I intend to have him shadowed. Can you get someone to shadow Roos, someone he won't recognize?"

"Where's he got to be shadowed to? Honolulu? In that case I'll volunteer myself."

"I'm serious," said Bulldozer.

Gunvald Larsson sighed. "I guess I'll have to arrange it," he said. "When's he to begin?"

"Now," said Bulldozer. "I'll let Roos go at once. He's off duty until Thursday afternoon, and before then he'll have shown us where Malmström and Mohrén are hiding out, just so long as we don't let him out of our sight."

"Thursday afternoon," said Gunvald Larsson. "Then we'll need at least two men who can relieve each other."

"And they'll have to be damned good at shadowing," said Bulldozer. "He mustn't notice anything, or all will be lost."

"Give me fifteen minutes," said Gunvald Larsson. "I'll call you when it's all fixed."

When Werner Roos climbed into a cab on Kungsholmsgatan twenty minutes later, Detective Sergeant Rune Ek was sitting at the wheel of a gray Volvo.

Rune Ek was a corpulent man in his fifties. He had white hair, glasses, and ulcers, and his doctor had just put him on a strict diet. This was why he didn't get much out of the four hours he spent at a table for one in the Opera Cellar restaurant, though Werner Roos and his red-haired lady friend apparently denied themselves nothing, whether dry or wet, at their window table on the veranda.

Ek passed the long, light summer night in an elder grove out at Hässelby, furtively watching the redhead's breasts, which were to be observed intermittently bobbing up and down on the waves of Lake Mälaren, as Werner Roos, like a latter-day Tarzan, did the crawl.

Later, as the morning sun shone down between the treetops, Ek continued this activity among some bushes outside a Hässelby bungalow. Having ascertained that the newly bathed couple were alone in the house, he devoted the following half hour to picking ticks out of his hair and clothes.

When, some hours later, Rune Ek was relieved, Werner Roos still hadn't put in an appearance. As far as anyone could see, it might take several hours before he dragged himself out of the redhead's arms in order, it was to be hoped, to look up his friends Malmström and Mohrén.

14

Anyone who had been in a position to compare the bank robbery squad to the robbers themselves would have found that in many ways they were evenly matched. The squad had enormous technical resources at its disposal, but its opponents possessed a large amount of working capital and also held the initiative.

Very likely Malmström and Mohrén would have made good policemen if anyone could have induced them to devote themselves to so dubious a career. Their physical qualities were formidable, nor was there much wrong with their intelligence.

Neither of them had ever occupied himself with anything except crime, and now, aged thirty-three and thirty-five respectively, they could rightly be described as able professional criminals. But since only a narrow group of citizens regarded the robbery business as respectable, they had adopted other professions on the side. On passports, driving licenses, and other means of identification they described themselves as "engineer" or "executive," well-chosen labels in a country that literally swarms with engineers and executives. All their documents were made up in totally different names. The documents were forgeries, but with a particularly convincing appearance, both at first and second sight. Their passports, for example, had already passed a series of tests, both at Swedish and foreign border crossings.

Personally, both Malmström and Mohrén seemed if possible even more trustworthy. They made a pleasant, straightforward impression and seemed healthy and vigorous. Four months of freedom had to some extent modified their appearance; both were now deeply tanned. Malmström had grown a beard, and Mohrén wore not only a moustache but also side-whiskers.

The suntan did not derive from any ordinary tourist trap like Majorca or the Canary Islands but from a three-week so-called photo safari in East Africa. This had been pure recreation. Later they'd made a couple of business trips, one to Italy to complete their equipment and the other to Frankfurt to hire a couple of efficient aides.

Back in Sweden they had carried out a few modest bank robberies as well as knocking off two check-cashing establishments, which, for fiscal reasons of a technical nature, had not dared to contact the police.

The gross income from this activity was considerable, but they had had large expenses and were looking forward to considerably more expenses in the near future.

A large investment, however, yields large dividends. So much they had learned from Sweden's half-socialist, half-capitalist economy, and the least one can say about Malmström's and Mohrén's goals was that they were extremely ambitious.

Malmström and Mohrén were working on an idea —an idea by no means new, but which did not for that reason lack appeal. They were going to do one more job and then retire. At long last they were going to stage their really big coup.

By and large their preparations were complete. All problems of finance had been solved, and the plan was as good as set. As yet they didn't know when or where; but they did know the most important thing: how. Their goal was in sight.

Though far from being criminals of the first order, Malmström and Mohrén were, as has been said, rather good at their job. The big-time criminal doesn't get caught. The big-time criminal doesn't rob banks. He sits in an office and presses buttons. He takes no risks. He doesn't disturb society's sacred cows. Instead he devotes himself to some kind of legalized extortion, preying on private individuals.

Big-time criminals profit from everything—from poisoning nature and whole populations and then pretending to repair their ravages by inappropriate medicines; from purposely turning whole districts of cities into slums in order to pull them down and then rebuild others in their place. The new slums, of course, turn out to be far more deleterious to people's health than the old ones had been. But above all they don't get caught.

Malmström and Mohrén, on the other hand, had an almost pathetic knack for getting caught. But they now believed that they had caught on to the reason for this: they had operated on too small a scale.

"Do you know what I was thinking about when I was taking a shower?" Malmström said. Emerging from the bathroom, he carefully spread a towel on the floor in front of him; he was wearing two others—one wound around his hips and the other draped over his shoulders. Malmström had a mania for cleanliness. This was already the fourth shower he'd taken today.

"Sure," said Mohrén. "Chicks."

"How could you guess?"

Mohrén was sitting by the window, looking intently out over Stockholm. He was dressed in shorts and a thin white shirt and was holding up a pair of naval binoculars to his eyes.

The apartment where they were living was in one of the large apartment houses on Danvik Cliffs, and the view was by no means bad.

"Work and chicks don't mix," Mohrén said. "You've seen how that turns out, haven't you?"

"I don't mix things, ever," Malmström said, offended. "Aren't I even allowed to think nowadays, huh?"

"Sure," said Mohrén magnanimously. "Just carry right on thinking; if you're up to it." He let his binoculars follow a white steamboat which was coming in toward The Stream.

"Yes, it's the 'Norrskär,' " he said. "Amazing that she's still on the job."

"Who's still on what job?"

"No one you're interested in. Which ones were you thinking about?"

"Those birds in Nairobi. Some sexpots, eh? I've

always said there's something special about Negroes."

"Negroes?" Mohrén corrected him. "Negresses, in this case. Absolutely not Negroes."

Malmström sprayed himself scrupulously under his arms and in certain other places.

"If you say so," he said.

"Anyway there's nothing special about Negresses," Mohrén said. "If you happened to get that impression it was just because you were suffering from sex-starvation."

"The devil I was!" Malmström disagreed. "By the way, did yours have a lot of hair on her cunt?"

"Yes," said Mohrén. "As a matter of fact she did, now that I think of it. A bewildering abundance. And it was very stiff. Bushy and nasty."

"And her tits?"

"Black," said Mohrén. "And lightly hung."

"I thought mine said she was a *maîtresse,* or else a mattress. Could that be right?"

"She said she was a waitress. I guess your English was a bit rusty. Anyway, she thought you were a train engineer."

"Yes, well, anyway she was a tart. What was yours?"

"Keypunch operator."

"Hmm."

Malmström picked up some sealed polyethylene bags containing underwear and socks, tore them open, and began to get dressed.

"You're going to waste your whole fortune on underpants," said Mohrén. "A most remarkable passion, I must say."

"Yes, it's goddam awful how expensive they've become."

"Inflation," said Mohrén. "And we're partly to blame."

"How the hell can that be?" asked Malmström. "We've been inside for years."

"We spend a lot of money unnecessarily. Thieves are always goddam spendthrifts."

"Not you."

"No, but I'm a shining exception. Though I do spend a fair amount on food."

80

"You didn't even want to fork out for those birds down there in Africa. That's why things turned out as they did. It was your fault we had to scrounge around for three days until we found a couple who'd do it free."

"That wasn't only for economic reasons," Mohrén said. "And certainly it wasn't to dampen inflation in Kenya. But as I see the matter, it's public thievishness that's undermining the value of money. If anyone should be put into Kumla it's the government."

"Hmm."

"And the tycoons. I've been reading about an interesting example of the way inflation begins."

"Oh?"

"When the British seized Damascus in October, 1918, the troops broke into the state bank and stole all the cash. Those soldiers hadn't any idea what it was worth. Among other things, an Australian cavalryman gave half a million to a kid who held his horse for him when he took a piss."

"Does a horse have to be held while it pisses?"

"Prices shot up a hundredfold, and only a few hours later a toilet roll was costing two hundred bucks."

"Did they really have toilet paper out there in Australia? In those days?"

Mohrén sighed. Sometimes he felt his intellect was becoming numb from never talking to anyone except Malmström. "Damascus," he said ponderously, "is in Arabia. Syria, to be more exact."

"No kidding." By now Malmström was dressed and was studying the results in a mirror. Muttering to himself, he fluffed up his beard and flicked some specks of dust, invisible to any normal person, off his blazer. Spreading out the towels side by side on the floor, he went over to the closet and got their weapons. Laying them out in a row, he got some cheesecloth and a can of cleaning liquid.

Mohrén cast a distraught glance at the arsenal. "How many times have you done that? It's all new from the factory, or almost, anyway."

"Have to keep our things in order," Malmström said. "Firearms need looking after."

They had enough there to start a minor war or, at the very least, a revolution. Two automatics, one revolver, two submachine guns, and three sawed-off shotguns. The submachine guns were standard Swedish Army equipment. All the others were foreign.

Both the automatics were of large caliber, a nine-millimeter Spanish Firebird and a Llama IX. The revolver, too, was Spanish, an Astra Cadix forty-five, and so was one of the shotguns, a Maritza. Both the others came from elsewhere on the Continent, a Belgian Continental Supra de Luxe and an Austrian Ferlach with the romantic name "Forever Yours."

Having cleaned the pistols, Malmström picked up the Belgian rifle. "The person who sawed off this rifle should be shot with it in the balls," he said.

"I guess he didn't acquire it like we did."

"What? I don't get you."

"Didn't acquire it honestly," Mohrén said seriously. "Probably he stole it." He turned back to the view of the river. "Stockholm sure is a spectacular city," he observed.

"How do you mean?"

"It needs to be enjoyed from a distance. So it's a good thing we don't have to go out much."

"Scared someone'll knock you off in the subway?"

"Among other things. Or else of getting a dagger in my back. Or an axe through my skull. Or being kicked to death by a hysterical police horse. Really, I feel sorry for people."

"People? What people?"

Mohrén made a sweeping gesture. "People down there. Imagine working your ass off to scrape together enough dough to pay off the installments on a car and a summer place while your kids are doping themselves to death. And your wife's only got to stick her nose outdoors after six in the evening to be raped. And yourself, you don't even dare to go to vespers."

"Vespers?"

"Just an example. If you've more than a ten-kronor bill on you, you get robbed; and if you've got less, the muggers stick a knife in your back out of sheer disappointment. The other day I read in the

82

newspapers that even the cops don't dare go out alone any more. There are fewer cops on the streets, and it's becoming harder and harder to keep order. Something like that. It was some big shot in the Ministry of Justice who said so. No, it'll be nice to get out of here and never come back."

"And never see the Rangers again," Malmström said gloomily.

"You and your vulgarity. Anyway, you're not allowed that in Kumla, either."

"Still we get a glimpse of it on TV, now and then."

"Don't mention our horrible cellmate," Mohrén said. He got up and opened the window. Stretching out his arms, he threw his head back—as if directly addressing the masses. "Hello down there," he shouted, "as Lyndon Johnson said when he held his election speech from a helicopter."

"Who?" Malmström asked.

The doorbell rang. The signal was a complicated one; they listened carefully.

"Guess it's Mauritzon," Mohrén said, looking at his watch. "He's even on time."

"I don't trust that bastard," Malmström said. "This time we're taking no chances." He slipped the magazine into one of the machine guns. "Here," he said.

Mohrén took the weapon.

Picking up the Astra, Malmström went out to the front door. Holding the revolver in his left hand he unlocked the various chains with his right. Malmström was left-handed. Mohrén stood six feet behind him.

Then, as abruptly as he could, Malmström jerked open the door.

The man outside had expected this. "Hello," he said, staring nervously at the revolver.

"Hi," said Malmström.

"Come in, come in," Mohrén said. "Dear Mauritzon, you are welcome."

The man who entered was laden with bags and packages of food. As he put down these groceries he cast a sideways glance at the display of weaponry.

"You guys planning a revolution?" he said.

83

"That's always been our line of business," Mohrén said. "Though right now the situation's not ripe for one. Did you get us any crawfish?"

"How the devil d'you expect me to get hold of crawfish on the fourth of July?"

"What d'you think we're paying you for?" Malmström said threateningly.

"A most legitimate question," Mohrén said. "That you can't get us what we tell you to is more than I can understand."

"But there are limits," Mauritzon said. "Haven't I got you everything, for God's sake? Apartments, cars, passports, tickets. But crawfish! Not even the king could fix himself some crawfish in July."

"I guess not," Mohrén said. "But what do you think they're doing out at Harpsund? The whole bloody government's probably sitting there gulping down crawfish. Palme, and Geijer, and Calle P.—the whole bunch of them. No, we're not accepting such excuses."

"As for that shaving lotion, it just doesn't exist," Mauritzon said hastily. "I've been rushing around town like a poisoned rat, but no one's heard of it for several years now."

Malmström's countenance darkened noticeably.

"But I've fixed everything else," Mauritzon went on. "And here's today's mail."

He brought out a brown unaddressed envelope and handed it to Mohrén, who stuffed it indifferently into his hip pocket.

This Mauritzon was a wholly different type from the others. A man in his forties, shorter than average, slim and well built, he was clean-shaven and had short blond hair. Most people, especially women, thought he seemed nice. His way of dressing and behaving suggested moderation in all things, and he was not remarkable in any way. As a type, he could have been called ordinary and was therefore difficult to remember or notice. All this had stood him in good stead. He hadn't been inside for several years, and at the moment he was neither wanted nor even under surveillance.

He had three different lines of business, all profitable: narcotics, pornography, and procurement. As a businessman he was efficient, energetic, and markedly systematic.

Thanks to an apparently well-meaning law, pornography of every conceivable form could now be produced perfectly legally and imported in unlimited quantities for re-export—mainly to Spain and Italy, where it sold at a good profit. His other line was smuggling, mainly amphetamines and other drugs, but he also accepted orders for weapons.

In inside circles Mauritzon was regarded as a man who could fix anything. A rumor was even going the rounds that he'd managed to smuggle in a couple of elephants he'd received from an Arabian sheik in part payment for two fourteen-year-old Finnish virgins and a drawerful of trick condoms. Moreover, the virgins were said to have been bogus—their maidenheads being a mixture of plastic and Karlsson's glue—and the elephants white. Unfortunately, there was no truth to this story.

"New shoulder holsters too?" Malmström asked.

"Sure. They're lying at the bottom of the food bag. May I ask what was wrong with the old ones?"

"Useless," Malmström said.

"Utterly worthless," Mohrén said. "Where did you get them?"

"Police Supply Division. These new ones are Italian."

"Sounds better," said Malmström.

"Will there be anything else?"

"Yeah, here's the list."

Glancing at it fleetingly, Mauritzon reeled off: "One dozen underpants, fifteen pairs of nylon socks, six net undershirts, a pound of black caviar, four Donald Duck rubber masks, two packets of nine-millimeter automatic ammunition, six pairs of rubber gloves, preserved Appenzeller cheese, one can of cocktail onions, cotton wool, one astrolabe . . . what in Christ's name is that?"

"An instrument for measuring the altitude of stars," Mohrén said. "I guess you'll have to look around in the antique shops."

"I see. I'll do my best."

85

"Exactly," said Malmström.

"Nothing else you want?"

Mohrén shook his head, but Malmström frowned thoughtfully and said: "Yes, foot spray."

"Any special kind?"

"The most expensive."

"I see. No chicks?"

No one answered, a silence which Mauritzon interpreted as hesitation.

"I can fix you up with any sort you want. It's not good for you guys sitting here every evening like a pair of owls. A couple of lively chicks would speed up your metabolism."

"My metabolism's real fine," Mohrén said. "And the only ladies I could think of are distinct security risks. No plastic hymens for me, thank you."

"Come off it, there's loads of crazy chicks who'd be more than pleased to . . ."

"I take that as a direct insult," Mohrén said. "No, and again no."

Malmström, however, still appeared to waver. "Though . . ."

"Yes?"

"This so-called assistant of yours, I'll bet she knows what she's doing." He made a deprecatory gesture.

Mauritzon said: "Monita? She's not your type, I'm sure. Not pretty or particularly good at it. General standard caliber. My tastes are simple when it comes to women. In a word, she's just average."

"If you say so," said Malmström, disappointed.

"Besides which she's gone away. She has a sister she visits now and then."

"So that's that," Mohrén said. "There's a time for everything, and the days are close at hand when . . ."

"What days?" said Malmström, mystified.

"The days when we shall once more be able to satisfy our lusts in a dignified manner and choose our own company. I hereby declare this meeting closed. Adjourned until the same time tomorrow."

"Okay," Mauritzon said. "Let me out, then."

"Just one more thing."

"What's that?"

"What d'you call yourself nowadays?"

"The usual. Lennart Holm."

"Just in case anything should happen, and we need to get hold of you quick."

"You know where I hang out."

"And I'm still waiting for those crawfish."

Mauritzon shrugged and left.

"Goddam sonofabitch," Malmström said.

"What was that? Don't you appreciate our trusty pal?"

"He smells of armpits," Malmström said condemningly.

"Mauritzon's a skunk," Mohrén said. "I don't dig his activities. Oh no, I don't mean him running errands for us, naturally. But this giving dope to kids and selling pornography to illiterate Catholics. It's dishonorable."

"I don't trust him," Malmström said.

Mohrén had taken the brown envelope out of his pocket and was scrutinizing it closely. "What's more, my friend," he said, "you're right. The guy's useful but not wholly reliable. Look, today he's opened this letter again. Wonder how he manages to get it unstuck? Some refined way of steaming it, I guess. If Roos didn't use this hair trick no one'd notice someone'd been messing about with the envelope. Considering what we're paying him it's really unjustifiable. Why's he so inquisitive?"

"He's a goddam louse," Malmström said. "It's as simple as that."

"I guess so."

"How many grand has he had off us since we started working?"

"About a hundred and fifty. Though of course he's had considerable expenses: weapons, cars, travel, and so forth. And then there's a certain amount of risk involved."

"The hell there is," Malmström said. "No one except Roos even knows we know him."

"And there's that woman with a name like a steamboat."

"Imagine him trying to palm off that ghost on me," Malmström said indignantly. "It's obvious she's

87

hardly up to it at all, and she probably hasn't washed since yesterday."

"Though to be objective, you're not being quite fair," Mohrén objected. *"Factum est,* he gave you an honest declaration of the nature of the goods."

"Est?"

"And as far as the hygienic details go you could easily have disinfected her first."

"The hell I could."

Mohrén extracted three sheets of paper from the envelope and laid them down on the table before him. "Eureka," he cried.

"Eh? What?"

"Here's what we've been waiting for, my lad. Come and take a look."

"I'll just wash up first," Malmström said, disappearing into the bathroom.

After ten minutes he was back. Mohrén rubbed his hands gleefully.

"Well?" said Malmström.

"Everything seems to be in order. Here's the plan. Perfect. And here are all the timings. Exact down to the last detail."

"What about Hauser and Hoff, then?"

"Coming tomorrow. Read this."

Malmström read. Mohrén burst out laughing.

"What're you laughing at?"

"The codes. 'Jean's got a long moustache,' for example. Do you know where he got it from and what it meant originally?"

"Search me."

"Oh well, it doesn't matter."

"Does it say two-and-a-half million?"

"Without any question!"

"Net?"

"Right. All the expenses have already been calculated."

"Minus twenty-five percent for Roos?"

"Precisely. We'll get exactly one million each."

"How much does this Mauritzon fathead know, then?"

"Not much—except the timings, of course."

"When's it to be?"

88

"Friday, 14:45. But it doesn't say which Friday."

"But the street names are here too," Malmström said.

"Forget Mauritzon," Mohrén said calmly. "Do you see what's written down here at the bottom?"

"Yeah."

"You don't happen to remember what it means, do you?"

"Sure," said Malmström. "Sure I do. And that puts a different complexion on things, of course."

"That's what I think, too," said Mohrén. "Jesus, how I long for those crawfish."

15

Hoff and Hauser were two German gangsters whom Malmström and Mohrén had employed in the course of their business trip to Frankfurt. Both had good recommendations, and indeed the whole matter could perfectly well have been negotiated by mail. Malmström and Mohrén, however, were as scrupulous as their plans were careful, and their German trip had been partially motivated by a desire to see what their prospective assistants looked like.

The meeting had taken place in early June. They contacted Hauser in the Magnolia Bar. Afterwards he introduced them to Hoff.

The Magnolia Bar, in downtown Frankfurt, was small and dark. The orange-colored lighting seeped out from concealed fixtures; the walls were violet, so was the wall-to-wall carpeting. The low armchairs, grouped around a few small circular plexiglass tables, were pinkish. There was a semicircular bar of polished brass, the music was soft, the barmaids blond, high-bosomed, and décolleté, and the drinks expensive.

Malmström and Mohrén settled down in a pink armchair by the only free table in the place, which, though it contained no more than a score of customers, seemed full to the bursting point. The fair sex was represented by the two blondes behind the counter. All the clients were male.

Coming up to them, the barmaid leaned over their table and gave them a glimpse of her large pink nipples and a sniff of her hardly pleasant odor of sweat and perfume. After Malmström had gotten his gimlet and Mohrén his Chivas without ice, they looked around for Hauser. They'd no idea what he looked like, though they knew he had a reputation as a tough customer.

Malmström caught sight of him first. He was standing at the far end of the bar, a long thin cigarillo in one corner of his mouth and a glass of whisky in his hand. Tall, slim, broad-shouldered, he was wearing a sandy-colored suede suit. He wore thick sideburns and his dark hair, thinning slightly at the crown, curled in at the nape of his neck. Leaning nonchalantly over the counter, he said something to the barmaid who, in a brief pause, came over and talked to him. He was strikingly like Sean Connery. The blonde gazed admiringly at him and giggled affectedly. Cupping her hand under the cigarillo that was glued between his lips, she tapped it lightly with her finger, and the long column of ash dropped into her hand. A gesture he pretended not to notice. After a while he swigged down his whisky and was instantly given another. His face was impassive, and the steely blue gaze was aimed at some point above and beyond the girl's bleached tresses. He did not so much as deign to graze her with his eyes. He just stood there looking as stony and tough as they'd heard he was. Even Mohrén was slightly impressed. They waited until he should look their way.

A small square man in an ill-fitting gray suit, a white nylon shirt, and wine-red tie came and sat down in the third armchair at their table. His face was round and rosy; behind thick rimless lenses his eyes were large and china blue, and his wavy hair was cut short and parted neatly on one side.

Malmström and Mohrén glanced at him indifferently and went on observing the James Bond character at the bar.

After a while the newcomer said something in a low voice, and it was some time before they realized he'd addressed them—still longer before it occurred to them that it was this cherubic person, not the tough over at the bar, who was Gustav Hauser.

A while later they left the Magnolia Bar.

Dumbfounded, Malmström and Mohrén followed Hauser who, dressed in a full-length dark green leather coat and a Tyrolean hat, marched on ahead of them, leading the way to Hoff's apartment.

Hoff was a cheerful man in his thirties. He received them into his family circle, which consisted of his wife, two children, and a dachshund. Later that evening the four men went out and had supper together and talked about their common interests. Both Hoff and Hauser turned out to be particularly experienced in this line of business, and each possessed special knowledge in several useful fields. Moreover, having just been released after serving a four-year sentence, they were in a hurry to get back to work.

After three days together with their new companions, Malmström and Mohrén went home again to continue their preparations for the big coup. The Germans promised to hold themselves ready and to be on the spot when the time came.

On Thursday, July 7, they were to be on location. They arrived in Sweden that Wednesday.

Hauser took the morning ferry over to Limhamn from Dragør in his car. It had been agreed he should fetch Hoff on Skeppsbron when the latter arrived by one of the Öresund Co.'s boats at noon.

Hoff had never been in Sweden before and was not even familiar with the appearance of a Swedish policeman. This, perhaps, explained his slightly confused and ill-mannered way of entering the country. As he walked down the gangway from the "Absalom" a uniformed customs officer approached him. Hoff immediately jumped to the conclusion that this man in uniform was a policeman, that something had gone wrong, and that they'd come to arrest him.

At the same moment he saw Hauser sitting in his car on the other side of the street, waiting for him with the engine running. In a panic Hoff pulled out his pistol and pointed it at the astonished customs official, who had been on his way to meet his fiancée, a young lady who, conveniently enough, worked in the "Absalom's" cafeteria. Before he or anyone else had time to do anything, Hoff had leapt over the barrier between the dock area and the sidewalk, dashed between a couple of cabs, jumped over yet another barrier, slipped in between two long-distance trucks, and, his pistol drawn, flung himself into Hauser's car.

Seeing Hoff rushing over towards him, Hauser had wrenched the door open, and the car was already moving before he got there. Then Hoff jammed his foot

92

down on the accelerator and vanished around the corner before it occurred to anyone to note the car's license number. He went on driving until he was sure no one was going to stop or follow him.

16

Good and bad luck notoriously tend to balance each other out, so that one person's ill luck turns out to be another's good luck, and vice versa.

Mauritzon was a man who did not regard himself as able to afford either and who therefore rarely left anything to chance. All his operations were characterized by a double security system, devised by himself, which guaranteed that only the most improbable combinations of various items of bad luck could precipitate a disaster.

Professional setbacks, of course, did occur at regular intervals, but they were only financial. Thus, some weeks earlier, an unusually incorruptible Italian lieutenant of Carabinieri had placed an embargo on a long-distance truckful of pornography; but for any detective to trace it back to Mauritzon, in person, was impossible.

On the other hand, a couple of months earlier, he'd become involved in a completely incomprehensible occurrence. Not even this, however, had had any consequences, and he felt certain many years would pass before anything similar would occur again. With good reason he deemed his chances of being arrested as even smaller than the chances of his getting thirteen right in his standing thirty-two-line soccer-pools system.

Mauritzon was seldom idle, and his Wednesday program was pretty full. First he was to accept a narcotics consignment at Central Station and take it to a storage locker at the Östermalm subway. Afterwards he planned to hand the key to a certain person in exchange for an envelope containing money. Then he would look up the contact where the mysterious letters addressed to Malmström and Mohrén were in the habit of appearing. It annoyed him slightly that, despite his ambitious attempts, he still hadn't managed to figure out the sender's identity. Then it would be time to do some shopping, buy some underpants, etc., and last on his program came his daily visit to the house on Danvik Cliffs.

The narcotics consisted of amphetamines and hash, ingeniously inserted in a loaf of bread and a piece of cheese, both in an ordinary shopping bag together with a variety of other objects of a particularly innocent nature.

He had already picked up the goods and was standing by the crosswalk outside Central Station, an insignificant but respectable-looking little man, holding a shopping bag.

On one side of him stood an old lady. On the other, a female crossing guard in a green uniform together with a crowd of other people. On the sidewalk, five yards away, two sheepish-looking policemen were standing with their hands clasped behind their backs. There was the usual—that is to say very heavy—traffic, and the air was saturated with enough gasoline fumes to make one gasp.

At length the lights turned green, and everyone began shoving and jostling, trying to beat the others across the street. Somebody bumped into the old lady, who turned around in horror and said:

"I see so badly without my glasses, but it's green now, isn't it?"

"Yes," Mauritzon said amiably. "I'll help you across, madam." Experience had taught him that a helpful attitude could often yield certain advantages.

"Thank you so much," the old lady said. "It's so seldom anyone gives us old people a thought."

"I'm in no hurry," Mauritzon said. Taking her lightly by the arm, he began to pilot her across the street. When they'd gone three yards from the curb another pedestrian in a hurry bumped up against the old woman again, so that she faltered. Just as Mauritzon prevented her from falling he heard someone shout:

"Hey, you there!"

He looked up and saw the crossing guard pointing at him accusingly and yelling: "Police! Police!"

The old lady looked around, bewildered.

"Grab that thief," the crossing guard yelled.

Mauritzon frowned but stood stock still.

"What?" said the lady. "What's the matter?"

Then she too squeaked: "A thief! A thief!"

The two policemen strode over. "What's all this, now?" asked one of them in an authoritative tone. Since he spoke in a Närke dialect of the most whining variety, he had some difficulty in producing the harsh strident tone supposedly required of a man in his position.

"A purse snatcher!" shouted the crossing guard, still pointing. "He tried to snatch that old lady's handbag."

Mauritzon looked at his antagonist, and a voice within him said: "Hold your tongue, you bloody ape."

Aloud he said: "Excuse me, but there must be some misunderstanding."

The crossing guard was a blonde of about twenty-five, who had contrived further to spoil her inherently unimpressive appearance with the aid of lipstick and powder.

"I saw it myself," she said.

"What?" said the old woman. "Where's the thief?"

"What's all this, now?" said the two patrolmen in unison.

Mauritzon remained completely calm. "It's all a misunderstanding," he said.

"This gentleman was just helping me across the street," said the old woman.

"Pretending to help you, yes," said the blonde. "That's how they do it. He snatched the old woman's ... I mean the old lady's bag so she almost fell over."

"You are misinterpreting the situation," Mauritzon said. "It was someone else who happened to bump into her. I just caught hold of her so she shouldn't fall over and hurt herself."

"Now don't you try that one," the crossing guard said stubbornly.

The policemen exchanged a questioning glance. The more authoritative of the two was evidently also the more experienced and enterprising. He reflected a moment, then delivered himself of the appropriate line: "You'd better come along with us."

Pause.

"All three of you. Suspect, witness, and plaintiff."

The old lady seemed utterly bewildered, and the crossing guard's interest immediately faded.

Mauritzon became even more diffident. "A complete misunderstanding," he said. "But one easily made, of course, with all these muggers roaming the streets. I've nothing against accompanying you."

"What is it?" asked the old lady. "Where are we going?"

"To the station," said the authoritative policeman.

"Station?"

"The police station."

The procession marched off under the gaping stare of hurrying citizens.

"I may have been mistaken in what I saw," the blonde said waveringly. She was used to taking down names and license numbers, but not to being taken down herself.

"That doesn't matter," said Mauritzon mildly. "It's quite right to keep your eyes peeled, especially at spots like this."

The police have an office right next to the railway station. Among many other things it's intended as a place where they can drink coffee. It's also for the temporary custody of detained persons.

The formalities became elaborate. First the names and addresses of the witness and of the old lady who had supposedly been robbed were taken down.

"I guess I was mistaken," the witness said nervously. "And I've my job to attend to."

"We must clear this matter up," said the more experienced of the policemen. "Search his pockets, Kenneth."

The man from Närke started searching Mauritzon, picking out various commonplace objects. Meanwhile the interrogation continued.

"What's your name, sir?"

"Arne Lennart Holm," said Mauritzon. "Known as Lennart."

"And your address?"

"Vickergatan six."

"Yes, the name's correct," said the other patrolman. "It's here on his driver's license, so it's perfectly correct. His name's Arne Lennart Holm. So that fits."

Next the interrogator turned to the old lady. "Have you lost anything, madam?"

"No."

"But I'm beginning to lose patience," the blonde said sharply. "What's *your* name?"

"That's irrelevant," the patrolman said bluntly.

"Oh, take it easy," Mauritzon said, relaxed.

"Have you lost anything, madam?"

"No. You've just asked me that."

"What articles of value did you have on you, madam?"

"Six thirty-five in my purse. And then my fifty-kronor card and pensioner's card."

"Do you still have these things?"

"Of course."

The patrolman closed his notebook, looked the assembled company over, and said: "The matter seems settled. You two may leave. Holm stays."

Mauritzon retrieved his belongings. The shopping bag was standing by the door. A cucumber and six rhubarb stalks protruded from it.

"What's in that shopping bag?" the policeman asked.

"Food."

"Really? You'd better check on that too, Kenneth."

The Närke man began plucking out the contents and laying them out on a bench by the door, used by off-duty policemen for putting down their caps and shoulder belts.

Mauritzon said nothing. He followed the process calmly.

"Yes," said Kenneth. "The bag contains food, exactly as Mr. Holm here said it did. Bread, butter, cheese, rhubarb, and coffee . . . and, yes, well, what Holm has said."

"Well," his colleague said conclusively, "then the

98

matter's settled. You can put all those things back again, Kenneth."

He thought for a moment, then turned to Mauritzon and said: "Well, Mr. Holm. This is an unfortunate affair. But as you may understand, we policemen have our job to do. We regret suspecting you of a criminal offense and hope we've not inconvenienced you."

"By no means," said Mauritzon. "Obviously you have your duties."

"Good-bye then, Mr. Holm."

"Good-bye, good-bye."

The door opened and yet another policeman came in. He was dressed in a blue-gray overall and was holding an Alsatian on a lead. In his hand he had a bottle of soda pop. "Bloody hell but it's hot," he said, slinging his cap down on the bench. "Sit, Jack."

Unscrewing the top, he put the bottle to his mouth. He paused, and again said irritably: "Sit, Jack!"

The dog sat down but almost immediately got up again and began sniffing at the bag against the wall. Mauritzon walked towards the door.

"Well, good-bye then, Mr. Holm," said Kenneth.

"Good-bye, good-bye," said Mauritzon.

By now the dog's head was completely submerged in the bag. Mauritzon opened the door with his left hand and reached out his right hand for the bag. The dog growled.

"Just a moment," said the policeman in overalls.

His colleague stared at him, uncomprehending. Mauritzon pushed away the dog's head and picked up the bag.

"Stop," said the third cop, putting down his bottle on the bench.

"Pardon?" inquired Mauritzon.

"This is a narcotics dog," the policeman said, moving his hand to the butt of his pistol.

17

The head of the narcotics squad was called Henrik Jacobsson. He'd held down the job for almost ten years and was a man under extreme pressure. Everyone thought he ought to have bleeding ulcers, or a nervous disorder, or should be running around chewing up curtains. But his constitution was up to most things and nowadays nothing so much as caused him to raise an eyebrow.

He contemplated the dissected cheese and the hollowed-out loaf, the bags of hash and the amphetamine capsules, also one of his assistants who was still standing there splicing up rhubarb.

Before him sat Mauritzon, apparently calm, but his mind in a turmoil. His double security system had been broken through in the most unlikely and idiotic fashion. How could such a thing happen? That it should happen once, he could accept; but something similar had happened to him only a couple of months ago. And that made twice. This week he'd presumably get thirteen right in the State Soccer Pools.

Already he'd said almost all that could be said. For example, that the unfortunate shopping bag wasn't his; that he'd been given it by a stranger at the Central Station to hand over to another stranger on Maria Square. It was true he'd guessed there was something shady about the transaction, but he hadn't been able to resist the hundred-kronor note the stranger had offered him.

Jacobsson had listened without interrupting or commenting, but also without appearing to be the slightest bit convinced. And now he said: "Well, Holm. You'll be taken into custody, as I said. You will probably be placed under formal arrest tomorrow morning.

100

You're allowed to make a phone call, providing it doesn't hinder or complicate the investigation."

"Is it so serious?" said Mauritzon humbly.

"Depends on what you mean by serious. We'll have to see what we find when we search your home."

Mauritzon knew precisely what they would find in the one-room apartment on Vickergatan, namely some very meager sticks of furniture and a few old clothes. So that didn't worry him. That they might ask him which locks his other keys fitted he also took fairly coolly, since he did not intend to answer. Consequently his other dwelling, on Armfeldtsgatan out at Gärdet, had every chance of remaining safe from poking cops and repugnant quadrupeds.

"Will there be a fine?" he asked, even more humbly.

"No, there won't, old boy," Jacobsson said. "This'll be prison, for sure. So you're in a pretty bad way, Holm. Incidentally, would you like some coffee?"

"Thanks, I'd prefer tea, if it's not too much trouble." Mauritzon was doing some sharp thinking. His position was worse than Jacobsson yet suspected. The fact was, he'd had his fingerprints taken. And very soon the computer would spew out a punch card on which was printed not the name "Lennart Holm," but quite different things—things that would give occasion for many questions he was going to find it hard to answer. They drank tea and coffee and ate half a cake while the assistant, with the air of a top-line surgeon at work, solemnly sliced up the cucumber with a scalpel. "Nothing else here," he said.

Jacobsson nodded slowly and said between bites: "As far as you're concerned, it'll make no difference."

A decision was ripening inside Mauritzon. True, he was down; but he was far from out for the count. And before he was counted out he had to get back up onto his feet—before the information from the identification bureau lay on Jacobsson's desk. After that no one would believe a word he said, no matter which line he adopted. He put down his paper cup, straightened his back, and said in a wholly new tone of voice: "I may as well lay my cards on the table. I'm not going to try to wriggle out of it any more."

101

"Thanks," Jacobsson said evenly.

"My name isn't Holm."

"No?"

"No, it's true I call myself that. But it isn't my real name."

"What is it then?"

"Filip Faithful Mauritzon."

"Is it a name you're ashamed of?"

"Truth to tell, I've been inside once or twice, a long time back. One gets to be known by the name one was convicted under. You know how it is."

"Sure."

"People get to know you've been inside, and then the cops come to check up. . . . Sorry, the police, I mean."

"Don't worry. I'm not touchy."

For a while Jacobsson said nothing. Mauritzon cast an anxious glance up at the clock on the wall. "I didn't get caught for anything serious, really," he said. "Just receiving a few stolen goods, fixing, possession of firearms, and so on. A breaking-and-entering job. But that was ten years ago."

"So you've been good since then, have you?" Jacobsson said. "Become a better person, perhaps? Or just learned a few more tricks?"

Mauritzon's reply to this was a rather crooked smile.

Jacobsson wasn't smiling at all. He said: "What are you driving at, really?"

"I don't want to go inside."

"But you've been inside already. And when all's said and done it isn't all that serious, is it? This town's full of people who've been inside. I meet them every day. A couple of months' rest, that never hurts."

Mauritzon had a strong feeling it was no brief vacation holiday that he was facing. He surveyed his fateful groceries and thought how if he really was arrested, the cops would soon be poking their noses into all sorts of matters and come across one thing or another, maybe; and that wouldn't be nice at all. On the other hand he had a fair amount of capital stowed away in certain banks abroad. And if he could slip out of his present quandary he'd lose no time in quitting first this town and then the country. After which everything would sort itself out. Anyway he was planning to retire from his line of business. He intended to finish with pornography and narcotics. Nor did he have any great desire to go on being an errand boy, however well paid, for people like Malmström and Mohrén. Instead he intended to get into the dairy business. Smuggling Danish butter into Italy was amazingly profitable. Moreover it was virtually legal; its only real risk lay in the possibility of being liquidated by the Mafia. Which was no small risk either, come to think of it. Anyway the time had come to resort to extraordinary methods. Mauritzon said: "Who's in charge of bank robberies?"

"Bulldo—" Jacobsson let slip.

"Bulldozer Olsson," said Mauritzon at once.

"District Attorney Olsson," said Jacobsson. "You thinking of squealing?"

"I might be able to give him some information."

"Couldn't you just as well give this information to me?"

"It's a rather confidential matter," Mauritzon said. "I'm sure a brief phone call is all that's needed."

Jacobsson considered this. He knew the National Police Commissioner and his assistants had declared bank robberies to be of prime importance. The only crime that could be considered more serious was throwing eggs at the United States ambassador. He drew the telephone toward him and dialed the direct number to the special squad's headquarters on Kungsholmen. Bulldozer himself answered.

"Olsson speaking."

"This is Henrik Jacobsson. We've arrested a pusher, who maintains he has something to say."

"About the bank robberies?"

"Apparently."

"I'll be right there."

And he was. Bulldozer entered the room stomping with enthusiasm. A brief conversation ensued.

"What is it you want to talk about, Mr. Mauritzon?" asked Bulldozer.

"Would you happen to be interested in a couple of guys called Malmström and Mohrén?"

"Sure," said Bulldozer. "Sure." He licked his lips.

103

"Tremendously interested. What exactly do you know, Mr. Mauritzon?"

"I know where Malmström and Mohrén are."

"Right now?"

"Yes."

Bulldozer rubbed his hands excitedly. Then he said, as if struck by an afterthought: "I presume you want certain concessions, Mr. Mauritzon?"

"I'd prefer to discuss the whole matter in more agreeable surroundings."

"Hmm," said Bulldozer. "Would my office on Kungsholmsgatan be more agreeable?"

"Sure thing," said Mauritzon. "But I guess, Mr. District Attorney, you'll have to talk the matter over with this gentleman here?"

Jacobsson's face as he had followed the discussion had been expressionless.

"Right," said Bulldozer eagerly. "We must have a little talk, Jacobsson. Can we talk in private?" Jacobsson nodded resignedly.

18

Jacobsson was a practical man. He took the matter coolly. His acquaintance with Bulldozer Olsson was superficial, but on the other hand he knew him by reputation. And that was reason enough to give up the fight before it even began.

The scene was simple. A cold room with a desk, two chairs, and a filing cabinet—not even a carpet on the floor. Jacobsson sat quite quietly at his desk.

Bulldozer rushed to and fro, head down, hands clasped behind his back. "Just one important technicality," he said. "Is Mauritzon under arrest?"

"No. Not yet."

"Perfect," said Bulldozer. "Splendid. Then we hardly need discuss the matter."

"Maybe not."

"If you like we could contact the National Commissioner . . . the Commissioner and the Chief Superintendent, too?"

Jacobsson shook his head. He knew everything about the potentates in question.

"Then the matter's clear?" said Bulldozer.

Jacobsson didn't reply.

"You've made a smart grab. You know who he is and can keep an eye on him. For the future."

"Yes. I'll have a word with him."

"Splendid."

Jacobsson went up to Mauritzon, looked at him for a moment, then said: "Well, Mauritzon, I've thought the matter over. You were given that bag by a stranger and were to hand it over to another stranger. Such things do happen sometimes in this business. It would be difficult to prove you're not telling the truth, so there's no need to arrest you."

"I see," said Mauritzon.

"Of course we'll keep the goods. We're assuming you acted in good faith."

"Are you letting me go?"

"Yes, providing you put yourself at Bull . . . District Attorney Olsson's disposal."

Bulldozer must have been listening at the door. It flew open and he entered headlong. "Come along," he said.

"Right away?"

"We can talk at my place," said Bulldozer.

"Sure," said Mauritzon. "It'll be a pleasure."

"That I'll promise you," said Bulldozer. "So long, Jacobsson."

Jacobsson said nothing. He looked after them vacantly. He was accustomed to this kind of thing.

Ten minutes later Mauritzon was indisputably the central figure at the special squad's headquarters. He sat down in the most comfortable chair that could be found as an illustrious group of detectives thronged about him.

Kollberg stared at his shopping list and said: "One dozen pairs of pants and fifteen pairs of socks. Who's supposed to use all that?"

"Mohrén'll take two pairs, and the other guy the rest, I guess."

"Does this Malmström guy eat underclothes?"

"I suppose not; but he always throws away the old ones when he changes. He likes a special kind, too. French ones. They're only obtainable at Morris's."

"No wonder he has to rob banks, with habits like that!"

Rönn, very inquisitive: "By the way, what's an astrolabe?"

"A sort of antique sextant, though different," Gunvald Larsson replied. Then he, too, contributed a question: "Why do two men need four Donald Duck masks?"

"Don't ask me. They've got two already anyway. I bought those last week."

Rönn said thoughtfully: "Yes, what's the meaning of 'six boxes nine'?"

"A special kind of contraceptive," said Mauritzon wearily. "When you put them on they look something like nightsticks, with dark blue uniforms and pink snouts."

"Quit bothering about that bit of paper now," Bulldozer Olsson said good-naturedly. "And Mr. Mauritzon does not have to contribute to the entertainment. We can provide our own."

"Can we?" asked Kollberg gravely.

"No, let's get down to brass tacks, instead," said Bulldozer, clapping his hands as if to inspire enthusiasm. Challengingly he surveyed his forces. Kollberg, Rönn, and Gunvald Larsson apart, the squad consisted of two younger detective sergeants, an expert on tear gas, a computer man, and an utterly incompetent patrolman named Bo Zachrisson. Everybody always felt they could dispense with him, so he was suitable for all sorts of special groups, even in these times when personnel were in such desperately short supply.

Neither the National Police Commissioner nor any other top brass had been seen or even heard from since their weird film show, a fact for which they were all grateful.

"Now we'll rehearse," said Bulldozer. "At six o'clock exactly Mauritzon will ring the doorbell. May we hear the signal once more?"

Kollberg tapped the table.

Mauritzon nodded. "Right," he said.

And then he qualified it: "At least it sounds right."

First a very short signal, immediately followed by a long one, pause, four short, pause, one long, followed directly by a very short one.

"I'll never be able to learn that tune," Zachrisson said dejectedly.

"We'll have to try and find you some other task, then," said Bulldozer.

"What might that be?" asked Gunvald Larsson. He was the only member of the squad who had made any previous attempts at collaboration with Zachrisson. They hadn't been especially successful.

"What am I to do, then?" asked the computer man.

"Yes. Actually, I've been wondering about that ever since last Monday," said Bulldozer. "Who sent you here?"

"Hard to say. It was some superintendent who called."

"Maybe you could figure something out," said Gunvald Larsson. "How to win the pools, for instance."

"That's impossible," said the expert gloomily. "I've been trying every week for a year."

"Let's think ourselves into the situation," Bulldozer said. "Who's going to ring the bell?"

"Kollberg," said Gunvald Larsson.

"Right. Perfect. Malmström opens. He expects to see Mauritzon with the astrolabe and underpants and all the rest of it. Instead he sees . . ."

"Us," said Rönn grimly.

"Exactly," said Bulldozer. "Both he and Mohrén'll be utterly perplexed. They'll be quite simply outwitted. Imagine the look on their faces!" He trotted about the room, smiling smugly. "And imagine how dumbfounded Roos'll be! Checkmate in one move." For a moment Bulldozer, envisaging these perspectives, appeared overwhelmed. But he quickly pulled himself together and went on: "The only problem is that Malmström and Mohrén'll be armed."

Gunvald Larsson gave an indifferent shrug.

"That doesn't matter too much," said Kollberg. If it came to blows, both he and Gunvald Larsson could put up a pretty good fight, and anyway Malmström and Mohrén probably wouldn't put up any opposition when they saw the size of their foe.

Bulldozer interpreted Kollberg's thoughts correctly and said: "We mustn't forget they may be desperate and try to shoot their way out. That's where you come in." He pointed at the tear gas expert, who nodded. "We'll also have a man with a dog ready outside the door," Bulldozer said. "The dog attacks. . . ."

"How does that hang together?" said Gunvald Larsson. "Is the goddam dog going to wear a gas mask?"

"Bright idea," Mauritzon said.

Everyone stared at him dubiously.

108

"So," said Bulldozer. "First possibility: Malmström and Mohrén try to resist, but, attacked by the dog and rendered harmless by tear gas, they are overpowered."

"All at once," said Kollberg skeptically.

But now Bulldozer was in full flight and was not concerned with objections. "Second possibility: Malmström and Mohrén don't put up any resistance. The police, pistols at the ready, force their way into the apartment and surround them."

"Not me," said Kollberg. He refused, on principle, ever to carry arms.

By now Bulldozer was almost lyrical. "The criminals are disarmed and handcuffed. Then I myself enter the apartment and warn them that they're under arrest. Then they're taken away." For a few moments he pondered these promising prospects. Then said animatedly: "Then we have the interesting third possibility: Malmström and Mohrén don't open up at all. They're extremely cautious and pay close attention to the doorbell signal. Now let's think about this. If they didn't answer, Mauritzon said the plan was for him to withdraw, wait nearby, return exactly twelve minutes later, and repeat the signal. And we'll do the same. Wait twelve minutes and ring again. Then either situation one or situation two will automatically occur. And we've already analyzed them."

Kollberg and Gunvald Larsson exchanged a glance of mutual comprehension.

"Alternative four . . ." Bulldozer began.

But he was interrupted by Kollberg, who said: "An alternative can only be one of two."

"I couldn't care less. Alternative four is that Malmström and Mohrén still don't open up. In that case you break down the door and—"

"And force our way in with our guns at the ready and surround the criminals," Gunvald Larsson finished with a deep sigh.

"Precisely," said Bulldozer. "That's precisely how it's going to be. Then I come into the room and arrest them. Perfect! You know this backwards. And all the possibilities have been exhausted. Right?"

For a while there was silence. Then Zachrisson

mumbled: "Fifth alternative: the gangsters open the door and mow us all down with their submachine guns, after which they take to their heels."

"Idiot," said Gunvald Larsson. "For one thing Malmström and Mohrén've been arrested any number of times without anyone ever getting hurt. For another, there's only two of them, and there's going to be six policemen and one dog outside the door, and ten more men in the stairway, and twenty out on the street, and a district attorney in the attic or wherever he figures on hanging out."

Zachrisson looked crestfallen but couldn't refrain from adding a final misanthropic word: "One can never be really sure about anything in this world."

"Shall I come too?" asked the computer man.

"No," said Bulldozer. "I don't see that there's anything for you to do."

"Without your machine you're helpless," Kollberg said.

"Perhaps we could hoist it up there for him with a crane," said Gunvald Larsson.

"You know all about the apartment's layout and existing entrances and exits," Bulldozer summed up. "The house has been under discreet observation for three hours and, as expected, nothing's happened. Malmström and Mohrén can't possibly know what's in store for them. Gentlemen, we are ready." He produced an antique silver watch from his breast pocket, flipped open the watchcase, and said: "In thirty-two minutes we strike."

"Isn't it conceivable that they'll try to beat it through the window?" Zachrisson suggested.

"Okay by me," said Gunvald Larsson. "The apartment's four flights up, as you know, and there's no fire escape."

"Alternative six in that case," said Zachrisson.

Bulldozer now turned to Mauritzon, who had been following the debate with indifference. "I don't suppose you'd care to accompany us, Mr. Mauritzon? Perhaps you'd like to meet your pals?"

Mauritzon answered with something between a shrug and a shudder.

"Then I suggest we put you somewhere nice and

peaceful until the matter's been cleared up. After all, you're a businessman, Mr. Mauritzon, and so you should understand that, in a manner of speaking, I am too. Should it appear you've tricked us in some way, our bargaining position will be a different one."

Mauritzon nodded. "All right," he said. "But I know they're there."

"I think Mr. Mauritzon's a goddam rat," said Gunvald Larsson to no one in particular.

Kollberg and Rönn studied the plans of the apartment one last time. The sketch had been drawn up according to Mauritzon's directions and was fairly accurate. Kollberg folded the paper and put it in his pocket. "Okay, then we'll get going," he said.

Mauritzon raised his voice and said: "As a friend, I'd just like to say Malmström and Mohrén are more dangerous than you think. They're sure to try and fight their way out. So don't take any risks."

Gunvald Larsson looked at Mauritzon grimly and said: "By that you mean you'd rather we shot both your pals dead on the spot, so you won't have to go around being scared to death of them for the rest of your life."

"I only wanted to warn you," said Mauritzon. "No need to take offense."

"Shut your face, you bloody pig," said Gunvald Larsson. He loathed being regarded as a colleague by people he despised. And that went for everyone, from informers to members of the National Police Board.

"Everything's ready," Bulldozer said with ill-concealed eagerness. "The action's on. Now we'll get going."

In the house on Danvik Cliffs all was as expected. What Mauritzon had said seemed to fit: for example, the name "S. Andersson" was on the doorplate.

Gunvald Larsson and Rönn were standing on either side of the door, pressed against the wall. Both had pistols in their hands: Gunvald Larsson his private Smith & Wesson thirty-eight Master, and Rönn his usual 7.65 millimeter Walther. Between them stood Kollberg, and the stairway behind him was crammed with people: Zachrisson and the tear gas man, the dog

111

handler and the dog, both the new detective sergeants, plus several uniformed patrolmen holding submachine guns and wearing bullet-proof vests. Bulldozer Olsson, supposedly, was in the elevator.

A world under arms, thought Kollberg, as his eyes followed the second hand on Gunvald Larsson's timepiece. He himself, of course, was unarmed.

Thirty-four seconds still to go. Gunvald Larsson's timepiece was a luxury watch. It always kept strict time.

Kollberg wasn't the slightest bit frightened. He'd been a cop far too long to be afraid of people like Malmström and Mohrén. On the other hand, he was wondering what they were thinking and talking about in there, isolated with their weapons, their supply of underpants, and mountains of goose-liver pâté and Russian caviar.

Sixteen seconds.

One of them, probably Mohrén, was obviously a gourmet of the first order, if Mauritzon was to be believed. Kollberg understood such an inclination very well: he himself was a lover of good food.

Eight seconds.

What would become of all that delicious grub when Mohrén and Malmström had been handcuffed and taken away? Maybe he could buy it off Mohrén cheap? Or would that be receiving stolen goods?

Two seconds.

Russian caviar, the kind with the golden lid, thought Lennart Kollberg.

One second.

Zero.

He put his right index finger on the doorbell: very short—long—pause—short—short—short—short—pause—long—very short.

Everyone waited.

Someone audibly drew his breath.

A shoe creaked.

Zachrisson, in some unknown way, managed to make his pistol rattle. How the hell can a pistol rattle? *Pistolrattle.* Interesting word, thought Kollberg. His stomach rumbled. Probably at the thought of Russian caviar. Something in keeping with Pavlov's dogs.

112

But this was all that happened. After two minutes there had still been no reaction to the bell from inside. According to the plan, they were now to wait ten minutes and then ring again.

Kollberg raised his right hand as a signal to those behind him to withdraw. Only Zachrisson, the dog, the dog handler, and the tear gas specialist remained within view; the first three went upstairs, and the latter down. Rönn and Gunvald Larsson stayed put.

Kollberg knew the plan down to the last detail, but he also knew Gunvald Larsson hadn't the faintest intention of following it. So he moved slightly to one side.

Gunvald Larsson also moved, placing himself right in front of the door and viewing it appraisingly. The thing didn't look impossible.

Larsson's got a mania for knocking down doors, thought Kollberg. True, he nearly always succeeded, but Kollberg disliked the method on principle and therefore shook his head and made a negative grimace.

As he expected, Gunvald Larsson took not the slightest notice. Instead, he backed away toward the wall and supported himself against it with his right shoulder.

Rönn appeared to be in on the idea.

Gunvald Larsson, hunched over and with his left shoulder protruding, made ready to fling himself against the door, a living battering ram—six feet three-and-one-half inches long and weighing 238 pounds.

Things having taken this turn, Kollberg too, of course, was in on it. No one, however, could have foreseen what was to happen within the next moment.

Gunvald Larsson flung himself forward, and the door, as though it hadn't even existed, flew open with inconceivable celerity.

This unexpected lack of any resistance caused Gunvald Larsson to rush straight through the entrance without any chance whatever of braking. Utterly off balance and in a pronouncedly forward-leaning posture, he flew straight across the room like a bolting crane and struck his head hard against the window frame opposite. The remainder of his enormous mass of mortal clay, however, went on following the laws of gravity. It swung around, unfortunately in the wrong direction, in such a manner that his backside, forcing out the windowpane, fell backwards out of the window in a cloud of splintering glass.

At the very last second he let go of his pistol and grabbed hold of the window ledge with his huge fist. He was thus left dangling five stories up from the ground with the larger part of his body outside the window—to which he clung desperately with his right hand and the hollow of his knee. Blood was already gushing from deep cuts in his hand, and his trouser leg, too, was beginning to turn red.

Rönn didn't move quite so fast but was still quick enough on his feet to get across the threshold the very second the door slammed shut again on its screeching hinges. It struck him with full force in the forehead. He dropped his pistol and fell backwards out onto the landing.

When the door flew open for the second time—after its collision with Rönn—Kollberg, too, succeeded in hurling himself into the apartment. A hasty survey showed that the only traces of human life in the room were one of Gunvald Larsson's hands and his right shank. Kollberg darted forward and grabbed hold of the leg with both hands.

There was imminent risk of Gunvald Larsson falling to his death. Kollberg leaned the considerable weight of his body against the leg and with his right hand succeeded in clasping his colleague's wildly gesticulating left arm. For a few seconds it seemed as though the weight ratio was wrong, and that they would both be catapulted out of the window. But Gunvald Larsson's lacerated right hand did not let go its grip, and, exerting all his strength, Kollberg finally succeeded in heaving up his distressed colleague to a point where he was at least halfway in again, torn to shreds and bleeding, but almost in safety.

By now Rönn, who had not lost consciousness, was crawling over the threshold on all fours, fumbling as he did so for his pistol which he'd dropped as he fell.

The next man to appear on the scene was Zachrisson, immediately followed by the dog, which bounded

114

forward. Zachrisson saw Rönn crawling around on all fours, blood dripping down from his head onto the pistol, which was lying on the floor. He also saw Kollberg and Gunvald Larsson bloodily intertwined by the smashed window and obviously out of action.

Zachrisson yelled: "Stop! Police!" Then he cocked his pistol and fired off a shot which hit the ceiling light. A white glass globe, it exploded with an ear-shattering report. Then, turning on his heel, he shot the dog. The beast sunk down onto its hind legs and gave a howl of agony, which pierced through bone and marrow. Zachrisson's third shot went through the open door of the bathroom, perforating the hot water pipe. A long jet of hot water spouted into the room. He fired another shot; but the pistol misfired and the mechanism jammed.

Wild-eyed, the dog handler rushed in. "The bastards have shot Boy," he yelled piercingly, drawing his regulation pistol. Flourishing it, he looked furiously around for someone on whom he could wreak vengeance.

The dog howled worse than ever.

A patrolman in a blue-green bullet-proof vest ran in through the open doorway with a loaded submachine gun but stumbled over Rönn and flopped to the floor. His weapon flew across the parquet flooring. The dog, obviously mortally wounded, sank its fangs into one of his thighs. The patrolman began yelling for help.

By now Kollberg and Gunvald Larsson were indoors again, lacerated and exhausted but with two conclusions lucidly in their heads. *Primo:* there hadn't been anybody in the apartment, neither Malmström nor Mohrén nor anyone else. *Secundo:* the door had not been locked nor presumably even properly closed.

By now the jet of hot water from the bathroom was scalding and steaming. It struck Zachrisson full in the face.

The policeman who was wearing the bullet-proof vest crawled over to his submachine gun. The dog, refusing to let go, snuffled after him, teeth sunk deeply into its victim's meaty leg.

Raising his bleeding hand, Gunvald Larsson roared: "Stop!"

And at that very instant the tear gas specialist hurled two grenades in quick succession through the door. They landed on the floor, between Rönn and the dog handler, and instantly exploded.

Somebody fired one last shot—who, it isn't known for sure. Probably the man with the dog. The bullet struck the heating radiator half an inch from one of Kollberg's knees, ricocheted whining out into the stairway, and hit the tear gas man in the shoulder.

Kollberg tried to yell: "We give in! We give in!" But he only produced a hoarse croak.

Spreading swiftly, the gas mingled with steam and the smoke of the grenades until it filled the room and no one could any longer see anyone else. Inside, six men and a dog were groaning, crying, and coughing.

Outside, on the stairs, the gas expert sat whimpering, the palm of his right hand pressed against his left shoulder.

Rushing down from the floor above, Bulldozer Olsson asked indignantly: "What's happened? What's going on? What's up?"

Horrible sounds were coming out of the gas-filled room: strangled howls, cries for help, and crude, incomprehensible curses.

"Stop the whole operation," Bulldozer ordered in a faint voice, himself beginning to cough hoarsely and shrilly. He retreated upwards out of the gas cloud, which followed him. Straightening his back, he turned to the now hardly discernible doorway. "Malmström and Mohrén," he said in a voice of authority, but with the tears streaming down his face, "throw away your guns and come out with your hands up. You're under arrest."

19

On the morning of Thursday, July 6, 1972, the members of the special squad were pale but composed. In their headquarters a glum silence reigned. No one felt particularly merry after yesterday's events. Least of all Gunvald Larsson. In a film, maybe, there's something comic about tumbling out of a window and dangling five stories above the ground. In reality there certainly isn't. Torn hands and clothes aren't particularly funny either.

Indeed, Gunvald was more annoyed about his clothes than about anything else. He was always scrupulous in the selection of his wardrobe, which also swallowed up a good slice of his salary. And now, for the umpteenth time, some of his most highly valued garments had fallen victim to his duties.

Nor was Einar Rönn happy. And even Kollberg was finding it hard to appreciate the comic elements in the situation, glaring though they were. He still recollected very clearly those butterflies in his stomach at the moment when he'd truly believed that both he and Gunvald Larsson only had five more seconds to live before being dashed to pieces on the ground. Nor was he religious. Kollberg did not believe in some huge police headquarters up in the sky, inhabited by winged detectives.

Though the battle of Danvik Cliffs had been analyzed in great detail, their written report was oddly vague and evasive. It was Kollberg who had written it.

But their losses could not be argued away. Three men had been taken off to the hospital, admittedly in no danger for their lives or with any risk of permanent harm. The tear gas expert had a flesh wound in his shoulder, and Zachrisson had burns on his face. The

117

doctors also alleged that he was suffering from shock, seemed "queer," and found it hard to give straight-forward answers to simple questions. This, however, might be because they didn't know him and over-estimated his intelligence—to underestimate it seemed virtually impossible. The patrolman who'd been bitten by the dog could look forward to several weeks' sick leave. Torn muscles and ripped tendons don't heal in a hurry.

Worst off was the dog. The Veterinary College surgical clinic reported that, although they had man-aged to remove the bullet, if infection were to set in they might still have to put him away. But Boy was a young and strong beast, they added, and his general condition was satisfactory. To anyone familiar with Veterinary College jargon this inspired little hope.

Rönn had an enormous bandage on his forehead and two magnificent bruises, which only lent added effect to the red nose with which nature had endowed him.

Gunvald Larsson should really have stayed at home. No one with a tightly bandaged right hand and knee can really be declared fit for duty. He also had a big lump on his head.

As for Kollberg, though troubled by a heavy, ach-ing head (due, in his view, to the unhealthy air of the battlefield), he was in somewhat better condition. A special cure chiefly consisting of cognac, aspirin, and his wife's loving and erotically tinged care, ably pro-vided, had had a positive—if transient—effect.

The enemy's losses, too, were insignificant. They had not even been present at the battle. Several objects in the flat had been seized, but not even Bulldozer Olsson could claim the loss of a roll of toilet paper, a cardboard box containing string, two jars of whortle-berry jam, and an improbable quantity of used under-pants was likely to upset Malmström and Mohrén to any serious degree. Nor would it place any grave ob-stacles in the way of their future operations.

At 8:52 Bulldozer Olsson stormed in through the door. Already he had attended two early morning meetings, one at the National Police Board and another with the people from Fraud, and by now he was well and truly on the warpath. "Good morning, good morning, good morning," he exclaimed merrily. "Well, boys, and how are you all?"

The boys felt more middle-aged than ever. Not one of them replied.

"Roos made some smart countermoves yesterday," Olsson said. "But that's nothing for us to cry over. Let's say we've lost a couple of bishops and a pawn."

"Looked more like stalemate to me," said Kollberg, who was a chess player.

"But now it's our move," cried Bulldozer. "Fetch in Mauritzon. Let's feel his pulse! He has something up his sleeve! And he's scared, gentlemen, scared! He knows Malmström and Mohrén'll be out for his blood now, and at this moment the greatest disservice we could do him would be to let him go. As he knows full well."

Red-eyed, Rönn, Kollberg, and Gunvald Larsson stared at their leader. The notion of again going into action on Mauritzon's instructions had little appeal.

Bulldozer studied them rather more carefully. His eyes, too, were swollen and red around the rims. "I thought of something last night, boys," he said. "What do you say? Shouldn't we employ rather younger and fresher forces for such operations from now on? I mean, like yesterday's?" After a brief pause he added: "It hardly seems right that middle-aged men who have long ago settled down and reached moderately high rank should be rushing about the place like this, firing off guns and so forth."

Gunvald Larsson gave a deep sigh and slumped down even more. He looked as if someone had just stuck a knife in his back.

Sure, thought Kollberg, that's dead right. But a second later he felt furious. Middle-aged? Settled down? What the hell?

Rönn mumbled something.

"What's that you said, Einar?" Bulldozer asked amiably.

"Well, it wasn't us who fired."

"Be that as it may," said Bulldozer. "Be that as it may. Well, now we must all pull ourselves together. Bring in Mauritzon!"

Mauritzon had spent the night in the cells—admittedly in greater comfort than usual. He had, for instance, been given a chamber pot to himself and even blankets, and the guard had inquired whether he'd like a glass of water.

Mauritzon had had nothing against these arrangements, and was said to have slept soundly. Not like the evening before, when he'd first been arrested. When they'd told him Malmström and Mohrén hadn't been there, he'd seemed troubled, not to say astounded.

C.I.D. methods, however, had revealed that they had been there only a little while earlier. There was an abundance of both men's fingerprints and traces of Mauritzon's right thumb and forefinger had even been found on one of the jam jars.

"You realize what that means?" Bulldozer Olsson said inquisitorially.

"Yes," said Gunvald Larsson. "That he's circumstantially linked to a jar of whortleberry jam."

"Right!" said Bulldozer, cheerfully surprised. "In fact, we've proof against him. Proof that'll even hold up in court. But that wasn't what I was thinking."

"What *were* you thinking?"

"That it shows Mauritzon's been telling the truth and will therefore probably go on telling us whatever he knows."

"Sure—about Malmström and Mohrén."

"And that's all we're really interested in just now, right?"

Once again Mauritzon was seated in their midst, the same insignificant mild little man, decent to the core.

"Well, my dear Mr. Mauritzon," said Bulldozer amicably. "Things failed to turn out quite as we'd expected."

Mauritzon shook his head. "Queer," he said. "I don't get it. They must have had some sort of sixth sense."

"Sixth sense," said Bulldozer dreamily. "Yes, at times one can almost believe it. Now if Roos . . ."

"Who's that?"

"Nothing, Mr. Mauritzon. Nothing. Just talking to myself. But there's something else worrying me. Our

120

private accounts don't quite balance. I've done you a big service, Mr. Mauritzon, and I'm still waiting, as it were, for a *quid pro quo.*"

Mauritzon thought long and deeply. Finally he said: "You mean that I'm still not at liberty?"

"Well," said Bulldozer, "yes and no. When all's said and done, dope pushing is a serious crime. I guess, Mr. Mauritzon, you'd get at least . . ." He broke off, counting on his fingers.

"Well, I guess I can promise you eight months. Or at least six."

Mauritzon regarded him calmly.

"But, on the other hand," Bulldozer went on, his tone becoming livelier, "I've promised you absolution for this time, haven't I? Provided I get something in exchange." Bulldozer straightened his back, smacked his palms together in front of his face, and said brutally: "In other words, if you don't immediately cough up everything you know about Malmström and Mohrén, we'll have you inside as an accomplice. Your finger-prints were found in the flat. And then we'll send you back to Jacobsson. And what's more, we'll see you get a damned good beating into the bargain."

Gunvald glanced appreciatively at the leader of the special squad and said: "Yeah, it'd be a personal pleasure for me to . . ." He left his sentence hanging in the air.

Mauritzon didn't bat an eyelash. "Okay," he said. "I've something I guess you can use on Malmström and Mohrén—and on a few others besides."

Bulldozer Olsson brightened. "Interesting, Mr. Mauritzon! And what is this choice tidbit?"

Mauritzon looked at Gunvald Larsson and said: "It's so simple your cat could fix it."

"My cat?"

"Sure. But don't blame me if you screw it up again."

"My dear Mr. Mauritzon, no harsh words now! We're all just as keen to get our paws on these lads as you are. But in heaven's name, what is it you have on them?"

"Their plan for their next job," Mauritzon said tonelessly. "Timings and all."

121

For just a moment District Attorney Olsson's eyes almost jumped out of his head. Three times he ran around Mauritzon's chair shouting like a maniac: "Tell us, Mr. Mauritzon! Spill the beans! You're already as good as free! We'll even give you a police escort if you like. But tell us. Please Mr. Mauritzon, tell us everything!"

Infected by his curiosity, the whole special squad had risen to their feet and were standing impatiently around the stool pigeon.

"Okay," Mauritzon said without more ado. "I'd promised to help Malmström and Mohrén with one thing and another. Purchases and so forth. They weren't too keen on going out, see? And every day I was to go to a cigar store in the Birka district and ask for Mohrén's mail."

"Which cigar store?" Kollberg demanded instantly.

"Oh, I don't mind telling you that too, though it won't do you any good knowing it. I've checked up on that already. The shop's kept by an old woman, and the letters had been handed in by old-age pensioners, a different one each time."

"Oh?" said Bulldozer. "Letters? What letters? How many letters?"

"Altogether only three," Mauritzon said.

"And you delivered them?"

"Sure. But not before I'd opened them."

"Didn't Mohrén notice?"

"No. People whose letters I open don't notice. I've a perfect way of doing it, see? Chemical."

"Indeed, and what was in the letters?" It was more than Bulldozer could do to stand still. He kept skipping about the floor like an overplump bantam cock on a hot grill.

"There was nothing at all interesting in the first two. They were about a couple of guys called 'H' and 'H' who were to come to a place called 'Q' and so forth. Just short messages. In some kind of a code. I stuck down the envelopes again and gave them to Mohrén."

"And the third one?"

"The third one came the day before yesterday. And that was most interesting, indeed. The plans for their next job, as I've already said. Detailed."

"And you gave the paper to Mohrén?"

"Papers. There were three big sheets. Sure I gave them to Mohrén. But not until I'd taken photostats, which I put away in a safe place."

"Oh, my dear Mr. Mauritzon," said Bulldozer, overwhelmed. "But which place? And how soon can you go and get them?"

"You can get them yourself. I don't feel like it."

"When?"

"As soon as I've told you where they are."

"And where's that?"

"Take it easy," Mauritzon said. "this is the genuine thing, don't you worry. But first there's a couple of things I want."

"And what are they?"

"First that paper from Jacobsson, the one you've got in your pocket. The one where it says I'm not suspected of narcotics offenses, and that the preliminary investigation's been abandoned for lack of evidence and so on."

"Sure, immediately," said Bulldozer, putting his hand into his inside pocket.

"Further, I want a similar paper, signed by yourself, about this business of my being an accomplice of Malmström and Mohrén. That the thing's been looked into and that I've been acting in good faith and so forth."

Bulldozer Olsson flew to his typewriter. The document was ready in less than two minutes. Mauritzon took both, read through their texts, and said: "Good. The letter with the copies is at the Sheraton."

"The hotel?"

"Yes. I sent it there. It's with the desk clerk. *Poste restante.*"

"Under what name?"

"Count Philip von Brandenburg," said Mauritzon bashfully. "Philip spelt with a 'ph.' "

They all looked at him astounded.

Then Bulldozer said: "Oh, my dear Mr. Mauritzon, admirable, admirable! Wouldn't you like to sit in another room just for a little while where you can have a cup of coffee and a Danish pastry or something?"

"Tea, thanks," said Mauritzon.

"Tea," said Bulldozer absent-mindedly. "Einar, would you kindly see to it that Mr. Mauritzon gets some tea and a Danish pastry . . . and . . . some company."

Rönn went out with Mauritzon and after less than a minute came back again.

"And what," said Kollberg, "do we do now?"

"Fetch that letter," said Bulldozer. "On the double. The simplest way would be if one of you went there and said you're Count von Brandenburg and asked for his mail. You for example, Gunvald."

Gunvald Larsson stared stiffly at him out of his china-blue eyes. "Me? Not on your life. I'd sooner hand in my resignation on the spot."

"Then you'll have to do it, Einar. If we tell the truth it'll only lead to a fuss. Maybe they'd refuse to hand over the Count's mail and so on. We can lose a lot of valuable time."

"Sure," said Rönn. "Philip von Brandenburg, Count. Here, I've got one of Mauritzon's calling cards he's given me. Had them in a kind of secret pocket in his wallet. They look most aristocratic."

The calling card was printed in a grayish print with a silver monogram in one corner.

"Get going," said Bulldozer impatiently. "Beat it!"

Rönn went.

"I'm thinking of something queer," Kollberg said. "If I go into the grocer's where I've shopped these ten years and ask to buy a pint of milk on account, they'll turn me down. But if a guy like Mauritzon walks into one of the smartest jewelers in town and says he's the Duke of Malexander he can walk out with two diamond rings and ten pearl necklaces on approval."

"Well, that's the way it is," said Gunvald Larsson. "We live in a class society . . . pure and simple."

Bulldozer Olsson nodded absent-mindedly. He wasn't interested in questions concerning the social structure.

The desk clerk looked at the letter he was holding in his hand, then at the visiting card, and lastly at Rönn. "Are you really Count von Brandenburg?" he asked suspiciously.

124

"Sure," said Rönn uneasily. "Or rather, that's to say . . . I'm his messenger."

"Aha," said the porter. "Like that, is it? Here you are, then. And tell the count we're always honored to have him as our guest."

Anyone who knew Bulldozer Olsson would probably have thought him seriously ill or at least out of his wits. For more than an hour he'd been in a state of utter euphoria. This feeling of abnormal well-being expressed itself less in his words than in his actions—or rather in his gestures and movements. It was more than he could do to sit still for more than three seconds at a time. He seemed to float about in the room, as if his crumpled blue suit had not been the envelope of a district attorney but of a zeppelin, and his plump little body had been filled with helium.

In the long run this little outburst of joy became trying. On the other hand, the three sheets of paper addressed to the "Count" were fascinating to study, and Kollberg, Rönn, and Gunvald Larsson were still examining them with quite as much interest as when their eyes had first fallen on them a good hour ago.

There could be no doubt about it. What lay on the special squad's table were photostats of virtually the entire plan for Malmström's and Mohrén's next bank robbery.

It was to be a robbery of no ordinary dimensions. It was a real knockout job, the one they'd been expecting for weeks. And now—all of a sudden—they knew almost everything! It was to take place on a Friday, at 2:45 P.M. In all probability either Friday the 7th— which was to say tomorrow—or else a week later, i.e. Friday, July 14.

There was much to suggest the latter alternative. This would give them a whole week, more than enough for all imaginable preparations. But even if Malmström and Mohrén went to work at once, the papers revealed so much that it would be mere routine to make a shambles of all their meticulous plans and grab them red-handed.

On one of the sheets was a detailed sketch of the bank itself, with every detail drawn in. This seemed to include everything related to the actual methods to be employed: the points at which the various individuals should stand, the location of the getaway cars, and their routes out of town. All was specified in detail.

Bulldozer Olsson, who knew everything about every bank in the entire Stockholm region, only needed to cast a glance at the sketch to be able to state on the spot which bank it was they intended to plunder: one of the largest and most modern in downtown Stockholm.

The plan, in all its simplicity, was so clever that it could only have one author: Werner Roos. Of that Bulldozer was sure.

The actual robbery was divided up into three independent actions. The first was to be a diversion.

The second was to be a prophylactic operation, aimed directly at the main enemy, viz., the police. The third was the robbery itself.

To carry out their plan, Malmström and Mohrén would need at least four field assistants. Of these, two were even mentioned by name: Hauser and Hoff. As far as could be seen, they were to stand guard during the actual coup. The two—or possibly more than two—others were to be responsible for the diversion and for the preventive aspect. These persons were described as "enterprisers."

The diversionary maneuver was to commence at 2:40 and take place on Rosenlundsgatan, on the South Side of the city. Included among the props were at least two cars and a very heavy charge of dynamite.

Everything suggested that this diversion was designed to draw maximum attention to itself, as well as almost all the patrol cars circulating in the center of the city and its southern suburbs. Precisely how it was to be carried out was not made clear. But there seemed to be every reason to suppose it would comprise a violent explosion, either at a gas station or inside a house. The man responsible for this was "Enterpriser A."

A minute later, as was tactically correct, the prophylactic measures were to be unleashed. This part of the plan was as ingenious as it was impudent. All the exits for the riot squads and other emergency vehicles always held in reserve at the Kungsholmen police station were to be blocked. Just how this was to be done was hard to imagine; but a central police force that was unprepared would certainly have some unpleasant surprises in store for it. Direct command of this part of the scheme lay with "Enterpriser B."

By 2:45, assuming these two primary operations had gone off according to plan, far and away the greater part of the mobile police forces would be tied up at the commotion on Rosenlundsgatan, on the South Side, while the tactical reserve of emergency personnel would be stuck in the central police building on Kungsholmen.

At that moment Malmström and Mohrén, assisted by the mysterious and unknown Messrs. Hoff and Hauser, would carry out the actual coup against the bank, with excellent prospects of remaining undisturbed by the police.

This, then, was to be the long-expected job, the job with a very big "J."

Two vehicles were to be employed as getaway cars and would later be exchanged for four others, with only one man in each. In view of the fact that by this time almost all mobile police would have been lured off to the southern parts of the city and the rest would be tied up on Kungsholmen, all four cars were to retreat northwards.

Even the booty's putative size was stated for the sake of completeness. It was estimated at a sum equivalent to two-and-a-half million Swedish kronor. It was this last detail that suggested Friday the 14th. A conversation with the bank had indicated that a sum of about that size would be easily accessible, in all kinds of currency, on that particular day. If, on the other hand, the gang struck tomorrow, its haul would be a good deal smaller.

Most of the instructions were in plain Swedish or were at least fairly easy to interpret.

"Jean has a long moustache," said Kollberg. "Everyone knows what that means. It was used over the radio to the French Maquis on the eve of D-day in World War II." Kollberg saw Rönn's inquiring glance and became explicit. "It means, quite simply: 'Okay, boys, let's get going.'"

"That last bit, too, is simple enough," Gunvald Larsson said. " 'Abandon ship.' That was the bit Mauritzon didn't get. Orders to clear out at once. Which is why that apartment was empty. Probably Roos suspected Mauritzon and had them change their hideaway."

"And immediately afterwards comes the word 'Milan,' " Kollberg said. "What's that mean?"

"Meet in Milan to split up the dough," Bulldozer said unhesitatingly. "But as things are, they won't even get out of the bank—that is, if we even let them get into it. The game's ours."

"Indubitably," Kollberg said. "At least, so it would seem."

Knowing all this, they easily drew up the countermeasures. Whatever might occur on Rosenlundsgatan, it was to be ignored as far as possible. As for the emergency vehicles on Kungsholmen, all that had to be done was to make sure that they were not there at the moment when the gangsters' preventive action was set in motion. On the contrary, they would be placed at strategic points around the bank.

"Well," Bulldozer said, more or less to himself, "this plan is clearly the work of Werner Roos. But how are we ever going to prove it?"

"The typewriter, perhaps?" said Rönn.

"Electric typewriting is almost impossible to trace to any particular machine. And he doesn't make any consistent typographical errors, either. So how are we to pin it on him?"

"Surely you can figure out a little thing like that," said Kollberg. "You who are a district attorney! Here in Sweden all you've got to do is bring charges against people in order to get them put away, even if they're innocent."

"But Werner Roos is guilty," Bulldozer said.

"What'll we do with Mauritzon?" Gunvald Larsson asked.

"Let him go, of course," Bulldozer said absentmindedly. "He's done his bit now and is out of the picture."

"Is he? I wonder," said Gunvald Larsson dubiously.

"Next Friday," said Bulldozer dreamily. "Think what's waiting for us!"

"Yes, just think," said Gunvald Larsson gruffly. The phone rang: bank robbery out at Vällingby.

As a bank robbery, it was nothing to write home about. A toy pistol and only fifteen thousand in booty. An hour later the culprit was found staggering around in Humlegården Park, trying to give away the cash. But at least he'd had time to get thoroughly drunk and, to cap it all, had been shot in the leg by an ambitious patrolman. The special squad dealt with the matter without even leaving the building.

"Could Roos be behind that, d'you think?" Gunvald Larsson asked maliciously.

"Well," said Bulldozer, cheered by the thought, "you've a bright idea there. Indirectly, Roos is guilty. His bank raids are an inspiration even to the ungifted. So indirectly, as I say, one could say . . ."

"Oh my God," said Gunvald Larsson. "Pack it in, will you?"

Rönn went to his own room. Inside sat someone he hadn't seen for a very long time: Martin Beck.

"Hello," Beck said, "been in a fight?"

"Yes," Rönn said. "Indirectly."

"Meaning?"

"I don't quite know," Rönn said vaguely. "Everything's so queer nowadays. What d'you want?"

20

Einar Rönn's room was at the rear of the central police building on Kungsholmsgatan. From the window he had a view out over an immense hole in the ground—out of which the gigantic showy building of the National Police Board would in due course rise up and obscure the view. From this ultramodern colossus in the heart of Stockholm the police would extend their tentacles in every direction and hold the dispirited citizens of Sweden in an iron grip. At least some of them. After all, they couldn't all emigrate or commit suicide.

The location and overwhelming dimensions of the new police headquarters had been violently criticized in many quarters; but in the end the police had had their way—as far as the building was concerned.

What the police, or to be more precise, some persons within its higher ranks, actually wanted, was power. This was the secret ingredient that in recent years had been guiding the department's philosophy. Since the police had never previously been an independent power factor in Swedish politics, only a few as yet understood which way the wind was blowing. The quest for power also explained why so many aspects of the never-ending forays made by the police in recent years had appeared contradictory and incomprehensible.

The new building was to be an important symbol of this new power. It was to facilitate a planned central directorate of a totalitarian type, and it was also to be a fortress against the prying eyes and ears of persons having no business there—which meant, in this case, the entire Swedish nation. In this context one line of thought was important: Swedes had gotten into the habit of laughing at the police. Soon no one would laugh any more. Or so it was hoped.

All this, however, was so far no more than a pious aspiration, screened from all except a few; something which, with a little luck and if the right political breezes blew, could ripen into a Ministry of Terror. As yet it was still little more than a big hole in Kungsholmen's rocky terrain.

From Rönn's window the view was still open toward the upper part of Bergsgatan and Kronoberg Park's leafy trees.

Now Martin Beck had gotten up from Rönn's desk and was standing by the window. From it he could see the window of the flat where Karl Edvin Svärd had lain dead for two months or so with a bullet through his heart and without anyone missing him.

"Before you became a specialist in bank robberies you investigated a death," Martin Beck said. "A man named Svärd."

Rönn gave an embarrassed titter. "Specialist!" he said. "Oh my!" Rönn was not a man with any grave defects; but his temperament was miles apart from Martin Beck's, and they'd always found it hard to collaborate. "Yes, it's true," Rönn said. "I was just busy with that death when I was detailed off."

"Detailed off?"

"Yes, to this special squad."

Martin Beck felt a very faint pang of irritation —perhaps at Rönn's unconscious use of military jargon. Two years ago he'd not have used such an expression. "Did you come to any conclusion?" Martin Beck asked.

Rönn rubbed his red nose with his thumb and said: "Didn't have much time to do anything about it, did I? Why're you asking?"

"Because, as you probably know, the case has been passed on to me—as some kind of therapy, I guess."

"Well," Rönn said, "it was a silly sort of a case. From the outset it looked like a detective story. Old man shot in a room locked from the inside. Added

131

to which . . ." He fell silent, as if ashamed of something. This was one of his more irritating tricks. You had to keep needling him all the time.

"What were you going to say?"

"Well, Gunvald said I ought to arrest myself at once."

"Oh? Why?"

"As a suspect. Don't you see? I could've shot him myself, here, from my room. Through the window." Martin Beck said nothing, and Rönn immediately became unsure of himself. "Well, of course he was just joking. Besides, Svärd's window was shut from the inside, and the blind was drawn down, and the pane hadn't been broken. Added to which . . ."

"What were you going to say?"

"Added to which I'm a terribly bad shot. Once I missed a moose at twenty-five feet. After which my dad never let me shoot again—only carry his thermos and brandy and sandwiches for him. So . . ."

"Yes?"

"Well, it's eight hundred feet away. And someone who can't hit a moose at twenty-five feet with a rifle certainly couldn't hit the building over there with a pistol. Well, I didn't mean . . . I'm sorry. . . ."

"What didn't you mean?"

"Well, it can't be very nice for you—me babbling away here about pistols and shooting and so forth."

"That's okay. Just how much work did you put into that case?"

"Only a little, as I said. I fixed up a criminological investigation, but by then people over there had been trampling every which way. And I rang up the lab and asked whether anyone had taken any paraffin tests of Svärd's hands. No one had, and to make matters worse . . ."

"Yes?"

"Well, the corpse had gone. Been cremated. A pretty story. What an investigation!"

"Did you look into Svärd's background at all?"

"No, never got that far. But there was one other thing I tried to arrange."

"And what was that?"

"Well, if he was shot, there must have been a

bullet. But there'd been no ballistic investigation, see? So I rang up the guy who did the postmortem. Well, as a matter of fact it was a girl; and she said she'd stuffed the bullet into an envelope and put it somewhere. Carelessness from beginning to end."

"Well?"

"She couldn't find it. The envelope, that is. I told her she had to try, and send it in for a ballistic examination. Then the case was taken out of my hands."

Martin Beck looked across to the distant row of buildings on Bergsgatan and thoughtfully rubbed the bridge of his nose with his right thumb and forefinger. "Einar," he said. "What's your private opinion about how it all happened? What do you think about it, personally?"

Only in the presence of his closest friends does a policeman ventilate his personal and private opinions about official investigations. Martin Beck and Rönn had never been either friends or enemies.

Rönn sat silent for a long while, apparently thinking unpleasant thoughts. Then he said: "Well, it's my belief that there was a revolver inside the apartment when the patrolmen got the door open."

Why just a revolver? The answer was simple: There'd been no cartridge case. Rönn's thinking was lucid, even so. A revolver must have been lying somewhere on the floor, for example underneath the corpse. In which case neither the patrolmen nor Gustavsson, who'd been there to take a look, would have seen it as long as the corpse was there. And it was not quite certain they'd examined the floor after the body had been taken away.

"Do you know Aldor Gustavsson?"

"Sure." Rönn squirmed unhappily in his chair.

But Martin Beck refrained from putting the disagreeable question. Instead he said: "There's one more important point, Einar."

"And what's that?"

"Did you have a chance to have a word with Kristiansson and Kvastmo? When I got here on Monday only one of them was on duty; and now one's on vacation and the other has a leave of absence."

"Sure, I called both of them to my office," said Rönn.

"And what did they have to say?"

"Obviously they stuck to what they'd written in their report. From the moment they'd got the door open until they'd left there'd only been five people in that apartment."

"That is, themselves, Gustavsson, and the two men who took the corpse away?"

"Exactly."

"And you asked them whether they'd looked under the corpse?"

"Sure. And Kvastmo said he had. Kristiansson kept on vomiting, so he mostly stayed outside."

Now Martin Beck didn't hesitate. He turned the screw. "And you think Kvastmo was lying?"

Rönn's answer was surprisingly long in coming. He'd said "A," Martin Beck thought; so there was hardly any reason why he shouldn't say "B" without more ado.

Rönn fingered the bandage on his forehead, and said: "I've always heard you were an unpleasant guy to be examined by."

"What do you mean?"

"Well, that those people who say so are right."

"And now be a good fellow and answer."

"I'm no psychologist when it comes to judging witnesses," Rönn said. "But to me Kvastmo seemed to be telling the truth."

"Your logic doesn't fit," Martin Beck said coldly. "How can you believe this revolver was in the room, and at the same time say you think the patrolmen were telling the truth?"

"Because there's no other explanation," said Rönn. "It's as simple as that."

"Okay, Einar, it's just that I, too, think Kvastmo was telling the truth."

"But didn't you say you hadn't spoken to him?" said Rönn, astonished.

"I said nothing of the kind. As a matter of fact I had a word with Kvastmo last Tuesday. But I wasn't in a position to speak to him in such calm circumstances as I guess you were."

Rönn looked hurt. "You really are unpleasant," he said. He pulled out the middle drawer of his desk and took out a spiral-bound notebook. He leafed through it a while and then ripped out a page, which he handed to Martin Beck. "I've one more bit of information that may interest you," he said. "Svärd hadn't been living very long out here on Kungsholmen. I found out where he'd been living before. But then I wasn't in a position to do anything more about the matter. Anyway, here's the address. You're welcome to it."

Martin Beck looked at the piece of paper. A name and address on Tulegatan—the district that, not without reason, had once been called Siberia. He folded the paper and put it in his pocket. "Thanks, Einar."

Rönn said nothing.

" 'Bye then," said Martin Beck.

Rönn replied with a curt nod.

Relations between them had never been particularly cordial. They now seemed to have deteriorated further.

Martin Beck left Rönn's room, and soon afterwards the building. He walked briskly through the town—along Kungsholmsgatan and on over Kungsbron along Kungsgatan to Sveavägen, where he turned north.

He could so easily have improved his relations with Rönn by saying something positive or at least friendly. He did not lack reasons for doing so. The investigation into Svärd's death had been messed up from the beginning. But from the moment when Rönn had taken it over, it had been dealt with promptly and with perfect correctness.

Rönn had instantly perceived that a revolver might have been lying underneath the corpse and that this was of crucial importance. Had Kvastmo really checked the floor after the remains had been removed? No one could really blame him if he hadn't. Gustavsson had appeared on the scene both in his capacity as Kvastmo's superior and as a specialist, and his self-assured way of assessing the situation had largely relieved both patrolmen of any further responsibility.

If Kvastmo *hadn't* looked, then matters at once assumed another aspect. After the corpse had been taken away, the men had sealed the apartment and gone off. But what, in this particular case, had been meant by "sealing"?

Since the police had not been able to get into the apartment without removing the door from its hinges, and then only after these had been more or less demolished, sealing had meant no more than tying a piece of string tightly between the doorposts and hanging up the usual printed notice saying the place was sealed off in accordance with the appropriate paragraph of the law. In practice, of course, this had meant nothing. And for several days almost anyone could have gotten in without the least difficulty. And various objects could have been removed, for instance a gun.

But all this implied, in the first place, that Kvastmo had been deliberately lying. And, further, it implied that he was a good enough liar to deceive not only Rönn but Martin Beck himself. Both Rönn and Martin Beck were old hands at the game, and neither had a reputation for being particularly easy to dupe.

Second, if Svärd had really shot himself, why should anyone have taken the trouble to filch the weapon? Here was an obvious contradiction. Nor was it limited to the fact that the man had been found lying in a room which, in fact, had been locked from within and where, to cap it all, no weapon had been found.

Svärd seemed to have no close relations. Nor, as far as anyone knew, had he kept any company. If no one knew him, who could have been interested in his death?

Martin Beck felt he must widen his knowledge on a number of points. Among other things, he would check up on one further detail concerning what had happened on Sunday, June 18. But above all he wanted to know more about Karl Edvin Svärd.

On the piece of paper he'd been given by Rönn was not only the address in "Siberia." There was another jotting. A name: "Landlady—Rea Nielson."

Now Martin Beck had reached the house on Tulegatan. A glance at the list of names in the hallway revealed that the landlady lived in the building. A remarkable fact in itself and perhaps fortunate for him.

He went up to the third floor and rang the bell.

21

The truck was gray, without any markings except its license plates. The men who used it were wearing overalls of much the same color as the truck itself. There was nothing about their appearance to indicate their occupation. They could have been repairmen of one kind or another, or perhaps city employees. Which in fact was precisely the case.

It was nearly six o'clock in the evening, and if nothing alarming had occurred within the next fifteen minutes they would soon be finishing their day's work and going off home to play with their kids for a while before settling down in front of the TV.

Martin Beck, having found no one at home in Tulegatan, had seized upon these two. They were sitting beside their Volkswagen van drinking beer out of bottles, while the vehicle spread a pungent odor of disinfectant. But above all there was another smell that no chemical on earth could overcome. The rear doors hung open. Understandably, the men were airing the inside of the vehicle at the first available opportunity.

In their beautiful city these men had a special and rather important function. Their daily task was to remove suicides and other unattractive persons who had departed this life to more suitable surroundings.

Some few people, for instance firemen and policemen as well as certain journalists and other initiates, were familiar with this gray truck. And when they saw it come driving down the street they knew what was amiss. But the great majority saw nothing peculiar about it; for them it was just another vehicle. Which was precisely the effect intended. After all, there was no reason to make people more dispirited and scared than they were already.

Like many others in slightly peculiar professions, these fellows took their job as it came and with great aplomb; they rarely or never overdramatized their task in the welfare machine. By and large, they only discussed it among themselves; they had long ago perceived that most listeners' reactions were highly negative—particularly when in jolly company, among friends, or at their wives' coffee tables.

Their contacts with the police, though everyday affairs, were always with cops of the most humdrum order. For a detective chief inspector to show interest in their doings, and even seek them out, was definitely flattering.

The more loquacious of the two wiped his mouth with the back of his hand and said: "Sure, I remember that one. Bergsgatan wasn't it?"

"Right."

"Though the name don't mean nothing. Stål, you say?"

"No, Svärd."

"Don't mean a thing to me. We don't often bother about names."

"I understand."

"That was a Sunday, too. Sundays is always busy, see?"

"Do you remember the policeman I named? Kenneth Kvastmo?"

"Nix. Name means nothing to me. But I remember a cop standing there, gaping."

"While you were taking out the body?"

The man nodded. "Sure. We thought he was one of the tougher sort."

"Oh, why?"

"There's two sorts of cops, see? Them as pukes and them what don't. That guy didn't even hold his nose."

"So he was there all the time?"

"Sure, I said so, didn't I? He made damn sure we did our job to satisfaction, so to speak."

The other tittered and took a swig of beer.

"Just one more question."

"And what might that be?"

"When you picked up the body, did you notice

138

whether there was anything lying underneath it? Any object?"

"And what might that have been, then?"

"An automatic, for instance. Or a revolver."

The man burst out laughing. "A pistol or a revolver," he roared. "Anyway what's the difference?"

"A revolver has a rotating chamber, which is turned by the mechanism."

"Like cowboys have, eh?"

"Sure, that's it. Not that it makes much difference. The main question is whether there could have been any kind of a weapon lying underneath the dead man."

"Now listen here, Chief Inspector. This customer was a middle-aged guy."

"Middle-aged?"

"Sure, about two months gone."

Martin Beck nodded.

"We lifted him over onto the plastic sheet, see, and while I sealed the cover around the edges, Arne here swept up the worms on the floor. We usually pour them into a bag with some stuff in it; snuffs 'em out on the spot, it does."

"Oh?"

"And if Arne had swept up a rod, too, he couldn't have helped noticing it, could he?"

Arne nodded and tittered. The last drops of beer stuck in his windpipe. "I sure would," he coughed.

"So—there was nothing there?"

"Nothing at all. Besides, that patrolman was standing there all the time, looking on. In fact, he was still there after we'd put our client into the zinc box and pushed off. That's right, Arne, isn't it?"

"Dead right," said Arne.

"You seem quite sure of yourselves."

"Sure? We're more than that. Underneath that client weren't nothing, see, except for a pretty collection of *cynomyia mortuorum*."

"What's that?"

"Corpse worms."

"And you're quite sure?"

"Sure as hell."

"Thanks," said Martin Beck. And left.

139

The men in gray overalls exchanged a few words. "You put him where he belonged," said Arne.

"How so?"

"With all that Greek of yours! Them big shots never thinks we're no good for nothing except packaging rotten corpses."

The mobile telephone buzzed in the front seat. Arne answered, grunted something, and put down the receiver. "Goddammit," he said. "Another bastard's gone and hanged himself."

"Oh well," his colleague said resignedly.

"I've never been able to stomach these guys as hangs themselves, to tell the truth. What do you mean by life, anyway?"

"Bah, come on, let's get going."

By now Martin Beck had a feeling of knowing, technically speaking, most of what was to be known about the queer death on Bergsgatan. At the very least the police activities seemed satisfactorily cleared up. But one important point remained. To get hold of the report from the ballistic investigation, if there'd been one.

About Svärd, personally, he still knew very little, even though he'd put a fair amount of work into finding out about the dead man.

The Wednesday of the stakeout of Malmström and Mohrén's apartment had hardly been eventful as far as Martin Beck had been concerned. He knew nothing about the bank robberies or the special squad's trials and tribulations; and for this he was mostly glad. After his visit to Svärd's flat on Tuesday afternoon he had first gone to the central police station on Kungsholmsgatan—where everyone else was deeply involved in his own problems and no one had any time for him —and thence to the National Police Board. There he had heard a rumor that at first seemed only ridiculous, but which, on reflection, had upset him.

It was being said he was to be promoted. But to what? Superintendent? Commissioner? Head of Section? Perhaps to health, wealth, and prosperity?

However, this was not the main point. Probably

the whole assumption was nothing but a product of backstairs gossip, for the most part baseless.

He'd been promoted to detective chief inspector as recently as 1967, and there were no real grounds for supposing he would ever reach the higher grades. Under no circumstances could there be any question of his being promoted to something better within four or five years, at the earliest. This was something that everyone should have known, for if there is one matter that bureaucrats are thoroughly acquainted with it's salary scales and promotions—matters where everyone keeps a jealous eye on his own and others' chances.

How could such a rumor have started? There must be some line of reasoning behind it. But what? As far as he could see, he could choose between two explanations.

The first was that they wanted to get rid of him as head of the National Homicide Squad, even to the point where they were prepared to kick him upstairs into the bureaucracy. That, after all, is the commonest way of getting rid of unpleasant or obviously incompetent officials. This, however, was improbable. True, he had enemies on the National Police Board, though to them he could hardly constitute a threat. Moreover, they could hardly avoid promoting Kollberg to succeed him, something which from their point of view would be quite as undesirable.

Therefore, the second alternative seemed the more probable. But unfortunately it was a good deal more humiliating for all parties. Fifteen months earlier he had been within an inch of losing his life: the only senior official in modern Swedish history to do so. He had been shot by a so-called criminal. The occurrence had drawn much attention, and what he had done had furnished him with a halo he certainly didn't deserve. However, for obvious reasons, heroes are in very short supply on the police force, and that was why the happy outcome of that drama had been grossly exaggerated.

So—there was now a hero on the force. And what can one do with a hero? He'd already been given a medal: and the least they could do with him now was promote him.

141

Martin Beck himself had had plenty of time to analyze what had happened on that fateful day in April, 1971. He had long ago come to the conclusion that he'd acted wrongly; not only morally but also professionally. He was also well aware that this reflection had also occurred to more than one of his colleagues long before he'd appreciated it himself. He'd been shot because he'd acted like an idiot. And on these grounds they were now about to give him a higher and more responsible position.

He had been contemplating his own situation on Tuesday evening, but as soon as he again sat down at his desk at Västberga, he had immediately stopped thinking about it. Instead, indifferent but ruthlessly systematic, he had devoted Wednesday to the Svärd case, sitting alone in his room and working his way through the investigation.

At one moment he had thought to himself that this was just about what he could henceforth hope to get out of his job when it was at its best. To be left alone to deal with a case in the approved manner, and without outside interference.

Somewhere inside him he still felt a faint nostalgia —for what, he couldn't say. Perhaps a genuine interest in what he was doing. He had always found solitude easy, and now he seemed definitely on his way to becoming a recluse who had no desire for others' company or any real will to break out of his vacuum. Was he turning into a serviceable robot, enclosed, as it were, under a casserole cover—a dome of invisible glass?

Where the present problem was concerned he had no professional doubts. Either he would solve it, or else he would not. The percentage of murders and manslaughters cleared up by his department was a high one. This was due to the fact that most crimes are uncomplicated and those persons who are guilty of them are usually disposed to throw in the sponge.

Further, the homicide squad was relatively well-equipped. The only segment of the force that had greater resources in proportion to the crimes it had to combat was the security police. Since they still mostly occupied themselves with keeping a register of communists, meanwhile obstinately averting their eyes from various more or less exotic fascist organizations, they really had no function anyway. Therefore they mostly spent their time dreaming up political crimes and potential security risks in order to have something to do. The results of their activities were just what one would expect: laughable. Nevertheless, the security police constituted a kind of tactical political reserve, always ready to be employed against disagreeable ideologies. And situations could easily be envisaged in which their activities would no longer be in the least bit laughable.

Sometimes, of course, the National Homicide Squad was also unsuccessful. Investigations became bogged down and were eventually filed away. Usually these concerned cases where the culprit was known but, because of his obstinate denials, could not be proven guilty. The more primitive a violent crime, the poorer, often, is the evidence.

Martin Beck's latest fiasco could serve as a typical example of this. An elderly man in Lapland had killed his wife, who was the same age as himself, with an axe. The motive was that he had long had a relationship with the couple's housekeeper, who was somewhat younger, and had finally tired of his old lady's nagging and jealousy. After murdering her, he had put the corpse out into the woodshed. Since it was winter and the cold had been severe, he had waited some two months before laying a door on a sled and taking her off to the nearest village, which lay more than twelve trackless miles from his farm. Whereupon he had simply declared that the old woman had fallen over and hit her head against the stove, and that he hadn't been able to take her to the village earlier because of the cold weather. Everyone in the place knew it was a lie; but the man had stuck to his tale and so did his housekeeper. The amateurish investigation of the local police had destroyed all traces of the crime. They then called in outside help, and Martin Beck had spent two weeks in a strange hotel before giving up and going home. In the daytime he had questioned the murderer, and in

143

the evenings had sat in the hotel dining room, listening to the locals laughing at him behind his back. Such reverses, however, were exceptional.

The Svärd story was odder and not really reminiscent of any case Martin Beck had ever handled. This should have been stimulating, but he had no personal interest in enigmas and did not feel stimulated at all.

His desk work on Wednesday had also yielded very little. The files of punished crimes contained no trace of Karl Edvin Svärd. In itself, this meant no more than that he'd never been convicted of any crime. But how many transgressors of the law get away without ever appearing before a court—quite apart from the fact that the law has been designed to protect certain social classes and their dubious interests, and otherwise seems mostly to consist of loopholes?

The report from the State Wines and Spirits Board drew a blank. This, presumably, meant that Svärd had not been an alcoholic. For a person of his social status would certainly have had his drinking habits scrutinized by the authorities. When the upper class drinks, it is known as "culture"; citizens of the other class having similar needs are immediately categorized as alcoholics, or as cases in need of care and protection. Whereafter they receive neither care nor protection.

All his adult life Svärd had been a warehouseman, and his last job had been with a forwarding agency. He'd had a bad back, a common enough thing in his profession, and at the age of fifty-six had been declared medically unfit.

Since then he had dragged out his days on his pension. In other words he belonged to that category for whom the chain stores maintain overstocked counters of dog and cat food.

A half-empty can of cat food, with the label "Miaow," had been the only apparently edible constituent of his larder.

Some data, certainly without significance: Svärd had been born in Stockholm; his parents had died in the forties; and he had never married or had to support anyone. He had not turned to the welfare authorities.

At the firm where he had had his last job there was no one who remembered him.

The doctor who had certified him as unfit for work fished out a few notes, in which it was said that the patient was not up to physical work and too old to be retrained. Further, Svärd had said he had no wish to work any more, "since it seemed senseless."

Perhaps it was also senseless to try to find out who might possibly have killed him, and if so, why. Since the manner of his killing seemed incomprehensible, the simplest procedure seemed to be to try and find the murderer first, and then ask him how he'd done it.

So now it was Thursday, and almost evening. Hardly an hour after his visit to the men with the evil-smelling truck, Martin Beck made a fresh attempt on the house on Tulegatan. His working day was really over, but he didn't feel like going home. So again he climbed the two flights of stairs and then waited a minute to get his breath back. As he did so he looked at the oval enamel doorplate with green letters on a white background: "Rhea Nielsen."

There was no doorbell button. Only a bell rope. He pulled it and waited. A bell tinkled. Otherwise nothing happened.

The tenement was an old one, and through the door's panes of frosted glass he saw a light shining in the vestibule. This indicated that someone was at home. At his previous visit all the lights had been out.

After a suitable interval he again pulled the bell rope; the tinkle was repeated, swift, shuffling footsteps were heard, and he glimpsed someone behind the opaque glass.

Martin Beck was used to the routine of swiftly summing up the people he met in the course of his duties, a kind of "preliminary description," to use the official term.

The woman who opened the door seemed at most to be thirty-five, but something told him she was actually a few years older. She was not very tall, only five foot two or so, he guessed. Though of compact build, she gave the impression of being lithe and shapely

145

rather than plump or clumsy. Her features were strong, somewhat irregular. The eyes were blue and uncompromising, the gaze steady, and she looked him straight in the eyes as if she were always ready to come to grips with things, of whatever sort they might be.

Her hair was straight, blond, cut short, though just then wet and tousled. She gave off a clean smell, very likely of herbal shampoo, and wore a short-sleeved knitted cardigan and faded blue jeans, suggestive of innumerable washings. The cardigan had not been on her more than a few seconds; large wet splashes were spreading over her shoulders and bosom. She was relatively broad across the shoulders, slender around the hips, with a short neck and dense, fine down on her sunburned arms. She had rather stubby bare feet with straight toes—as if accustomed to walking in sandals or clogs and as often as possible in nothing at all.

Aware that he was examining her feet with the same professional meticulousness that he was accustomed to devoting to bloodstains and marks on corpses, he raised his eyes to her face.

Now the eyes were searching and the brow slightly ruffled. "I was just washing my hair," she said. Her voice was hoarse; perhaps she had a cold, or was a chain smoker, or just naturally spoke like that.

He nodded.

"I shouted 'come in' twice. The door's not locked. I don't usually lock it when I'm at home. Not unless I want to be in peace and quiet, that is. Didn't you hear me call out?"

"No. Are you Rhea Nielsen?"

"Sure. And you're a policeman, eh?"

Though Martin Beck's powers of observation functioned unusually swiftly, for once he had an immediate sense of having met someone who in this respect was his superior. In a few seconds she had pigeonholed him correctly; and further, the look in her eyes suggested that she had already summed him up. Though that remained to be seen.

The explanation of her quick assessment of him might, of course, be that she was expecting a visit from the police, though he didn't think so. As he took out his wallet to show his identity card, she said: "It's quite enough if you tell me your name. Goddammit, man, come in! There's something you want, I guess, and neither of us likes standing talking out here on the stairs."

Though Martin Beck felt he had only slightly been thrown off his guard, it was a feeling he very rarely had occasion to feel.

Turning abruptly, she led the way into her apartment. At first its size and layout were beyond him. But the rooms were pleasantly furnished with old odds and ends of furniture. Some children's drawings, stuck up with drawing pins, indicated she had some kind of a family. Otherwise the decorations on the walls were mixed. There were oil paintings, and drawings, and old photos in oval frames, but also newspaper clippings and posters—among them portraits of Lenin and Mao, though these, as far as he could see, were mostly without political implications. There were also a lot of books, on bookshelves or piled up here and there, as well as a respectable collection of records, a stereo set, a couple of old and apparently much-used typewriters, and above all papers, most of them stenciled and clipped together, which almost looked like police reports. He concluded that they were notes of one sort or another and that she was busy with some kind of studies.

He followed her in, past what could only be a nursery. But the beds were so tidily made up that the room's usual occupants could hardly be in the vicinity. Well, it was summer of course, and the children of all parents who could afford it were in the country, out of reach of the city's polluted air and absurd living conditions.

She threw him a glance over her shoulder, not a particularly appreciative one, and said: "Do you mind if we sit here in the kitchen? If you do, just say so." The tone of voice, not exactly friendly, was not exactly hostile either.

"This'll do fine."

"Take a seat, then."

They had come into the kitchen, and he sat down at a large round table. There were six chairs of various kinds, painted in gay colors, with room for more.

147

"Wait a second," she said.

She seemed nervous and restless, but behaved as if it were her normal condition. In front of the stove was a pair of clogs. She climbed into them and tramped off out of sight. He heard her busy herself with something, and at the same moment as an electric motor started up she said: "You didn't tell me your name."

"Beck. Martin Beck."

"And you're a policeman?"

"Yes."

"What kind?"

"National Criminal Police."

"Salary scale twenty-five?"

"Twenty-seven."

"See there! Not so bad."

"Not too bad, no."

"And how do I address you?"

"Detective chief inspector."

The motor hummed. The sound was familiar from his past, and he realized almost immediately what she was doing: quickly drying her hair with the aid of a vacuum cleaner.

"Rhea," she said. "That's me. Though of course I don't have to say so. The name's on the door."

The kitchen was a big one, as it so often is in older houses, and despite the table and its many chairs there was not only a gas stove and a dishwasher but also a refrigerator, a freezer, and plenty of room left over. On a shelf above the sink were pots and kettles, and on nails beneath them hung various natural products: for instance, twigs of wormwood and thyme, bunches of mountain ash berries, ribbons with dried mushrooms, and three long twists of garlic—objects which, though they create an atmosphere and give off an aromatic scent, are not altogether indispensable in a household. Wormwood and mountain ash berries are good spices to add to brandy, and thyme can be put into pea soup—though Beck, in the days when his stomach had been equal to that Swedish delicacy, had preferred sweet marjoram. Mushrooms are always good to have about if one knows how to use them. But the garlic could only be regarded as a decoration,

148

since the quantity would have been enough to last any normal consumer a lifetime.

She came back into the kitchen, combed her hair, saw instantly what he was looking at, and said: "To keep away the vampires."

"The garlic?"

"Sure. Don't you ever go to the movies? Peter Cushing knows everything about vampires."

She had swapped the wet knitted cardigan for a sleeveless turquoise-colored garment, in all essentials reminiscent of a slip. He noticed she had blond hair under her arms, little breasts, and no need of a bra. Nor was she wearing one, and her nipples were clearly visible under the cloth.

"Police," she said. "Detective chief inspector." She looked at him with that straight look of hers and furrowed her brow: "I didn't think that officers on salary scale twenty-seven made visits."

"Not usually, no," he said.

She sat down at the table but immediately got up again, biting on her knuckles.

Martin Beck realized the moment had come for some kind of initiative. He said: "If I understand you correctly, you're not especially positive in your attitude to the police."

She threw him a quick glance and said: "No. I can't say I've ever had any use for them. Nor do I know anyone else who has. On the other hand I know a lot of people to whom they've caused suffering and unpleasantness."

"In that case I'll do my best to trouble you as little as possible, Mrs. Nielsen."

"Rhea," she said. "Everyone calls me Rhea."

"If I understand things correctly, you are the owner of this building?"

"Yes. I inherited it a few years ago. But there's nothing here to interest the police. No dope sessions, no gambling dens, not even any prostitutes or thieves." She paused briefly. "Perhaps a little subversive activity goes on here from time to time. Mental crimes. But you aren't on the political side."

"How can you be so sure?"

149

She laughed, suddenly and heartily. A gay infectious laugh. "I'm not all that dumb," she said.

No, certainly not, thought Martin Beck. Aloud he said: "You're right. I'm only concerned with crimes of violence. Murder and manslaughter."

"We've had neither the one nor the other here. Not even a fight for the last three years. Though last winter it's true someone broke into the attic and ripped off a lot of rubbish. I had to report it to the police, since the insurance people insist on it. No policemen turned up, they hadn't time for it; but the insurance company paid up. All that about reporting it to the police was obviously only a formality." She scratched her neck, and said: "Well, and what do you want?"

"To talk about one of your tenants."

She raised her eyebrows. "One of mine?" she asked, laying heavy emphasis on the word "mine," as if worried and astonished.

"Not one of those you've got now," he said.

"Only one has moved out during the last year."

"Svärd."

"Right. A man called Svärd used to live here. He moved out last spring. What's up with him?"

"He's dead."

"Did someone do him in?"

"Shot him."

"Who?"

"It's possible he committed suicide. But we're not sure of it."

"Can't we talk a little more relaxed?"

"By all means. But what do you mean, relaxed? Call each other by our Christian names?"

The woman shook her head. Then she said: "Formal talk is hopeless. I loathe it. Though I can behave in the most correct manner if I have to. And I can play the flirt, and dress myself up, and use eye shadow and lipstick."

Martin Beck felt strangely unsure of himself.

Suddenly she said: "Like a cup of tea? Tea's good."

Though he would dearly have liked a cup of tea, he said: "Please don't bother for my sake. I don't need anything."

150

"Nonsense," she said. "Hot air. Wait a minute, and I'll fix you something to eat, too. A grilled sandwich would do us both good."

Immediately he felt he wanted one too. And before he could say he didn't she was chattering on.

"It won't take more than ten minutes at most. I can serve up food in two shakes of a cat's tail. No bother at all. And it's good. One must try to make the best of everything. Even if everything looks as if it's going to the devil, one can always cook something nice. Tea and a sandwich in the oven, then we can talk."

To refuse seemed impossible. He became aware of something new about her. An obstinate trait, a strong-willed streak, which could be hard to resist.

"Yes, thanks," he said lamely.

But before he'd even had time to say the words she was already busy. Banging about a lot, but also astonishingly quick and efficient. As a matter of fact he'd never seen anything like it, at least not in Sweden.

During the seven minutes it took her to get the food ready she didn't say a word. Six hot sandwiches with slices of tomato and grated cheese and a big pot of tea. He watched her making her improvised meal, wondered how old she was.

At the same moment, as she sat down in front of him, she said: "Thirty-seven. Though most people think I'm younger."

He was too astonished to hide his amazement.

"That was what you were thinking, wasn't it? Eat up."

It tasted fine.

"I'm always hungry," she said. "I eat ten to twelve times a day."

People who eat ten or twelve times a day usually find it hard to keep their weight down.

"And it doesn't make me the least bit fatter," she said. "Makes no difference anyway. A few pounds one way or the other don't change a human being. I'm always myself. Though I go nuts if I don't get any food."

She gulped down three sandwiches. Martin Beck ate one, and after some hesitation a second. "I see you've certain opinions about Svärd," he said.

"Yes, one could say that."

151

They found it easy to understand each other. Strangely enough neither was surprised at this. It seemed self-evident.

"So there was something odd about him?" he said.

"Yes," said Rhea. "He was a queer one, he was. A very queer guy indeed. Couldn't make head or tail of him. So, if the truth be told, I was happy when he moved out. By the way, how did he die?"

"He was found in his flat on the eighteenth of last month. By that time he'd been dead at least six weeks. Probably longer. At a guess, about two months."

She shook herself and said: "Goddammit, I don't want to know the details. I'm hypersensitive to the more advanced class of gory details, if you know what I mean. Dream about them afterwards."

It was on the tip of his tongue to say she would not be exposed to any unnecessary descriptions. But he saw it was superfluous.

Instead it was she who said: "One thing's clear, anyway."

"Oh, and what's that?"

"It could never have happened while he was living here."

"Couldn't it? Why not?"

"Because I wouldn't have allowed it to."

She put her chin in her hand, her nose between her forefinger and middle finger. He noticed she had quite a big nose and strong hands with very short nails and was looking at him seriously.

Then she suddenly got up again and poked about on the kitchen shelf until she'd found some matches and a pack of cigarettes. She smoked, inhaling deeply. Then she stubbed out her cigarette, ate up the fourth sandwich, and sat there with her elbows on her knees and her head bowed. She threw him a glance and said: "It's possible I couldn't have prevented him from dying. But he wouldn't have stayed there for two months without me noticing it. Not even two days."

Martin Beck said nothing. She was certainly only telling the truth.

"Landlords in this country are the last things God

152

created," she said. "But the system encourages them to exploit people."

He chewed his lower lip. Martin Beck had never made his political opinions public and always tried to avoid conversations of political import.

She said: "No politics, eh? Okay, we'll skip the politics. But I happen to be a landlord myself . . . just happen to be. I inherited this dump, as I've said before. Actually it's a good building, but when I inherited it and moved in it was a bloody rat hole. My dad certainly hadn't changed a light bulb or paid to have a broken window mended in ten years. He lived miles away from here and was only interested in collecting the rents and kicking out tenants who couldn't pay on time. Then he divided the apartments up into bed spaces and rented them out at swinishly high prices to foreigners and others who had no choice. They've got to live somewhere too, haven't they? In almost all these old houses it's the same story."

Martin Beck heard someone open the front door and come in. The woman didn't so much as react.

A girl came into the kitchen. She was wearing a housecoat and carried a bundle. "Hello," she said. "Can I use the washing machine?"

"Sure, go ahead."

The girl paid no attention to Martin Beck; but Rhea said: "I guess you two don't know each other. This is . . . well, what did you say your name was, again?"

Martin Beck got up and shook hands. "Martin," he said.

"Ingela," said the girl.

"She's just moved in," Rhea said. "Lives in the flat Svärd used to have." She turned to the girl with the bundle. "How do you like it?" she asked.

"It's sure fine," the girl said. "But there's trouble with the toilet again today."

"Hell. I'll ring the plumber first thing tomorrow."

"Otherwise everything's lovely. By the way . . ."

"Yes?"

"I don't have any detergent."

"It's behind the bath."

"I'm stone broke."

"Okay. Don't take more than fifty öre's worth. You can do me some little fifty-öre service sometime. Lock the street door, for instance."

"Nice of you." The girl went out into the bathroom.

Rhea lit a fresh cigarette. "That's one thing. Svärd's was a good flat. I had it done up two years ago. It only cost eighty kronor a month. Yet he moved out, even so."

"Why?"

"Couldn't say."

"No trouble?"

"None. I don't have trouble with people who live here. No need for it. Everyone's got his own little ways, naturally. But that's just fun."

Martin Beck said nothing. He felt he'd begun to relax. He also noticed that he didn't need to put questions to her.

"Svärd's queerest trait was that he used to have four locks on his door. In a house where almost no one ever locks his door except when he absolutely needs to be in peace. When he moved out he unscrewed all his chains and bolts and took the whole lot with him. He was as strongly protected as little girls are nowadays."

"You mean—metaphorically?"

"Sure. Sexually. Here our pillars of society go crying out in horror because kids, girls particularly, begin feeling their oats when they're thirteen. Idiots. Everyone knows we begin getting sexy when we're thirteen or so, and with the pill and all that a girl's as safe as Fort Knox. So what's there to be afraid of nowadays? In our day a girl was dead scared of getting pregnant. Anyway, how did we come to talk of such things?"

Martin Beck laughed. He was astonished. But it was a fact. He had laughed. "We were talking about Svärd's door," he said.

"Yes. And you laughed. I didn't think you knew how. Or that you'd forgotten the trick of it."

"Maybe I happen to be in a bad mood today," he conceded.

154

But it was the wrong line; it achieved the opposite effect from what he'd intended. A faint expression of disappointment flitted over her face. She had been right and she knew it.

To try to fool each other was stupid, and he said: "I'm sorry."

"Though it's true I didn't really fall in love until I was sixteen. But things were different in those days." She killed her cigarette and said in a matter-of-fact voice: "I talk a hell of a lot too much. Always. But that's only one of my many weaknesses. Though it's not exactly a flaw of character, is it?"

He shook his head.

She scratched her neck and said: "Did Svärd still have all those lock gadgets?"

"Yes."

She shook her head, kicked off her clogs, put her heels on the floor, and turned her feet inwards so that the toes rubbed each other.

"Couldn't understand it. Must have been a phobia with him. But sometimes it worried me. I've spare keys to all the doors. Some of the people here are old. They can fall ill and need help. And then one must be able to get in. But what's the use of a spare key if the door's barricaded from inside? And Svärd was fairly old, of course."

The noises from the bathroom changed character, and Rhea shouted out: "Need some help, Ingela?"

"Yes . . . I guess so. . . ."

She got up and was out a while. When she came back she said: "Now that's fixed. Apropos this age question, we must be about the same."

Martin Beck smiled. He knew that almost everyone took him for about five years less than the fifty he'd soon be.

"Svärd really wasn't all that old, though," she said. "But he wasn't well. Apparently pretty ill. He didn't count on living all that much longer, and when he moved he went into the hospital for a checkup. What the result was I don't know. But he was in the radium clinic and that doesn't sound too good, it seems to me."

155

Martin Beck pricked up his ears. This was news. But now the front door opened again. Someone said in a bright voice: "Rhea?"

"Yes. I'm out here in the kitchen."

A man came in. Seeing Martin Beck, he hesitated a moment, but at once she pushed him a chair with her foot and said: "Sit down."

The man was fairly young, perhaps twenty-five, of medium height and normal physique. Oval face, fair hair, gray eyes, and good teeth. Clothes: a flannel shirt, corduroy trousers, and sandals. In his hand he held a bottle of red wine. "I've brought this with me," he said.

"And I who'd meant to stick to tea today," she said. "But okay. You can get yourself a glass. Four, while you're at it. Ingela's in there, doing her wash."

She bent forward, scratched her left wrist, and said: "One bottle won't go far with four of us. I've got some too. You can get one out of the pantry. On the left inside the door. The corkscrew's in the top drawer below and to the left of the dishwasher."

The newcomer followed her instructions. He seemed accustomed to obey. When he'd sat down, she said: "I guess you've never met Martin . . . Kent."

"Hi," said the man.

"Hi," said Martin Beck.

They shook hands.

She poured the wine and called out in her hoarse voice: "Ingela, we've some wine in here when you've finished." Then, troubled, she looked at the man in the flannel shirt and said: "You look wretched. What's up? Something more gone wrong?"

Kent took a swig of the wine and put his face in his hands. "Rhea," he said, "what am I going to do?"

"Still no job?"

"Not a ghost of one. So here I am, with my exam in my pocket and no job. The devil only knows whether there'll ever be one, either." He reached out and tried to take her hand. This irritated her, and she withdrew it. "I'd a desperate idea, today," he said. "I must ask you what you think about it."

"And what does your idea look like?"

"To enter the Police Academy. Anyone can get in

there, even if he's retarded. They're short of people, and with my credentials I ought to get in easily, as soon as I've learned to knock drunks on the head."

"Do you feel like beating people up, then?"

"You know very well I don't. But maybe one can do some good, somehow. Reform from the inside, after one's got over the worst."

"Though their activities are hardly aimed at drunks," she said. "And meanwhile how are you going to support Stina and the kids?"

"I'll have to borrow. I found out all about it today when I was there getting the application forms. Here, I've got them with me. I thought you'd like to look through them . . . you who understand everything."

He took some folded forms and a recruiting brochure out of his hip pocket, pushed them across the table, and said: "If you think it's crazy, say so."

"Rather, I must say. On the whole I shouldn't say the police are a scrap interested in people who use their brains, or who want to reform from within. How about your papers, politically? Are they clean?"

"Oh, I was in a leftist student group once, but that's all, and now they're accepting everyone, except members of left-wing parties . . . actual communists, that is."

She reflected, took a big gulp of wine, and shrugged. "Why not? It seems crazy, but I guess it could be interesting."

"The chief question is . . ." He drank. Then he said "skål" to Martin Beck, who also drank, cautiously to begin with.

"What's the question?" she asked, irritated.

"Well, Rhea. Can anybody stand it in the long run? Can they?"

She threw Martin Beck a cunning look. Her irritation had been wiped out by a smile. "Ask Martin here. He's an expert."

The man looked at Martin Beck with an astonished and dubious expression. "D'you know something about this?"

"A little. The truth is the police need all the good applicants they can get. It's a profession with plenty of variety to it, as you see from that brochure there, and

157

with many forms of special duties. Anyone who's interested in helicopters, for instance, or machinery, or organizational problems, or horses . . ."

Rhea struck the table with the flat of her hand so that the glasses jumped. "Don't talk rubbish now," she said angrily. "Goddammit, man, give him an honest answer!"

To his own astonishment Martin Beck replied: "You've a chance of sticking it out the first few years, if you're prepared to associate with numbskulls and be shouted at by your superiors, who are either climbers, or obsessed by a sense of their own importance, or just idiots. You can't have any opinions of your own. Afterwards you've every prospect of becoming one yourself."

"Obviously you've no use for the police," said Kent despondently. "But it can't be as crazy as all that. There's too much unmotivated hatred of the police, and that's for sure. Or what do you think, Rhea?"

She gave an unusually hearty laugh. The she said: "Try it. You'll make a fine policeman. I'm sure. Everything else seems to be out of the question. And the competition is said to be not overwhelming."

"Can you help me fill in the application?"

"Give me a pen."

Martin Beck had one in his breast pocket and gave it to her at once.

The girl called Ingela had finished her washing and came in and sat down. She talked a bit about things in general, mostly food prices and the way they were cheating with the date marks in the dairy department. Obviously she worked in a supermarket.

The bell tinkled, the door opened, and someone came in with dragging footsteps. It was an elderly woman. She said: "The reception on my TV is awful."

"If it's the aerial I'll get Eriksson to look at it tomorrow. Otherwise I guess we'll just have to repair the set. It's worn out, of course, but I've some friends who've got a spare one. If worst comes to worst we can borrow their old one. I'll see to it tomorrow."

"I've been baking today, and I've brought you a loaf, Rhea."

158

"Thanks. Very nice of your. I'll fix that TV of yours, auntie, you'll see."

She had finished the application forms and gave them to the man in the flannel shirt. She had filled them in with amazing swiftness.

Now she looked at Martin Beck again, the same steady gaze as before. "As a landlord one has to function as a caretaker," she said. "You see? It's needed, but not many people think like that. Almost everyone speculates and is stingy as can be. They don't think any further than their noses, and that's swinish. I try to do my best here; people who live in the same building must feel they belong together and that it's their home. These apartments are fine now, but I can't afford repairs to the outside. Naturally I don't want to raise the rents more than necessary this autumn. Though I'll have to put them up a bit. If a house is to be looked after properly there's a lot to see to. After all, one is responsible to one's tenants."

Martin Beck felt in a surprisingly good mood. He had no desire to leave this kitchen. He was also a trifle sleepy. Due to the wine. For fifteen months he'd drunk nothing.

"Oh yes, to be sure," she said. "This business about Svärd."

"Did he keep any valuables at home?"

"No. Two chairs, and a table, and a bed. A filthy carpet, and only the most indispensable things in the kitchen. Hardly any clothes, even. That's why that lock business can only have been a phobia. He avoided everyone. It's true he used to talk to me, but only when it was absolutely necessary."

"He was as poor as can be, as far as I know."

She looked meditative, filled her glass, and drank. "I'm not so sure about that," she said. "Mostly he seemed stingy to the point of lunacy. True, he always paid his rent, though he grumbled about it. Even though it was only eighty a month. And as far as I know he never bought himself anything but dog food. Well, cat food. Didn't drink. Had no expensive habits at all. So even if he only had his old-age pension he ought to have been able to indulge in a sausage now and again. It's true all too many old people live on dog food, but

159

usually they have higher rents to pay and place rather higher demands on existence, for example half a bottle of wine with their dinner sometimes. Svärd didn't even have a radio. When I was studying psychology I read about people who live on potato peelings, and go about in fifty-year-old clothes, and have hundreds of thousands of kronor stuffed inside their mattress. Well, everyone knows about them. A psychological phenomenon, I forget what it's called."

"But there was no money in Svärd's mattress."

"And he moved out, which wasn't like him. His new place must have cost him more, and to move his belongings must have cost something too. It doesn't make sense."

Martin Beck emptied his wineglass. He would have liked to have stayed among these people; but now he had to be off. He had got food for thought. "Well, I'm off now."

"I was going to make spaghetti bolognese. It's not bad when one makes the sauce oneself. Stay, by all means."

"No. I must go now."

She followed him out on her bare feet. They passed the nursery, and he cast a glance inside.

"Yes," she said. "The kids are out in the country. I'm divorced." After a moment's pause, she added: "You too, eh?"

"Yes."

At the door she said: "So long, then. Come back. I've lectures at the summer university in the daytime, but I'm always home after six." Brief pause. She threw him an intriguing glance and said: "We can talk about Svärd, can't we?"

A fat man in slippers and unpressed gray trousers came down the stairs. He was wearing a red-yellow-and-blue Viet Cong badge on his shirt. "Rhea," he said, "the light in the attic's gone out."

"Get a new bulb from the cleaning cupboard," she said. "Seventy-five watts'll do."

"You want to stay," she said to Martin Beck. "So stay."

"No. I'm off now. Thanks for the tea, sandwiches, and wine."

He saw that for just a moment she was thinking of exerting some kind of influence over him, presumably using the spaghetti as a lever.

But she refrained and said: "Well, good-bye, then. Again."

" 'Bye."

Neither of them said, See you again.

He was thinking of Svärd. He was thinking of Rhea. He was in a more cheerful mood than he'd been in for a long time, a very very long time; though as yet he was not conscious of it.

22

Kollberg and Gunvald Larsson were sitting facing each other at the latter's desk. Both looked thoughtful.

It was still Thursday and they had left Bulldozer Olsson alone with his dreams of the impending day of happiness when he'd be able to put Werner Roos behind bars.

"What the devil's up with Bulldozer?" Gunvald Larsson said. "Is he really thinking of letting Mauritzon go, just like that?"

Kollberg shrugged. "That's the way it would seem," he said.

"But not even having him shadowed, that's what I don't understand," Gunvald Larsson went on. "There's every prospect of it yielding high dividends. Or do you think Bulldozer's got his sights on something even more brilliant?"

Kollberg shook his head thoughtfully and said: "No, it's like this, I guess: Bulldozer'd sooner sacrifice what he might gain by shadowing Mauritzon than lose something else he values more."

Gunvald Larsson frowned. "And what might that be?" he asked. "Surely no one's more eager to get his mitts on this gang than Bulldozer."

"No, that's for sure," Kollberg said. "But has it occurred to you that hardly any of us has such first-class sources of information as Bulldozer? He knows any number of informers and crooks, and they really trust him because he never cheats them and always keeps his word. They rely on him and know he never promises something he can't perform. Bulldozer's stool pigeons are his chief asset."

"What you mean to say is, if it gets around that

he tails his stool piegeons when they've been here giving him some tips, that'll be the end of their confidence in him and all those nice tips too?"

"Precisely," Kollberg said.

"Anyway I think it's goddam stupid to let this opportunity slip," Gunvald Larsson said. "Suppose we keep a quiet check on where Mauritzon goes and what he gets up to next. That needn't trouble Bulldozer, need it?" He threw Kollberg a questioning glance.

"Okay," Kollberg said. "I too am pretty curious as to what Mr. Faithful Mauritzon has in mind. By the way, is Faithful a Christian name or a surname?"

"It's a dog's name," said Gunvald Larsson. "Maybe he sometimes disguises himself as a dog. But we'll have to get started, because I imagine he's being let out any moment now. Who starts?"

Kollberg looked at his new wristwatch, which was of the same make and model as the one that had gone through the washing machine. He hadn't eaten for a couple of hours and had begun to feel ravenous. Anyone who's trying to get his weight down, he'd read somewhere, should eat a little, but often; the latter part of this advice he had accepted with pleasure.

"I suggest you do," he said. "I'll stick around the phone here, so you just call me if you need any help or want me to relieve you. Take my car. It's not such an eyesore as yours." He took out his keys and handed them to Gunvald Larsson.

"Good," said Gunvald Larsson. He got up and buttoned his jacket. In the doorway he turned and said: "If Bulldozer asks after me, think of something. You'll be hearing from me. So long."

Kollberg waited two minutes, then went down to the cafeteria for his dietetic repast.

Gunvald Larsson didn't have to wait very long. Mauritzon came out onto the stairway, hesitated a moment, and set off for Agnegatan. He turned off to the left, and went on to the bus stop on Kungsholmstorg, where he stood waiting.

In a doorway, not far off, Gunvald Larsson also waited. He was well aware of the difficulty of this enterprise. For one thing, his height and build were not easily concealed, even in a crowd. And for another, Mauritzon would recognize him if he so much as looked in his direction. If Mauritzon was thinking of taking the bus, Gunvald Larsson could hardly get on the same one without being recognized. At the taxi stand, diagonally across the street, an empty cab was waiting, and he hoped no one would take it before he needed to.

The Sixty-two stopped at the bus stop and Mauritzon got on.

Before going over to the cab Gunvald Larsson waited until the bus had gone far enough for Mauritzon not to recognize him through the rear window. He left Kollberg's car standing where it was.

The cab driver was a young woman with tousled blond hair and lively brown eyes. When Gunvald Larsson showed her his identity card and asked her to follow the bus, she lit up with enthusiasm.

"Great!" she said. "This guy you're chasing, is he a dangerous gangster?"

Gunvald Larsson didn't reply.

"I understand—it's secret. Don't worry, I'll be as silent as the grave."

Silence, however, turned out to be the one thing she was incapable of.

"We'd better take it easy," she said, "so we can stay behind that bus at the bus stops."

"Yes," Gunvald Larsson said, as curtly as possible. "But keep your distance."

"I get it," she said. "You don't want to be seen. Pull down the sun visor so you can't be seen from above."

Gunvald Larsson pulled it down. She threw him a conspiratorial glance, caught sight of his bandaged hand, and exclaimed: "How did that happen? Been in a fight, eh?"

Gunvald Larsson grunted.

"It's a dangerous profession, being a policeman," she went on. "But terribly exciting, of course. Before I started driving a cab I thought of joining the force. Best of all I'd have liked to be a detective, but my husband was against it."

Gunvald Larsson said nothing.

"Though it can have its moments of excitement, driving a cab, too. Like now, for instance." She beamed at Gunvald Larsson, and with an effort he smiled back a twisted smile.

All the time she was keeping a medium distance from the bus. Altogether, she drove exceptionally well, and this had to make up for her talkativeness.

Gunvald Larsson uttered no more than an occasional monosyllable, while his driver had time for no small amount of talk before Mauritzon finally got off the bus on Erik Dahlbergsgatan. He was the only passenger to do so, and while Gunvald Larsson was taking out his money the girl at the wheel gave Mauritzon a curious stare.

"He doesn't look at all like a crook to me," she said, disappointed. She took her money and quickly scribbled a receipt. "Anyway, good luck," she added, and slowly drove off.

Mauritzon crossed the street diagonally and turned off onto Armfeldtsgatan. When he'd disappeared around the corner, Gunvald Larsson made haste to reach it and peeped around just as Mauritzon was vanishing into a doorway.

After a while Gunvald Larsson opened the door. Somewhere inside the building he heard another door slam. Then he went in and inspected the list of tenants.

At once his glance was caught by the name Mauritzon. Astonished, he raised his eyebrows. So—Filip Faithful Mauritzon lived here under his own name! Gunvald Larsson recalled that while he'd been questioned he'd given an address on Vickergatan, where he lived under the name of Lennart Holm. Most practical, Gunvald Larsson thought to himself. Hearing the elevator start up, he hastily betook himself out into the street again.

Not daring to cross the street for fear Mauritzon might catch sight of him through a window, he hugged the wall of the building as he made his way back to the corner of Erik Dahlbergsgatan. There he took up his post, peeping cautiously out to keep an eye on Mauritzon's doorway.

After a while the cut under his knee began to
165

ache. It was too early to ring Kollberg, and anyway he didn't dare leave his observation post in case Mauritzon should put in an appearance.

When Gunvald Larsson had been standing there waiting at the street corner for three-quarters of an hour, Mauritzon suddenly emerged from the doorway. Gunvald Larsson just had time to realize that the fellow was walking towards him before pulling abruptly back out of sight. Hoping Mauritzon hadn't seen him, he ran limping down the street and into the nearest doorway.

Mauritzon, looking straight ahead of him, walked briskly by. He had changed his suit and was carrying a little black suitcase. He crossed Valhallavägen, and Gunvald Larsson followed at as great a distance as possible without losing sight of him.

Mauritzon went quickly down towards Karlaplan. Twice he turned and looked nervously behind him; the first time Gunvald Larsson took cover behind a parked truck, and the second time he dived into a doorway.

As Gunvald Larsson had already guessed, Mauritzon was on his way to the subway. Only a few people were waiting on the platform, and Gunvald Larsson found it hard to keep out of sight. But there was nothing to suggest Mauritzon had spotted him. He boarded a southbound train, and Gunvald Larsson got into the next car.

At Hötorget they both got off, and Mauritzon disappeared into the crowds.

Gunvald Larsson looked around, trying to find him on the platform. But it was as if the man had been swallowed up. He searched each exit without catching sight of Mauritzon, and in the end he took the escalator to the upper level. He went around to the five different exits. No Mauritzon. Finally he came to a standstill outside Ström's shop window, swore, and wondered whether Mauritzon hadn't seen him after all. In which case he could have given him the slip by running across the platform and jumping on a northbound train.

Gunvald Larsson looked somberly at a pair of Italian shoes that were lying in the window and whose owner he would gladly have been had they existed in his size. Several days earlier he had been in and inquired.

Now he turned to go up and take the bus to Kungsholmen. Suddenly he caught sight of Mauritzon at the other end of the station. He was on his way towards the Sveavägen exit. Besides his black suitcase he was now carrying a package tied with a large and elaborate ribbon with bows. After he had disappeared up the stairs, Gunvald Larsson followed.

Mauritzon went on southwards down Sveavägen and entered the downtown air terminal. Gunvald Larsson took up his observation post behind a truck on Lästmakargatan. Through the huge windows he could see Mauritzon go up to the counter and talk to a tall blonde in uniform. Gunvald Larsson wondered where Mauritzon was thinking of going. South, of course, perhaps to some spot on the Mediterranean. Or still further—Africa was popular nowadays. For obvious reasons Mauritzon was scared of staying in Stockholm; yet the moment Malmström and Mohrén realized he'd split they certainly wouldn't be feeling kindly towards him either.

He saw Mauritzon open his suitcase and put the box of chocolates, or whatever it was, inside. Then he got his tickets, stuffed them inside his jacket, and emerged onto the pavement.

Gunvald Larsson watched him stroll slowly away in the direction of Serbelstorg; then he went inside. The girl who had helped Mauritzon was standing leafing through a card index. She threw Gunvald Larsson a quick glance, went on leafing, and said: "Yes sir, what can I do for you?"

"I should like to know whether that gentleman who was here just now bought a ticket," Gunvald Larsson said. "And if so, where to."

"I don't know whether I should tell you that," the blonde said. "Why do you ask?"

Gunvald Larsson laid his identity card on the counter. The girl looked at it, then at Gunvald Larsson, and said: "I guess you mean Count von Brandenburg? He bought a ticket to Jönköping and reserved a seat on the 14:50 flight. He was planning to take the airport bus, because he asked what time it went. It leaves from Sergelstorg at five minutes to two. What has Count von . . . ?"

"Thank you, that was all I wanted to know," said Gunvald Larsson. "Good day."

He went towards the door, wondering what business Mauritzon might have in Jönköping. Then he recalled seeing in Mauritzon's file that he was born there and that his mother was still living in that town. So—Mauritzon was going home to hide away with his mom!

Gunvald Larsson emerged onto Sveavägen. At a distance he could see Faithful Mauritzon Holm von Brandenburg slowly sauntering along the street in the sunshine. Gunvald Larsson went off in the opposite direction to find a phone and call Kollberg.

23

When he came to meet Gunvald Larsson at the appointed time and place, Lennart Kollberg had brought with him every thinkable jimmy and other tool for opening the door of the Armfeldtsgatan apartment. What he should have been supplied with, however, but wasn't, was a search warrant issued by District Attorney Olsson. But neither he nor Gunvald Larsson were unduly troubled by the notion that they were about to commit an offense in the course of their duties. They were quietly counting on Bulldozer being so delighted if they found anything that could be of use that he'd forget all about the breach of regulations. And if they didn't find anything, there'd be no reason to tell him about it. Anyway, the concept of a breach of regulations was without relevance nowadays. It was the regulations which were all wrong.

By this time Mauritzon would be on his way south; not to Africa, admittedly, but far enough to let them work in peace.

The doors to the apartment house were fitted with standard locks. So was Mauritzon's; and it didn't take Kollberg long to open it. On the inside, the door was equipped with two safety chains and a fox-lock, designed to lock only from within. These devices suggested that Mauritzon counted on receiving—or not receiving—guests a good deal more obstinate than the salesmen and peddlers whose visits he declined by means of a little enamel notice on the door.

His apartment consisted of three rooms plus a kitchen, a hallway, and a bathroom. In itself it was rather elegant. But though its furniture was quite expensive, the overall impression was of tasteless banality. They went into the living room. In front of them was a

169

teak wall unit consisting of bookcases, cupboards, and a built-in writing desk. One shelf was full of paperbacks, while the others were heaped with all kinds of bric-a-brac: souvenirs, pieces of china, little vases and bowls, and other ornaments. On the walls hung a few imitation oil paintings and reproductions of the sort commonly sold in dime stores. The furniture, curtains, and carpets, though they seemed by no means cheap, appeared to have been selected at random, and their patterns, materials, and colors did not go together.

In one corner was a little cocktail bar. The mere sight of it would have been enough to make anyone feel sick, let alone the smell of the contents of the bottles behind the mirrored doors of the cabinet. The front of the bar was covered in oilcloth of a very peculiar pattern: yellow, green, and pink figures reminiscent of amoebas, or possibly highly magnified spermatozoa, were floating about on a black background. The same pattern, albeit on a considerably smaller scale, was repeated on the plastic surface of the bar.

Kolberg went over and opened the cocktail cabinet. It contained a half-empty bottle of Parfait d'Amour, a virtually empty bottle of Swedish dessert wine, an unopened half-bottle of Carlshamns Punch, and a completely empty bottle of Beefeater Gin. Shuddering, he shut the doors of the cabinet and went into the next room.

There was no door between the living room and the next room, only an arch supported by two pillars. Presumably the space beyond was intended to serve as a dining room. It was fairly small and had a bay window overlooking the street. In here was a piano and, in one corner, a radio and record player.

"Aha, so here we have the music room," said Kollberg, with a grand gesture.

"Somehow I find it hard to imagine that rat of a fellow sitting here playing the *Moonlight Sonata*," said Gunvald Larsson. He went over and lifted the piano lid, inspecting the instrument's interior. "At least there are no corpses here," he said.

Having made the preliminary tour of inspection,
170

Kollberg took off his jacket and they began going through the apartment in detail. They started in the bedroom where Gunvald Larsson immediately began ransacking the closet while Kollberg attacked the chest of drawers. For a while they worked in silence. It was Kollberg who broke it.

"Gunvald," he said.

A muffled reply came from the depths of the closet.

Kollberg went on: "They didn't have much success shadowing Roos. He flew out from Arlanda a couple of hours ago, and Bulldozer got in the final report just before I left. He was deeply disappointed."

Gunvald Larsson grunted. Then he stuck his head out and said: "Bulldozer's optimism and wild expectations expose him to constant disappointments. But he soon gets over them, as no doubt you've noticed. Well, what was Roos up to on his days off?" He disappeared into the closet again.

Kollberg shoved in the lower drawer and straightened his back. "Well, he didn't meet up with Malmström and Mohrén, as Bulldozer hoped," he said. "The first evening, day before yesterday that is, he went to a restaurant with some dame and went skinny-dipping with her afterwards."

"Yes, I heard about that," Gunvald Larsson said. "And then?"

"He stayed with this dame until the afternoon and then drove into town and wandered about, apparently aimlessly and all by himself. Yesterday evening he went to another restaurant with another girl but didn't go for a swim, at least not outdoors. He took her home with him to Märsta. Yesterday he took her in a taxi to Odenplan, where they parted. Then he drifted about on his own, went into a few shops, drove home to Märsta again, changed his clothes, and drove out to Arlanda Airport. Not very exciting! And above all not particularly criminal."

"If the skinny-dipping isn't to be regarded as an offense against public decency," Gunvald Larsson said, "and Ek, who was sitting there in the bushes watching, doesn't report him for committing a nuisance." He came out of the closet and shut the door. "Nothing in there except for a lot of incredibly ugly clothes," he said, going out to the bathroom.

Kollberg went on to study a green cabinet that did duty as a bedside table. The two uppermost drawers contained a welter of objects, all more or less used: crumpled Kleenex, cuff links, a few empty matchboxes, half a bar of chocolate, safety pins, a thermometer, two packages of cough drops, restaurant bills and cash-register receipts, an unopened pack of black condoms, ball-point pens, a postcard from Stettin with the message: "Here's vodka, women, and song, what more can one want? Nils," a cigarette lighter that didn't function, and a blunt peasant knife without a sheath.

On top of the bedside table lay a paperback, the cover of which showed a bandy-legged cowboy holding a smoking revolver in his hands.

Kollberg leafed through the book, which was entitled *The Gunfight at Black Ravine,* and a photo fell out onto the floor. A color snapshot, it showed a young woman sitting on a jetty wearing shorts and a short-sleeved white sweater. She was dark, and her appearance was humdrum. Kollberg turned the photo over. Along the top edge was written in lead pencil: "Möja, 1969," and under it in blue ink and another handwriting, "Monita." Kollberg stuck the photo back among the pages and pulled out the lower drawer.

It was deeper than either of the others, and when he'd pulled it out he called for Gunvald Larsson. They looked down into the drawer.

"Queer place to keep a grinding machine," said Kollberg. "Or maybe it's some advanced kind of a massage apparatus?"

"Wonder what he used it for?" said Gunvald Larsson thoughtfully. "He doesn't quite seem the type to have hobbies, does he? Though of course he could have stolen it or been given it in payment for dope." He went back to the bathroom.

Little more than an hour later their search of the apartment and its contents was finished. They had found little of special interest: no money stowed away, no incriminating correspondence, no weapons, and no medicines stronger than aspirin and Alka-Seltzer.

Now they were standing in the kitchen, where they had rummaged through all the drawers and closets. The refrigerator, they noticed, had not been turned off and was full of food, which meant that Mauritzon wasn't intending to stay away for long. Among other things, a smoked eel lay staring up challengingly at Kollberg, who ever since the day he'd decided to get his weight down had suffered continuously from hunger, However, he got control of himself and with a grumbling stomach turned away from the refrigerator and its temptations. He caught sight of a key ring with two keys, which was hanging from a hook behind the kitchen door. "Keys to the roof," he said, pointing.

Gunvald Larsson went up to the key ring and unhooked it. He said: "Or to the basement. Come on, let's take a look."

Neither of the keys fitted the door to the roof, so they took the elevator down to the ground floor and went downstairs to the basement. The largest of the keys opened the lock of the fire door.

First they entered a short hallway with doors on either side. Opening the door on the right they looked into the garbage room. The building had a garbage chute, at the mouth of which stood a metal container on wheels, lined with a large yellow plastic bag. Three more containers with bags—one filled to the brim with garbage and two empty—stood by the wall. In one corner stood a brush and pan.

The door opposite was locked, and a notice said it led to the washroom.

The corridor led into a long passageway stretching in both directions. Along its walls were rows of numbered lockers, all fitted with various types of padlocks.

Kollberg and Gunvald Larsson tried out the smaller key in several of them and finally found the right one. There were only two things in Mauritzon's locker: an ancient vacuum cleaner without a nozzle, and a large chest, which was locked. While Kollberg picked the lock Gunvald Larsson opened the vacuum cleaner and looked inside.

"Empty," he said.

Kollberg opened the lid of the chest and said: "But not this one. Take a look."

173

Inside the chest were fourteen unopened bottles of 130 proof Polish vodka, four cassette tape recorders, an electric hair drier, and six electric shavers, all brand new and still sealed in their original packages.

"Smuggled," said Gunvald Larsson. "Or else stolen goods."

"They're certainly stuff he's been given in exchange," Kollberg said. "I wouldn't mind seizing the vodka, but I suppose we'd better leave it all where it is."

He shut the chest and locked it, and they went out again into the passage.

"Well, that was something, at least," Kollberg said. "But not much to bring home to Bulldozer. I guess we'd better put the keys back where we found them and beat it. Nothing more to be done here."

"Cautious bastard, that Mauritzon," said Gunvald Larsson. "Maybe he's even got a third apartment." He stopped, nodding toward a door at the far end of the passage. Across the door the words "Air Raid Shelter" were stenciled in red paint. "Let's see if it's open," he said. "While we're at it."

The door was open. The air raid shelter seemed to be used as a bicycle storage room and general junk heap. Besides the bikes and dismantled motor scooter there were a couple of baby carriages, a sled, and an old-fashioned toboggan with a steering wheel. Against one wall was a carpenter's workbench, and on the floor beneath it lay a couple of window frames without any glass in them. In one corner stood an iron spike, a couple of brooms, a snow shovel, and two pitchforks.

"I always get claustrophobic in places like this," Kollberg said. "During the war, when we had air raid practice, I always sat trying to imagine what it'd feel like to sit there underneath a bombed building and never be able to get out. Goddam awful."

He looked around. In the corner behind the bench stood an old wooden box with the hardly visible word "sand" painted on its front. On the lid was a galvanized bucket. "Look," he said. "There's one of those old sand boxes from the war."

He went over, lifted off the bucket, and opened
174

the lid of the sand box. "There's still some sand in it," he said.

"We never needed it," said Gunvald Larsson, "anyway not to put out incendiary bombs with. What's that?"

Kollberg had bent down over the box. Shoving his hand into it he picked something out and placed it on the bench. It was a green American army-type shoulder bag.

Kollberg opened the satchel and laid out its contents on the workbench:

A crumpled pale-blue shirt.
A blond wig.
A blue denim hat, wide-brimmed.
A pair of sunglasses.
And a pistol: a forty-five-caliber Llama Auto.

24

The girl who called herself Monita had not met Filip Faithful Mauritzon on that summer day three years ago when she was photographed on a jetty on Möja—an island in the Stockholm Archipelago.

That summer had been the last in her six years of marriage to Peter; in the autumn he met another woman, and just after Christmas had left Monita and their five-year-old daughter Mona. She did what he asked and applied for a quick divorce on grounds of his infidelity: he was in a hurry to marry his new woman, who was already in the fifth month of pregnancy when the divorce went through. Monita kept the two-room apartment in Hökarängen, out in the suburbs, and there had never been any question that the child remain in her care. Peter relinquished his rights to have regular contacts with his daughter; later it was to turn out that he also defaulted on his duty to contribute to the child's support.

The divorce not only led to a sharp deterioration in Monita's finances, it also forced her to break off her studies, which she had only recently begun. And this depressed her more than anything else in the whole wretched story.

As time passed she had begun to feel handicapped by her lack of education. For she had never really had a chance to go on studying or to learn a profession. When she had finished her nine-year compulsory schooling she had wanted to take a year off before entering college. And when that year was at an end she had met Peter. They had gotten married, and her plans for higher education had been put on the shelf. The following year their daughter had been born. Peter had started night school. Not until he had completed his education—the year before their divorce—was it to have been her turn again. When Peter had left her, her educational prospects had been destroyed: it was impossible to get hold of a regular baby-sitter, and even if one had been available the expense would have been too much for her.

The first two years after her daughter had come into the world Monita had stayed at home, but as soon as she had been able to place the child in a day care center she had begun working again. Earlier, that is to say from the month after she had left school up to a few weeks before the child's delivery, she had held a number of different jobs. During those years she had been a secretary, a cashier at a supermarket, a stock clerk, a factory worker, and a waitress. She was a restless soul. As soon as she didn't feel happy or felt she needed a change, she'd quit her job and look for a new one.

When, after the two-year involuntary interruption, she again began looking for a job, she discovered that the labor market had grown tighter and that there wasn't much for her to choose from. Lacking any professional education or useful contacts, only the worst-paid and least-stimulating occupations were open to her. Now it was not so easy to change jobs as soon as the boredom became excessive, but when she had begun to study again the future looked brighter and the soul-killing monotony of work on an assembly line became easier to put up with.

For three years she had stayed at her job in a chemical factory in the southern suburbs of Stockholm. But when the divorce had gone through and she'd been left alone with her daughter, she was forced to take a shorter and worse-paid shift. She felt caught in a trap. Suddenly, in despair, she quit her job—without knowing what she was going to do next.

Meanwhile unemployment had become steadily worse, and the lack of jobs was so severe that even academically educated and highly qualified professional people were fighting over ill-paid jobs that were far beneath their qualifications.

For a while Monita had been out of work. She received a meager income from unemployment insurance but became steadily more depressed. All her thoughts went to the problem of how to make ends meet; rent, food, and clothes for Mona swallowed up everything she could scrape together. She couldn't afford to buy any clothes for herself and had to give up smoking. The pile of unpaid bills just grew and grew. In the end she had swallowed her pride and asked Peter to help her; after all, the law obliged him to contribute to Mona's support. Though he complained that he now had his own family to think of, he gave her five hundred kronor. She had used it immediately to pay off some of her debts.

Except for three weeks when she worked as an office temporary and a couple of weeks picking out loaves in a big bakery, Monita had no steady job during the fall of 1970. She hadn't found this lack of work disagreeable in itself. It was nice to be able to sleep late in the mornings and be with Mona in the daytime, and if she'd not been weighed down with all these money worries, lack of work wouldn't have bothered her. As time went by, her desire to continue her education had waned. What was the sense of wasting time and energy accumulating debts, when all one got for one's pains were worthless exams and the dubious satisfaction of having slightly enriched one's store of knowledge? Furthermore, she'd begun to suspect that something more than higher wages and pleasanter working conditions would be needed before there would be much sense in participating in the industrial-capitalist system.

Just before Christmas she went with Mona to visit her sister in Oslo. Their parents had died in a car crash five years ago, and this sister was the only close relative she had. After their parents' death it had become a tradition with them to celebrate Christmas at her sister's place. To get the money for her ticket she went to a pawnshop with her parents' wedding rings and a few other pieces of jewelry she'd inherited from them. She stayed in Oslo for two weeks, and when she got back to Stockholm again after New Year's she'd gained six pounds and felt more cheerful than she had for a long time.

In February, 1971, Monita celebrated her twenty-fifth birthday. A year had now passed since Peter had left her, and Monita thought she'd changed more during that single year than during her entire marriage. She had matured, discovered new aspects of herself, and that was to the good. But she had also grown harder, more resigned, and a trifle bitter. And that was not so good. Above all, she had become very lonely.

As the solitary mother of a six-year-old who demanded all her time, and with her home in a big housing project out in the suburbs where everyone seemed to be erecting barriers around his own privacy, she had no chance to break out of this isolation.

Little by little her former friends and acquaintances had drawn away and ceased to show up. Not wishing to leave her daughter alone, she could only rarely go out, and for lack of money couldn't afford entertainment. During the first period after her divorce some friend or other would come out and look her up; but it was a long way out to Hökarängen, and they soon got tired of the trip. She was often down in the dumps and very depressed, and presumably the impression she'd made on her friends had been so dismal that she'd scared them away.

She took long walks with her daughter and brought home bundles of books from the library, reading them during the silent solitary hours after Mona had gone to sleep. It was rare for her phone to ring. She herself had no one she could call; and when the phone was finally cut off because she hadn't paid her bill, she didn't even notice the difference She felt like a prisoner in her own home. But gradually her imprisonment began to feel like security, and existence outside the walls of her dreary suburban apartment seemed steadily more unreal and remote.

Sometimes at night, as she wandered aimlessly between the living room and the kitchen, too tired to read and too nervous to sleep, it would seem to her that she was going out of her mind. It was as if she only had to let go a little, and the barriers would fall and madness would burst through.

Often she contemplated suicide, and many times her feelings of hopelessness and anxiety were so acute that only the thought of her child prevented her from taking her own life.

She worried deeply about the child. She would weep tears of helpless bitterness when she thought of her daughter's future. She wanted her child to grow up in a warm, secure, humane environment—one where the rat race after power, money, and social status did not make everyone into an enemy, and where the words "buy" and "own" weren't regarded as synonymous with happiness. She wanted to give her child a chance to develop her individuality and not be shaped to fit into one of the pigeonholes society had prepared for her. She wanted her child to feel the joy of working, of sharing life with others, of security; and she wanted her to have self-respect.

Such elementary demands on existence for her daughter did not seem to her presumptuous; but she clearly saw that she'd never realize these hopes as long as they went on living in Sweden. What she couldn't figure out was how to get the money to emigrate; and her despair and despondency threatened to turn into resignation and apathy.

When she'd come home after her visit to Oslo, she had decided to pull herself together and do something about her situation. To enlarge her own freedom and also save Mona from becoming too isolated, she tried —for the tenth time—to get her a place in a day care center quite near the building they lived in. To her astonishment a place was available, and Mona was able to start at once.

Very much at random, Monita had begun answering the want ads. And all the while she was brooding on her main problem: *What was she to do to get some money?* That she'd need a great deal of it if she was ever to radically alter her situation was something she clearly realized. She wanted at all costs to go abroad. She felt less and less content—and had begun to hate this society, which boasted of a prosperity actually reserved for a small privileged minority while the great majority's only privilege was to keep moving on the treadmill that turned the machinery.

Again and again in her thoughts she turned over the various ways of getting some capital. She found

180

the problem insoluble. To earn it by honest work was out of the question. Even when she was working she had never managed to make her after-tax earnings suffice for much more than rent and food.

Her chances of winning the soccer pools seemed improbable, but every week she went on handing in her thirty-two-line system, if only to be able to go on hoping.

There was no one she could expect to leave her a fortune. Nor was it likely that some mortally ill millionaire would propose marriage and then give up the ghost on their wedding night.

There were girls, of course, who earned a lot of money as prostitutes. She even knew one personally. Nowadays there was no need to walk the streets; you just called yourself a model and rented a studio or took work in some massage parlor or elegant sex club. But she found the mere thought of it repulsive.

The only way left, then, was to steal it. But how, and where? Anyway, she was certainly too honest to carry it off. So for the time being she decided to try to get herself a decent job. This proved easier than she'd dared hope.

She got a job as a waitress in a busy well-known downtown restaurant. Her hours were short and convenient, and there were excellent prospects of doing well out of tips. One of this restaurant's many habitués was Filip Faithful Mauritzon.

One day he was sitting, an insignificant but decent-looking little man, at one of Monita's tables, where he ordered pork and mashed turnips. He had said some friendly words to her and joked as she took his order; but there was nothing about him to merit Monita's particular attention. Neither, on the other hand, was there anything about Monita to arouse Mauritzon's special interest, at least not that time.'

Monita's appearance, as she herself had gradually come to realize, was commonplace. People she'd met only once or twice rarely recognized her the next time. She had dark hair, gray-blue eyes, good teeth, and regular features. She was of medium height—five feet five inches—normal physique, and weighed about one hundred and twenty pounds. There were men

181

who thought her beautiful, but that was only after they had come to know her well.

When Mauritzon, for the third time in a week, sat down at one of her tables, Monita recognized him and guessed that he was going to order the *plat du jour:* sausages and boiled potatoes. Last time he'd taken pork pancakes.

He did order the sausages, and a glass of milk to drink. When she brought him his food, he looked up at her and said: "You must be new here, miss?"

She nodded. It wasn't the first time he'd spoken to her, but she was used to anonymity, and her waitress's uniform did nothing to facilitate recognition.

When she brought him his bill he gave her a substantial tip and said: "I hope you'll like it here, miss, because I do. And the food's good, so watch your figure." Before leaving he winked at her in an amiable manner.

During the following weeks Monita noticed how the tidy little fellow who always ate the simplest of food and never drank anything but milk began to select one of her tables. Before sitting down, it became his habit to stand over by the door and look to see which tables she was serving. This astonished her, but she also felt faintly flattered.

She did not regard herself as any great shakes as a waitress. She found it hard to maintain a mask of impassivity toward querulous or impatient customers, and whenever anyone annoyed her, she'd snap back. She also had the habit of getting lost in her own thoughts and was often distraught and forgetful. On the other hand she was strong and worked quickly, and to such customers as she thought deserved it she was friendly without being obsequious or silly like some of the other girls.

Each time Mauritzon came in she'd exchange a few words with him. Gradually she came to regard him as an old acquaintance. His polite, slightly old-fashioned manners—which seemed in some way out of harmony with the pithy views on everything between heaven and earth that he often expressed—fascinated her.

Though Monita was not happy in her new job,

182

she did not find it altogether a bad one. She finished before the day care center closed, so she was able to pick Mona up on time. And she no longer felt so desperately isolated and lonely, though she still entertained the same wild hope that one day she'd be able to leave Sweden for some other more friendly climate. By now Mona had found several new playmates in the day care center and could hardly wait to get there every morning. Her best friend lived in the same building, and Monita had gotten to know the parents —who were young and friendly. With them she had made a mutual arrangement whereby they each looked after the other's daughter at nights, when an evening out became imperative. Several times she had had Mona's playmate as her overnight guest, and Mona had twice slept at her friend's place—even though Monita had found nothing better to do on those occasions than to go into town to a movie. Even so, it was an arrangement that gave her a sense of freedom and that was later to prove a most practical one.

One April day, when she'd been working at her new job for a little more than two months, she was standing there with her hands clasped under her apron, dreaming, when Mauritzon summoned her over to his table. She went up to him, nodded at his plate of pea soup, which he'd barely had time to taste, and asked: "Is there something wrong with it?"

"Excellent, as usual," Mauritzon said. "But something has occurred to me. Here I sit stuffing myself day after day while you just run about working. I was going to ask whether I could invite you out to have a bite to eat with me, for a change. In the evening, of course, when you're free. Tomorrow, for instance?"

Monita didn't hesitate long. She had long ago summed him up as honest, sober, and hard-working, a trifle eccentric but certainly not dangerous, even quite nice. Besides, this move of his had long been in the air, and she'd already made up her mind what she'd answer when he asked her. So she said: "Oh well, why not?"

After passing that Friday evening in Mauritzon's company Monita only needed to revise her opinion in two respects. He was not a teetotaler, and presumably he wasn't very hard-working either; but neither of these facts made him any less nice. Indeed, she found him really interesting.

Several times that spring they went out to restaurants together. Each time Monita, in a friendly but firm manner, turned down Mauritzon's invitation to come home with him for a nightcap, nor did she allow him to see her home to Hökarängen.

In the early summer she saw nothing at all of him and for two weeks in July was herself away on vacation with her sister in Norway.

The first day after her return Mauritzon came in and sat down at his usual table. The same evening they met again. This time Monita went home with him to Armfeldtsgatan. It was the first time they went to bed together. Monita found he was as sociable in bed as elsewhere.

Their relationship developed to their mutual satisfaction. Mauritzon was not too demanding and did not insist on meeting her more often than she herself wished, namely a couple of times a week. He was considerate toward her, and each found the other's company agreeable.

For her part she showed him the same delicacy. He was extremely taciturn, for instance, about his occupation, about how he earned his living; but though she wondered a good deal about this she was never inquisitive. Neither did she want him interfering too much in her own life, least of all where Mona was concerned. So she took care not to poke her nose into his affairs. He didn't seem particularly jealous—no more than she was. Either he realized he was her only lover, or else he was indifferent to whether she went with other men. Nor did he ever ask her about her earlier affairs.

When autumn came they went out on the town together less frequently, preferring to stay at his place, where they had something nice to eat and passed the greater part of their evenings and nights together in bed.

Now and again Mauritzon vanished on some business trip, though he never said where or what sort of business it was. Monita was not stupid. She'd quite soon come to realize his activities must be criminal

184

in some way, but having satisfied herself that he was basically decent and honest she assumed his criminality to be of an innocuous kind. She thought of him as a Robin Hood who stole from the rich to give to the poor. That he was a white slaver or that he sold narcotics to children was something that never occurred to her. As soon as the opportunity presented itself she tried in a veiled way to let him know that she was not disposed to moralize about crime aimed at the rich or against an exploitative society in general. She did this to get him, if possible, to reveal some of his secrets.

And indeed, around Christmas, Mauritzon found himself obliged to initiate Monita to some small extent into his affairs. Christmas was always a busy time in Mauritzon's line of work, and now, in his enthusiasm not to let slip any opportunity to make a dollar, he had taken on many more jobs than he could handle. Indeed, it was a physical impossibility. A highly complicated transaction required his presence in Hamburg the day after Christmas, though he had also promised that same day to make a delivery at Fornebu Airport outside Oslo. Since Monita was to spend Christmas in Oslo as usual, the temptation to ask her to act as his stand-in and courier was more than he could resist. No great risks were attached to the job, but the arrangements in connection with the delivery were so unusual and so involved that he could hardly fool her into thinking it was just an ordinary Christmas present. He gave her detailed instructions but, knowing she took a dim view of the drug business, told her that the package contained some forged forms to be used in a post office job.

Monita had nothing against acting as his assistant and carried out her task without complications. He paid for her journey and gave her a few hundred kronor by way of a fee.

Though this extra income, so easily earned but so sorely needed, should have whetted her appetite, Monita, after she'd had time to think the matter over, was very much of two minds about undertaking anything similar in the future.

She had nothing against the money. But if it entailed a risk of ending up in jail, she at least wanted to know what it was all about. She regretted not having taken a look at the contents of the package and began to suspect Mauritzon had fooled her. Next time he asked her to act as his emissary she'd made up her mind to refuse. To run about with mysterious parcels containing anything from opium to time bombs was quite simply not up her alley.

Mauritzon must have understood this intuitively, for he asked no more services of her. Though his attitude remained the same, as time went by she began to become aware of aspects of his nature that she'd not perceived before. She discovered that he often told her lies—quite unnecessarily, since she never asked him what he was up to or tried to put him on the spot. She also began to suspect that he was not a gentleman thief—rather, a petty retailer in crime who would do virtually anything for money.

During the first months of the year they met less frequently, not so much because Monita was resisting him but because Mauritzon was unusually busy and was often away.

Monita did not think he'd grown tired of her; any evening he had to himself he was only too glad to spend with her. On one occasion when she was at his place he had some visitors. It was an evening in early March. His visitors, whose names were Malmström and Mohrén, were somewhat younger than Mauritzon and seemed to be business associates of his. She had taken a particular liking to one of them, but they'd not seen each other again.

For Monita the winter of 1971 was grim. The restaurant where she'd been working changed hands. Converted into a pub, it lost its former customers without managing to attract new ones, and in the end the staff had been fired and the place turned into a bingo hall. Now she was out of work again, and, with Mona in the day care center by day and out playing with her friends on weekends, she felt more lonely than ever.

She found it irritating not to be able to put an end to her affair with Mauritzon, an irritation that increased during his absences. When they were together she still enjoyed his company. Besides being the only person in the world apart from Mona who seemed to have any need for her, he was obviously in love with her—and this of course was flattering.

Sometimes, having nothing to do in the daytime, she'd go up to the Armfeldtsgatan apartment at times when she knew he wouldn't be at home. She liked to sit there alone, reading, listening to records, or just being among his things, which still seemed strange to her though by now she should have gotten used to them. Apart from a couple of books and some records, there was nothing in his flat she would ever have dreamed of possessing in her own home. Nevertheless, in some queer way, she felt at home there.

He'd never given her a key to his apartment. It was she who had a copy made one time when he'd lent her his. This was the only liberty she'd ever taken with him, and at first it had given her a bad conscience.

She always made sure to leave no telltale traces and only went there when she was quite sure he was away. How would he react if he knew? Sometimes, of course, she snooped about his belongings but never found anything that seemed particularly incriminating. She'd had the extra key made not in order to pry, but just to be able to go there in privacy—not that anyone was looking for her or had any interest in her whereabouts. Even so, it gave her a feeling of inaccessibility, a sense of sovereignty reminiscent of what she had known when playing hide-and-seek as a child. She would always choose such a good hiding place that no one in the whole world could ever find her. If she'd asked him, he'd probably have given her a key of her own. But then there'd have been no fun in it.

One day in mid-April Monita, feeling unusually restless and troubled, went to the apartment in Armfeldtsgatan. She was going to sit in Mauritzon's ugliest and most comfortable armchair, play some Vivaldi on the phonograph, and hope that that wonderful feeling of peace and total indifference to everything would come over her.

Mauritzon was away in Spain, and wasn't due back until the next day.

She hung up her coat and shoulder bag on a hook
187

in the hallway and after taking out her cigarettes and matches went into the living room. It was its usual tidy self. Mauritzon did his own cleaning up. When they had first become acquainted she'd asked him why he didn't hire a cleaning woman. He'd answered that he liked tidying up and had no desire to hand over that pleasure to someone else.

Putting down her cigarettes and matches on the broad arm of the armchair, she went into the other room and set the record player going. She put on *The Four Seasons*. Listening to the first notes of Vivaldi, she went out into the kitchen to get an ash tray from the closet, then went back with it into the living room. Curling up in the armchair, she placed the ash tray on its arm.

She thought about Mauritzon and their poverty-stricken relationship. Though they'd known each other for a year it had grown no deeper, nor had it matured. Rather the contrary. She could never remember what they talked about when they met, presumably because they never talked about anything of importance. Sitting there now in his favorite chair and looking at the bookcase with all its silly little pots and vases, she thought him an unusually absurd character. And for the hundredth time she asked herself why she even bothered with him, why she didn't get herself a proper man instead?

She lit a cigarette, blew the smoke out in a thin jet up at the ceiling, and reflected that she must stop thinking about that half-wit before she fell into a really bad mood.

Making herself comfortable in the chair she closed her eyes and tried to stop thinking, slowly moving her hand meanwhile in time with the music. In the middle of the *largo* she knocked over the ash tray, which fell to the floor and smashed.

"Dammit," she muttered. She got up, went out into the kitchen, and opened the closet under the sink —fumbling for the brush, which normally stood to the right of the garbage bag. It wasn't there. So she bent down and looked inside. The brush was lying on the bottom, and as she reached for it she caught sight of a briefcase. The briefcase stood behind the garbage bag. Old and worn; she'd never seen it before. He must have put it in there intending to take it down to the basement. It looked too bulky to go into the garbage chute.

At that moment she noticed that a thick piece of string was wound around it many times and that it had been tied in several efficient knots. Lifting out the briefcase, she put it down on the kitchen floor. It was heavy.

Now she was curious. Cautiously, she undid the knots, trying to remember how they had been tied. Then she unwound the string and opened the briefcase.

It was full of stones; flat pieces of black shale, which she recognized. It seemed to her she'd recently seen them somewhere. She furrowed her brow, straightened her back, flung her cigarette butt into the sink, and stared thoughtfully at the briefcase. Why should he have packed an old briefcase with stones, tied it up with string, and put it under the sink?

Now she examined the briefcase more carefully. Genuine leather—it had certainly been elegant and rather expensive when new. She inspected the inside of the flap: no name. Then she noticed something peculiar: someone had cut off the four bottom corners with a sharp knife or razor blade. What was more, it had been done quite recently. The slashed surfaces of the leather were quite fresh.

All at once she realized what he'd intended to do with this briefcase: throw it into the sea. Why? Bending down, she began picking out the slabs of shale. As she laid them out in a heap on the floor she remembered where she'd seen such stones. Down in the hallway, just inside the door to the yard, there'd been a heap of these slabs. Presumably they were to be used for surfacing the yard at the rear of the building. That's where he must have gotten them.

Just as she was thinking there couldn't be many left in the briefcase, her fingertips touched something hard and polished. She took it out and stood there holding it in her hand, contemplating it. Slowly a thought that had long been gnawing away in the depths of her mind took shape.

189

In this black steel thing, perhaps, she had the solution—the freedom she'd been dreaming of.

The pistol was about seven-and-a-half inches long, of big caliber, and had a heavy butt. On the blueish shining steel above the breach was engraved the name: Llama. She weighed the weapon in her hand. It was heavy.

Monita went out into the foyer and put the pistol in her bag. Then she went back into the kitchen, replaced all the stones in the briefcase, rewound the string around it—trying to duplicate the original knots —and finally put the briefcase back where she'd found it.

She took the brush, swept up the fragments of the ash tray in the living room, went out into the hallway, and poured them down the garbage chute. When she came in again she turned off the record player, put the record back where it belonged, and went out into the kitchen. She took her cigarette butt out of the sink and flushed it down the toilet. Then she put on her coat, snapped her bag closed, and hung it over her shoulder. Before leaving the apartment she made a quick tour of the rooms to make sure everything was in its place. She felt for the key in her pocket, slammed the door behind her, and went downstairs.

As soon as she got home she planned to do some serious thinking.

25

On Friday morning, July 7, Gunvald Larsson got up very early. Not precisely at sunrise, that would have been excessive. The name of the day in the Swedish calendar was "Klas," and the rim of the sun appeared over the Stockholm horizon as early as eleven minutes to three.

By half past six he had taken a shower, eaten his breakfast, and dressed, and half an hour later he was already on the front stoop of the little house on Sångarvägen, in Sollentuna, already visited by Einar Rönn four days before.

This was the Friday when everything was going to happen. Once again Mauritzon was to be confronted by Bulldozer Olsson, it was to be hoped under less cordial circumstances than last time. Perhaps, too, the moment had arrived for them to lay their hands on Malmström and Mohrén and intervene in their big coup.

But before the special squad went into action Gunvald Larsson had it in mind to solve a little problem that had been irritating him all week. Seen in a broader context, perhaps, it was a mere trifle, yet an annoying one. Now he wanted to dispose of it once and for all and also to prove to himself that his own thinking had been correct, and that he'd drawn the right conclusion.

Sten Sjögren had not gotten up with the sun. Five minutes passed before, yawning and fumbling with the belt of his dressing gown, he came down and opened the door.

Gunvald Larsson was not unfriendly, but he came straight to the point. "You've been lying to the police," he said.

"Have I?"

"A week ago you twice described a bank robber, who at first glance appeared to be a woman. Further, you gave a detailed description of the car that person used in the getaway, and of two men who were also in the car, a Renault 16."

"Quite right."

"And on Monday you repeated the same story, word for word, to a detective inspector who came here and talked to you."

"That's true, too."

"What is also true is that the whole thing was nothing but a pack of lies."

"But I described that blonde as best I could."

"Yes, because you knew several other people had seen the robber. You were also smart enough to figure out that a film had probably been taken inside the bank."

"But I'm certain it was a woman!"

"Oh? Why?"

"I'm not sure, but I've got a kind of instinct where dames are concerned."

"This time, as it happens, your instinct has failed you. But that's not what I've come here about. I want you to admit that your tale about the car and those two men was made up."

"Why do you want me to do that?"

"My reasons have no bearing on the matter. Anyway, they're of a purely private nature."

Sjögren was no longer half-asleep. With a curious look at Gunvald Larsson he said slowly: "As far as I know it's not a crime to give incomplete or inaccurate information, as long as one isn't under oath."

"Quite right."

"In which case this conversation is meaningless."

"Not to me. I very much want to check upon this matter. Let us say I've reached a certain conclusion, and I want to be sure it's the right one."

"And what conclusion is that?"

"That you conned the police with a bunch of lies for your own advantage."

"Plenty of people in this society think only of their own advantage."

192

"But not you?"

"At least I try not to. Not many people understand. My wife, for instance. Which is why I haven't got her any longer."

"So you think it's right to break into banks? And regard the police as the natural enemy of the people?"

"Something of that sort, yes. Though not quite so simple."

"To rob a bank and shoot the director of a gymnastics institute isn't a political act."

"No, not here and now, it isn't. But one can take an ideological view of the matter. Look at it in its historical perspective. Sometimes bank robberies have been politically motivated—during the Irish troubles, for instance. But the protest can also be unconscious."

"So—it's your view that common criminals can be regarded as revolutionaries?"

"That's a thought," Sjögren said, "though it's one that most prominent so-called socialists reject. Ever read Artur Lundkvist?"

"No." Gunvald Larsson mostly read Jules Régis and similar authors. At the moment he was ploughing through S. A. Duse's output. However, this had nothing to do with the matter. His literary habits were dictated by a need for amusement; he had no longing for a literary education.

"Lundkvist got the Lenin Prize," said Sten Sjögren. "In an anthology called *A Socialist Man*, he writes like this—and I quote from memory: 'Sometimes it goes so far that simple criminals are made to look as if they were consciously protesting against the miserable state of affairs as if they were almost revolutionaries . . . something that would least of all be tolerated in a socialist country.' "

"Go on," said Gunvald Larsson.

"End of quote," said Sjögren. "Lundkvist is a jerk. His whole line of reasoning is imbecilic. In the first place, people can be driven to protest against their state of affairs without being ideologically awake. And secondly, that bit about the socialist countries . . . there's not an ounce of logic to it. Why the devil should people rob themselves?"

193

Gunvald Larsson said nothing for a long while. Finally he said: "So—there was no beige-colored Renault?"

"No."

"Nor any unnaturally pale driver in a white T-shirt, nor any guy in black who looked like Harpo Marx?"

"No."

Gunvald Larsson nodded to himself. Then he said: "The fact of the matter is that the man who broke into that bank seems to be done for. And so far from being some kind of an unconscious revolutionary, he was a bloody rat who was hitchhiking on the capitalist bandwagon and lived by peddling dope and pornography—without a thought to anything except his own profit. Self-interest, that is. Furthermore, he has squealed on his pals in an attempt to save his own skin."

Sjögren shrugged his shoulders. "There's plenty of that kind about, too," he said. "Put it whichever way you like, but the guy who robbed that bank was some kind of underdog—if you see what I mean."

"I see exactly what you mean."

"How could you figure all this out?"

"Try it yourself," said Gunvald Larsson. "Put yourself in my shoes."

"Why the devil did you ever become a policeman?" asked Sjögren.

"Sheer chance. Actually I'm a seaman. Anyway, all that was so long ago, and many things looked quite different in those days. But that's neither here nor there. Now I have what I wanted."

"And that was all?"

"Exactly. Good-bye."

"Good-bye," said Sjögren. He looked utterly astounded. But Gunvald Larsson didn't notice. He was already on his way to his car. Nor did he hear Sjögren's parting shot:

"Anyway, I'm dead sure it was a girl."

At that same early hour of the morning Mrs. Svea Mauritzon was standing baking in her kitchen on Pilgatan, in Jönköping. Her prodigal son had come home and was to be regaled with fresh cinnamon buns

194

with his morning coffee. She was blissfully unaware of the terms in which her son was at that moment being described by a policeman a hundred and eighty miles away; if she had ever heard anyone call the apple of her eye a rat she would instantly have given that person a taste of her rolling pin.

A sharp ring on the front doorbell broke the morning silence. Laying aside her tray of freshly iced cinnamon twirls on the sink, she dried her hands on her apron and shuffled hurriedly out to the front door in her down-at-the-heels slippers. She noticed that the clock only showed 7:30 and threw an anxious glance toward the closed bedroom door.

In there her boy was sleeping. She had made up a bed for him on the sofa in the living room, but the clock had disturbed him and in the middle of the night he'd woken her up and asked her to switch beds with him. Poor child, he was working himself to death. What he needed was a real good sleep! For her part, being almost stone deaf, she did not hear the ticking of the clock.

Outside her front door stood two big men.

She didn't quite hear all they said, but they were extremely insistent. They must be allowed to speak to her son. In vain she tried to explain it was too early and that they could come back a little later when he'd finished sleeping.

They were implacable, maintaining that their errand was of the very greatest importance. Finally, very reluctantly, she went in to her son and gently awakened him. Raising himself on his elbow, he looked at the clock.

"Are you out of your mind? What do you want to wake me up like this for in the middle of the night? Didn't I say I wanted to have a good sleep?"

She gave him an unhappy look. "There are two gentlemen who want to see you," she said.

"What!" he yelled, jumping out of bed. "You haven't let them in, have you?"

Mauritzon knew it must be Malmström and Mohrén. They had realized he'd betrayed them, figured out where he was hiding, and were here seeking revenge.

195

His mother shook her head and stared at him in amazement as he flung on his clothes without even taking off his pajamas. At the same time he rushed around the room, collecting his scattered belongings and flinging them into his bag.

"What's it all about?" she asked, anxiously.

He snapped shut the bag, grabbed her by the arm, and hissed: "You must get rid of them! Tell 'em I'm not here. Say I've gone to Australia, anything!"

Not hearing what he'd said, she noticed her hearing aid was lying on the bedside table and put it on. Mauritzon tiptoed over to the door, pressed his ear against it, and listened. Not a sound. They were standing out there waiting for him, probably with a whole arsenal of guns ready to fire.

His mother came up to him and whispered: "What is it, Filip? What kind of men are they?"

"Just you get rid of them," he whispered back. "Tell 'em I've gone abroad."

"But I've already told them you're here. How could I know you didn't want to see them?"

Mauritzon buttoned up his jacket and grabbed his bag.

"Are you going already?" his mother asked, disappointed. "And I who've baked you some buns. Cinnamon snails, which you're so fond of . . ."

He turned to her and said indignantly: "How can you stand here babbling about cinnamon buns when . . ." He broke off, cocking his ear toward the vestibule. He heard a vague mumble of voices. Now they were coming in to get him—or liquidate him on the spot. He broke into a cold sweat, looking desperately around the room. His mother lived on the seventh floor, so there was no question of jumping out the window; and the only door gave out onto the vestibule where Malmström and Mohrén were waiting for him.

Going over to his mother, who was standing by the bed looking bewildered, he said: "Go on out. Tell 'em I'm coming, that I'll only be a minute. Try to get 'em out into the kitchen. Offer them some buns. Hurry up. Get going!"

He shoved her toward the door and stood with his

back to the wall. After she'd gone out, closing the door behind her, he again pressed his ear against it. He could hear voices, and after a while footsteps coming closer. When they stopped outside the door instead of going on out toward his mother's buns in the kitchen as he'd hoped, he suddenly knew the full meaning of the expression "my hair stood on end."

Silence. A metallic sound, perhaps a magazine being inserted into a pistol. Someone cleared his throat. Then a hard knock and a voice that said: "Come on out now, Mauritzon. This is the C.I.D."

Mauritzon opened the door and with a groan of relief practically fell into the arms of Detective Inspector Högflykt of the Jönköping C.I.D., who was standing there with the handcuffs ready for him.

Half an hour later Mauritzon was sitting on the plane to Stockholm with a large bag of cinnamon buns on his knee. He had convinced Högflykt that he was only too glad to cooperate, and the handcuffs had been removed. Staring down over the sunny plains of Östergötland he munched his buns. All things considered, he felt at peace with the world.

Every once in a while he offered his bag to his companion, who shook his head more grimly each time: Detective Inspector Högflykt, always panic-stricken in airplanes, wasn't feeling at all well.

The plane landed on the dot at 10:25 at Bromma Airport, and twenty minutes later Mauritzon was once again inside the police headquarters on Kungsholmen. While the police car was driving into town he had anxiously begun to speculate over what Bulldozer might have in store for him; by now the feeling of liberation and relief that had followed the shock of his awakening that morning had completely gone—giving place to grim apprehensions.

Bulldozer Olsson—in the company of select elements from the special squad, to wit Einar Rönn and Gunvald Larsson—was impatiently awaiting Mauritzon's arrival. Under the direction of Kollberg, the squad's other members were busy preparing their afternoon operation against the Mohrén gang. A complicated maneuver, it called for careful organizing.

Bulldozer, informed of the find in the air raid shelter, had been almost beside himself with joy. He'd hardly slept a wink all night, so excited and expectant was he as the great day approached. Already he had Mauritzon where he wanted him—and Malmström and Mohrén as well, from the moment when they tried to stage their big grab. If it didn't happen this Friday, then it certainly would the next, in which case today's operations could be regarded as a useful general rehearsal. Once he had the whole Mohrén gang under lock and key it certainly wouldn't be long before he also had Werner Roos on the hook.

Bulldozer's rosy dreams were interrupted by the telephone. He grabbed the receiver, listened for three seconds, and yelled: "Bring him in this moment!" He banged down the receiver, clapped the palms of his hands together, and said energetically: "Gentlemen, he is on his way. Are we ready?"

Gunvald Larsson grunted, and Rönn said without much enthusiasm: "Sure."

Rönn knew very well that he and Gunvald Larsson were there mainly to act as an audience. Bulldozer loved to perform in front of an audience, and today the performance was unquestionably his. He was not only playing the leading role, he was also the producer. Among other things he had adjusted the position of his fellow actors' chairs at least fifteen times until they were completely to his satisfaction.

Bulldozer was now sitting in the judgment seat behind his desk. Gunvald Larsson sat in the corner over by the window, and Rönn was at the end of the table to his right. Mauritzon's chair was placed directly in front of Bulldozer, but so far back from the table that it stood right in the middle of the open floor.

Gunvald Larsson was picking his teeth with a fragment of matchstick, meanwhile casting surreptitious glances at Bulldozer's gay summer getup: a mustard-yellow suit, blue-and-white-striped shirt, and a tie with a pattern of green Michaelmas daisies on an orange background.

There was a knock at the door, and Mauritzon

was brought in. By this time he had begun to feel rather ill at ease, and the sight of the now familiar faces in Bulldozer's room did nothing to calm him. They all looked grim.

That big blond guy, Larsson or whatever his name was, did not entertain very warm feelings towards him; so much he had already realized. As for that northerner with the drinker's nose, he seemed to be a glum fellow at best. What boded no good, however, was that even Bulldozer, who at their last meeting had been as benign as Father Christmas, was now contemplating him with harsh disapproval.

Mauritzon sat down on the chair indicated, looked around the room, and said: "Good morning."

No one returned his greeting. He went on: "There was nothing in those papers you gave me, Mr. District Attorney, which said I couldn't leave town, and as far as I know there was nothing of that sort in our agreement, either."

Bulldozer raised his eyebrows, and Mauritzon added hastily: "But naturally I'll help you in any way I can."

Bulldozer leaned forward, clasped his hands on the desk top, looked at him a while, and said in a mild voice: "Really, Mr. Mauritzon? So you will help us in any way you can. That is really most kind of you, Mr. Mauritzon. But now we have no more services to ask of you, Mr. Mauritzon. No! Now it's our turn to do *you* a service. You have not been quite honest with us, Mr. Mauritzon, have you? We realize how heavily this must weigh on you, and that is why we have gone to the trouble of arranging this little meeting—so that you can unburden yourself to us in peace and quiet."

Mauritzon threw an uncertain look at Bulldozer and said: "I don't understand. . . ."

"No? If I say that it's about last Friday, then perhaps, Mr. Mauritzon, you will understand."

"Last Friday?" Mauritzon's gaze wavered. He wiggled in his chair. He looked from Bulldozer to Rönn and back to Bulldozer, met Gunvald Larsson's cold china-blue gaze, and finally looked down at the floor. It was dead silent in the room.

199

Bulldozer went on: "Last Friday, a week ago, yes! Surely it's impossible, Mr. Mauritzon, that you don't recall what you were up to then? If nothing else, Mr. Mauritzon, you can't have forgotten the day's take. Ninety thousand isn't peanuts, whichever way you look at it. Or what do you say?"

"Ninety thousand . . . ninety thousand what? I don't know about any ninety thousand."

Mauritzon sounded bolder now, and Bulldozer's voice was not quite so silky-smooth as he said: "Naturally, Mr. Mauritzon, you haven't any idea what I'm talking about?"

Mauritzon shook his head. "No," he said. "I haven't."

"Perhaps, Mr. Mauritzon, you would like me to express myself more clearly? Would you?"

"Yes, please," said Mauritzon humbly.

Gunvald Larsson straightened his back and said irritably: "Don't sit there playing dumb! You know very well what it's all about."

"Of course he does," Bulldozer said good-naturedly. "Mr. Mauritzon is only trying to show us how smart he can be. It's all part of the game, as it were. But it'll soon pass over. Of course he may be experiencing some difficulty in expressing himself."

"He didn't have any when it was a question of squealing on his pals," Gunvald Larsson said acidly.

"Well, we'll see," Bulldozer said. He leaned forward and looked Mauritzon between the eyes. "You want me to express myself more clearly? Okay, then I shall. We know very well that it was you who robbed that bank on Hornsgatan last Friday, and you'll get nowhere by denying it, since we've got proof. Regrettably, however, you didn't stop at robbery, something which in itself is a pretty serious matter, and I hardly need to point out what a very nasty situation you're in. Now, of course you can maintain that you were taken by surprise, didn't shoot to kill. The fact nevertheless remains: the man is unquestionably dead."

Mauritzon had turned pale. Little beads of sweat began to break out around his hairline. He opened his mouth to say something, but Bulldozer went on:

200

"I hope you appreciate that your situation is so serious that nothing is to be gained by playing tricks, and that the best you can do not to make things worse is to show a willingness to cooperate. Do I make myself clear?"

Mauritzon, gaping, shook his head. Finally he said, stammering: "I . . . I don't know what . . . what you're talking about."

Bulldozer got up and began walking to and fro in front of Mauritzon. "My dear Mauritzon. I have endless patience when patience is necessary. But sheer stupidity is something I find hard to tolerate," he said in a tone of voice that implied that even the most infinite patience has its limits.

As Bulldozer went on speaking, pacing gravely to and fro between Mauritzon and the desk, Mauritzon again shook his head.

"I fancy I've expressed myself with all possible clarity, but I repeat: We know that you, alone, went into that bank on Hornsgatan, that you shot and killed a male customer, and that you managed to get away with ninety thousand in cash. We know this, and you will gain nothing by denying it. On the other hand, you can to some extent—not very much, admittedly, but to some extent—improve your situation by confessing without more ado and by also showing a little good will. You will do best by giving us a full account of the events of that day—by telling us what you've done with the money, how you got away from the scene of the crime, and who your accomplices were. Well, have I expressed myself clearly enough?"

Breaking off his promenade, Bulldozer sat down again behind his desk. He leaned back in his chair and threw a glance first at Rönn and then at Gunvald Larsson—inviting their silent applause. Rönn merely looked dubious, and Gunvald Larsson absent-mindedly picked his nose. Bulldozer, who had been expecting their faces to light up with admiration at this model of a concise and psychological harangue, thought resignedly: "Pearls before swine." Again he turned to Mauritzon.

The latter stared at him with mingled suspicion and terror.

"But I've nothing to do with all that," he said excitedly. "I haven't the faintest idea about any bank robbery."

"Don't beat around the bush, now. You heard very well what I said. We have proof."

"What sort of proof? I haven't robbed any bank or shot anyone. The whole thing's grotesque."

With a sigh Gunvald Larsson got up and stood in front of the window with his back to the room. "It's senseless, trying to talk in a friendly way to a guy like that," he said over his shoulder. "A smack in the face is the only thing he'll understand."

Bulldozer waved a calming hand at him, and said: "Wait a little, Gunvald." Placing his elbows on the desk he put his chin in his hands and gazed in a troubled way at Mauritzon.

"Well, Mauritzon? It's up to you."

Mauritzon threw out his hands. "But I haven't done it. I promise you! I swear!"

Bulldozer went on looking at him in a troubled manner. Then, bending down, he pulled out the bottom drawer of his desk as he said: "Really? But I reserve at least the right to doubt it." Straightening his back, he flung the green American army shoulder bag on the table and looked triumphantly at Mauritzon, who looked at the bag, astounded. "As you see, Mauritzon, we've got it all here."

One at a time he took the things out of the bag and set them out on the table in a row. "The wig, the shirt, the glasses, the hat, and last but not least, the pistol. Well, what do you say now?"

At first Mauritzon stared uncomprehendingly at the various objects. Then his expression changed and he stared at the table, turning slowly whiter in the face. "What . . . what's all that?" he said. His voice did not quite convince. He cleared his throat, repeated his question.

Bulldozer threw him a weary look and turned to Rönn. "Einar," he said. "Would you go and check that our witnesses are here?"

"Sure," said Rönn. He got up and went.

After a few minutes he came back, stopped in the doorway, and said: "Sure."

Bulldozer flew up out of his chair. "Good," he said. "Then we're on our way."

Rönn disappeared again, and Bulldozer put the things back into the bag. He said: "Come along then, Mauritzon. We're going across to another room. We're going to have a little fashion show. Coming, Gunvald?" He rushed to the door, clutching the bag. Gunvald Larsson followed him, pushing Mauritzon roughly ahead of him. They went into a room further down the corridor.

The room differed little from the other offices. There was a desk, chairs, a filing cabinet, and a typewriter stand. A mirror was mounted on the wall. On the other side of the wall this mirror acted as a window, so that it was possible to watch from the next room.

Einar Rönn was standing in that room, watching unobserved as Bulldozer helped Mauritzon put on the blue shirt, stuck the wig of long blonde hair onto his head, and gave him the hat and sunglasses. Mauritzon went up to the mirror and stared bewildered at his own image; while Rönn on the other side of the wall had an unpleasant feeling of invisibility as he looked straight into the other man's eyes through the back of the mirror. Then Mauritzon donned the sunglasses and hat. Everything seemed to fit perfectly.

Rönn went out and fetched the first witness— the woman who was chief cashier at the Hornsgatan bank. Mauritzon stood in the middle of the floor with the bag hanging over his shoulder, and when Bulldozer said something to him he began walking to and fro in the room.

The witness looked at him through the glass pane, then looked at Rönn and nodded.

"Take a good look," Rönn said.

"It's certainly her," the cashier said. "There's no question of it. I think she had narrower pants on then. That's the only difference."

"Are you quite sure?"

"Oh yes. One hundred percent."

The next witness was the bank manager. He threw a glance at Mauritzon. "It's her," he said, without a trace of doubt in his voice.

203

"You must take a careful look," Rönn said. "We don't want any mistakes."

The bank manager looked at Mauritzon for a while as he walked about in the other room. "Sure, sure. I recognize her. The walk, the attitude, the hair . . . sure, I'm certain." He shook his head. "Pity," he said. "Such a pretty girl."

Bulldozer devoted the rest of the morning to Mauritzon, but as one o'clock approached he broke off the examination without having gotten a confession out of him. But Bulldozer was counting on Mauritzon's defenses collapsing soon, and anyway the evidence against him was certainly adequate. Mauritzon was allowed to call a lawyer, whereafter he was put into custody until such time as he could be formally placed under arrest.

All things considered, Bulldozer felt happy about his morning. He grabbed a quick lunch of flounder and mashed potatoes in the canteen and with renewed energy flung himself into his next task: the capture of the Mohrén gang.

Kollberg had had his work cut out. Major forces had been mobilized at the two main spots where the attack was expected: Rosenlundsgatan and the vicinity of the bank.

The mobile forces had orders to stand by around these two areas and at the same time to avoid drawing attention to themselves. Along the getaway route, too, vehicles were stationed that could quickly block it if the bank robbers, against all expectations, should get that far.

In the police headquarters on Kungsholmen there was not so much as a motorcycle. Parking lot and garage stood empty. All vehicles had been stationed in tactical positions about the town.

At the critical moment Bulldozer was to be in the police building, where he would be able to follow events over the radio and also receive the gangsters when they were brought in.

The members of the special squad were to be in and around the bank itself—all but Rönn. It was to be his job to keep an eye on Rosenlundsgatan.

At two o'clock Bulldozer drove around on a tour

of inspection in a gray "T"-registered Volvo Amazon. Perhaps there were a few too many police cars to be seen in the streets around Rosenlundsgatan, but around the bank there were no signs at all that it was under observation, and police cars were not noticeably numerous. Fully satisfied with these arrangements, Bulldozer drove back to Kungsholmsgatan to await the critical hour.

Now it was 2:45; but at Rosenlundsgatan all was quiet. One minute later nothing had happened at the police headquarters. When it was 2:50 and the bank, too, had not been attacked, it was clear this was not the day of the big coup.

For safety's sake Bulldozer waited until 3:30 before calling off the operation, whose planning and details they now had a whole week to polish up and correct. They all agreed, however, that things had gone according to plan: they all had done their jobs satisfactorily; the time schedule had worked; everyone had been at the right place at the right moment.

Only the day was wrong. But in a week's time it would all be repeated—if possible with even greater precision and efficiency.

Then, it was to be hoped, Malmström and Mohrén, too, would put in an appearance.

On that Friday, however, the very thing that everyone feared most of all occurred. The National Police Commissioner got it into his head that someone was going to throw an egg at the United States ambassador, or perhaps a tomato at the embassy, or set fire to the Star-Spangled Banner.

The security police were worried. They lived in a world of spooks, a world that swarmed with dangerous communists and bomb-throwing anarchists and hooligans who were trying to bring society to its senses by protesting against plastic milk bottles and the vandalization of the urban environment. The security police got most of their information from Ustasja and other fascist organizations, with whom they were delighted to collaborate in order to gain information about alleged left-wing activists.

The National Police Commissioner, personally,

was even more worried. For he knew something that even the security police still had not got wind of. Ronald Reagan was turning up. That hardly popular governor had already popped up in Denmark, where he had lunched with the Queen. It was not out of the question that he might drop in on Sweden, too, in which case his visit could hardly be kept a secret.

This was why the Vietnam demonstration, planned for that evening, came at a most inopportune moment. Many thousands of people were indignant about the bombing of North Vietnam's dikes and wholly unprotected villages, which for reasons of prestige had to be blasted back into the Stone Age. Some of these people had gathered at Hakberget to adopt a resolution. Afterwards it was their intention to hand the document to some doorman at the United States Embassy.

This must not be allowed to happen. The situation was delicate, the chief of the Stockholm Police was off duty, and the head of the riot police was away on vacation. Thousands of disturbers of the peace were threateningly close to the city's most sacrosanct building: the glass palace of the United States. In this situation the National Commissioner of Police made a historic decision. He was going to see to it, in person, that the demonstration went off peacefully. He personally would lead the procession to some safe spot, far from the dangerous neighborhood. This safe place was Humlegården Park, in the center of Stockholm. There the goddam resolution was to be read aloud, after which the demonstration was to be dissolved. The demonstrators, for their part, were peaceful enough and agreed to everything. The procession got going along Karlavägen. Every able-bodied policeman within in reach was mobilized to supervise the operation.

For example, Gunvald Larsson suddenly found himself sitting in a helicopter, staring down at the long line of people with banners and Viet Cong flags proceeding at a snail's pace northwards. He clearly saw what happened but could do little or nothing about it. Nor did he want to.

At the junction of Karlavägen and Sturegatan the National Police Commissioner, in person, led the procession straight into a large and extremely disgruntled crowd of soccer fans who were pouring out of the civic stadium, greatly displeased at the poor showing of the home team. The melee that ensued was reminiscent of the rout after Waterloo or the Pope's visit to Jerusalem. Within three minutes policemen of every kind were striking out right and left against everything and everyone: soccer fans, people taking a stroll in Humlegården, and pacifists—all of whom suddenly found nightsticks raining down on them, and motorcycle police and mounted detachments brutally forcing their way among them. Demonstrators and fans began fighting without knowing why, and in the end the uniformed police were knocking down their plainclothes colleagues. The National Police Commissioner himself had to be evacuated by helicopter.

Not, however, the one Gunvald Larsson was sitting in; for after a minute of this hullaballoo he said: "Fly off, dammit, anywhere you like, as long as it's far away."

A hundred people were arrested and many more were injured. None of them knew why. Stockholm was in chaos. And the National Police Commissioner said, out of pure habit: "None of this must be allowed to come out."

26

Martin Beck rode again—crouching low and at a gallop across a plain—surrounded by men in raglan coats. In front of him he saw the Russian artillery emplacement; the muzzle of a gun stuck out between the sandbags, staring at him. Death's black eye. He saw the shell coming straight toward him. It grew. It became bigger and bigger until it filled his whole field of vision —and then the image blackened. This must be Balaklava. Then he was standing on the bridge of "H.M.S. Lion." The "Indefatigable" and the "Queen Mary" had just blown up and been swallowed by the sea. A messenger rushed up and yelled: " 'Princess Royal' has blown up!" Beatty bent forward and said in a loud, calm voice, above the roar of battle: "Beck, there seems to be something wrong with our bloody ships today. Steer two points closer to the enemy."

Then came the usual scene with Garfield and Guiteau. He jumped off his horse, rushed through the railroad station, and caught the bullet in his body. At the very moment when he was breathing his last, the National Police Commissioner came up and affixed a medal to his shattered chest, unrolled something resembling a scroll of parchment, and said, rolling his *r*'s: "You've been prromoted to the rrank of Commissioner, salarry grrade B-thrree." The President lay in a heap on the platform, wearing his top hat. Then a wave of burning pain passed through him, and he opened his eyes.

He was lying, soaked in sweat, in his own bed. The clichés were getting worse and worse. This time Guiteau had looked like ex-Patrolman Eriksson, President Garfield like an elegantly turned out elderly gentleman, the National Police Commissioner like the National Police Commissioner, and Beatty as he did on the 1919 Peace Mug—surrounded by a laurel wreath and exuding a faintly arrogant air.

Otherwise his dream, this time too, had been full of absurdities and misquotations.

David Beatty had never said: "Turn two points nearer to the enemy." According to all available sources, his order had been: "Chatfield, there seems to be something wrong with our bloody ships today. Turn two points to port." In itself, of course, this made no difference. Two points to port, in this context, was the same as two points toward the enemy.

And in the previous dream, when Guiteau had looked like John Carradine, the pistol was a Hammerli International. Now, when he had resembled Eriksson, his gun had been a derringer. Furthermore, only Fitzroy James Henry Somerset, surely, had worn a raglan coat at Balaklava. There was neither rhyme nor reason to these dreams of his.

He got up, shed his pajamas, and took a shower. As the cold water gave him gooseflesh he thought of Rhea.

On his way to the subway he thought about his own odd behavior yesterday evening.

At his desk out at Västberga, all of a sudden he felt unpleasantly alone.

Kollberg came in and asked him how he was. It was a tricky question, and all he managed to reply was: "Oh, not too bad."

Kollberg left again, almost at once. He was sweating and was in a big rush. In the doorway he said: "That job on Hornsgatan seems to have been cleared up. What's more, we've a fine chance to catch Malmström and Mohrén red-handed. How's your locked room coming along, by the way?"

"Not too bad. Anyway, better than I'd expected."

"Really?" said Kollberg. Lingering a couple of seconds longer, he said: "I think you're looking a bit brighter today. So long."

"So long."

Then he was alone again. He began thinking about Svärd.

At the same time he thought about Rhea. She had

given him much more than he'd expected. From a policeman's point of view, that is. Three lines of thought, maybe four. Svärd was pathologically miserly. Always, at least for years, he had barricaded himself inside his apartment even though it had contained nothing of any value. Svärd had been ill and not long before his death had been admitted to a radium clinic.

Could Svärd have had some money stowed away somewhere? And if so, where?

Had Svärd been frightened of something? And if so, what? The only thing of any putative value inside his lair, barred and bolted, had been his own life.

What the devil had Svärd suffered from? The radium clinic suggested cancer. But if he had been a doomed man anyway, why had he been so concerned to protect himself against someone or something? Perhaps he'd been afraid of one particular person? In which case—of whom?

And why had he moved to a more expensive and presumably inferior apartment if he was really as stingy as everyone made out?

Questions—hard ones, but not altogether insoluble—questions hardly to be resolved in a couple of hours. More likely they'd take days. Why not weeks or months? Perhaps several years. Or maybe forever.

And what about that ballistic investigation? That's where he should make a start. Martin Beck reached for the phone. It was not in a helpful mood today. He had to dial six times, four of which ended with a "just a moment, please," and then went dead. But finally he got hold of the girl who had opened up Svärd's chest seventeen days earlier.

"Sure," she said. "Now I remember. There was a policeman who called me, grumbling about that bullet."

"Detective Inspector Rönn."

"I guess that was his name, yes. Don't remember. Anyway, it wasn't the same guy who had charge of the case earlier, Aldor Gustavsson, I mean. This one didn't seem so experienced. He began all his sentences with 'sure' or 'well.' "

"What happened then?"

"Well, as I told you last time, the police didn't seem all that interested to begin with. No one had

210

asked for a ballistic investigation until that northerner called up. I didn't really know what to do with the bullet. But . . ."

"Yes?"

"It seemed wrong to throw it away, so I stuffed it into an envelope and added my own comments, what it was all about, and so forth. Exactly as if it had been a real murder case. But I didn't send it over to the lab since I happen to know how overwhelmed with work they are there."

"What did you do then?"

"Put the envelope aside. Then I couldn't find it immediately. I'm new here, and I don't have a filing cabinet of my own, and so forth. But anyway I found it and sent it in."

"To be examined?"

"Well, it's not my business to ask for that kind of thing. But I assume that if the ballistics people get hold of a bullet they examine it, even when it's suicide."

"Suicide?"

"Sure, I made a note of that. The police said at once it was suicide."

"Well, in that case I'll have to call the lab," Martin Beck said. "But there's one more thing I wanted to ask you."

"What's that?"

"During the autopsy, did you notice anything special?"

"Sure, that he'd shot himself. That was in the police report."

"I was mostly thinking of something else. Did you find anything to suggest that Svärd had suffered from any serious illness?"

"No. His organs seemed healthy. But . . ."

"But?"

"But I didn't examine him all that closely. Just confirmed the cause of death. That was why I only looked at the thorax organs."

"Which means?"

"Heart and lungs, mostly. Nothing wrong with them. Apart from the fact that he was dead, that is."

"Otherwise he could have suffered from almost anything?"

211

"Certainly. Anything from gout to cancer of the liver. Say, why're you asking me so much about this? It was just a routine case, wasn't it?"

"Questions are part of our routine," Martin Beck said. He brought the conversation to an end and tried to contact one of the ballistics experts at the lab. He had no success and was finally obliged to call the head of the department himself. This was a man called Oskar Hjelm who, though he was an eminent criminologist, was above all a person disinclined to conversation.

"Oh, so it's you, is it?" Hjelm said sourly. "I thought you were going to be promoted to commissioner. But perhaps that was a vain hope."

"How so?"

"Commissioners sit thinking about their own careers," said Hjelm, "when they're not out playing golf or talking nonsense on television. Above all they don't ring me up and ask a lot of obvious questions. What is it now?"

"Just a ballistic checkup."

"Just? And which one, if I may ask? Any lunatic can send us something. We've heaps of objects under study here and no one to study them. The other day we received a toilet bucket from Melander. He wanted to know how many different individuals had shat in it. It was full to the brim, certainly hadn't been emptied for a couple of years."

"Not very nice."

Fredrik Melander was a detective working on the homicide squad who for many years had been one of Martin Beck's most valuable assistants. Some time back, however, he'd been transferred to the burglary squad, presumably in hopes that he might be able to do something about the total confusion prevailing there.

"No," said Hjelm. "Our work isn't nice. But no one seems to understand that. The National Police Commissioner hasn't so much as set foot in this place for several years, and when I asked to speak to him last spring he sent a message saying he was occupied for the foreseeable future."

"I know your life's hell," said Martin Beck.

"To say the least," said Hjelm, a trifle conciliatory

212

now. "You can hardly imagine how things are here, but we're always grateful for the least little bit of encouragement or understanding. Though we never get any, of course."

The fellow was an incurable grumbler, but clever and susceptible to flattery.

"It's a wonder you get by at all," Martin Beck said.

"More than that," said Hjelm, thoroughly amiable now. "It's a miracle. And now, what was this ballistic question?"

"It was about a bullet from a guy who was killed. A man called Svärd. Karl Edvin Svärd."

"Sure," said Hjelm. "I know that one. Typical story. Suicide, so it was alleged. The autopsy people sent it here without telling us what to do with it. Shall we have it gold-plated and sent to the police museum, or what? Or was it just a polite hint that we can just as well give up and shoot ourselves?"

"What sort of bullet was it?"

"A pistol bullet. Used. Haven't you got the weapon?"

"No."

"Then how can it be suicide?"

A good question. Martin Beck made a note on his pad. "Any special characteristics?"

"Well, one might suppose it came from a forty-five automatic. There are so many makes of them. But if you'll send us the empty cartridge we can tell you more about it."

"I haven't found the cartridge."

"Haven't you? What did this Svärd guy do after he'd shot himself, may I ask?"

"Don't know."

"People who have that kind of a bullet in their guts aren't usually so nimble," said Hjelm. "They don't have much choice, just lie down and die, for the most part."

"Yes," said Martin Beck. "Thanks very much."

"For what?"

"For your help. And good luck."

"No macabre jokes, if you please," Hjelm said. He put down the phone.

So that was that. Whether Svärd himself or some-one else had fired the lethal shot, he hadn't taken any risks. With a forty-five one can be pretty sure of obtain-ing the desired results, even if one doesn't quite hit the heart.

But what had this conversation yielded, really? A bullet isn't much in the way of evidence as long as one hasn't got the weapon or at least the cartridge. But there was one positive detail. Hjelm had said it was a forty-five automatic, and he was known for never mak-ing statements he couldn't substantiate. Therefore Svärd had been shot with an automatic.

All the rest was just as incomprehensible as be-fore. Svärd didn't seem to have committed suicide and no one else could have shot him.

Martin Beck went on with his work. He began with the banks, since experience had taught him this always took a lot of time. Though it's true bank secrecy in Sweden isn't what it should be, there were still hun-dreds of financial institutions to check. And with in-terest rates being so wretchedly low, many small savers preferred to place their funds in some other Scandina-vian country, usually Denmark.

He went on phoning: It was the police. It was about a person called so-and-so and with one or an-other of these addresses and the following social-secur-ity number. Had this person any kind of account or perhaps a safe deposit box?

Simple though this question was, there were many people it had to be put to. Besides which it was Friday, and the hour was approaching for all banks to close. To count on getting any answer before the be-ginning of next week at the earliest seemed unrealistic.

He would also like to know what the hospital Svärd had been admitted to had to say. But that would have to wait until Monday.

Now Friday was over as far as his duties were concerned. By this time Stockholm was in utter chaos. The police were hysterical, and large parts of the public were panic-stricken. Martin Beck didn't even know. That segment of the landscape he could see from his window consisted of a stinking highway and an industrial park, and—as a view—it was no more confused or repulsive than usual.

By seven o'clock he still hadn't gone home, even though his working day had ended two hours ago and there was nothing more he could do to further his investigations. The day's efforts had yielded only scanty results. The most tangible consequence was a slight pain in his right forefinger, from all his dialing.

His last official action of the day was to look up Rhea Nielsen in the telephone directory. Sure enough, her name was there. But there was no indication of a profession. His hand was already hovering over the dial when he realized there was nothing he could ask her about, at least not concerning the Svärd case.

As an official act, this call was sheer self-deception. The simple truth was, he wanted to hear whether she was at home; and the only question he really wanted to ask her was equally simple: Can I come over for a while?

Martin Beck removed his hand from the phone and stacked up the telephone directories in their usual place. Then he tidied up his desk, threw away pieces of paper bearing superfluous jottings, and put his pencils where they belonged, namely in their tray.

All this he did slowly and carefully, and in fact managed to take an astoundingly long time at it. He devoted the best part of half an hour to a ball-point pen whose retracting mechanism was broken before deciding it was useless and flinging it into the wastepaper basket.

The South Police Station was by no means deserted. Somewhere not far away he could hear a couple of colleagues discussing something in shrill, indignant voices. He was not the least bit curious about whatever it was they were talking about.

Leaving the building, he went to Midsommarkransen subway station, where he had to wait a rather long time for a train. It looked good enough on the outside, but the interior had been grossly vandalized —its seats were slashed and anything that could be removed, unscrewed, or ripped off was gone. He got off in the Old City, and went home.

215

After he had put on his pajamas he looked for some beer in the icebox and wine in the kitchen closet, knowing full well that he would find neither.

Martin Beck opened a can of Russian crab, made himself a couple of sandwiches, and took out a bottle of mineral water. There was nothing wrong with the food. But to sit there chewing it all alone was goddam dreary. Admittedly, it had been just as dreary late Wednesday; but then it hadn't mattered, so to speak.

Seized with a desire for activity, he went to bed with one of his many unread books. It happened to be Ray Parkins' documentary novel about the Battle of Lake Java. He read it through from start to finish and thought it poor. He couldn't understand why it had been translated into Swedish and looked to see which publisher was responsible. Norstedts. Odd.

In *The Two-Ocean War* Samuel Eliot Morison had treated the same subject more exhaustively and in an infinitely more exciting manner in nine pages than Parkins had succeeded in doing in two hundred and fifty-seven.

Before dropping off to sleep he thought of spaghetti bolognese. At the same time he felt something like expectation about the next day.

It must have been this unmotivated feeling that caused Saturday and Sunday to seem so insufferably empty of all content. For the first time in years he felt restless and painfully shut in. He went out. On Sunday he even took the steamer out to Mariefred, though that did not help. Even outdoors he still felt just as shut in. Something was basically wrong with his existence, something he wasn't prepared to accept as equably as he had before. Observing people all around him, he gained the impression that many of them were in the same predicament he was, though they either didn't realize it or wouldn't admit it to themselves.

On Monday morning he rode again. Guiteau looked like Carradine and shot with a forty-five automatic, and when Martin Beck had carried out his ritual sacrifice Rhea Nielsen came up to him and asked: "What the hell are you up to?"

Later he was sitting in the South Police Station belaboring the telephone. He began with the radium clinic.

In the end he got his answer, but it was not a very satisfactory one. Svärd had been admitted on Monday, March 6. But the following day he had been transferred to the communicable disease clinic of South Hospital. Why?

"Not easy to say, so long afterwards," said the secretary who had finally managed to find Svärd's name among her papers. "He was obviously no case for us. We haven't got his records here, just a note that he'd been sent to us by a private doctor."

"Which private doctor?"

"Dr. Berglund, a general practitioner. Yes, here it is. Can't read what's written on the admittance slip, you know what doctors' handwriting is like. And it's a bad photostat anyway."

"But the address?"

"His office? Odengatan 30."

"So that's legible, at least," said Martin Beck.

"It's embossed," said the secretary laconically.

Dr. Berglund's automatic telephone-answering machine informed him that the office was closed and would not be opening again until the fifteenth of August. The doctor, of course, was on vacation.

Martin Beck, however, was not disposed to wait for more than a month to find out what illness Svärd had suffered from. So he called up South Hospital, which is an enormous place with heavy telephone traffic. It took him more than two hours to get it confirmed that Karl Edvin Svärd had in fact been admitted to the communicable disease clinic in March—to be precise, from Tuesday the seventh to Saturday the eighteenth, when, as far as could be determined, he had gone home.

But had he been released as healthy or mortally ill? To get an answer to this question seemed impossible: the doctor in charge was on duty, but busy, and couldn't come to the phone. The time had obviously come for Martin Beck to resume his visits.

He took a taxi to South Hospital and after wandering around for a while found the right corridor. Only ten minutes later he was sitting in the office of the person who ought to know all about Svärd's state of health.

The doctor was a man of about forty, small of stature, dark-haired, and with neutral-colored eyes—blue-gray with a touch of green and light brown. While Martin Beck searched his pockets for some non-existent cigarettes, the man put on a pair of horn-rimmed spectacles and became absorbed in his records. After ten minutes of total silence he pushed his spectacles up onto his forehead, looked at his visitor, and said: "Yes, yes. And what was it you wanted to know?"

"What was Svärd's illness?"

"None at all."

Martin Beck pondered this somewhat surprising statement. Then he said: "Then why was he in here for almost two weeks?"

"Eleven days, to be exact. We gave him a thorough checkup. For he had certain symptoms and had been sent to us by a private doctor."

"Dr. Berglund?"

"Right. The patient himself thought he was seriously ill. He had a couple of minor swellings on his neck and a lump on the left side of his midriff. It could be felt clearly, even by pressing it only lightly. Like so many other people, he'd got it into his head that he had cancer. He went to a private doctor, who found the symptoms alarming. The fact is, general practitioners rarely have access to the equipment necessary to diagnose cases of this kind. Nor is their judgment always of the best. In this case an erroneous diagnosis was made, and the patient was immediately sent to the radium clinic. There they could only note that no valid diagnosis had been made, and so he was sent to us. Here he went through a whole series of examinations. We always examine patients very thoroughly."

"And the result was that Svärd had nothing wrong with him?"

"By and large, yes. Those things on his neck we could dismiss at once. They were just ordinary fat formations, quite harmless. The lump on his midriff needed more careful investigation. Among other things we had a complete aortography done and also X-rayed his whole digestive system. Further, we made a complete liver biopsy and—"

"What's that?"

"Liver biopsy? To put it simply, we put a tube into the patient's side and extract a piece of his liver. As a matter of fact, I did it myself. Then the sample was sent to the laboratory, and they looked to see whether there were, for example, any cancer cells. Well, we found nothing of that kind. The lump turned out to be an isolated cyst on the colon—"

"I beg your pardon?"

"The gut. A cyst, as I say. Nothing to imperil his life. In itself, it could be removed by an operation, but we didn't think such intervention necessary. The patient suffered no discomfort from it. True, he said he had earlier had severe pains, but those were obviously of a psychosomatic nature." The doctor paused, threw Martin Beck a glance of the kind one usually reserves for children and other hopelessly uneducated people, and explained: "Imaginary pains, that is."

"Did you have any personal contact with Svärd?"

"Sure. I spoke to him every day, and before he was allowed to go home we had a long talk."

"How did he react?"

"First he behaved as if he was suffering from the disease he imagined. He was convinced he was suffering from incurable cancer and would die very soon. Didn't think he had much more than a month to live."

"And in fact he didn't," said Martin Beck.

"Really? Was he run over?"

"Shot. It's possible he committed suicide."

The doctor took off his glasses and wiped them thoughtfully on a corner of his white coat. "The latter suggestion strikes me as utterly improbable," he said.

"Oh, and why?"

"Before we let Svärd go home I had, as I've already said, a long talk with him. He was enormously relieved when it dawned on him he was healthy. Earlier, he'd been in a terrible state. But now he changed altogether. He became happy, quite simply. We had already seen how his pains disappeared as soon as we'd given him some very weak pain killers. Pills that—just between ourselves—cannot alleviate any real physical pain whatsoever."

"So you think he can't have committed suicide?"

"He wasn't the type."

"What type was he, then?"

"I'm not a psychiatrist, but mostly I got the impression of him being a hard, shut-in man. I know the staff here had a certain amount of trouble with him and thought him demanding and querulous. But these traits didn't appear until the last few days, after he'd realized his complaint constituted no threat to his life."

Martin Beck pondered. Then he said: "I suppose you don't know whether he had any visitors while he was here?"

"No. I can't say I do. He told me he had no friends."

Martin Beck got up. "Thanks," he said. "That's all I wanted to know. Good-bye."

He got as far as the door when the doctor said: "About visitors and friends, there's something I've just thought of."

"What's that?"

"Well, Svärd had a relative, whom he heard from. A nephew. He called up during my telephone hour and asked how his uncle was."

"And what did you reply?"

"This nephew of his called just at the moment our examinations were finished. So I could give him the happy news that Svärd was in good health and still had every prospect of living for many years."

"How did the man react?"

"He seemed astonished. Obviously Svärd had convinced him, too, that he was gravely ill and would hardly survive his hospitalization."

"Did this nephew tell you his name?"

"Presumably, but I don't remember it."

"One other thing strikes me," Martin Beck said. "Don't people usually give the name and address of their next of kin when they enter the hospital, or some friend, just in case they . . ." He left his sentence hanging in the air.

"Sure. Quite right," said the doctor and put on his glasses again. "Let's see. There ought to be a name here. Yes, here it is."

"What is it?"
"Rhea Nielsen."

Martin Beck walked through Tantolunden Park, deep in thought. No one robbed him, or clobbered him on the head. All he saw were flocks of drunks, who lay spread out there behind the bushes, presumably waiting to be taken care of.

Now he really had got something to think about. Karl Edvin Svärd had not had any brothers or sisters. So how could he have a nephew?

Now Martin Beck had a reason to go to Tulegatan, this Monday evening, and he was in fact almost there.

But when he'd gotten as far as Central Station, where he was to change trains, he changed his mind and went back two stations to get off at Slussen. Then he walked along Skeppsbron Quay to see whether there were any interesting boats to look at. But few were in.

Suddenly he noticed he was hungry. Since he'd forgotten to do his shopping, he went to a restaurant called The Golden Peace and—under the gaze of a number of tourists who kept on tormenting the personnel with idiotic questions about which famous people were seated where—ate some ham. Last year he had himself contrived to become rather well-known, but people's memories are short, and by this time his celebrity had had time to fade.

As he paid his bill, he had reason to note that this was his first restaurant meal for some time. During his period of abstinence the prices, already exorbitant, had gotten ridiculous.

Home again, he felt more restless than ever and wandered about the little apartment for a long while before retiring with a book; a book that was neither boring enough to send him to sleep nor interesting enough to keep him awake. About three o'clock he got up and took a couple of sleeping pills, something from which he usually abstained. They quickly knocked him out, and when he woke up he still felt groggy. Yet he had long overslept his usual hour and hadn't dreamt at all.

Once back in his office he began the day's investigations by thoroughly reading through his own notes. This kept him busy until lunch, which consisted of a cup of tea and some dry toast.

Then he went to the bathroom and washed his hands. When he came back, something happened: the phone rang.

"Inspector Beck?"

"Yes."

"This is Handelsbanken." The man said which branch of the bank he worked at and went on: "We received an inquiry from you about a client called Karl Edvin Svärd."

"Yes?"

"He has an account with us."

"Is there any money in it?"

"Yes. A considerable sum."

"How much?"

"About sixty thousand. It's . . ." The man fell silent.

"What were you about to say?" Martin Beck asked.

"Well, in my opinion there's something odd about this account."

"Have you got the papers there?"

"Certainly."

"Then I can come and look at them at once?"

"Naturally. Just ask for me. My name is Bengtsson. I'm the manager."

It was a relief to get moving. The bank was on the corner of Odengatan and Sveavägen. In spite of all the traffic he was there in less than half an hour.

The manager was right. There was something odd about Svärd's account.

Martin Beck sat at a table behind the counter, studying the documents and for once feeling grateful for a system that gave the police and other authorities unrestricted access to people's private affairs.

The bank manager said: "The striking thing about it, of course, is that this client has a checking account. It would have been more natural for him to have, for instance, a savings account, which yields a higher rate of interest."

This observation was correct. But even more striking was the regularity with which the sum of seven hundred and fifty kronor had been deposited. The entries were always made between the fifteenth and the twentieth of every month.

"As far as I can see," Martin Beck said, "this money was not paid in directly to this branch."

"No, never. The deposits were always made somewhere else. If you'll take a look, Inspector, you'll see they were always made at other branches, often branches of banks other than ours. Technically it makes no difference, since the money always ended up in Svärd's checking account here with us. But there almost seems to be a system behind these constant changes."

"You mean Svärd put the money in himself but didn't want to be recognized?"

"Well, that would be the first thing one would think of, yes. When you put money into your checking account, after all, you don't have to state who made the deposit."

"Though you have to fill in a deposit slip, don't you?"

"Not necessarily. Plenty of people are unfamiliar with the system, and in that case the teller usually fills in the name, the account number, and the number of the branch. It's all part of our service to our clients."

"But what happens to the slip?"

"The client gets a copy, which is his receipt. When the payment is made into the client's own account the bank doesn't send him any notification. Notifications are only sent when asked for."

"Then where are all the originals?"

"They are filed centrally."

Martin Beck let his finger run down the rows of figures. Then he said: "Didn't Svärd ever take out any money?"

"No, and in my view that's the oddest thing of all. He has never drawn a single check on this account, and now that I've looked into the matter it also appears he never even had a checkbook. At least not for years."

Martin Beck rubbed his nose energetically. No checkbook had been found at Svärd's place, nor were there any copies of deposit slips or notifications from the bank.

"Was Svärd known by sight here?"

"No. None of us had ever seen him."

"How old is this account?"

"It seems to have been opened in April, 1966."

"And since then seven hundred and fifty kronor have been coming in every month?"

"Yes. Though the last deposit is dated March 16." The man looked at his calendar. "That was a Thursday. The next month no money came in."

"The explanation is quite simple," Martin Beck said. "It was about then that Svärd died."

"Oh? We've had no notification to that effect. In such cases the deceased's relatives usually communicate with us."

"He doesn't seem to have had any."

The bank manager looked bewildered.

"Until now," Martin Beck said. "Good morning."

He realized he'd better get going before the bank was robbed. If that were to happen while he was on the premises he could hardly help becoming entangled in the activities of the special squad. And that kind of entanglement he'd certainly rather avoid.

New aspects to the case. Seven hundred and fifty a month for six years! That was a singularly regular income, and since Svärd had never taken anything out, quite a large sum of money had gradually accumulated in the mysterious account: Fifty-four thousand kronor.

To Martin Beck that was a lot of money. For Svärd it must have been even more, almost a fortune.

So Rhea had not been that far from the truth when she'd talked about money in his mattress. The only difference was that Svärd had been more rational; he had kept up with the times.

This new development spurred Martin Beck to fresh activity. The next step would be to have a word with the tax authorities, for one thing; and, for another, to take a look at such deposit slips as might have been filed.

The Internal Revenue people knew nothing of Svärd. There he had been regarded as a pauper, and the authorities had contented themselves with that refined form of exploitation called value-added tax on foodstuffs—a tax that has been arranged with a special view to hitting those who have already been knocked out.

Well, Svärd had certainly not earned his money by hard work, and the notion that anyone in his position could have saved it from his pension was absurd.

And the deposit slips, then?

The head office of the bank quickly produced the last twenty-two of them—all in all there should have been seventy-two, if he had counted correctly—and that same afternoon Martin Beck was already sitting and staring at them. They all came from various branch offices, and they all looked as if they had been written in different handwritings, accepted without question by as many different cashiers. By and by it would of course be possible to visit these people and ask whether they remembered the client. But this would consume an enormous amount of time, without any great likelihood of yielding results.

Who could be expected to remember a person who had deposited seven hundred and fifty kronor into his own checking account many months before? The answer was simple: no one.

A little later Martin Beck was home again, drinking tea out of his 1919 Peace Mug. He looked at it and thought that if the mysterious man who had made all these payments into his account looked like Field Marshal Haig, anyone would have been able to recognize him. But who looked like Haig? No one, not even in the most pretentious films or plays.

This evening, again, things were somehow different. He was still restless and unsatisfied, but this time it was due in some way to his not being able to tear his thoughts away from his job: Svärd; that idiotic locked room; the mysterious man who had paid in all that money.

Who was he? Could it have been Svärd himself, in spite of everything? No. It seemed most improbable that Svärd should have put himself to all that trouble. And it also seemed improbable that Svärd himself, a mere warehouseman, would ever have hit on the idea of opening a checking account.

No, the money had been paid in by someone else. Probably a man, since it was less likely that a woman had gone into the bank, given her name as Karl Edvin Svärd, and said she wanted to put seven hundred and fifty kronor into her own checking account. . . .

But why should anyone want to give Svärd money, anyway? That was a question he must leave temporarily unanswered.

Then there was another misty figure he had to reckon with. The mysterious nephew.

And least tangible of all was the person who— sometime in April or early May—had managed to shoot Svärd, even though the latter was in a veritable fortress, a room locked from the inside.

Was it possible, perhaps, that these three had all been the same person? The man who had made the payments, the nephew, and the murderer? Well, that was a question worth brooding on at some length.

He put aside his mug and looked at the clock. Time had passed quickly—half past nine already. Too late to go anywhere. Anyway, where had he been thinking of going?

Martin Beck picked out a Bach record and turned on the record player. Then he went and lay down.

He went on thinking. If all gaps and question marks were ignored, a story could be assembled out of what he now knew. The nephew, the man who had paid in the money, and the murderer were one and the same person. Svärd was a petty blackmailer who for six years had been forcing this person to pay him seven hundred and fifty kronor a month. But being pathologically stingy, Svärd had never used any of the money, and his victim had gone on paying, year after year. But in the end the latter had had enough.

Martin Beck found no particular difficulty in imagining Svärd as a blackmailer. But a blackmailer must have something on his victim, must constitute a latent threat to the person he extorts money from. In his own apartment Svärd had had nothing that could incriminate anyone. Of course, he might have rented a safe-deposit box in some bank. In which case it would soon come to the attention of the police.

In any case, a blackmailer had to be in possession

226

of some kind of information. Where could a warehouseman get such information? Where he worked. Possibly in the house he lived in. As far as anyone knew, these were the only two places where Svärd had any human contact. At home and at his job.

But Svärd had stopped working in June, 1966; two months earlier the first payment had been made into his checking account. All this had happened more than six years ago. What had Svärd been doing since?

The record was still going around and around when he woke up. If he'd dreamed anything, he'd forgotten it.

Wednesday—and he was quite clear how his work should start: with a walk.

But not to the subway. His office at Västberga did not attract him, and today he felt he had excellent reasons for not going to it. Instead, he thought he'd take a little stroll along the quays, and began by walking southwards along Skeppsbron, across Slussen and on eastwards along Stadsgården Quay.

This was the part of Stockholm he'd always been fondest of. Particularly when he was a child—when all the ships had tied up here with their cargoes from near and far. Nowadays the real ships were few and far between, their day was past, and the Åland ferries, with their bars and drunks, had replaced them. A poor substitute. The old guard of stevedores and seamen, too, who in those days had given this part of the harbor much of its charm, were beginning to die out.

Today, again, he was feeling a little different. He enjoyed, for example, walking in the fresh air, walking briskly, knowing where he was going and letting his thoughts run free.

He reflected on the persistent rumors about his own promotion and felt more troubled about them than before. Right up to his wretched mistake, fifteen months ago, Martin Beck had been afraid of precisely this: that he'd be given a job that would tie him to his desk. He'd always liked working out in the field—or at least to be able to come and go as he wished.

The thought of an office with a conference table, two "genuine oil paintings," a swivel chair, armchairs for visitors, a cheap rug, and his own private secretary,

227

all this was a good deal more terrifying today than it had been a week ago. Not because the rumors struck him as well-founded, but because he had begun to think about the consequences. Perhaps, in spite of everything, what he made of his life wasn't entirely meaningless?

Half an hour of brisk walking and he reached his goal. The warehouse was an old one. Not being designed for container traffic or suitable to modern requirements, it was soon to be torn down.

Inside, very little was going on. The office where the chief warehouseman should have been sitting was empty, and the glass panes through which that important personage had formerly supervised the work were dusty. One was broken, in fact, and the calendar on the wall was two years out of date.

A forklift truck was standing beside a not very impressive stack of piece goods, and behind it were two men—one wearing orange overalls and the other a gray coat.

Each was sitting on a plastic beer case, and another case, upside down, stood between them. One of the two men was quite young; the other looked as if he might be about seventy, though that seemed improbable. The younger man was reading yesterday's evening paper as he smoked a cigarette. The older was doing nothing at all.

Both looked up at Martin Beck lackadaisically, and the younger marked his arrival by dropping his cigarette on the floor and stamping it out with his heel.

"Smoking in the warehouse," said the older man, shaking his head. "That would have been . . ."

"In the old days . . ." the young man said, bored. "But we aren't living in the old days, now; haven't you dug that yet, you old thief?" Turning to Martin Beck, he said in an unfriendly voice: "What do you want? This is private property. It's even written on the door. Can't you read?"

Martin Beck took out his wallet and showed his card.

"Cop," said the younger man with distaste.

The other said nothing, contenting himself with staring at the floor, clearing his throat, and spitting.

"How long have you been working here?" Martin Beck asked.

"Seven days," the younger man said. "And to-morrow it's over. I'm going back to the truck terminal. But what d'you want here?"

Martin Beck didn't reply.

Without waiting for him to speak, the man went on: "Soon all this'll be over and done with, see? But my friend here can remember when there was twenty-five men and two bosses inside this goddam old shack. Don't you, grandpa?"

"Then he probably remembers a man named Svärd. Karl Edvin Svärd."

The older man threw Martin Beck an empty glance and said: "What of it? I don't know nothing."

It wasn't hard to explain the old man's attitude. Someone from the office must already have told him the police were looking for people who'd known Svärd.

Martin Beck said: "Svärd's dead and buried."

"Oh? Dead, is he? In that case I remember him."

"Don't sit there boasting, grandpa," the other man said. "When Johansson was here asking questions the other day, you didn't remember a bloody thing about it. Anyway, you're gaga." Obviously regarding Martin Beck as utterly harmless, he shamelessly lit another cigarette and added, by way of information: "The old boy's gaga, that's for sure. Next week he's getting laid off, and starting in January he'll be getting his pension. If he lives that long, that is."

"I've a very good memory," the old man said, somewhat offended. "You bet I remember Kalle Svärd. But no one told me he was dead."

Martin Beck said nothing.

"Even the cops can't push dead people around," the man said philosophically.

The younger man got up and, taking the beer case he'd been sitting on with him, went over to the door. "Isn't that goddam truck coming soon," he snorted, "so I can get out of this old-age home?" He went outside and sat down in the sunshine.

"What kind of a guy was Kalle Svärd?" Martin Beck asked.

The man shook his head. Again he cleared his

229

throat and spat; but this time it wasn't by way of innuendo, though his phlegm landed only an inch or so from Martin Beck's right shoe.

"What kind of a guy . . . is that what you want to know?"

"Yes."

"Sure he's dead?"

"Sure."

"In that case I can tell you, sir, that Kalle Svärd was the biggest goddam pain in the ass I've ever met."

"How so?"

The man gave a hollow laugh. "In every goddam lousy way a man can be! I've never worked together with worse, and that's saying a lot, seeing as I'm a man who's sailed the seven seas, yessir! Not even drones like that guy out there could match Kalle Svärd. And yet it's types like that who've turned a decent profession into donkey work." He nodded toward the door.

"Was there anything special about Svärd?"

"Special? Sure he was special, like hell he was! First and foremost he was the laziest bastard there ever was. No one could wriggle out of work like he did. And no one was so stingy, or less willing to stick up for his mates. He wouldn't have given a dying man a drop of water, he wouldn't." The man fell silent. Then he added slyly: "Though he was good in some ways."

"In which ways?"

The man's gaze wavered a little, and he hesitated before answering: "Bah! Licking the foremen's asses, he was good at that. And letting others do his job for him. And making out he was ill. Didn't he get himself pensioned off before his time, even before they started laying people off?"

Martin Beck sat down on the beer case. "There was something else you were going to say," he said.

"Was I?"

"Yes, what was it?"

"Is it sure Kalle's kicked the bucket?"

"Yes, he'd dead. Word of honor."

"Cops ain't got no honor, and one shouldn't really talk ill of the dead. But I've always thought it don't make no difference, much, providing a guy stands solid with them as is alive."

"My view exactly," Martin Beck said. "What was it Kalle Svärd was so good at?"

"He was real smart at breaking into the right crates, see. Though he usually did it during his overtime, so no one else didn't get nothing out of it."

Martin Beck got up. This was news; and certainly the only news this man had to give him. To know which crates to break into had always been a matter of importance in this job—something of a professional trick and trade secret. Liquor, tobacco, and foodstuffs can so easily get damaged in transit. Also various salable articles of the right size.

"Sure, sure," said the old man. "So that slipped out of me, did it? And I guess that's what you wanted to know. And now you can beat it. So long, comrade."

Karl Edvin Svärd might not have been popular, but no one could say his mates hadn't stood up for him, at least as long as he was alive.

"Good-bye," the man said. "Good-bye, good-bye."

Martin Beck had taken a step toward the door and was already opening his mouth to say "thanks very much" or something of that sort. Instead he halted and went back to the case. "I think I'll just sit here and talk a while," he said.

"What's that?" said the man, looking up.

"Pity we haven't a couple of beers. But I can go and get some."

The old man stared at him. Gradually the resignation drained from his eyes and was replaced by astonishment. "What's that?" he said again, suspiciously. "You want to sit and talk with me?"

"Sure."

"I've got some," the man said. "Beer, that is. Under that case you're sitting on."

Martin Beck got up, and the man took out a couple of cans of beer.

"Is it okay if I pay?" Martin Beck asked.

"To me it seems goddam okay. Though it's all the same."

Martin Beck took out a five-kronor bill, handed it over, sat down, and said: "So you've been at sea, you said. When did you first sign on?"

"Nineteen twenty-two, in Sundsvall. On a schooner called 'Fram.' Skipper's name was Jansson—a bastard, if ever there was one."

After they'd chatted a while, and each had opened another can of beer, the younger man came back, stared at them in amazement, and said: "Are you really a cop?"

Martin Beck didn't reply.

"You ought to be bloody well reported," he said and went back to his place in the sun.

Martin Beck didn't leave until the truck had arrived, more than an hour later. Their talk had been rewarding. It was often interesting, listening to old workers, and Martin Beck couldn't understand why almost no one took time to do so. This man had seen a lot of things, both ashore and at sea. Why didn't such people ever get a word in on the mass media? Didn't politicians and technocrats ever listen to what they had to say? Certainly not; for if they did, many fateful errors in matters to do with employment and the environment could have been avoided.

As for the Svärd case, here was another loose end for him to look into. But at this particular moment Martin Beck didn't feel up to it. He wasn't used to drinking three cans of beer before lunch, and already they had begun to take effect in a faint dizziness and an aching head.

At Slussen he took a taxi to the Central Baths, where he sat in the sauna for fifteen minutes, then for ten more, and took two snorting headers into the cooling bath—concluding these exercises by sleeping for an hour on the pallet in his cubicle.

The cure had the desired effect. When, shortly after lunch, he arrived at the forwarding agent's office on Skeppsbron, he was once again perfectly lucid. He had a request to make, a request he didn't expect anyone to understand. And in fact they reacted as he'd expected.

"Damages in transit?"

"Precisely."

"Well, of course things get damaged in transit. Naturally! Do you know how many tons of goods we handle every year?"

A rhetorical question. All they wanted was to get rid of him as quickly as possible. But he wasn't letting go.

"Nowadays of course, with the new systems, much less gets damaged, though when it does happen it's more costly. Container traffic. . . ."

Martin Beck wasn't interested in container traffic. What he was curious about was the goings-on in Svärd's day.

"Six years ago?"

"Yes, or earlier. Let's say during nineteen sixty-five and sixty-six."

"It's very unreasonable of you to expect us to answer questions like that. As I've said, goods were much more often damaged in the old warehouses. Sometimes whole cases got smashed, though of course the insurance always took care of the losses. It was rare for any individual warehouseman to be called to account. Now and again, I guess, someone was fired, though usually it was the temporary hands. Anyway, accidents simply couldn't be avoided."

Nor did he want to know whether anyone had been fired. Instead, he asked whether any record had been kept of the damages that had occurred, and if so by whom.

"Sure. By the foreman, of course. He made a note of it in the warehouse daybook."

"Do you still have these daybooks?"

"Possibly."

"In that case, where?"

"In some old box up in the attic. It would be impossible to find them, at least not straight off the cuff like this."

The firm was antediluvian. Its head offices had always been in this building in the Old City. They must have tons of old papers stowed away. But Martin Beck went on insisting. He quickly became highly unpopular. It was a price he didn't mind paying. After another brief altercation concerning the exact meaning of the word "impossible," the people in the office realized that probably the simplest way to get rid of him was to do what he asked.

A young man was sent up to the attic. Almost
233

immediately he returned empty-handed and with a look of resignation on his face. Martin Beck noticed that the young man's jacket wasn't even dusty. He offered to accompany him personally on his next foray.

It was extremely hot up in the attic, and the dust swirled around them like fog. Otherwise it all went easily enough. After half an hour they'd found the right box. The daybooks and ledgers were of the old-fashioned clothbound type, with cracked cardboard covers. Their labels bore the numbers of the various warehouses as well as the years. All in all they found five volumes with the right numbers and dates—from the second half of 1965 and the first six months of 1966.

The young clerk did not look so tidy now. His jacket was ripe for the cleaners, and his face was streaked with dust and sweat.

Down in the office everyone looked at the daybooks with amazement and distaste. No, they didn't want a receipt for them; indeed they couldn't care less whether they ever saw them again.

"I do hope I've been no trouble," Martin Beck said blithely.

They stared listlessly after him as he departed, his booty under his arm.

He made no pretense of having increased the popularity of the country's "largest public service organization," as the National Police Commissioner, in a statement that—even within the force—had aroused an amazement bordering on dismay, had recently called the police.

At Västberga Martin Beck took the volumes out to the bathroom and wiped them off. Then he washed himself, went to his room, and sat down to read them. It was three o'clock when he began, and five when he felt he'd finished.

Though largely incomprehensible to any uninitiated person, the warehouse ledgers had been fairly well kept. The jottings went on from day to day, noting in abbreviated terminology the quantities of goods handled.

But what Martin Beck was looking for was there too. At irregular intervals there were notes of goods damaged. For example:

Gds dmgd in transit, 1 case cans of soup, fr recptn
Svanberg Wholesalers, Huvudstagat. 16, Solna.

Such a note always indicated the type of merchandise and who it was for. On the other hand, there was never any note of the extent of the damage, its nature, or who had caused it.

Admittedly, such accidents had not happened very often. But liquor, foodstuffs, and other consumer articles constituted the overwhelming majority.

Martin Beck transferred all the damage reports into his own notebook. And their dates. Altogether they added up to some fifty entries. When he'd done with the ledgers, he carried the whole pile out to the office and wrote on a slip of paper that they were to be mailed back to the forwarding agents. On top of it all he put one of the white police correspondence cards with the message: "Thanks for your help! Beck."

On his way to the subway station he reflected that this would give the forwarding agency another shipment to handle, a sadistic thought that he was surprised to note aroused in him a certain childish glee.

While waiting for a vandalized subway train he reflected on modern container traffic. To lose a steel container full of bottles of cognac and then smash it in order to lovingly gather up the fragments that remained in buckets and gasoline cans was now out of the question. In containers, on the other hand, today's gangster syndicates could smuggle in literally anything, and were daily doing so. The Customs Bureau had lost all control over these events and therefore occupied itself with senselessly persecuting individual travelers who might have a few packs of cigarettes or an undeclared bottle of whisky in their baggage.

He changed trains at Central Station and got off at the College of Commerce.

In the state liquor store on Surbrunnsgatan the woman behind the counter stared suspiciously at his jacket, dusty and crumpled from his foray into the basement.

"I'd just like a couple of bottles of red wine, please," he said.

Instantly her hand went under the counter to press

the button that lit up the red control light. "Your identity card, please," she said grimly.

He showed his card, and she blushed slightly, as if victimized by an unusually stupid and indecent practical joke.

Then he went home to Rhea.

After pulling the bell rope once, Martin Beck felt if the door was open. It was locked. But inside the foyer the light was on, and after half a minute or so he tried again.

She came and opened. Today she was wearing brown corduroy trousers and a funny sort of pale-mauve shift that reached halfway down her thighs. "Oh, it's you, is it?" she said grumpily.

"Yes. May I come in?"

She looked at him. "Okay." She turned her back.

He followed her into the foyer. After two steps she halted and stood there, her head bowed. She went back to the door and unlocked it—then changed her mind and locked it again. Finally she went ahead into the kitchen.

"I've bought a couple of bottles of wine."

"Put them in the closet," she said, sitting down at the kitchen table. On it lay two open books, some papers, a pen, and a pink eraser. He took his bottles out of the bag and put them away.

With a sideways glance she said, annoyed: "What d'you want to go and buy such expensive wine for?"

He sat down opposite her. Looking him straight in the eyes, she said: "Svärd, eh?"

"No," he said at once. "Though I'm using him as a pretext."

"Do you have to have a pretext?"

"Yes, I do."

"Okay," she said. "Then we'll make some tea." She pushed aside her books and began banging about with her pots and pans. "Actually I'd intended to study this evening," she said. "But it doesn't matter. It's so goddam miserable being on one's own. Had dinner?"

"No."

"Good. Then I'll make us something." She stood with her legs apart, one hand on her hip, with the other scratching her neck. "Rice," she said. "That'll do fine.

I'll make some rice, and then we can mix it up with something to make it taste better."

"Sure, that sounds fine."

"It'll take a little while, though. Twenty minutes maybe. We'll have tea first." She set out some cups, poured the tea, and sat down, Holding the cup in her broad hands she blew on her tea, meanwhile peering at him over the rim—still a trifle glum.

"By the way, you were right about Svärd. He had money in the bank. Quite a lot."

"Mmm," she said.

"Someone was paying him seven hundred and fifty kronor a month. Have you any idea who that could have been?"

"No. He didn't know anyone, did he?"

"Why did he move out?"

She shrugged her shoulders. "The only explanation I can think of is that he didn't like it here. He was a queer guy. Several times he complained of my not locking the street door earlier in the evenings. I guess he thought the whole house existed only for him."

"Sure, that's about right."

She sat silent a long while. Then she said: "What's right? Is there anything interesting about Svärd?"

"Whether you'll think it's interesting or not I can't tell," said Martin Beck. *"Someone* must have shot him."

"Queer," she said. "Tell me." Again she began busying herself with her saucepans, but at the same time she listened carefully to what he had to tell her. From time to time, though she didn't interrupt, she frowned. When he'd finished, she burst out into uproarious laughter. "Marvelous!" she said. "Don't you ever read detective stories?"

"No."

"I read heaps of them. Anything. And forget most of it as soon as I've finished. But that's a classic. A room locked on the inside—there are some major studies of just that kind of thing. I read one not long ago. Wait a moment—and get out some bowls. Take the soya from the shelf. Lay the table nicely."

He did his best. She was out of the room for a few minutes. When she came back she had some kind of a magazine in her hand. Laying it open beside her bowl, she began spooning out food. "Eat," she commanded. "While it's hot."

"Tasty," he said.

"Mmmm," she said. "Success again." She gulped down a sizable portion, then looked into the magazine and said: "Listen to this. 'The Locked Room: A Study.' It contains three possibilities, A, B, and C. A: The crime has been committed in a locked room, which is really and truly locked and from which the murderer has disappeared, since there's no murderer inside it. B: The crime has been committed inside a room, which only seems to be hermetically closed and from which there is some more-or-less ingenious way of getting out. C: The crime has been committed by a murderer who stays inside, hidden.

She spooned up some more food. "Category C seems to be out of the question," she said. "No one can remain hidden for two months with only half a can of cat food to live on. But there are lots of subsections. For example, A5: Murder with the help of animals. Or B2: Someone has gotten in through the hinge side of the door, leaving lock and bolt intact, after which the hinge is again screwed back into place."

"Who wrote it?"

She looked. "Göran Sundholm, his name is. He quotes others too. A7 isn't so bad either: Murder by illusion, by erroneous sequence in time. A good variant is A9: The victim is dealt the deathblow somewhere else, whereupon he goes to the room in question and locks himself in before dying. Read it for yourself."

She handed him the magazine. Martin Beck glanced through it, then laid it aside.

"Who's doing the dishes?" she asked.

He got up and began clearing the table.

She lifted up her legs and sat with her heels on the seat of her chair and her arms around her knees. "After all, you're the detective," she said. "It ought to amuse you when something out of the ordinary

238

happens. Do you think it was the murderer who called the hospital?"

"Don't know."

"Seems likely to me." She shrugged. "Of course the whole thing's as simple as can be," she said.

"Probably." He heard someone at the front door: but the bell didn't ring, nor did she react. There was a system here that worked. If she wanted to be in peace, she locked herself in. If anyone had an important errand, he rang. All this, however, called for confidence in one's neighbors. Martin Beck sat down.

"Perhaps we can have a taste of that expensive wine," she said.

And it tasted good. Neither of them said anything for a long while.

"How can you stand it, being a policeman?"

"Oh, I manage. . . ."

"We can talk about it some other time."

"They're thinking of promoting me to commissioner."

"And you don't want it," she declared.

Somewhat later she asked: "What kind of music d'you like? I've every sort you can think of."

They went into the room with the record player and the assortment of armchairs. She played something.

"Take off your jacket, goddam it," she said. "And your shoes." She had opened the second bottle, but this time they drank slowly.

"You seemed annoyed when I turned up," he said.

"Yes and no."

Not a word more. The way she had behaved then had meant something. That she wasn't an easy lay. She saw he'd understood; and he knew she saw it. Martin Beck took a sip of his wine. Just now he was feeling unashamedly happy. He peeked at her where she sat with a downcast expression on her face and her elbows on the low table.

"Like to do a jigsaw puzzle?" she said.

"I've got a good one at home," he said. "The old 'Queen Elizabeth.' "

That was true. He'd bought it a couple of years ago but had never given it a thought since.

"Bring it next time you come," she said. Quickly and suddenly she changed her posture. Sitting with her legs crossed and her chin on her hands, she said: "Perhaps I should inform you that for the time being I'm no sort of a lay."

He threw her a quick glance, and she went on: "You know how it is with women—infections and such."

Martin Beck nodded.

"My sex life is without interest," she said. "And yours?"

"Nonexistent."

"That's bad," she said.

She changed the record and they drank some more.

He yawned.

"You're tired," she said.

He said nothing.

"But you don't want to go home. Okay then, don't go home."

And then: "I think I'll try and study a bit longer anyway. And I don't like this goddam shift. Tight and silly."

She peeled off her clothes and flung them in a heap on the floor. Then she put on a dark-red flannel nightgown, which reached down to her feet and looked very odd in every way.

As she changed he observed her, interested.

Naked, she looked exactly as he'd imagined. Firmbodied, strong, and well-built. Fair hair. Bulging stomach, flat rounded breasts. Rather large, light-brown nipples.

He didn't think: No scars, blemishes, or other identifying marks.

"Why don't you lie down a while?" she said. "You look really beat."

Martin Beck obeyed. He really did feel beat and dropped off almost at once. The last thing he saw was her sitting at the table, her blond head sunk over her books.

When he opened his eyes she was bending over

him, saying: "Wake up now. It's twelve o'clock. I'm as hungry as can be. Go down and lock the street door, will you, while I put a sandwich in the oven. The key's hanging on the left side of the door—on a bit of green string."

27

Malmström and Mohrén robbed the bank on Friday, July 14. At 2:45 exactly they marched in through the doors wearing Donald Duck masks, rubber gloves, and orange overalls.

In their hands they held high-caliber pistols, and Mohrén immediately fired a shot at the ceiling. Then, so that all present should understand what was happening, he shouted in very broken Swedish: "This is a bank robbery!"

Hauser and Hoff were wearing their usual outdoor clothes and enormous black hoods with holes for their eyes. Hauser was also equipped with a Mauser and Hoff with the sawed-off Maritza shotgun. They stood at the doors to keep open their retreat to the getaway cars.

Hoff let the muzzle of the shotgun sway to and fro, to warn outsiders away, while Hauser took up his planned tactical position in such a way as to be able to fire either into the bank or out at the sidewalk.

Meanwhile Malmström and Mohrén began systematically emptying all the cash drawers.

Never had anything worked so perfectly or gone so completely according to plan.

Five minutes earlier an old car had exploded outside a garage on Rosenlundsgatan, on the south side of the city. Immediately after the explosion, someone had fired a series of shots in various directions, and a house had burst into flames. Enterpriser A, who had staged these spectacular events, ran off through an alley to the next street, where he got into his car and drove home.

One minute later a stolen furniture truck backed

obliquely into the driveway of the central police building and broke down. Its rear door opened and scores of cartons of oil-soaked cotton came spewing out and immediately caught fire.

Meanwhile, Enterpriser B walked calmly away down the sidewalk, apparently unconcerned at the chaos he'd caused.

Yes, everything went off precisely as planned. Every detail was carried out on the dot, according to schedule.

From the point of view of the police, too, everything worked out more or less as they had expected. Everything happened as had been foreseen, and at the proper time.

With one little hitch.

Malmström and Mohrén didn't rob a bank in Stockholm. They robbed a bank four hundred miles away, in Malmö.

Per Månsson of the Malmö C.I.D. was sitting in his office drinking coffee. He had a view out over the parking lot, and when the explosion came and great clouds of smoke began rolling in from the driveway, his Danish pastry stuck in his throat. At the same moment Benny Skacke, a young hopeful who, despite his careerist ambitions, had still gotten no further than detective sergeant, jerked open his door and shouted that the catastrophe alarm had gone off. A bomb had exploded in Rosenlundsgatan, where it was also said that that wild firing was going on and at least one building was in flames.

Though Skacke had been living in Malmö for three and a half years, he had never so much as heard of Rosenlundsgatan and did not know its whereabouts. But Per Månsson did. He knew this town inside out, and it struck him as exceedingly peculiar that such a bombing should occur in that forgotten street in the peaceful district called Sofielund.

As it turned out, neither he nor any other policeman was given much of a chance for this kind of musing. At the same time as all available personnel were directed southwards, the police headquarters themselves seemed to be threatened. It took some time before

243

they realized that the whole tactical reserve had quite simply been shut up inside the parking lot. Many of them sped over to Rosenlundsgatan by taxi or in private cars that had no radio.

Månsson, for his part, got there at 3:07. By then the city fire department, which moved fast, had put out the fire. Obviously the whole thing was a bluff and had only caused insignificant damage to an empty garage. By this time large numbers of police were in the area, but apart from a badly damaged old car they found nothing remarkable. Eight minutes later a motorcycle policeman picked up a radio message that a downtown bank was being robbed.

By that time Malmström and Mohrén had already left Malmö. They had been seen driving away from the bank in a blue Fiat but had not been followed. Five minutes later they had separated and changed over to two other cars.

When, after a while, the police had managed to clear up the mess in their own parking lot and rid themselves of the furniture truck and the troublesome cartons, roadblocks were put up at all exits to the city. The alarm went out nationwide, and a search began for the getaway car.

Three days later it was found in a shed near the docks, together with the overalls, Donald Duck masks, rubber gloves, pistols, and various other accouterments.

Hauser and Hoff did a good job for the lush fees that had been deposited in their wives' checking accounts. After Malmström and Mohrén had vanished, they kept guard over the bank for nearly ten minutes and indeed didn't leave until the first policeman hove into view. As it happened, it was two patrolmen walking their beat who first chanced upon the bank. Their experience of anything except school kids who drank beer in public places was almost nil. And their only contribution was to yell themselves hoarse into their walkie-talkies. By that time there was hardly a policeman in all Malmö who wasn't yelling into a walkie-talkie, and almost no one who was listening.

Hauser even got clean away, something that no one, least of all himself, had really expected. Shortly afterwards he left Sweden via Helsingborg and Helsingør without even being accosted.

Hoff, however, was caught—owing to a peculiar oversight. At 3:55 he boarded the ferry "Malmöhus" wearing a gray suit, a white shirt, a tie, and a black Ku Klux Klan hood. A trifle absent-minded, he'd forgotten to take it off. The police and the customs men, imagining some costume party was being held on board, let him pass. But the crew of the vessel felt there was something strange about him, and on arrival at Frihavnen he was handed over to an elderly, unarmed Danish policeman. He almost dropped his beer bottle in amazement when his prisoner affably brought out two loaded pistols, a bayonet, and a primed hand grenade and laid them all down on the table in a little room at the Frihavnen station. The Dane, however, soon pulled himself together; there was something peculiarly agreeable about arresting a prisoner with such a nice name. "Hof," in Danish, means "restaurant."

Apart from a ticket to Frankfurt, Hoff had a certain amount of money on him: to be exact, forty German marks, two Danish ten-kronor notes, and about four kronor in Swedish money. That was all the loot that could be found.

It reduced the bank's losses to 1,613,496 kroner and 65 öre.

Meanwhile in Stockholm the strangest things were happening. The worst of them befell Einar Rönn.

Together with six patrolmen he had been assigned the less important task of keeping an eye on Rosenlundsgatan and grabbing Enterpriser A. Since the street is quite long, he had spread out his little force as cleverly as possible: a flying squad of two men in a car and the others placed at strategic points along the way. Bulldozer Olsson had told him to take it easy and above all, whatever happened, not to lose his nerve.

At 2:38 he was standing on the pavement opposite Bergsgruvan and feeling fairly tranquil, when two young men came up to him. Their appearance was similar to most people nowadays: dirty.

"Got a light?" one of them asked.

"Sure, no," Rönn said peacefully. "That is to say, I haven't. No."

A second later a dagger was pointing at his belly at the same time as a bicycle chain was being swung around in disturbing proximity to his head.

"Now, you bloody fucking goddamn cop," said the young man with the dagger. And in the same breath, he said to his mate: "You take his wallet. I'll take his watch and ring. Then we'll slice him up."

Rönn had never been a jujitsu or karate champion, but he still remembered a little of what he'd once learned in the gymnasium.

Putting out his foot he neatly tripped the guy with the dagger so that he sat down astonished on his ass. The rest, however, didn't come off quite so well. Though Rönn jerked his head as quickly as he could, he still got a nasty bang of the bicycle chain above his right ear; as everything went black before his eyes he grabbed assailant number two and, as he fell, pulled him down onto the pavement.

"And that's your last little fling, you bastard," hissed the guy with the dagger.

But at that moment the flying squad turned up, and by the time Rönn could see again the patrolmen had already given the two prostrate thugs a thorough beating with nightsticks and pistol butts and had handcuffed them as well.

The one with the bicycle chain was the first to recover. Blood streaming down his face, he looked around and said, as usual: "What happened?"

"You walked straight into a police trap, my lad," said one of the patrolmen.

"Police trap? For us? Are you out of your mind? We were just going to have some fun with a cop."

Once again Rönn had gotten a lump on his head. It was the only physical injury suffered by any member of the special squad that day. All their other wounds were of a purely psychological nature.

In the gray bus that, equipped to the teeth with every thinkable device, was his operational headquarters, Bulldozer Olsson could hardly sit still from excitement—something that seriously disturbed not only the radio operator but also Kollberg.

At 2:45, after the tension had reached its peak, the seconds began to draw out and pass with agonizing languor.

At 3:00 the staff of the bank began to make arrangements to close, and the sizable police unit inside the bank, led by Gunvald Larsson, could hardly object to them getting on with their work.

A feeling of great emptiness had begun to overcome them all, but Bulldozer Olsson said: "Gentlemen, we have only temporarily been outwitted. Werner Roos has guessed we've figured out something, and is hoping we'll give up. He'll have Malmström and Mohrén strike next Friday, a week from today, that is. Well, it's he who's losing time, not us."

At 3:30 the first really disturbing report came in. It was so alarming that all withdrew at once to Kungsholmen, there to await further developments. During the next few hours the telex never ceased tapping out new messages.

Gradually the picture cleared, though it took some time.

" 'Milan' obviously didn't mean what you thought it did," said Kollberg coldly.

"No," Bulldozer said. "Malmö. That was smart." For some considerable time now he'd been sitting quite still.

"Who the hell could have known the streets in Malmö have the same names," Gunvald Larsson said.

"Or that almost all the new banks have the same interior design," said Kollberg.

"We should have known it, gentlemen," shouted Bulldozer. "Roos knew it. It's cheaper to build all the banks the same. Roos pinned us down in Stockholm. But next time he won't get away with it. We'll just have to wait till next time."

Bulldozer had apparently recovered. He got up and said: "And where is Werner Roos?"

"In Istanbul," said Gunvald Larsson. "Where he's taken a few days off, to rest up."

"Sure," said Kollberg. "Where d'you think Malmström and Mohrén are resting up?"

"Makes no difference," said Bulldozer, some of his

old fire returning. "Easy come, easy go. They'll soon be back again. Then it'll be our turn."

"D'you think so?" Kollberg said dubiously.

The situation was no longer particularly mysterious, but the hour was late.

Malmström, for instance, had already reached his hotel in Geneva, where he'd had a room booked for the last three weeks.

Mohrén was in Zurich. But he was going on to South America the next day.

In those last few minutes in the shed where they'd swapped cars, they hadn't had much time to talk.

"Now don't go and throw away all your hard-earned money on underpants and loose women," Mohrén admonished.

"What a hell of a lot of bread!" Malmström said.

"And what shall we do with the hardware?"

"Deposit it in some bank, of course," Mohrén said. "Where else?"

A day or so later Werner Roos was sittting in the bar of the Istanbul Hilton sipping a daiquiri and reading the *Herald Tribune*. It was the first time he had managed to draw the attention of this haughty news organ to himself. It was a single-column article, quite short, under the laconic heading: "Swedish Bank Robbed." The text mentioned the more important facts: for example, the amount of money. At least half a million dollars. And one less important piece of information: "A representative of the Swedish police said today that they think they know the organization behind the coup."

A little further down came another Swedish news item. "Mass escape from prison. Fifteen of Sweden's most dangerous bank robbers today escaped over the wall of Kumla Prison, hitherto regarded as escape-proof."

This latter bit of news reached Bulldozer Olsson just as, for the first time in several weeks, he had gone to bed with his wife. Instantly jumping out again, he began traipsing about the bedroom, repeating the same delighted words: "What possibilities! What fantastic possibilities! It's war to the death, now! War to the death!"

248

That same Friday, Martin Beck arrived at the house in Tulegatan at 5:15. He had his jigsaw puzzle under his arm, and in his hand was a bag containing some bottles from the State Liquor Monopoly. He met Rhea on the ground floor. She came tramping down the stairs in her red clogs, with nothing on but her long pale-mauve cardigan. She was carrying a garbage bag in either hand.

"Hi," she said. "Glad you've come. I've something to show you."

"Let me take those," he said.

"It's just garbage," she said. "And anyway you've got your hands full. Is that the puzzle?"

"Yes."

"Fine. Open the gate, will you?"

He held open the gate to the yard and watched her go over to the garbage cans. Her legs were like everything else about her: solid, muscular, shapely. As the lid of the garbage can fell with a bang she turned and ran back. She ran like a sportswoman, straight forward, head down, knowing where she was going. She also half-ran up the stairs, so that he had to take several steps at a time to keep up with her.

Two people were sitting in the kitchen, drinking tea: one was the girl called Ingela, the other was someone he didn't know.

"What was it you were going to show me?"

"Here," she said. "Come."

He followed her.

She pointed at a door. "There you are," she said. "a locked room."

"The nursery?"

"Dead right," she said. "There's no one in there, and it's locked from inside."

He stared at her. Today she looked happy—and extremely healthy. She began to laugh, a hoarse hearty laugh. "The kids've got a hook on the inside," she said. "I put it on myself. After all, they've a right to be in peace and quiet when they want to, too."

"But they aren't at home."

"You're dumb," she said. "I was in there with the vacuum cleaner, and when I was through I slammed the door behind me. A bit too hard, maybe.

249

So the hook flew up and dropped into the eye. Now I can't get it open again."

He felt the door. It opened outwards but seemed impossible to budge.

"The hook is on the door, and the eye's on the doorpost," she said. "They're both made of heavy metal."

"How're we to get it open?"

She shrugged and said: "By force, I guess. It's all yours. That's what one needs a man about the house for, so they say."

He must have looked unusually dumb standing there, for she laughed again. Then, passing the back of her hand swiftly over his cheek, she said: "Don't worry. I can fix it just as well myself. But anyway, it's a locked room; which subsection I couldn't say."

"Can't we slip something in through the crack?"

"There isn't any crack. I told you I mounted that hook myself. I did it right."

So she had. The door yielded no more than a tiny fraction of an inch.

She seized the doorknob, kicked off her right shoe, and put her foot against the doorpost.

"No, hang on," he said. "Let me."

"Okay," she said and went back to join the others in the kitchen.

Martin Beck took a good long look at the door. Then he did the same as she had. He put his foot against the doorpost and grabbed the doorknob, which seemed old and dirty. The fact was, there was no other way. Unless you wanted to smash the pegs of the hinges.

The first time he didn't exert all his strength. The second time he did. But he wasn't successful until his fifth try. The screws came out of the timber with a whining sound and the door burst open.

It was the screws of the hook that had pulled out. The eye still sat firmly anchored to the doorpost. It was cast in one piece with a four-hole base plate. The hook was still hooked into the eye. It too was thick and seemed impossible to bend. Steel, probably.

Martin Beck looked around him. The nursery was empty, and its window was firmly closed.

To fix the hook arrangement again, both hook and eye had to be moved an inch or so. The woodwork around the old screw holes had been destroyed.

He went out into the kitchen where everyone was talking at once, discussing the genocide in Vietnam.

"Rhea," he said. "Where are your tools?"

"Over there in the chest." She pointed to it with her foot, her hands being full. She was demonstrating a crochet stitch to one of the others.

He got a screwdriver and awl.

"There's no hurry," she said. "Get yourself a cup and come and sit down. Anna here has been baking. Buns."

He sat down and ate a freshly baked bun. Though he followed what they were talking about, his thoughts were elsewhere. Then he turned to something else.

He sat silent, listening to memory's tape recorder —a conversation from eleven days ago.

Conversation in a corridor in the Stockholm City Hall, Tuesday, July 4, 1972.

MARTIN BECK—*So when you'd smashed the pegs and got the door open you entered the apartment?*
KENNETH KVASTMO—*Yes.*
MARTIN BECK—*Who went in first?*
KENNETH KVASTMO—*I did. Kristiansson felt sick from the smell.*
MARTIN BECK—*What did you do, precisely, when you came in?*
KENNETH KVASTMO—*There was a horrible stench. The light was poor, but I could see the corpse lying on the floor, two or three yards away from the window.*
MARTIN BECK—*And then? Try and remember it in detail.*
KENNETH KVASTMO—*You could hardly breathe in there. I walked around the body and over to the window.*
MARTIN BECK—*Was it shut?*
KENNETH KVASTMO—*Sure. And the window shade was down. I tried to pull it up but couldn't. The spring was uncoiled. But I figured we'd just have to get that window open and get some air.*
MARTIN BECK—*What did you do then?*

251

KENNETH KVASTMO—*I pushed the shade aside and opened the window. Then I wound up the shade and set the spring—though that was afterwards.*

MARTIN BECK—*And the window was closed?*

KENNETH KVASTMO—*Sure. At least, one hook was on properly. I unhooked it and opened the window.*

MARTIN BECK—*Do you remember whether it was the upper or the lower hook?*

KENNETH KVASTMO—*Not absolutely for certain. The upper, I guess. What the lower one was like I don't remember. I guess I opened that one too —no, I'm not sure.*

MARTIN BECK—*But you are sure the window was hooked on the inside?*

KENNETH KVASTMO—*Sure, one hundred percent. I'm absolutely sure.*

Rhea gave him a playful kick on the shin. "Take a bun, for God's sake," she said.

"Rhea," he said. "Have you got a good flashlight?"

"Sure. It's hanging on a nail in the cleaning closet."

"May I borrow it?"

"Sure you can."

"Then I'm going out a while. I'll be back soon and fix that door."

"Fine," she said. "So long."

"So long," said Martin Beck. He got the flashlight, called for a taxi, and drove to Bergsgatan.

He stood a while on the sidewalk, looking up at the window on the other side of the street. Then he turned around. Behind him Kronoberg Park lay on rising ground. The slope was rocky and steep, covered with bushes.

He clambered up until he'd reached a position opposite the window. He was almost on level with it, and the distance was at most twenty-five yards. Taking a ball-point pen out of his pocket he pointed it at the window's dark rectangle. The shade was drawn down; the landlord, to his intense annoyance, had been forbidden to rent the apartment until the police said he could.

Martin Beck moved around until he'd found the very best spot. He was nothing of a marksman, but if his ball-point pen had been a forty-five automatic he could have hit anyone who'd shown himself at that window. Of that he was sure.

He was well hidden here. Naturally, in mid-April the vegetation had been a good deal sparser, but even then it should have been possible to hide without drawing attention—as long as you didn't move.

Now it was broad daylight, but even late in the evening the street lighting should have been enough. Darkness would also have offered better protection to anyone standing on the slope. Even so, no one would be likely to fire from here without a silencer on his pistol.

Once again he considered closely which spot was best. And using it as his starting point he began his search. Few people were passing by beneath him. Those who did halted when they heard him poking about in the shrubs. But only momentarily. Then they hurried on their way, anxious not to get involved.

He searched systematically. He began to his right. Almost all automatics reject their cartridges to the right, but how far and in what direction? It was a job that called for patience. Close to the ground, he was glad he had the flashlight. Martin Beck did not intend to give up. At least not for a long time.

After an hour and forty minutes he found the empty cartridge. It was lying between two stones, partially covered by leaves and dirt. Plenty of rain had fallen since April. Dogs and other animals had been trampling about up here; certainly humans too—for example, those who took it into their heads to break the law by drinking beer in a public place.

He pried out the little brass cylinder, wrapped it in a handkerchief, and put it in his pocket.

Then he walked eastwards along Bergsgatan. Near City Hall he found a cab and drove out to the criminology lab. At this time of day they would probably be closed, but he was counting on someone being there. Almost always nowadays someone was working overtime. But he had to do a lot of talking before anyone even agreed to accept his find.

In the end, however, he talked them into it. He put it in a plastic box and carefully filled in the details on a card.

"And of course you're in one hell of a hurry for it," said one of the technicians who was working overtime.

"Not particularly," Martin Beck said. "In fact not at all. I'd just be grateful if you'd take a look at it when you get the chance."

The technician contemplated the cartridge case. It wasn't much to look at, squashed and dirty. It didn't seem too hopeful. "Just because you said that," the technician said, "I'll look at it just as soon as I can. We're fed up to here with all you guys who come in saying there's not a precious second to lose."

By now it was so late he felt he must call Rhea.

"Hi," she said. "I'm all by myself now. The street door's locked, but I'll throw down the key."

"I'll fix that door."

"I've already done that myself. Have you done what you wanted?"

"Sure."

"Good. Then you'll be here in half an hour."

"Just about."

"Just give a shout from the sidewalk. I'll hear you."

He got there just after eleven and whistled. At first nothing happened. Then she came down herself and opened the door, barefoot, wearing her long red nightie.

Up in the kitchen she said: "Did you use the flashlight?"

"Sure. A helluva lot."

"Shall we open the wine now? By the way, have you had anything to eat?"

"Nope."

"That's no good. I'll fix something. Won't take long. You're starving?"

Starving. Yes, perhaps he was.

"How're things going with Svärd?"

"Seem to be getting clearer."

"How so? Tell me. I'm so goddam curious about everything."

254

By one o'clock the wine bottle was empty.

She yawned.

"By the way," she said, "I'm leaving town tomorrow. Back on Monday. Maybe not until Tuesday."

He was about to say: "Now I'll be off."

"You don't want to go home," she said.

"No."

"Then you can sleep here."

He nodded.

She said: "But it's not easy sleeping in the same bed as me. I kick around all the time, even while I'm asleep."

He undressed and got into bed.

"Would you like me to take off my nice nightie?" she said.

"Sure."

"Okay."

She did so and lay down beside him. "But that's the end of the fun," she said.

He reflected that two years had gone by since he'd shared a bed with another human being. Martin Beck didn't reply. She was warm and very close.

"We didn't have time to start on that puzzle," she said. "It'll have to be next week."

Whereupon he dropped off to sleep.

28

Monday morning. Martin Beck was humming to himself as he turned up at Västberga. A clerk stared at him in astonishment as he walked down the corridor. All weekend he'd been feeling fine, even though he'd spent it alone. In fact he could hardly recall when he'd last felt so optimistic. The summer of 1968 hadn't been too bad.

At the same time he was breaking into Svärd's locked room he was also breaking out of his own.

He spread out the excerpts from the warehouse ledgers in front of him, putting a check mark beside the names that seemed most worthy of consideration. Then he attacked the telephone.

Insurance companies have one urgent task: to earn as much money as possible. So they keep their personnel up to their ears in work. For the same reason they keep all their documents in apple-pie order, in a constant panic that someone may swindle them and gnaw unpunished into their profits. Nowadays this mad working tempo had tended to become an end in itself: "Impossible, we haven't got the time."

There were various types of countermeasures he could apply, e.g., the one he'd used on the lab technicians on Friday evening. Another was to pretend to be even more pressed for time than they were; this often worked if one represented some branch of the bureaucracy. As a policeman it's tough trying to speed up other policemen. But in certain other cases it works admirably.

"Impossible, we haven't time. Is it urgent?"

"Fantastically urgent! You've just got to find the time."

"Who's your immediate superior?"

And so forth.

The answers gradually began coming in, and he noted them on his list: compensation paid; incident closed; the insured died before the debt could be settled.

Martin Beck went on phoning and making notes. By now the margins of the ledgers had begun to look really full, though of course he didn't get answers to everything.

During his eighth conversation a thought struck him. He said: "What becomes of the damaged merchandise after the company has paid out the insurance?"

"Naturally, we inspect it. If the merchandise can still be used we sell it to our employees at a discount."

Yes, yes. And that, too, meant a small profit. Naturally.

Suddenly he remembered his own experiences in this field. Almost twenty years ago, right after he got married, he'd been very hard up. Before Inga—the cause of the marriage—was born, his wife had been working for an insurance company. There she had been able to buy at a discount a great number of cans of unusually foul-tasting consommé damaged in transit. They'd lived on them for months. Since then he'd never really liked consommé. Maybe the loathesome liquid had already been tasted by Kalle Svärd or some other expert and found unsuitable for human consumption.

Martin Beck never got as far as dialing his ninth call. The phone squawked. Somebody wanted something of him. Surely it couldn't be . . .

"Yes, Beck here."

"Mmmm, Hjelm here."

"Hi, nice of you to call."

"It sure is. But you seem to have behaved decently out here, and anyway I was thinking of doing you one last service."

"A last service?"

"Before you're promoted to commissioner. I see you've found that cartridge."

"Have you looked at it?"

257

"Why else do you think I'm phoning?" Hjelm said irritably. "We've no time here for unnecessary phone calls."

He must have something up his sleeve, Martin Beck thought. If Hjelm called, it was always to triumph in one way or another. Ordinarily you heard from him in writing. Aloud he said: "That's damn decent of you."

"One might say that," Hjelm agreed. "Well, that cartridge of yours is in pretty bad shape. Very hard to get anything out of it at all."

"I understand."

"I doubt it. I guess you want to know whether it matches that suicide bullet, eh?"

"Sure."

Silence.

"Sure," Martin Beck said. "That's just what I'd like to know."

"It matches," said Hjelm.

"For sure?"

"Haven't I told you, once and for all, that we don't deal in guesswork here?"

"Sorry."

"I suppose you haven't got the gun too?"

"No. I don't know where it is."

"But it so happens I do," said Hjelm dryly. "At this moment it's lying right here on my desk."

In the special squad's lair on Kungsholmsgatan there was nothing that could be said to indicate optimism. Bulldozer Olsson had rushed off to the National Police Board for consultations. The National Police Chief had told them nothing must be allowed to come out, and just now Olsson was urgently trying to find out what it was that mustn't come out.

Kollberg, Rönn, and Gunvald Larsson were sitting silent in postures reminiscent of parodies of Rodin's "The Thinker."

There was a knock at the door, and at virtually the same moment Martin Beck was standing inside the room. "Hi," he said.

"Hi," said Kollberg.

258

Rönn nodded, and Gunvald Larsson didn't even bother.

"You guys don't seem too happy."

Kollberg stared at his old friend and said: "We have our reasons. And what brings you here? No one ever comes here of his own free will."

"I did. Unless I'm wrongly informed, you've got a joker here by the name of Mauritzon."

"Sure," said Rönn. "The Hornsgatan murderer."

"What do you want him for?" said Kollberg, suspicious.

"Just to meet him."

"How so?"

"I'd like to have a little talk with him—assuming he knows how to talk."

"Not much point in that," Kolberg said. "He's a chatterbox, but not in the right way."

"Won't he confess?"

"You can be goddam sure he won't. But the circumstantial evidence'll be too much for him. We've found his disguise in the house where he lives. Plus the murder weapon. And we've tied him to it."

"How?"

"The serial number on the gun had been filed off. And the marks on the metal come from a grinding machine that is demonstrably his and that was found in his bedside table. The grinding pattern agrees with the microscopic image. It's airtight. And yet he goes on denying it."

"Sure. And he's been identified by witnesses," said Rönn.

"Well . . ." Kollberg began. But he immediately broke off, pushed down some buttons on his phone, and barked some orders into the mouthpiece.

"They're bringing him down."

"Where can we talk?"

"Take my room," Rönn said.

"Take good care of that idiot," said Gunvald Larsson. "He's all we've got."

Within five minutes Mauritzon appeared, handcuffed to a guard.

"That seems superfluous," Martin Beck said.

"We're just going to have a little talk. Unlock him and wait outside."

The warder fiddled with the handcuffs. Mauritzon irritably rubbed his right wrist.

"Please sit down," said Martin Beck.

They sat down opposite each other at the desk.

Martin Beck had never seen Mauritzon before and noticed, though it did not astonish him, that the man seemed to be emotionally disturbed and exceedingly nervous—on the verge of collapse.

Perhaps they'd beaten him up. But probably not. It was all too common for murderers to have an unstable disposition and lose their heads as soon as they were caught.

"I'm the object of a diabolical conspiracy," Mauritzon said in a shrill voice. "The police or someone else has planted a lot of false evidence in my home. But when that bank was robbed I wasn't even in town, though even my own lawyer doesn't believe me. What the hell am I to do?"

"Are you a Swedish-American?"

"No. Why?"

"You said 'planted.' That's not a Swedish word."

"Well, what in God's name can you call it when the police come breaking into your home and put wigs, and sunglasses, and pistols, and God knows what else there and then pretend to have found them? I swear I've never robbed a bank. But even my own lawyer says I haven't a chance. What do you want me to do? Confess to a homicide I've absolutely nothing to do with? I'm going crazy."

Martin Beck put his hand under the desk and pressed a button. Rönn's desk was a new one, cunningly equipped with a built-in tape recorder. "The fact is," said Martin Beck, "I've nothing at all to do with all that."

"Haven't you?"

"No. Nothing at all."

"So what do you want?"

"To talk about something else."

"And what could that be?"

"A story I imagine you are familiar with. It begins in March, 1966. With a crate of Spanish liqueur."

260

"What?"

"The fact is, I've documented almost everything. Quite legally, you imported a case of liqueur, declared it to the customs, and paid the duty. Above all the duty; but also the freight? Is that correct?"

Mauritzon didn't answer. Martin Beck looked up and saw the fellow was gaping at him, astounded.

"I've got all the papers," Martin Beck repeated. "So I assume it's correct."

"Yes," Mauritzon said, at length, "that is correct."

"But you never received that consignment. If I understand the matter correctly, the crate was destroyed by accident while in transit."

"Yes. Though I wouldn't exactly call it an accident."

"No, you're right enough on that point. I believe that a warehouseman, by the name of Svärd, smashed it intentionally to get at the liqueur."

"You believe bloody right. That was exactly what happened."

"Mmmm," Martin Beck said. "I realize you're tired from all these other matters. Perhaps you'd prefer not to talk about this old story?"

After a very long while Mauritzon said: "Sure. Why not? It's good for me to talk about something that's really happened. Otherwise I'll go out of my mind."

"As you wish," Martin Beck said. "Now, in my view those bottles didn't contain liqueur."

"And you're still right."

"What they really did contain we can leave for the moment."

"If you're interested, I can tell you. The bottles had been fixed in Spain. Though they looked perfectly authentic they contained a morphine-based solution of phenedrin, a commodity much appreciated in those days. The consignment was quite valuable."

"Yes. And as far as I know, this abortive piece of smuggling—for it was abortive—is highly criminal."

"You're right there," said Mauritzon, as if this was an angle he'd been overlooking.

"Further, I have reason to assume that you were blackmailed by this guy Svärd."

261

Mauritzon didn't reply. Martin Beck shrugged and said: "As I've already said, you needn't answer if you don't want to."

Mauritzon still seemed as nervous as before. He kept altering his position and couldn't keep his hands still.

They must really have been putting psychological pressure on him, Martin Beck thought, faintly astonished. He knew Kollberg's methods and knew they were almost always humane.

"I shall reply," Mauritzon said. "Don't stop. This brings me back to reality."

"You paid Svärd seven hundred and fifty a month."

"He wanted a thousand. I offered five hundred. Seven hundred and fifty was a compromise."

"Why don't you tell me all about it yourself," Martin Beck said. "If there's anything you don't understand we can reconstruct it together."

"You think so?" said Mauritzon. His face twitched. He mumbled: "Is that possible?"

"Sure," said Martin Beck.

"Do you think I'm insane, too?" Mauritzon asked suddenly.

"No. Why should I?"

"Everyone seems to think I'm crazy. I've almost come to believe it myself."

"Just tell me what happened," Martin Beck said. "There's certainly an explanation to everything. So —Svärd squeezed you for money."

"He was a bloodsucker," Mauritzon said. "When that happened I simply couldn't afford to be put away. I'd been inside before and been given a couple of suspended sentences and was under surveillance. Though of course you know all that."

Martin Beck said nothing. As yet he had not checked up too carefully on Mauritzon's criminal record.

"Well," said Mauritzon. "Seven hundred and fifty a month isn't the whole world. Nine thousand a year. That crate alone was worth a lot more." He checked himself and added in consternation: "I don't get it. How can you know all this?"

"Most things in a society like ours are documented," Martin Beck said amiably.

"But those bastards down at the docks must have been smashing up crates every goddam week," Mauritzon said.

"Sure. But you were the only one who didn't claim any insurance money."

"That's true. I almost had to beg them not to get it for me. Otherwise we'd have had the insurance adjustors there, poking their noses into things. Svärd was quite enough."

"I understand. And you went on paying."

"After a year or so I tried to cut him off, but I only needed to be a few days late for the old boy to start threatening me. And my affairs weren't of a kind that could withstand inspection."

"You could have reported Svärd for blackmail."

"Of course. And been put away for several years myself. No. There was only one thing I could do. Pay up. The bastard gave up his job and used me as some kind of a pension fund."

"But in the end you'd had enough of it?"

"Yes." Mauritzon twisted his handkerchief nervously between his fingers. "Between ourselves," he said. "Wouldn't you have, too? Do you know how much I paid that guy?"

"Yes. Fifty-four thousand kronor."

"You seem to know everything," Mauritzon said. "Say, can't you take over that bank robbery from those lunatics out there?"

"That, perhaps, would be difficult," Martin Beck said. "But you didn't pay up without protest, did you? Now and again you threatened him?"

"How can you know that? A year or so ago I began thinking of all that money I'd paid to that thief over the years. Last winter I got in touch with him."

"How?"

"I met him in town and told him to stop it. But the old skinflint just said I knew what would happen if the money wasn't paid in on time."

"What would happen?"

"He'd rush straight to the police. Admittedly this

business with the case of liqueur was ancient history. But that wouldn't have stopped the police from snooping into my affairs. Some of what I was busy with wasn't legal. Besides, I found it hard to explain why I'd gone on paying him all these years."

"Anyway, Svärd told you something to calm you down, didn't he? He said he'd die soon."

Mauritzon sat silent a long while. "Has Svärd told you all that? Or have you got it in writing?"

"No."

"Are you some kind of a mind reader, or what?"

Martin Beck shook his head.

"Then how can you know every goddam detail? He said he had cancer in his guts and wouldn't live longer than six months. Anyway, I guess he was a bit scared. And I thought to myself, if I've been keeping him for six years, six months more one way or the other doesn't matter."

"When did you last speak to him?"

"It was in February. Then he was whining and complaining, you'd have thought I was some kind of a goddam relative. He said he was going into the hospital—the 'death factory,' he called it. The radium clinic, that is. He seemed finished. Just as well, I thought to myself."

"But you called up the hospital and checked?"

"Sure. He wasn't there. They said he was in some clinic on the South Side. Then I began to suspect something was up."

"I see. So you called up the doctor there and said Svärd was your uncle."

"There doesn't seem much sense in my telling you anything, does there? I can't say anything you don't know already."

"Oh yes . . ."

"And what might that be?"

"What name you gave, for example."

"Svärd, obviously. How could I be the bastard's nephew if I didn't call myself Svärd? Haven't you thought that one out?" Mauritzon threw Martin Beck a glance of happy surprise.

"No, as a matter I hadn't. You see?"

Some kind of relationship was beginning to grow up between them.

"The doctor I talked to said the old boy was well and certainly wouldn't kick the bucket for another twenty years. I figured that . . ." He fell silent.

Martin Beck made a swift calculation and said: "That would mean a hundred and eighty thousand kronor more."

"Sure, sure. I give up. You're too clever for me. That same day I paid in the money for March, so that the goddam deposit slip would be lying there waiting for him when he got home. At the same time . . . Well, d'you know what I did at the same time?"

"You decided it was to be the last time."

"Precisely. I'd heard he was going to leave the hospital on Saturday, and as soon as he stuck his nose into the shop to buy his lousy cat food I grabbed him and told him it was all over. But he was just as impudent as always, said I knew what would happen if he didn't get a notification from the bank on the twentieth of next month at the latest. Yet he was real scared, even so. For d'you know what he did then?"

"He moved."

"Of course you knew that too. And what I did then?"

"Yes."

There was a moment's silence. Martin Beck reflected that the tape recorder really was completely soundless. Before receiving his visitor he'd checked that it was working and put on a new reel. Now he must choose his tactics.

Martin Beck said: "Sure, I know that too, as I've said. By and large we can regard this conversation as over."

Mauritzon looked obviously upset. "Wait a moment," he said. "Do you really know?"

"Sure."

"Because, you see, I don't. Goddam it, I don't even know whether the old boy's alive or dead. And this is where the spooky stuff begins."

"Spooky stuff?"

"Yeah, and since then everything has gone to . . ."

265

yes, gone to hell, you might say. And in two weeks time I'll be sentenced to life for something only the devil himself could have fixed up. There's no goddam lousy sense in it."

"You're from Småland."

"Sure, didn't you notice it until now?"

"No."

"Queer. You who understand everything. Well, and what did I do?"

"First you tracked down Svärd's new apartment."

"Sure, that was simple. I kept an eye on him for a few days, noticed when he went out, and so forth. It wasn't often. And the shade of his window was always drawn down, even when he was airing out the apartment in the evenings. I checked on that, too."

"Checked" was an "in" word; everyone was using it to death. It had begun with children and then spread to almost everyone in Sweden. Even Martin Beck used it sometimes, though he did his best to speak pure Swedish.

"You thought you'd give Svärd a real fright. If worst came to worst, you'd kill him."

"I didn't much care which. But he was hard to get at. So I thought up a simple way of doing it. Of course you already know which way I mean?"

"You thought you'd shoot him through his window, either when he opened it to air the apartment or else as he closed it."

"There you are, you see! Those were the only times he showed himself. And I found a fine spot. Obviously you know where."

Martin Beck nodded.

"I can just imagine it. There's only one place if one doesn't want to go into the house. The slope up to the park on the other side of the street. Svärd opened his window at nine every evening and shut it at ten. So I went there to put a bullet into the old guy."

"Which day?"

"Monday the seventeenth. I did it instead of going to the bank, as it were. Ten in the evening. Now the spooky stuff begins. You don't believe me? Hell, I can't prove it. But first let me check up on something. D'you know what I thought I'd do him in with?"

"Yes. A forty-five automatic—Llama 9-A."

Mauritzon put his head in his hands and said: "You're in this conspiracy too. That's something, as far as I see, that you couldn't possibly know. Yet you do. It's not in nature."

"So that the shot wouldn't attract people's attention, you put a silencer on it."

Mauritzon nodded, amazed.

"I assume you did it yourself. The usual type, which can only be used once."

"Sure, sure, that's right," said Mauritzon. "That's right, that's right, that's right. But now *you* tell *me* what happened."

"You begin," said Martin Beck. "And I'll explain the rest."

"Well, I went there. Drove there in my own car. It was dark. Not a soul about. Inside the apartment the light was out. The window was open. The shade down. I took up my position on the slope. After a few minutes I looked at my watch: 9:58. Everything turns out precisely as I'd imagined. The goddam old bastard pushes the blind aside, appears in the window, and I guess he thought he'd close it. As it happened, though, I still hadn't quite made up my mind. But I guess you know that."

"You hadn't made up your mind whether you'd kill Svärd or just warn him with a shot in the arm or maybe in the window frame."

"Self-evident," said Mauritzon in despair. "That you know that, too, is self-evident. After all, these are just things I thought to myself and which were never anywhere except inside here." He thumped his knuckles against his forehead.

"But in a flash you make up your mind."

"Yeah. Seeing him standing there I think to myself it's just as well to put an end to him once and for all. So I fire." He fell silent.

"What happened?"

"Well, what happened then? I don't know. It seems impossible that I could have missed, though at first I thought so. He disappears, and to me it looks as though the window is being shut. Quick as can be.

The shade's hanging down. Everything looks as it usually does."

"What did you do then?"

"I drove home. What the hell else could I do? Then, day after day, I look at the newspapers; but there's nothing in them. Everything seems incomprehensible—so I figured then. But it's nothing compared to what I'm thinking now."

"How was Svärd standing when you fired?"

"Leaning forward a bit, and his right arm raised. He must have been holding the window hook with one fist and leaning against the sill with the other."

"Where did you get the gun from?"

"Some guys I know had bought some weapons abroad, on an export license. I arranged for them to be brought into the country. At the same time I thought it might be a good idea to have a gun myself. So I bought an extra pistol. They already had one. I'm no expert on firearms, but I thought it looked okay."

"Are you sure you hit Svärd?"

"Sure I am. Anything else is unthinkable. But all the rest is beyond me. Why hasn't anyone ever bothered about it, for example? I used to drive past and take a look up at the window. Always just as closed, with the shade still pulled down. So I began to wonder whether I hadn't missed, even so. After that the strangest things began happening. Oh my God, what a mess. I don't understand a thing. And then here you are, all of a sudden, and understand everything."

"Some things I guess I can explain," said Martin Beck.

"May I ask you a few, just for a change?"

"Sure. Go ahead."

"First, did I hit the bastard?"

"Yes. You killed him on the spot."

"That's something anyway. I'd begun to think he must be sitting in the next room here, reading a newspaper, laughing till he pissed in his pants."

"So," said Martin Beck seriously, "you've committed a murder."

"I guess so," said Mauritzon, unconcernedly.

"That's what those bright boys in there are saying, too. My lawyer, for instance."

"Any other questions?"

"Why didn't anyone bother about him being dead? There hasn't been a line in the papers."

"Svärd wasn't found until long afterwards. At first various circumstances suggested that he had committed suicide."

"Suicide?"

"Yes, the police are careless too, sometimes. The bullet had hit him from directly in front, which is understandable because at that moment he was leaning forward. And the room where he was lying had been locked from inside, the window too."

"He must have pulled it after him as he fell, and the hook dropped into the ring."

"That's the conclusion I've come to, too. More or less. Anyone who's hit by such a big-caliber projectile is flung several yards backwards. Even if Svärd wasn't exactly holding the window hook, it could very well have fallen into place when the window slammed shut. I've seen similar things. Quite recently." Martin Beck smiled to himself. "And so the whole affair's pretty well cleared up," he said.

"Pretty well cleared up? How could you know what I was thinking just before I fired?"

"That," said Martin Beck, "was pure guesswork. Anything more you want to ask about?"

Mauritzon stared at him in amazement. "Anything more? Are you making fun of me?"

"Not in the least."

"Then would you be so good as to explain the following. That evening I drove straight home. I put the gun in an old bag I'd filled with stones. Then I shook it up, goddam thoroughly, and put it in a safe place. First I take off the silencer and hammer it out flat. It was the kind you can only use once, but I hadn't made it myself. As you said, I'd bought it with the automatic. Next morning I drive to the station and take the train to Södertälje. On the way I walk into a house like any other house and chuck the silencer into the garbage chute. I don't even recall exactly which house it was. At Södertälje I get my motor boat, which I keep moored there. I bring it up to Stockholm and arrive in the evening. Next day I take the bag with the automatic and head the boat out to sea—towards Vaxholm—and I chuck the bag overboard. In the deepest part of the channel."

Martin Beck frowned.

"All *that* I know for certain I've done," said Mauritzon excitedly. "No one can get into my apartment while I'm away. No one has ever had a key to it. And just before I settled my account with Svärd I told the very few acquaintances who know where I live that I'd gone to Spain."

"Did you?"

"But goddam it, there you sit, even so, knowing everything. You know all about the automatic, which quite obviously can't be lying anywhere except at the bottom of the sea. You knew all that about the silencer, too. Will you please be so goddam kind now as to explain all this."

Martin Beck pondered. Finally he said: "You must be in error somewhere."

"Error? But haven't I told you all this in detail? Hell, I know what I do, don't I? Or . . ." Mauritzon began laughing shrilly. He broke off suddenly and said: "You're just sitting there fooling me, you too. And don't kid yourself I'm going to repeat all this in court."

Again the man began laughing uncontrollably.

Martin Beck got up, opened the door, waved to the patrolman on duty, and said: "I'm finished. For the moment, anyway."

Mauritzon was led out. Still laughing. It sounded unpleasant.

Martin Beck opened the drawer of the desk, ran off the rest of the tape, took it in his hand, and went out to the special squad. Rönn and Kollberg were there.

"Well," said Kollberg. "Did you like Mauritzon?"

"Not particularly. But he's confessed to murder."

"Who's he murdered now?"

"Svärd."

"Really?"

"Without any question."

"Oh, that tape," Rönn said. "Is it from my recorder?"

"Yes."

"I won't do you much good. It's not working."

"But I tested it."

"Sure, it works for the first two minutes. After that you won't hear a squeak. A repairman's coming tomorrow to fix it."

"Oh." Martin Beck looked at the tape and said: "It doesn't matter. Mauritzon's had it. Circumstantial evidence. We've tied the murder weapon to him, as Lennard pointed out before. Did Hjelm tell you there'd been a silencer on it?"

"Yes," Kollberg said, yawning. "But in the bank he didn't use one. Why're you looking so strange?"

"There's something odd about Mauritzon," Martin Beck said. "Something I don't understand."

"What are you asking for?" Kollberg said. "Complete insight into the human psyche? Are you thinking of writing a thesis on criminology?"

"So long," said Martin Beck. He left.

"Well," Rönn said. "He'll have plenty of time for that when he's a commissioner."

Mauritzon was brought up before the Stockholm District Court, accused of murder, manslaughter, and armed robbery, as well as narcotics offenses and various other matters.

To all these charges he pleaded not guilty. To every question he replied that he knew nothing about the matter and that the police had picked him out as a scapegoat and planted the evidence.

Bulldozer Olsson was at the height of his form, and the accused constantly found himself hard-pressed. In the course of the proceedings the prosecutor even went so far as to change the manslaughter charge into a second count of murder.

After only a three-day trial, the verdict was given. Mauritzon was sentenced to hard labor for life for the murder of the gymnastics instructor and the bank robbery on Hornsgatan. He was also found guilty of various other offenses, including a conspiracy charge in connection with other Malmström-Mohrén jobs.

The charge of having murdered Karl Edvin Svärd, on the other hand, was dropped. The defense lawyer who, in the early stages of the trial, had acted apathetically, suddenly woke up and made havoc of the circumstantial evidence. Among other things he called in experts of his own who threw doubt on the ballistic investigation and pointed out, correctly, that the cartridge had been too seriously damaged to be linked with any certainty to Mauritzon's automatic.

Martin Beck testified, but what he had to say was found to be full of gaps and to be based to some extent on absurd assumptions.

From the point of view of justice, so called, this made little difference. Whether Mauritzon was condemned for one murder or two had no effect on the consequences. Formally, life imprisonment is the harshest penalty permitted under Swedish law.

Mauritzon listened to his sentence with a wry smile. Altogether, throughout the trial, he had behaved a trifle oddly.

When the judge asked whether the accused had understood his sentence, Mauritzon shook his head.

"In principle it means you have been found guilty of the Hornsgatan bank robbery and the murder of Mr. Gårdon, the gymnastics instructor. On the other hand the court has acquitted you of the charge of murdering Karl Edvin Svärd. To sum up, you have been condemned to imprisonment for life and will now be taken back into custody until your sentence becomes final and beyond appeal."

As the guards were taking him away, Mauritzon laughed. Those who noticed it thought this man—who showed neither remorse not any respect for the law or the court—was an unusually hardened criminal.

Monita was sitting in a shady corner of the hotel terrace with the Italian grammar book from her adult-education course on her knee.

In the little bamboo grove at the bottom of the garden Mona was playing with one of her new-found

272

friends. They were sitting on the sun-speckled ground between the slender bamboo trees, and Monita, hearing their bright cheerful voices, was amazed at the ease with which children communicate even if they don't understand a word of each other's language. Anyway, Mona had already learned a number of words, and Monita was sure her daughter would learn this foreign tongue a good deal more quickly than she would. In fact, she had about decided it was hopeless.

Here in the hotel she managed very well with English and a few halting words of German; but she wanted to talk to other people besides the hotel staff. That was why she had started to learn Italian, which seemed a good deal easier than Slovene and which she hoped she'd be able to use since they were near the Italian border.

It was terribly hot, and the heat was making her feel sleepy, even though she was sitting in the shade and only a quarter of an hour had passed since she'd gone up and, for the fourth time this morning, taken a shower. She closed her book and stuffed it into her handbag, which was standing on the stone paving beside her chair.

On the street and the sidewalk outside the hotel garden, lightly clad tourists were strolling to and fro. Among them were many Swedes. Too many, Monita thought. In the crowd it was easy to distinguish the little town's regular inhabitants. Their movements showed they felt themselves at home and knew what they were about. Many of them were carrying various objects: baskets of eggs or fruit, large loaves of dark bread from the bakery on the pier, fishing nets, or their own children. And a while back a man had walked past with a freshly slaughtered pig on his head. Most of the older people were dressed in black.

She called to Mona, who came running—her new playmate at her heels.

"I thought we'd take a little walk," Monita said. "Just up to Rozeta's house and back. Want to come?"

"Do I have to?" Mona said.

"No, of course not. Stay here and play if you like. I'll soon be back." Monita began walking up the hill behind the hotel.

Rozeta's house stood on the mountainside, a quarter of an hour's walk from the hotel. It was still called that, though Rozeta herself had died five years ago, and the house was now owned by her three sons—all of whom had houses of their own down in the town.

Monita had already made the oldest son's acquaintance during her first week here. He kept a bodega down by the harbor and it was his daughter whom Mona most liked playing with. By now Monita had gotten to know his whole family but could only converse with the husband, who had been at sea and spoke good English. It cheered her to have made friends in town so quickly; but best of all, she had arranged to rent Rozeta's house in the fall, when the American who was living there during the summer had gone home. Since the house had not been promised to anyone else until next summer, she and Mona would be able to live there during the winter.

Rozeta's house—whitewashed, spacious, and comfortable—was situated in a big garden with a fantastic view out over the mountains, the harbor, and the bay.

Sometimes Monita would go there and sit in the garden a while and talk to the American, a former army officer who had settled in the house during his retirement to write his memoirs.

As she went on up the steep slope Monita again reviewed the events that had brought her here. How many times she had done this in the last three weeks she couldn't say. And presumably she'd never cease to be astonished that once she had made up her mind to act, everything had happened so quickly and with such self-evident simplicity. Nor would she ever quite get over the fact that, to achieve her end, she had killed someone; but no doubt, as time passed, she would become reconciled to the memory of that unintentional but definitive shot—which, during sleepless nights, still echoed through her head.

Finding that gun in Filip Mauritzon's kitchen closet had decided matters. Actually, it was as she'd stood there in his kitchen with his automatic in her hand that she'd instantly made up her mind. Afterwards it had taken her two and a half months to decide on a plan of action and to summon her courage. Ten weeks—when she'd thought of nothing else.

When at last she'd acted, she'd thought over every situation that could conceivably arise, including all those that might occur while she was still inside the bank.

What she'd never reckoned with was the possibility of being taken by surprise. Which was exactly what had happened. She knew nothing about firearms. Since she was only planning to use the automatic to frighten people, she hadn't even examined it very closely. That it could suddenly go off, just like that, had never really occurred to her.

Seeing that man come toward her, she'd involuntarily squeezed the trigger. That the gun had gone off was something she'd been totally unprepared for. Seeing him fall and realizing what she'd done, she'd been scared out of her wits. That she should have had the presence of mind to act more or less according to plan, even so, was still a source of amazement to her. Internally, she'd been paralyzed by shock.

After taking the subway home she'd stashed the bag with the money among Mona's clothes in one of the suitcases she'd already begun packing the previous day.

But after that she'd begun to act irrationally. Changing her dress and sandals, she'd taken a taxi to Armfeldtsgatan. This had not been part of her original plan. But all at once she'd begun to feel that Mauritzon, at least in part, was guilty of the murder she'd committed. And she intended to put the gun back where she'd found it.

But when she again found herself standing in his kitchen she'd realized the unreasonableness of this notion. She'd panicked and run away. Reaching the ground floor she'd noticed the door to the cellar standing wide open. Down in the cellar she'd been just about to open the door and dump the bag among all the garbage there when she'd heard voices. Realizing it had to be the garbage men who'd come to empty the sacks, she'd run farther down the passage and found herself in a kind of storeroom. There she'd hidden the bag in a wooden box that was standing in one corner, waited until the door had slammed behind the garbage men, and then quickly left the building.

Next morning she'd left Sweden.

Monita had always dreamed of seeing Venice. Less than twenty-four hours after her bank robbery she'd found herself there, with Mona. They'd only stayed two days. Hotel rooms had been hard to find, the heat had been oppressive and—combined with the canal stench—almost unbearable. They could come back again after the worst of the tourist season was over.

They'd taken the train to Trieste and thence on to the little Istrian town in Yugoslavia where they now were.

In one of the suitcases standing in the clothes closet in her hotel room lay the nylon bag containing eighty-seven thousand kronor in Swedish banknotes. Several times it had occurred to her that perhaps she ought to keep the money somewhere safer. One day she'd go over to Trieste and put it in a bank.

The American wasn't in, but Monita went out into the garden and sat down with her back against a tree, which she guessed must be a pine.

She drew her legs up, rested her chin on her knees, and screwing up her eyes looked out across the Adriatic.

It was an unusually clear day; she could see the horizon and a little white passenger steamer that was heading for the harbor.

In the noonday heat the rocks down there, the white shore, and the gleaming blue bay all looked inviting. In a while she'd go down there and swim.

The National Police Commissioner of Police had summoned Superintendent Malm to his large bright corner room in the oldest part of the police headquarters building. The sun was casting a rhomboid of light on his raspberry-red carpet, and through the closed windows could be heard faint noises from the construction of the subway line outside. They were discussing Martin Beck.

"Well, you've been in a much better position to

appraise him than I have, both while he was on sick leave and these two weeks he's been on duty," the National Police Commissioner said. "How do you find him?"

"It depends what you mean," Malm replied. "Do you mean his state of health?"

"The doctors are the best judges of his physical condition. As far as I understand, he's recovered completely. Rather, I mean what impression you have of his psychological state."

Superintendent Malm passed his hand over his well-combed locks. "Hmm," he said. "I find it hard to say. . . ."

Silence fell in the room, and the National Police Commissioner waited a while for him to go on. Then he said with a trace of irritation in his voice: "I'm not asking you for a detailed psychiatric analysis. I merely thought you could tell me what sort of an impression he makes on you just now."

"I haven't met him all that often, either, sir," Malm said evasively.

"But you've more to do with him than I have," the National Commissioner persisted. "Is he really his old self?"

"You mean, like he was before he was wounded? No, maybe not. But of course he's been ill for some time and away from the job, and maybe it'll take a little while before he's back in harness again."

"In what way do you think he's changed?"

Malm threw his boss an uncertain look and said: "Well, not for the better, anyway. Of course he's always been a bit strange and difficult to understand. And naturally he's often been a trifle too inclined to take matters into his own hands."

The National Commissioner leaned forward and frowned: "You think so? Well, I suppose it's true. But up to now his work has always produced good results. Are you implying that his highhandedness has grown worse?"

"Well, sir, I don't know. After all, he's only been back at work a couple of weeks."

"My impression is that he's absent-minded," the National Commissioner said, "that he's lost his sting.

Just look at this latest investigation into the Bergsgatan death."

"Yes," Malm said. "He's made a mess of that."

"A scandalous mess. And not only that! The whole thing seems utterly confused. We can only be grateful the press hasn't shown any interest in the case. Admittedly, it's still not too late. The story can leak out, and that wouldn't be good for us; least of all for Beck."

"I don't know what I should say," Malm said. "Some aspects of that investigation seem to be products of sheer fantasy. As for that alleged confession . . . well, one doesn't know what to think."

The National Police Commissioner got to his feet, went over to the window, and looked out toward Agnegatan and the City Hall across the way. After a few minutes he went back to his chair, laid the palms of his hands on his desk, scrutinized his nails, and said: "I've given a lot of thought to this Beck business. And as you'll understand, it's been worrying me not least in view of our earlier decision to promote him to commissioner."

He paused, and Malm waited attentively.

"Now this is how I see the matter," the National Commissioner went on. "Beck's manner of handling this Sköld story . . ."

"Svärd," Malm interposed. "Svärd, his name was."

"What's that? Ah yes, yes. Svärd then. Beck's behavior seems to suggest he isn't quite balanced, or what do you say?"

"In a way he seems raving mad, I think," said Malm.

"Oh, let's hope it isn't as bad as all that. But psychologically he's unbalanced, and my view is that we ought to wait and see whether this is permanent, or just a transient effect of his illness."

The National Commissioner lifted his hands an inch or so above the desk top and then let them fall again. "In other words," he said, "in this situation I think it would be a bit risky to recommend his promotion. He'd better stay where he is, and we'll see how things turn out. His promotion, after all, has only been suggested. Nothing has gone up to the Board. So I suggest we quite simply drop the whole matter and for the time being let it rest. I've other suitable candidates to propose for that job, and Beck himself need never know his name was ever put forward, so no damage has been done. Shall we put it like that?"

"Yes, sir," said Malm. "I'm sure that's a sensible decision."

The National Commissioner got up again, went over to the door, and opened it for Malm, who jumped up from his chair.

"I think so too," the National Police Commissioner said and closed the door behind him. "A most sensible decision."

When, a couple of hours later, the rumor of his inhibited promotion reached Martin Beck, he for once had to agree with one of the National Commissioner's utterances.

Unquestionably, the latter had made a singularly wise decision.

Filip Faithful Mauritzon was pacing his cell. He found it was physically impossible to sit still. His thoughts, too, found no rest. But as time had passed they'd become more simplified. Nowadays they limited themselves to a little set of questions.

What had happened, really?

And how?

To neither of these questions could he find an answer.

Already the guards who were keeping an eye on him had had a word with the prison psychiatrist. Next week they'd tell the chaplain too.

Mauritzon kept on asking for explanations. Explaining things was something the chaplain was good at. Maybe he could be of some use.

Now the prisoner was lying quite still in the dark. He couldn't sleep.

He thought:

What the devil happened, really?

And how?

Someone must know.

Who?

PER WAHLÖÖ and MAJ SJÖWALL, his wife and co-author, wrote ten Martin Beck mysteries. Mr. Wahlöö, who died in 1975, was a reporter for several Swedish newspapers and magazines and wrote numerous radio and television plays, film scripts, short stories and novels. Maj Sjöwall is also a poet.